SO-BIZ-212

THE
PHAROS
OBJECTIVE

A MORPHEUS INITIATIVE THRILLER

DAVID SAKMYSTER

DEVIATION

AN IMPRINT OF VARIANCE PUBLISHING

ISBN: 1-935142-15-1
ISBN-13: 978-1-935142-15-7

Published by Deviation Books (USA) an imprint of Variance LLC.
www.variancepublishing.com

Library of Congress Catalog Number: 2010929957

Visit David Sakmyster on the World Wide Web at:
http://www.sakmyster.com
You may also email him at
dsakm@rochester.rr.com

Cover design by Jeremy Robinson,
www.findtheaxis.com
Interior design by Stanley Tremblay

Printed in the USA

10 9 8 7 6 5 4 3 2 1

Printed on acid-free paper.

For Amy

ACKNOWLEDGMENTS

This is the part of the book that I like to think of as the author's Oscar acceptance speech. It's our chance (and obligation) to thank everyone who's ever touched our careers, nurtured our souls, flexed our literary muscles and given us hope that our Olympian-sized dreams might actually have a chance of coming true someday.

And since for more than one reason I can't go all Jack Palance on you and do a set of one-armed push-ups, I'll follow the typical tradition and give well-earned thanks to a bevy of folks without whom I'd still be lost in a mountain of rewrites and half-finished dreams:

To Tim Schulte and the Variance team for seeing the potential in my little slush pile submission, and to Shane Thomson for helping improve the work and creating such an excellent final product. To my agent, Hannah Brown-Gordon, for taking a chance on me and jump-starting my career.

To Tim Powers, KD Wentworth and all the classy people at The Writers of the Future organization for all the wisdom they impart. And to Nancy Kress and my hometown writing group heroes at Writers&Books for their endless encouragement.

To my parents, for their unfailing support,

advice and inspiration (and all those early-morning emails that begin with, "Here's a story idea . . ."). And of course to my wife—my eternal muse and most-appreciated critic. You're all indispensible.

And finally, a shout-out to the dedicated people at the Sodus Bay Historical Society who run and maintain the Lighthouse Museum at Sodus Point. Thanks for the history lessons, the technical explanations and for patiently answering a myriad of research questions. If one warm summer day you find yourself up that way, grab a delectable cheeseburger at Zoot's, eat at the picturesque bayfront park, then walk off the calories with a climb to the top of the lighthouse and enjoy the view.

Okay, okay, I hear the orchestra cueing up. Time for me to shut up, exit stage left and let the show begin.

THE PHAROS OBJECTIVE

A MORPHEUS INITIATIVE THRILLER

MORPHEUS (Greek: Μορφέας, Μορφεύς, "he who forms, shapes, moulds"). The Greek god of dreams, Morpheus is the son of Hypnos, the god of sleep, and Pasithea, the goddess of hallucination, her name meaning "acquired sight."

PROLOGUE

PHAROS ISLAND, ALEXANDRIA, EGYPT—
861 A.D.

One hundred sleek Arabian horses and their dark riders, carrying torches and armed with hammers, pikes and rusty axes, thundered across the wave-battered promontory toward the lighthouse. The riders roared past Dakhil, who stood upon the crumbling red granite stairs between two colossal statues with missing limbs and fractured torsos. In the shadow of the towering Pharos Lighthouse, Dakhil imagined that the sun had been anchored permanently behind the massive structure, unable to escape its dominion.

He trembled as the riders headed straight into the arched doorway—the toothless, yawning mouth of the Pharos—and he shivered as the Mediterranean winds tugged at his black robes and snatched at his turban. The ancient lighthouse stood in silent indifference, and by a trick of light and shadow it appeared to be expanding, calmly breathing in the Muslim riders, inhaling men and horses alike.

"I hope you have been true to me," said a voice at his shoulder. Dakhil turned to face Barraq Najdeelen, caliph of Alexandria and commander of the military forces occupying the city.

Alexandria had fallen to the Muslims two hundred years earlier with little resistance from the Christians. Once the jewel of the Roman-Egyptian era, an unparalleled center of wealth and knowledge, the gods had all but abandoned Alexandria; and now the once-proud cosmopolitan city was a mere strategic port, valued only for its access to the rich interior trade routes. And of course, for its military potential. This harbor, well-protected by jagged reefs and low-lying shoals, had seen fleet after fleet sail against Constantinople while enjoying the defense of the marvelous Pharos Lighthouse.

Barraq knew his enemy would eventually seek to recapture the city. "The infidel King Michael despises the Pharos. It is a sign of our strength and a looming reminder of Christian impotence." He breathed in the sea air, and his long, oily beard whipped over his shoulder.

"I have spoken only the truth," Dakhil said, nervously taking a step back. High above, the great mirror, a twenty-foot disc of reflective metal, scratched and clouded with age, winked at him, threatening to expose his lies.

Barraq tilted his head back. "You have been in Constantinople two years, my friend. Perhaps they found you out as my spy, and in exchange for your life you offered to come back here with malicious rumors?"

"No, My Lord. I am ever your loyal servant."

"We shall see." Barraq let his fingers drop to his belt and carefully trace the hilt of his scimitar. "This treasure—you do not have further specifics?"

"My Lord?" Dakhil trembled again, and wished he could step out of the shadow of the lighthouse. All the way up its precipitous walls, the crumbling statues of the ancient gods of Egypt, Greece and Rome pointed accusingly at him while the tower itself appeared to lean over for a closer look.

"What is it exactly? The men speak of Alexander the Great's lost hoard. Is it gold and silver? Jewels beyond compare . . . ?"

"More valuable still," Dakhil said, and again offered a prayer to all the gods that were ever dreamed up by men, hoping the legends were true. The timing for this had to be perfect. He had inherited certain knowledge, information that was beyond the understanding of popes, kings or caliphs. Information, he had been told, that must remain hidden until directed otherwise.

But Dakhil was not one for patience. The title of *Keeper* did not suit him. Life was short, and who knew if the world would continue to exist after his own breath expired? So he had decided to release just a hint of what he knew, disguised as a rumor from the enemy's camp, hoping to excite the caliph's men to do what he himself could not. Brute force would surely succeed where patience had failed.

"What could be more valuable?" Barraq asked. Suspicion flashed in his eyes.

Just then, a muffled cry reached their ears from above. A shout, then a horrifying scream. Barraq and Dakhil looked up and shrank back, although they were in no danger. The huge mirror had been wrenched free of its mounts in the zeal of the treasure-seekers and rolled out one of the porticos and over the edge hundreds of feet up. It took two men with it, rotating end over end as it plummeted from the top spire and slammed onto a ledge, crushing one man and dislodging a hail of stone and debris before it bounced off and plunged another two hundred feet. Finally, upon the limestone blocks of the courtyard, it shattered in an eruption of glass and metal, releasing a tortured cry—a lament for the end of its twelve-hundred-year existence.

Dakhil cursed. "Why did they go *up*? That was not the way. The secret tunnels . . . the chambers are below the foundation!"

Barraq waved away his protests. "I instructed my men to be thorough."

"Fools," Dakhil whispered. He now began to fear that the caliph's men were not up to the task.

Barraq withdrew a stick of dried wheat from his saddlebag and chewed its tip. "Tell me, Dakhil, what reward would you ask if we find this treasure?"

Still ruing the loss of such a mighty artifact, the great mirror that had reflected the sights of a millennium, Dakhil said, "I would ask, My Lord, for but one item."

"One only?"

"Yes, if I may have first pick. A little thing, of no use to anyone."

Barraq studied him. "If no one else has use for it, why would you?"

Dakhil shrugged. "To own something from a lost age . . . such a possession would be priceless." He hoped his answer would satisfy the caliph. Of course, Dakhil knew exactly what he wanted: the most powerful item in the collection. He had done his research, he had memorized the catalog, he knew right where it was. The trick would be to find it and take it before the wrath of the soldiers and the caliph descended on him.

However, if the legends were correct and the lighthouse defenses truly existed as rumored, his job might be easier. He felt the metal edge of his sword against his hip, and the two daggers in his boots chafed against his skin.

I shall have to be quick.

Barraq made a sound like a mocking laugh, but before he could speak, an ominous roar came from the lighthouse. This time, it was accompanied by a rumbling under the earth. The tower itself began to tremble and a great dust cloud burst from the doorway and hissed from the hundred windows and cracks in the lower section.

Dakhil started to run toward the entrance with Barraq close behind. They climbed the flight of eroded stairs, raced past toppled statues and across an overgrown courtyard toward the door, where three men just now emerged, black-faced and covered with dust. Coughing, they dropped to their knees, one man holding up his hand. Blood oozed from his ears and his nose, one eye ruined.

"Gone, gone!" he cried, even as his comrades fell, spitting up blood and then lying still.

Barraq grabbed the survivor and shook him to his feet. "Speak, fool! What happened?"

"A door—" He coughed out blood, speckling Barraq's face. "—strange signs upon it . . . twisting serpents and a staff. We could not open it. We three returned to seek your advice, to call for the Magi. But the others . . . they would not wait."

Barraq shook him again, harder. "What happened?"

"Hammers! I heard hammers striking the door, then"—he gasped and clawed at Barraq's face—"they screamed, 'Trap! It's a trap!' The walls shook, the floor gave way. Then the sound"—another coughing fit seized his body—"of a roaring wave."

Barraq slowly turned to Dakhil as he let the man drop to the ground. "A trap . . ." he echoed, just as other men began streaming out of the doorway.

Dakhil reached for his sword, and they fell upon him before it cleared the sheath.

The seventeen men who survived had been higher up in the tower. The other eighty-three, including their horses, had, by some unknown device, been swept out into the harbor.

Dakhil was led to the rocky shore east of the lighthouse and was forced to watch the bodies of those he had betrayed wash up against the stones, forced to stare at those he had sent to their deaths, their bloated, battered corpses a testament to his impatience.

He looked on, attempting stoicism, even as Barraq's men set about sawing off his hands at the wrists and his feet at the ankles. Amidst his screams, they cauterized the stumps with flames from an oil-soaked torch and then chained him to the rocks in the water at the base of the lighthouse, facing west, away from Mecca.

At one point during the ensuing days of agony, as the gulls and the ravenous fish came to feast on his flesh, Dakhil recalled the old Greek legend of Prometheus. He had, after all, merely longed to bring light into the world, to present a powerful gift to mankind. Unlike Prometheus, he had failed; but like the Titan, he had nevertheless been ruthlessly punished.

Barraq left him there after retrieving the dead and placing a team of six men at the summit to staff a continually burning pyre. They could not afford to lose any more ships in the treacherous harbor, and their vigilance against Constantinople must not cease. He rode off on the tenth day of Dakhil's slow death, too soon to see the lone boat steal across the harbor through the moonless night.

A man in a gray cloak stepped out onto the embankment and calmly traversed the rocks until he reached the dying man. "It seems," he said after a moment of contemplation, "your father chose poorly."

Dakhil moaned. His chewed-out eye sockets, above the ragged flesh and protruding cheekbones, turned toward the sound. His lungs choked on seawater and congealed blood. "No . . ."

"We are Keepers," said the stranger. "*Keepers*. A

sacred trust we have held for centuries. I cannot forgive what you have done."

"Believed . . . it was time," Dakhil muttered as the water crashed over his emaciated body and the cloaked form bent over him.

"It is not for us to decide the time. Only to keep the secret until the world is ready." The words, spoken deeply, powerfully, came from within the folds of his hood. "In the meantime, the Pharos protects itself. The Pharos has always protected itself."

Dakhil moaned.

The cloaked stranger moved in closer. "While I cannot forgive, I can be merciful."

A thin blade cut through Dakhil's throat with almost no resistance and produced very little blood. A soft gasp wheezed into the surf.

The man stood up. He bowed his head toward the flickering beacon high above in a final sign of respect and a renewed commitment to its protection. Then, with a heavy sigh, he made his way back into his boat and sailed into the shadows.

BOOK ONE
—THE LIGHTHOUSE—

Whoever wants to conquer Egypt has to conquer Alexandria, and whoever wants to conquer Alexandria has to conquer the Harbor.
— Julius Caesar, *The Alexandrian War*

Sixty feet under the harbor's churning waves, his blue fins kicking just above the reef's dangerous uppermost protrusions, Professor Caleb Crowe held the grapefruit-sized marble head in his bare hands, letting the colder currents wash off the sediment and muck. He turned the sculpture around, marveling at the late classical Egyptian artistry—the perfect symmetry, the deep-set, thoughtful eyes.

Isis.

The headdress and the Sothis star on her forehead placed this artifact in the Ptolemaic Dynasty—just about the right age. He reached for the camera hanging from his neck, considering how he might use this photo in a series of Ancient History lectures he was currently preparing for the spring semester at Columbia.

In the shadowy depths, the reefs and amphorae intermingled with the huge rocks, immense pillars and chunks of masonry thrust between the long-forgotten shipwrecks. Caleb's breathing quickened, echoing in his ears even as the Mediterranean's pressure squeezed his head in its grip. The current tugged him sideways into a massive block of moss-coated basalt.

He let go of the camera and reached out to steady himself. And as Isis looked on, the bare skin on his fingers touched the ancient slab—

—and something like an electric jolt ripped through his nervous system, starting at the base of his spine and spearing out in all directions. The water shimmered, the sea bottom shuddered, and a red-hot pain tore open the doors to his mind, barged inside and exploded in a blast of golden light like a swarm of maddened yellow jackets on fire, careening off the insides of his skull.

Caleb hadn't had a clairvoyant vision in more than four years, and to have it strike now, of all times, at the bottom of Alexandria's harbor, with his air running out and his dive partner wandering off on his own somewhere beyond the dim shadows, was about as dangerous as it was startling. The vision ripped through him like a teasing jolt of pleasure, then just as quickly left him alone again in the cold water, with Isis's eyes looking upon him with pity.

There was a brief moment of confusion, then it returned with a vengeance. He doubled over, hyperventilating, burning through his oxygen, *seeing* . . .

His mind reeled and his stomach twisted. An armada of bubbles surrounded his head like ravenous fish, nipping at his skin, shouting out alarms. But his eyes, wide open, no longer perceived what lay before him, for they strode with his mind . . .

. . . to the tower . . . the lighthouse . . . the Pharos . . . there it is, rising before him, a three-stage construction, almost four hundred feet high, tapering to a glorious spire that seems to challenge the simmering Egyptian sun itself. The tower's outer casing glitters on the western side, reflecting the sun with the light of a thousand stars, and all along its ascent hang statues of divinities and mythical guardians, peering down from their lofty perches.

He tears his eyes away and blinks, bringing into focus the man standing on the steps, welcoming him. A man he instinctively knows as the architect of the Pharos: Sostratus of Cnidos.

"Welcome, Demetrius," he says. "Come, I have much to show you."

Seeing through Demetrius's eyes, Caleb speaks as if following a well-rehearsed script. His voice cracks and the words spill like gravel off his parched tongue. "Sostratus, engineering wonder this may be, yet it has the imposing grandeur, aura and beauty of the divine. My friend, this lighthouse will be adored for ages."

Sostratus turns and looks up at his handiwork. "I hope you are right, and humbly, I trust in the gods that I have built it well enough to last." He helps Demetrius up the final steps into the courtyard, where doves and sparrows coo in transplanted palm trees and fountains pour out fresh reservoir water at each of the cardinal points.

"And it is not yet done." Sostratus raises his hand to the distant, dwindling spire atop the converging stages; past the mammoth two-hundred-foot rectangular lower section, pierced with three hundred windows; beyond the octagonal second stage, rising a hundred feet more, to the last part ascending the final hundred feet. Tiny forms climb on ropes and chisel at sections on the spire, at the cupola and the pillars around the beacon, working like industrious ants.

"I apologize that the masons have not yet removed the scaffolding. We are still hauling up stone for the outer casing and, of course, the great golden statue of Poseidon has yet to arrive by barge from Memphis. I have invited Euclid to pay me a visit and calculate how best to raise it to the apex."

Demetrius makes a grunting sound, then reaches over and clasps his friend. "By Jupiter, you have done it."

"Why so shocked, my friend? Surely you have watched my progress from your precious library across the harbor?"

Demetrius stops and teeters as he cranes his neck and gazes up. "In the scroll rooms, there are few windows. We need to safeguard the world's most important books, not expose them to the elements."

Sostratus chuckles. "Well said. And of course, in all your courtyard festivals you never thought to lift your head over the wall and glance westward to admire my creation?"

Demetrius looks down at his sandaled feet, taking strange comfort from such a common sight. "I have, my friend, I have. A remarkable achievement, your lighthouse has become an integral part of the landscape in the mere twelve years it has taken to build. Alexandrians may take it for granted, yet they speak of little else but its completion and the coming festivals Ptolemy has planned for its dedication day. Your lighthouse has, in fact, become synonymous with Alexandria. The thousands of daily visitors to our harbors are awestruck by its magnificence. Indeed, it is the first thing they see, well before the coast even appears."

Sostratus smiles. "I hear they are already calling it 'The Pharos,' after the island itself."

"True, Homer's little epilogue in the Odyssey *granted us fame enough."*

"Even if he had it wrong. Egyptian settlers at Rhakotis told Menelaus the island belonged to Pharaoh, and out of ignorance, the name stuck. Pharos Island."

Demetrius nods, waving off the same boring discussion he's endured uncounted times. "Believe me, I know the tale well. We have over ninety copies, translated into fourteen languages, with scholars working on the Iliad *now."*

"Wonderful ambitions you have," Sostratus says, intending the complement to be genuine, however eliciting a wounded look from Demetrius. "Or is it our king's ambition?"

"A little of both. Although, from time to time I have to fuel our benefactor's interests." Sostratus nods in empathy. "Now, my friend, do I get the promised tour, or must I wait another twelve years?"

"In just a moment. First I want you to look up, right there." He points to a low-level scaffold, untended for the moment, above which a lengthy inscription is chiseled in Greek letters large enough to be seen by arriving ships in the Eastern Harbor.

Demetrius squints and reads it aloud:

"SOSTRATUS OF CNIDOS, SON OF DEXIFANOS, DEDICATES THIS TO THE SAVIOR GODS ON BEHALF OF THOSE WHO SAIL THE SEAS."

He blinks. "All honor to Castor and Pollux aside, I think Ptolemy Philadelphus may have something to say about your name on his monument."

"Indeed he would," Sostratus says, his lips curling into a grin, "if this were what he saw. Our king wants his credit, and he shall have it. I am humble and patient. My thoughts are ever in the future, beyond the horizon of mere generations."

"What are you going to do?" Demetrius asks, genuinely confused.

"Tonight, when the sun's heat diminishes, my slaves will cement over this inscription and carve into it all the credit due our great king."

A smile creeps across Demetrius's face. "Ah, ingenious! Assuming your slaves are mute, or you have them killed, in time, the cement will crumble and erode away, revealing your name."

Sostratus spreads out his arms and closes his eyes, basking in some private, faraway vision. "I shall be immortal."

"I had not thought you so vain. Is it so vital that you are remembered?"

"Only for what I have done. It is the same with your books, no? Those authors, their wisdom must

endure. Hence the need for your library."

Demetrius nods. "Of course, but—"

"This tower is important in more ways than are immediately obvious. Beyond safety, beyond practicality, beyond a mere symbol of our grand city and a testament to Alexander's genius. Beyond all that, I intend it to house something even more precious, something that, like my inscription above, will emerge in time and bring truth to a clouded world."

"Then by all means, sir." Demetrius bows. "Now . . . the tour?"

High above, the sun peeks through the open-air cupola between gilded pillars supporting the roof where Poseidon's feet are destined to stand. A lone hawk circles the mid-section, vainly beating its wings to ascend farther.

Caleb gagged, reached for the fading vision and saw his fingers spear through a cascade of bubbles—bubbles spewing from his own throat. He'd spit his mouthpiece out! The world was darkening, his mouth filling with foul water.

For so many years he had pushed this power away, dreading the visions that came: horrific sights of metal cages in the mountains, of emaciated hands reaching through the bars, of whimpers and moans and cries for help. Visions dredged up by a talent he couldn't control, alive with sights, sounds and smells. A gift he'd never wanted.

A curse.

But today was different. What he saw was new—an original, unprovoked vision. Too bad it would be the last vision he ever saw. Then it surged back, and . . .

. . . *Demetrius whispers, "It's marvelous." He shuffles around two slaves at work polishing a marble Triton as he exits the hydraulic lift, the water-powered elevator that has shot them up three levels in less than a minute. He steps up to the terrace's southern wall. Mouth open, he gapes at the view: the sprawling twin harbors below, the Heptastadion connecting the mainland to Pharos Island, the hundreds of multicolored sails dotting the sea and the boats anchored at the docks, the wide stretch of the magnificent Imperial Palace, and behind it, the gymnasium, the Temple of Serapis . . . and there, the shining walls and columns and the golden domed roof of the museum. Inside its walls are the library and the mausoleum of Alexander, whom Ptolemy buried there, establishing his direct connection to the legend.*

"Incredible, seeing it from this vantage." His gaze follows the Street of Canopus from the Moon Gate by the sea across Alexandria and through the Gate of the Sun, parallel to the canal connecting to the Nile, then weaving across the sands back through the haze and dust of the desert toward Memphis and Upper Egypt. The fierce cobalt sky

engulfs all else, until the startling turquoise sea grazes at the horizon and consumes everything beyond. Over the dark blue waves, the shadow of the Pharos arches to the east as a lone marker etching its imprint upon nature as it would graft itself onto human consciousness for millennia to come.

"You were saying?" Demetrius takes great gulps of air and slowly backs away from the edge.

Sostratus takes his arm and leads him inside the spire to a staircase weaving in a double spiral up the last hundred feet. "I was speaking of impermanence and of a future that is even beyond the sight of the oracles."

"If even the gods are blind to it, then what must we fear?"

"The unknown." Sostratus speaks as they make the same ascent he has made three or four times a day for the past three years. His friend, unconditioned to the exertion necessary for such a climb, needs to rest.

"Must we continue to the top?"

"I wish to show you something before we go back down—down into the very bowels of the earth to illuminate the real reason you are here."

Demetrius shoots him a look. "What, was it not for the view?"

"Not entirely. Come, we are almost there."

Caleb bolted back to the present, fighting the

brackish, cold water rushing into his lungs. He screamed—or tried to—dimly aware of another figure swimming toward him. The darkness softened until it gave way to the bright light of day, and a familiar man in white robes . . .

. . . *emerges alone at the top. Sostratus climbs inside the "lantern," a thirty-foot-wide cupola, where four marble pillars, fitted with rare gems and studded with embroidered gold, support a domed roof twenty feet overhead. In the center of the floor, the empty brazier stands ready for its sacred task of alerting and guiding ships safely into the harbors past the deadly silt banks, shoals and reefs that for centuries have been the bane of seafarers. Sailors will be guided by fire at night, and by smoke during the day, the black coils visible long before even the tower emerges into view.*

A noise at his back makes him smile. Demetrius appears from the trap door, holding his side and wheezing. He sits on the top step and glances around while wiping thick beads of sweat from his forehead. "I don't believe I'll look over the edge. Maybe next time."

"Entirely understandable. But come,"—he motions to Demetrius to get up—"witness these automatons." Great statues, twice the size of men, stand at three of the corners of the platform. "I'm sure you are familiar with Heron's designs and inventions outlined in the Pneumatica."

Demetrius nods, even though he'd had time only for a perusal of Heron's work before other scholars, including Hipparchus, snatched it up to examine and debate with its author on the principles of hydraulics and thermodynamics.

"This one," Sostratus says, pointing to a muscled statue in the likeness of Hermes with his finger outstretched along his angled arm, "was designed with help from your resident astronomer Aristarchus. It tracks the daily path of the sun, precisely mirroring its trails and changing with the seasons. "That one there"—he points to the western edge, where a silver-plated robed female faces the Imperial Palace and leans forward with hands cupped around her mouth—"screeches out a warning of the presence of a hostile fleet if one of the attendants trips that switch. The whole city can be mobilized hours before invading ships can be seen from the shore."

Demetrius mumbles something lost in the winds, then rises to his feet. "And that last one?"

Sostratus laughs. "A trivial magician's trick. It calls out the hours of the day. But here is what I am most proud of." He lifts a heavy tarp, releases it from its bindings, and lets the wind rip it free, flinging it from the spire to sail with the winds out over the hills and the rooftops of Alexandria. "The great mirror."

Demetrius gasps at the immense circular sheet

of polished glass adhered to a thick layer of metal. He looks into its surface, and sees himself reflected back, but at reduced size.

"A finely polished lens." Sostratus smiles. "It will direct the beacon's fire by night, sending a beam out to sea to guide ships or, perhaps, harness the rays of the sun and set them to flames."

"Apollo's blood," Demetrius whispers, hands shaking. "And you can move it, direct it?"

"We will have that capability, yes. Once mounted on the outstretched hand of Poseidon, we will control the statue by means of gears and levers."

"Fantastic." Demetrius involuntarily glances down—all the way down—where his gaze settles on the tiny dome of his library. "So, my friend, why did you really call me here if not for the enviable experience of being the first to have such a tour?"

Sostratus turns his back on his guest and stares out to sea, arms folded. "This was merely prelude, so that you could understand the extent of my tower's defenses, the sturdiness of its construction, how I have built it to withstand the elements and the ire of the earth itself."

"Fine, I have witnessed it. To what end?"

Sostratus coughs. "Do you know what the high priest of Memphis said when Alexander's funeral procession passed through his city?"

"No."

"He said, 'Bury him not here, for where that man lies only war and strife will endure.'"

Demetrius remains silent, and listens only to the sound of the wind rustling through his clothes. "I'm sorry, my friend, I cannot fathom what this has to do with me. I understand your fears of war and how this lighthouse has been outfitted as more than a mere beacon, but—"

Sostratus turns abruptly. "Come with me back to the ground floor, then below it, beyond the hydraulic workings and through the tunnels under the harbor. There I will show you the true function of this tower."

"But why me?" Demetrius asks, struggling to keep up as Sostratus starts back down. Immediately, he is pleased to find the descent infinitely more comfortable than the climb.

"Patience, my friend. You are about to see." Sostratus leads the way, and they descend in silence, circling, moving ever deeper with each successive stage. "And before you glimpse into the vault that will house the greatest treasure ever assembled, I ask only for one thing—your pledge to guard its secret with your life."

Caleb saw it all in a flash, as though time had altogether stopped its forward march while his mind processed the visions breath by breath, full of all the sense and clarity of lived experience.

But then it moved on and everything shifted

back into place.

The water slammed him into reality. The bubbles, the currents, the mouthpiece flailing in the spirals of muck rising from his thrashing feet . . . the statue head falling from his grasp. And then other hands on him, holding him, forcing a spare mouthpiece between his lips. Gagging, choking, coughing.

He kicked away.

Disoriented, his mind still straddling two millennia, he broke free and sped upward, heedless of everything but the need to break the surface, to thrust his head out and see—see if it was true. To see the reality of the vision still locked in his mind's eye of that glorious spire, that transcendent tower.

The lighthouse.

The Pharos.

Was it really there? A towering colossus dominating the harbor, all of Egypt, just as he had seen it?

He kicked and thrashed and ignored the raging fire burning his skull, in his blood, until a wall of pain halted his ascent. And then, fully believing it would be his final wish, he thought, *Phoebe, forgive me!* before his lungs died and he fell into a chasm of pain and mindlessness.

For the past ten years Caleb had been waiting for a miracle—for his father to dramatically stride back into their lives with grand stories of adventure and escape from that horrible Iraqi torture cell in the mountains, the one Caleb had seen time and again in his nightmares.

His father had been shot down in an Apache helicopter during the First Gulf War, and his body had never been recovered. It wasn't long before everyone had moved on—everyone but Caleb, that is—who, although only five at the time, had already started having visions, a power his mother claimed to share, despite never witnessing the same things Caleb had seen every night: his father, very much alive, very much tortured, begging, pleading for help, for acknowledgment, for salvation. Images of things done to him—wooden shards under his fingernails, wires attached to the place between his legs—would wake Caleb screaming. He'd reach for the pencil and pad of paper he kept by the bed and scramble to draw the horrific visions that lingered, clinging to him in the waking world. He'd see . . .

. . . *some kind of great enclosure, a fence or a gate, and a burning five-pointed star above it. Sometimes an eagle's head, flying over a sun. And his father's arms, bleeding from a hundred cruel cuts, reaching out, bloody fingers clasping at nothing, his voice a barely audible whisper, "Caleb . . . Caleb . . ."*

And then a word he couldn't make out.

But instead of even the slightest acknowledgment of his remote-viewing talents, his mother had sent Caleb to therapy. That had been the beginning of his split with her. With both of them, even his sister Phoebe, to some extent. His mother had refused to believe that his dreams could be populated by such personal revelations, especially in light of their terrifying nature, so she attributed them to childhood delusions, feelings of paternal loss and grave emotional trauma.

"It's true!" Caleb had yelled one time when he was twelve, when it had all come to a head. Standing up to her, but only coming to her shoulder. In that moment he'd seen a flicker of fear in her eyes. Or was it a flash of respect?

Her eyes had snapped to the drawings on his bed, and she seemed to deflate, shrinking to his level. She gripped his shoulders. "I don't see those things," she whispered, and her eyes softened and seemed to implore, *and neither should you.*

Tears had spilled down Caleb's cheeks as he tried to pull away from her. He wanted to shout that she was wasting her talents by drawing stupid old buildings and ancient shipwrecks. Those things didn't matter. And the people in her so-called 'psychic' group, the members of the Morpheus Initiative, who came by the house to sit with her and go into their trances and talk to the spirits or whatever—they were leeches and imposters.

And so was she.

How could she have any real power? How could

she be a true remote viewer if she couldn't even perceive what Caleb, a child, had seen so clearly, if she couldn't tell that her husband was crying out in pain, a prisoner forgotten by his country, and worse, by his own family? No, instead, his own wife had chosen to spend her time with strangers, helping them find useless old artifacts or sunken wrecks.

Caleb had pushed her away and run out the door. He raced along Sodus Bay in a cool November rain, ran past that decrepit lightship he and Phoebe had affectionately named Old Rusty. He ran until he was too tired to keep running. And then, when he had spent his anger, he turned back and walked to the entrance of their own lighthouse—the historic landmark his family had managed for two generations—and climbed the narrow metal stairs to the very top, where he sat beneath the old burned-out light, the great lamp that had been decommissioned just after his father's disappearance.

Hugging his knees, he'd stared out over Sodus Bay until the sun finally burrowed beneath the horizon and hid itself for another night.

And now, all these years later, in a rush of frothing bubbles, Caleb burst from the depths of Alexandria's Eastern Harbor, expelling a lungful of acrid water, coughing as the other divers rushed him to the waiting yacht. He briefly regained consciousness and gasped when he perceived the grand lighthouse as it stood over two thousand years ago, leaning over as if to inspect his condition for itself. And at the very top, at the apex, Caleb imagined he could see someone gripping the railing and peering over the side, a man who looked, not surprisingly, like his father.

At the first bend on the promontory, just above a jumble of boulders and red stone rocks rising out of the sea, a man stood, watching. He wore a black tie and Ray-Ban sunglasses. His hair, trimmed short, had gray streaks that flecked his temples, matching the color of his just-pressed Armani suit. He held a paper bag full of stale bread crumbs, handfuls of which he tossed absently into the frothing sea while he stole glances at the scene in the harbor.

"It's happening," he said into the wind. Then he cocked his head, listening to the answer returned to a tiny plastic receiver in his left ear.

He tossed a few more crumbs out to birds that warily kept their distance. "Yes, I'm sure," he said. "The young professor from Columbia. They just pulled him out of the harbor. Probably ascended too fast . . . No, Waxman's yacht is right there, and my guess is he'll have Caleb in the recompression chamber in minutes . . . If you recall, when we learned Crowe would be diving, a few us felt this possibility was not unexpected, yet our warnings were overruled." The man paused, listening, then shook his head. "No. I can't get closer, not without risk." Another handful of bread crumbs launched into the wind blew back onto his starched pants and his polished leather shoes. "Yes, we have a microphone on the yacht as ordered. Fortunately, it's in the same room with the hyperbaric oxygen chamber." He made a scowling face. "Well, at least we did that right." He nodded, coughed and then tossed the bag, crumbs and all, into the sea. "All right. I'll wait here and listen in, but I won't risk exposure. If Crowe has that kind of talent, and he happens to sense something . . ."

The wind kicked up and whipped his jacket open, flinging his tie over his shoulder. Head down, he walked behind two tourists snapping pictures. He opened a pack of cigarettes and spent some time and difficulty lighting one as he walked toward the fortress.

He switched the channel on his earphone's receiver, and while he waited for the sounds from the boat, he kicked at a rock, sending it off the edge and into the sea. He walked along the breakwater stones toward the vacant citadel, pretending to admire its immense sandstone walls, its grand colonnades, gates and towers.

As if this decrepit hovel could compare with the Pharos.

He risked a backward glance. The activity on the yacht continued, with the other divers surfacing, climbing up to check on their team member. *All aboard*, he mused, smiling as he adjusted his glasses. Then he tapped his ear, increasing the volume. He listened, hearing the tension in their voices, the conflict between the members of the Morpheus Initiative and their leader, George Waxman. *Conflict is good*, he thought. *Might even be in our best interest to get them working at odds, coming at this from different angles.* God knew it was going to be hard enough as it was.

For two thousand years the Keepers had waited, but patience was running thin. He and his fellow Keepers were convinced that the time for passivity had long since passed. A combination of dedicated research and luck had finally led them to the *Key*. And now, knowing it was only a matter of time— time measured in years, not centuries—plans were set in motion.

The Key.

Several reliable sources had confirmed that it was close: one of the members of the Morpheus Initiative had it. Now, it was only a matter of finding out which one and answering the larger question of determining if whoever had it even knew what it was.

He turned and looked out across the sea, his gaze sweeping the harbor like a lighthouse beacon. Two millennia. Indeed, patience was running out. But still, they had to be careful.

The Pharos protects itself.

The yacht waited above the dive site, more or less, depending on the drift and the currents that had buffeted Caleb and the other four members of the group that had gone down with him. They had sailed out just a short distance from the promontory at the edge of the Ras el-Tin peninsula, and had anchored just beyond the shadow of the sandstone towers and imposing walls of Sultan Qaitbey's fifteenth-century fortress—the castle some claimed had been built on the foundation of the Pharos Lighthouse.

And some, like George Waxman, believed the Pharos, one of the Seven Wonders of the Ancient World, had crumbled and plunged into the sea at this very spot. And here it remained—or at least, its pieces—preserved in the muck on the earthquake-rattled seafloor, inviting discovery for those with the resources to get past the Egyptian authorities and brave the currents, the treacherous reef's minimal visibility, and pollution.

Holding a tumbler of hundred-fifty-year-old Grand Marnier, George Waxman watched from the railing as they hauled Caleb up over the side.

"Recompression chamber!" Elliot James yelled up to him.

Waxman stifled the urge to celebrate. *Is this it?* "What happened?"

"He touched something," Elliot said, ripping off Caleb's mask, pulling off the fins, the weight belt and the buoyancy vest. Elliot was a forty-two-year-old diver from St. Thomas, with a scar on the right side of his neck—a souvenir from a brush with a school of young tiger sharks.

"Looked like the head of a sphinx, or a goddess," said the other diver, Victor Kowalski. Victor was a New Orleans native, bald and black as night, a veteran Navy Seal, and not without a bit of clairvoyant talent himself. Waxman had found him quite valuable over the years, in more ways than one. Everyone on his team had their talents.

Victor and Elliot had solid scuba expertise and physical strengths to complement their psychic abilities, while the other team members that comprised the Morpheus Initiative—Nina Osseni,

Amelia Gaines, Xavier Montross, Tom Ellis, Dennis Benford and Mary Novaka—were all powerful remote viewers. But the members Waxman really had his eye on were the Crowes. Caleb and his mother, Helen, were here while Caleb's younger sister, Phoebe, the final member of the Initiative, remained back at their home in Sodus, confined to a wheelchair after an unfortunate accident several years earlier. Even so, she managed to be somewhat useful. At times.

A whole family of psychics. Talented remote viewers. Just as he had expected when he first recruited them for the Initiative almost fifteen years ago. He had brought in Helen first, knowing that she would only come with her children. And if either child had any hereditary powers, Waxman would be able to discern that along the way. But after the tragic incident in Belize, everything changed. Helen was still more than willing, but Caleb . . . he blamed himself for Phoebe's injury. Promptly at eighteen, he'd left the Morpheus team and gone his own way.

Bright kid, scholarship to anywhere he wanted, Waxman recalled. Cruised through Columbia. Teaching now—a professorship in Ancient History. At least he kept that interest alive. And he was here, wasn't he?

Of course, that was partly a result of Waxman's doing. He had pulled some strings with Columbia's

Board, then maneuvered Caleb into a slot on a research dive in Alexandria during the same time the Morpheus Initiative would begin phase two of their Pharos Project. Once he'd arrived, Helen had been more than persuasive and convinced Caleb to at least take advantage of Waxman's offer to use his boat and resources to conduct his own research. Together again. And if Waxman got his way, it would just be the start. He needed Caleb, but he wasn't about to let on just how much.

Waxman finished his drink and headed down into the lower level, where Victor and Elliot were just closing the door, sealing the tank and setting the dials on the recompression chamber. They stepped away, breathing heavily, and dripping all over his hardwood floors. Scowling, Waxman handed Victor his empty glass. "Fill that." He approached the chamber and peered inside at Caleb's twisted body on the cot. The kid's eyelids were flickering.

Still dreaming? Still seeing visions? "We need to know what he saw. How long is he going to be in there?"

"Six hours at least today," said Elliot. "And probably a few hours each for the next couple days until—"

Waxman waved away the details. "He can hear me?"

"Yep, just hit the intercom switch."

He moved in closer, then turned back. "Oh and Victor, when you return with my drink, bring Caleb a pad of paper and a box of pencils."

Waxman pulled up a chair and yelled over his shoulder, "And find me that statue's head!"

4

Caleb awoke with a wheezing, breathless gasp and immediately sat up but reeled suddenly as his head spun in flaring pain. He was in what looked like the inside of a space capsule: all white and padded, one narrow cot to sleep on, and a tiny porthole window. A pad of paper, thick, with about a hundred sheets, lay on the floor next to his uncomfortable sleeping accommodations along with a dozen sharpened pencils, all bundled together with a rubber band.

The he heard it: *knock, click, knock, click*. He looked up and nearly blacked out again. He put his head back down and groaned. The air was thin, pure, almost cold.

"That's right," came a voice he recognized only too well from the small intercom speaker on the wall. "Concentrated oxygen to go with the pressure treatment."

Caleb grunted. "Hi, George." His voice sounded nasally, cartoonish, a by-product of the oxygen inhalation.

"Hello Caleb. Sorry about your predicament. Lucky I was here, and lucky I brought my own recompression chamber. Saved you a trip to the local hospital, where you'd be more likely to die from something other than what got you there in the first place."

"Yeah, I'm so lucky."

"Why'd you rise so fast, Caleb? Did you *see* something?"

Caleb rubbed his temples. *A flash of light, the burning Egyptian sky suddenly turning dark as he stepped into the shadow of the Pharos.* He blinked. "Where's my mother?"

"In talks with the Egyptian Council of Authorities, trying to secure access to the catacombs along the old Canopic Way. Assuring dive permits—"

"A little late for that."

"We used yours," Waxman said. Caleb now noticed the face leering in at him from the porthole window. Hair the color of rock salt, wavy and slicked back over a high, triangular forehead; narrow cheekbones and a hard, pointed jaw set below pencil-thin lips. A cigarette dangled from his lips, and from the tip hung a long spindle of ash about to fall. Tendrils of smoke coiled around his face, obscuring his eyes and fogging the window. "Remind me," Waxman continued, "to thank Columbia for their assistance in our little quest."

"*Your* quest," Caleb corrected, trying to sit up as the pressure chamber did its work. "I opted out of the Morpheus Initiative four years ago. Remember?"

"I seem to recall something about that," Waxman said with a grin. "And again, for what it's worth, I'm sorry."

"Tell it to Phoebe."

"I did. I do . . . every time I see her."

Caleb narrowed his eyes. "When do you—?"

"Didn't your mother tell you? We've been using your home on Sodus Bay as our new headquarters."

"She must've left that out," Caleb said with some bitterness. "But then again, we don't talk much." And Caleb didn't want to ask, *So where do you sleep?*

"Pity. You'd be proud of your sister. Even from her wheelchair, she's become quite an asset. Her access to the University of Rochester archives and labs has proven invaluable, and the way she manages the sessions, catalogs the drawings, comes up with the targets and tests the group members . . . she's really something."

"Good for her." Caleb wanted it to come out sarcastically, but he also meant it. He had known about her success at her first year in the university, but had limited his correspondence with her. The past was too much, the guilt too intense. He wouldn't even pick up the phone when she called— at first, several times a week, then after his lack of response, once a month. Her messages piled up in the voicemail cache until he would be forced to delete them to free up space.

Waxman tapped on the door. "And something about being there, in your childhood home, with its tiny lighthouse overlooking the bay, I don't know . . ."—he grinned and stepped back so only the streaky window remained visible—"it helps focus the visions, directs the team toward the proper mind frame for its mission."

"And what exactly is the mission this time, George?" Caleb always called him George to his face. Maybe he was being unfair, but the man had inserted himself into their lives, into his family, like a splinter under a fingernail, and so soon after Dad had been lost. At the time, even at such a young age, Caleb had known the story of Odysseus. Enamored by his father's bedtime tales of Greek tragedies and classical literature, Caleb imagined Waxman as one of Penelope's suitors to his father's Odysseus; and he kept alive a fantasy that his father would one day return with vengeance in his heart and rout anyone foolish enough to have tried to take his place.

Waxman's face returned to the window, and his

voice crackled over the knocking sounds. "Our project—our objective, this time—is the search for the perfect testable scenario; an archaeological enigma that, if solved, could once and for all, scientifically prove the validity of remote viewing." He paused, taking another drag on the cigarette. Caleb could almost smell the menthol through the door. Waxman's favorite brand, it was the smell he always associated with George's presence, and with his father's absence.

Waxman continued. "The Pharos Lighthouse! If we can locate it through psychic means, just think what that will prove. Imagine it: a documented success case, a melding of archaeology and para-psychology. It would open up so many avenues of research, generating interest and—"

"Grants . . . Money . . ."

"Yes, of course. But I'm not in it for wealth, Caleb."

"No? Then what was the Bimini dive all about back in 2003? I seem to recall that Mom and your other psychic crackpots happened to pinpoint the exact location of three sunken ships and quite a bit of salvage."

"That was different."

"And what about Belize, George? Why did we go there, if not for the promise of the treasure Elliot drew in one of his trances? Why did we enter Tomb Fifteen?"

George remained silent for a long while. "Caleb, believe me, this is different."

"Is it?" Caleb stood up, wobbly, biting his lip against the pain surging through his muscles due to the nitrogen narcosis, microscopic bubbles warring in his veins. He staggered and leaned against the wall. "Let me see if I can explain how it's different. You're here not to locate one of the lost Seven Wonders of the World or to prove the validity of something we already know is real, but to locate only one thing."

Waxman was silent.

Caleb inched closer, sliding along the wall until his face was in front of the glass, his eyes locked on Waxman's. "You know the legends. You've studied the same stories I have, the same rumors my mom was always on about, the same stories my dad told me as a kid." He swallowed, his mouth dry. "You want the treasure. You want the lost treasure of Alexander the Great."

"I'd be lying," Waxman said, "if I said that thought hadn't crossed my mind."

Caleb sat back down, holding his throbbing head. "Good, finally you've said something I can believe."

"But Caleb, think about it. We can do it! We're better suited than anyone else. Why? Because we can *see*, truly see. The other archaeologists, they're blind, just going on old words, faded texts or ancient relics, some of them two thousand years old. While they're struggling with government officials and museum curators, we're seeing beyond it all, far into the past, hoping to glimpse exactly where and how to get to it."

"If it exists."

"Caleb, like you said, you've read the same texts I have. And you've read your father's notes. I know you have."

Caleb lifted his head. Yes, his father's notes. For a moment, he had a flash to a night seventeen years ago, his father in a room surrounded by stacks of old books, newspapers and magazines. And drawings—hundreds of drawings. Some of them Helen's, some his father's. . .

. . . and there he stands in his military uniform a week before shipping off, looking over his shoulder at five-year-old Caleb standing in the doorway, holding up one sheet of paper—a drawing of the Pharos, at night, besieged by an armada of Roman ships.

Caleb blinked, and he was back in the recompression chamber, listening to Waxman drone on about his father's research.

". . . his obsession, which became your mother's. I thought it quaint that your father, the son of a lighthouse keeper in Upstate New York, should adopt as his life's passion the very first lighthouse, researching and learning everything about it."

"Yeah," Caleb said, "quaint. Like it was 'quaint' that his children should follow you around the world, risking their lives in the pursuit of whatever treasure you thought you could get your hands on."

"Your mother—"

"—should have known better. We lost our father, and then, as if that wasn't enough, we lost our childhood, tramping around through bug-infested jungles and submerged wrecks, all for your cause."

"I won't apologize for that. A better education you couldn't have asked for."

"I *didn't* ask for this. Phoebe didn't—"

"Caleb, enough. Listen. We'll have to clear out of this area soon, so let's get to the point. What did you see down there?"

Caleb hung his head.

"Draw it, if you like," Waxman ordered, pointing to the paper and pencils.

"Don't need to," Caleb whispered.

"What?"

"I don't need to draw it. And it's nothing. It was nothing."

"So, 'nothing' almost got you killed?"

Caleb looked up. "Nothing that will help you. All I saw was the lighthouse. The Pharos. The day before its dedication." Waxman was silent—a breathless silence. "And . . ."

"And nothing. Sostratus, the architect, was there, and I was, I don't know, somehow I was seeing through the eyes of Demetrius—"

"The librarian?"

"Yes, I suppose."

"Fascinating."

"Yeah, whatever. So Sostratus showed Demetrius around. It was . . . beautiful, majestic, soaring. But, I saw no treasure. I—"

"But it was here, the lighthouse?"

Caleb nodded. There had been enough speculation through the ages, since the remnants of the tower, long-wracked by earthquakes and disuse, had at last been shaken loose and crashed into the sea, as to where exactly it had stood. But Caleb's vision had made it clear. "Yes, the view I had from the top—the orientation of the coast, the landmarks—yes, it was here, at the tip of the peninsula."

"Where Qaitbey's fortress stands?"

Caleb nodded.

"Anything else?"

"No. Yes. I saw the inscription. Sostratus signed the monument, then plastered over it."

"Ah," Waxman grinned. "I read about that, one of the anecdotes in Heinrich Thielman's study. So it's true."

"If you believe my visions."

"Why should I doubt them?"

Caleb shrugged, thinking of his father, of countless drawings of a man, possibly still alive, held captive in the mountains of Iraq. "Others have."

"Well, Caleb, consider me your number-one fan, then. I'm in your corner, I believe you. And I confess, now that I've got you here, locked in my vault for the next six hours. I don't want to let you go, not without something in return."

"How about a kick in nuts when I get out of here?"

"Really, is that all the thanks I get?"

"Thanks," Caleb said, turning and limping back to the cot. He lay down. "I'm going to try to sleep it off, and when this is done, I'd like to get back to my hotel. I have a plane to catch in the morning."

"No you don't." Waxman's face disappeared. "I, uh, took the liberty of calling the university and explained the situation, explained your near-death experience—"

"You what?"

"—and the fact that you have nitrogen narcosis, a life-threatening condition. Air transportation is out of the question. Besides, you need rest. A minimum of two weeks. And your colleagues, they quite agreed."

"No, no, no."

"Yes, Caleb, it's for your own good. And your mother, she'll be here in a few hours to take care of you."

"Great." Caleb sat back, fuming, but he knew Waxman was right. He'd never be able to fly in this condition. He should, by rights, be in a hospital.

As if reading his mind, Waxman said, "The offer still stands, I can drop you off at the local infirmary and you can take your chances."

"All right, what the hell do you want?"

"I want two weeks, Caleb, just two weeks."

"Of what?"

"Your time." His face at the window again, beaming. "Your talents. The paper, the pencil . . . your visions. That's all. Join the Morpheus Initiative again, just on a temporary basis."

Caleb shook his head. "I'd be a waste. This is the first vision I've had since . . . since Belize."

"It's like riding a bike, I hear." Waxman grinned. "You never really lose it."

"What makes you think I can help?"

"Call it a hunch. Come on, kid. Spend some time with your mom, live in luxury on my yacht or at the five-star hotel in the city, not that dump you've been staying at. Just come to the sessions, try to remote view the targets, and let's see if together we can't solve one of the greatest mysteries of the ancient world."

Caleb held his head as the knocking sounds intensified and his temples throbbed in time to the pulsing of the boat's engines. Again he thought of his father, surrounded by all those dusty texts; he thought of the two-story lighthouse above his childhood home, the long shadow it threw over the grass on summer days when he and Phoebe would chase each other on the hill over the bay.

"All right, I'll help," he whispered.

"Fantastic—"

"But not for you."

"Fine," Waxman said.

"And not for Mom, or even for Phoebe." He looked up. "I'm doing this for my father. If I find it, if I help locate the entrance, the passageway or whatever it is you're all looking for, I'll have done it for him. For his memory."

Waxman nodded, grinning. "Whatever works. Glad to have you back, kid."

"Where's Helen?" George called out when he returned to the yacht's lounge. The motors were running, with Elliot at the wheel, turning the ship back toward the harbor as the sun started its long descent over the spires and mosques, over the scintillating glass dome of the newly completed Alexandrian library. In the lounge he found Victor and Mary watching the LCD screen, catching up on CNN. Behind the bar sat the dark-skinned Italian, Nina Osseni, with short curly hair and piercing green eyes. She wore a tank top that exposed her shoulder tattoos: Egyptian symbols, the two eyes of Horus, left and right. She leaned over in a pose at once seductive and restrained.

She was young but perfectly suited to Waxman's

needs. He had recruited her right out of Annapolis, where she had been planning for a career at the FBI. She knew seven languages besides her native Italian, including Egyptian and Saudi; she was skilled in hand-to-hand combat; proficient in most firearms, with a specialty in handguns; and to top it all, her psychic scores were off the charts.

"Haven't seen Mrs. Crowe yet," Nina said. "But we have another . . . situation." She showed him two small dime-shaped objects with wires sticking out of them. "Found these on the boat just after the last sweep. We must have been careless."

Waxman bristled. "What else?"

Nina angled the silver-plated Dell laptop slightly so that only Waxman could see the screen. It displayed a familiar man, the one on the pier, in his gray suit. "I took this with the zoom lens while you were talking with the Crowe kid. He's on shore, trying to be discreet."

Waxman smiled. "Not too good at it. You run the facial-recognition program against our data-base?"

"Of course."

"And?"

"It's Wilhelm Miles."

"Ah, Miles." Waxman filled his drink, took a long sip. "Must be the son. The father took ill last year."

"Died two weeks ago," Nina said.

"Very good. So, this is indeed a lucky break. Gives us the edge." He met Nina's eyes. "You know what to do?"

Nina's upper lip curled slightly and her eyes sparkled. "Looking forward to it."

She closed the laptop, nodded to Elliot and Victor, who were busy talking about the dive, and left the room. Waxman walked outside and watched the approaching shore, keeping his focus on the waving flags over the Qaitbey fortress. He blinked, narrowed his eyes and, in the heat, imagined the Pharos, imagined it as Caleb had seen it—nearly complete, with the scaffolding tracking up along the sides, the great mirror settling into place, and Sostratus at the base, arms folded, smirking with the knowledge of a secret he alone held.

But not for much longer.

Waxman thought of his most valued passenger, down in the recompression chamber. Two thousand years was long enough. Some secrets were not meant to last.

Five hours to go.

Caleb dreaded what was to come, alone in his chamber for five more hours. Nothing to do but think. And possibly . . . He eyed the sketchpad. Waxman had sent the other divers out looking for the statue's head that he'd dropped. If they could find it, or some other relic, maybe he could spend this time productively, trying to return to the vision to finish it.

Caleb sighed. He probably didn't need the head. His visions had never been dependent on touch or proximity. The images of his father, tortured in that Iraqi cell, were proof enough of that. Although, back then he had been at home, sometimes in his father's room, among his books, his precious books and notes and drawings. Maybe there was a connection.

He reached for the pad, pulled out one pencil. He pressed the graphite tip to the page, closed his eyes, took a deep breath, and started. He would let his subconscious be the artist; and once set free, it would steer wherever it willed, wherever . . .

Caleb opened his eyes. His hand, pausing only for a moment, went right to work, sketching a distinctly Mayan pyramid set among roughly drawn jungles. A stone staircase, worn and chipped, leading up to a great door, a door Caleb feverishly colored in, dark.

Black.

Onyx.

He broke out in a sweat, blinked, and the drawing took on a life of its own, tugging him into it.

A humid blast of air, the scent of cocoa and papaya, the buzzing of insects, the wind through the palms.

He gasped, and his eyes rolled back in his head. "No," he whispered, but then he realized this, too, was inevitable. He wasn't done suffering, paying for his mistakes.

"No . . ."

"Yes! Come on!" Phoebe bounds up the steps ahead of him. She's only twelve, but she is so quick. Her auburn hair is tied back in a pink scrunchy,

her t-shirt stained with mud and dust, her jeans rolled up over her ankles. Caleb follows more cautiously, seeking precise footholds on the crumbling stairs. He pauses and looks back down, forty feet below, to where the jungle greedily consumes everything beyond the base of the pyramid, stretching for miles in every direction.

Back to the north, almost half a mile, is their base camp. Their mother is there with George Waxman and two others. They are all so excited; this is the first inland mission for the Morpheus Initiative. Last month they spent a week in seclusion in Mexico City while Phoebe and Caleb stayed in their room, subsisting on enchiladas and bad attempts at American hamburgers, doing nothing but playing War and Go Fish, and reading, of course. Caleb was always reading. Seven books that week, much to Phoebe's dismay. But then it happened: Helen came in one morning, looking haggard, but excited.

"We found it!" she exclaimed, and then brought Caleb and Phoebe into the smoke-filled conference room they'd reserved, a room full of drawings, taped sequentially on the walls, all showing a pyramid and a black door. Then distant shots of landscape, and colored thumbtacks placed on geological maps.

"Found it," she repeated, and approached Waxman where he pored over a map with a compass *and a protractor.*

"Here!" he announced. "We'll make our approach along this trail, then plot out the course to the tomb."

"Tomb?" Phoebe asked, eyes brightening. She was definitely her father's child. She loved anything ancient, especially anything that might be full of mummies and treasure.

Now, a month later, in the heart of the darkest, deepest valley in the jungle, they've found the small pyramid, the tomb of the sixth-century Mayan King Nu'a Hunasco, inside of which lies the vast wealth he had entombed with himself and his wives.

The knocking sounds of the recompression chamber thrummed in his skull. White walls bleached over the jungle hues for a moment, and Caleb tried to focus, making a half-hearted attempt to re-entangle himself in the present. *Focus on the vibrations here, in this chamber, the subtle movements of the waves tugging at the hull.* But it was no use. The white chipped away, layer by layer, revealing the alluring scene painted behind it, impatient to be viewed . . .

Caleb and Phoebe wait on the stones at the top of the tomb an hour after dawn, surrounded by bugs, swarms already alert and hungry, while their mother and the others are still back in their tents, just waking up. "Bug spray's wearing off."

Caleb slaps at plump mosquitoes with annoyance, trying to imagine some purpose to their lives, some ultimate destiny determining the course of their aerial struggles. He sighs and approaches his sister, and then they both put their hands, palms out, on the cool onyx slab that served as the door to Nu'a Hunasco's tomb.

"So now what?"

Phoebe grins. "We both saw it, right?"

"I saw something," Caleb admits. "You were the one that drew it." He looks around, checking the vine-consumed alcoves, the shadows deep with mystery.

"There, I think." Phoebe points to the upper-most stone on the left side of the door—an octagonal block, coated with moss. Caleb pulls out his pocket knife and tries to reach it.

"Too high."

"Let me get on your shoulders."

Caleb sighs. "All right, but hurry. I don't want Mom and George to find out we're gone."

"Having second thoughts?" He bends down and she climbs on his shoulders.

"About stealing the glory from George? Not at all. But Mom . . ."

"She'll be pissed."

"Yeah, but she'll get over it if we find the treasure."

"We'll find it, you and me. We're a great team.

And we'll show them we're just as good, that we saw it when they couldn't."

"We did." Caleb wobbles, trying to keep her stead. "Jeez, you got heavy."

"Shut up, I'm in a growth spurt."

"Too many Doritos, if you ask me."

"What else are we going to eat down here? Now, hold still, I think I've got it."

Caleb tries to look up into the shadows where her hands are fumbling around the octagonal stone. Then he has the sudden fear that something bad is about to happen—that Phoebe is going to trigger some trap, like in the Indiana Jones movies, and spring-loaded darts will riddle their flesh before a giant boulder pulverizes their bones.

"Got it!" she shouts, and Caleb hears something above turn with a grating sound that releases a cascade of dust. Coughing, Caleb lets Phoebe down and drops to his knees, just as the stone slab shakes and slides sideways into a thick groove in the stone wall.

Phoebe quickly pulls out two flashlights from her backpack and hands the bigger one to Caleb. "Ready, big brother?"

Caleb glances back, expecting a horde of spear-wielding Mayans to burst from the thicket at any moment, but the trees sway and the cicadas sing and the sun glares with blind ferocity that all but pushes him inside the sheltering darkness after Phoebe.

They descend a straight, narrow staircase, stepping carefully around rubble where the jungle has found its way inside. Vines and roots hug the walls and smother the ceiling. Further down, the steps seem to grow steeper, and Caleb and Phoebe take their time with their footing, shining their lights ahead and, occasionally, back.

"Thinking about Dad?"

Caleb looks up, surprised. She rarely mentions Dad, and barely even remembers him. He was shot down when she was only three, but Phoebe has been watching Caleb intently over the past couple years, sympathetic to the internal conflict her older brother has been struggling with. He continues following, then pulls ahead, shining his light into the gloom, adding his brilliance to Phoebe's steady beam. "Let me lead."

"I think I've seen him too." Phoebe touches his shoulder.

He pauses. The cool air is musty, a little rank, full of dust, and the walls are cracked where brown vines protrude. The back of Caleb's neck breaks out in a cold sweat. He turns, shines the light on her face.

"When?"

She chews on her lower lip and it reminds him of how, as a baby with two new teeth, she used to nibble on a piece of cheese. "Sometimes I feel, I don't know, dizzy, and I sit and the world kind of disappears and then I see this bright white room, and this Middle Eastern man walks in, carrying something shiny and I scream . . ."

Phoebe's eyes glaze over.

". . . and the walls change color. And suddenly I'm in a desert, and there's a man in a rusty cage and a dirty dish filled with little white worms and there are scorpions and then . . ."

Caleb's mouth is dry as sand. He tries to reach for her but can't move. "What then?"

She shrugs, blinks. "I don't know. Sometimes it all just vanishes and I'm back in the present. Other times I look up and I see the sun, except on top of it there's this bird's head and a beak and tiny brown eyes looking down at me."

Caleb's fingers go to his mouth. "The eagle and the sun! The same thing I've seen, that I've drawn! And Dad . . . tortured in that place." He wants to run screaming to anyone who will listen—to the police, to the American embassy, to anyone but his mother, who won't hear of it. But then he tells himself to relax. Maybe Phoebe has just been influenced by his vivid descriptions, and subconsciously she has begun experiencing the same things.

She squints. "I don't get this vision often, and it's not very strong. Mom says it's nothing. You'll outgrow it, too, she says, eventually."

"I won't."

"You will." Phoebe gives him a nudge back down the stairs. "And Mom says someday you'll learn to separate the . . . the objective dreams from the others."

Caleb scowls. "You even sound like Mom."

She shrugs. "You're my big brother, and even though you're a real nerd sometimes, I still like you." She stares at her shoes. "I don't want you to hate me, too."

"I don't hate Mom."

"Yes you do."

"I hate that she won't believe me. She won't look for Dad. He's been calling for our help all this time and we're ignoring him, hoping he'll just die."

"He might be dead," Phoebe whispers as they start descending again. Too eager, she squeezes past him, determined to go first. "Did you ever think of that? Maybe it's like Mom says, and you're just picking up on stuff from the past."

"Maybe, but—"

Something shifts, a barely perceptible sound, but in this hollow passageway it echoes in Caleb's ears like a thunderclap. He shines his light down to Phoebe's foot and illuminates the step sinking beneath her weight.

Another spring.

She freezes, turns back with a look of surprise, a look that begs her big brother to say everything *is all right, that it's just a weak step.* "Caleb?"

He reaches for her—

—just as she drops into the darkness, the entire stairwell suddenly falling away, and everything beyond Caleb's step just vanishes, sucked into the distant floor, somewhere in all that darkness. But he catches her, barely. Just her wrist. Her scream pierces his ears and lets loose a hailstorm of dust and rocks from the walls and the high, tapering ceiling.

"Don't let go!" *she shrieks.*

"Got you, I've got you." *He sets down the light, which promptly rolls and spills off the step, turning end over end, then clanking and winking out below as the darkness claims it. Only Phoebe's light remains, spinning wildly in her free hand.*

"Drop the light, Phoebe, and grab my arm with both hands!" *He has a hold on the upper stair with his left hand while clinging to Phoebe with his right.*

"Wait. Just hold on. I think . . ." *She steadies her light, aims it down, where it highlights something that glints like the sun about twenty feet away. The beam, full of captured dust, plays slowly over the chamber below, tracing objects that flash back at them. Heaps of golden ingots, statues, jade and ruby necklaces; monkey gods with sapphire eyes holding plates heaped with golden cups and chains, coins and spheres; and in the center, a gold-inscribed crypt. And there . . . a mosaic face, pierced nose and ears, and slanted eyes leering up at them, mocking their predicament.*

"Phoebe!"

She looks back, eyes glazed, as her hand slips.

"Drop the flashlight! Come on Phoebe, come on! Reach for me. We'll get the others and come back."

She drops the light, and the seconds drag out until the flashlight smashes on the hard rock floor below. "We found it," she whispers and lifts her hand, reaching for Caleb. He feels her palm, sweaty from holding the flashlight, slipping along his skin. Her other hand, the fingers sliding down and then through his—

"NO!"

—then his empty hand, fingers open, snatching at nothing but swirling dust. The darkness swallows her up, greedily enveloping everything, it seems, but her fiercely shining blue eyes and the words screaming from the depths.

"Big brother!"

Caleb clenches his eyes . . .

. . . and opened them, to see his etchings of the pyramid, the door, the stairs, and page after page, roughly torn from the pad and scattered across the cot and the floor of the recompression chamber. And the last one, still on his pad: a hand reaching out to him from the darkness beyond a broken stairwell. Caleb tore it out, crumpled it into a ball and brought it to his mouth, chewing into the edge to stop from screaming.

When the thrumming in his ears subsided and only the knocking and whirring of the chamber remained, he glanced at his watch.

Only two hours to go.

7

The Keeper stepped out of the white and blue cab, buttoned his suit coat and strode toward the crowded sidewalk. Somehow, in this sweltering city, the temperature had actually managed to rise since the sun dipped below the hillside rooftops. He noted their silhouettes, squat rectangular eyesores where there once stood magnificent temples, royal palaces and centers of learning.

He grumbled as a mob of unwashed, barefoot kids ran past him. Brushing off his suit and checking to make sure none of them had picked his pockets, he shuffled into an alley that smelled of human waste. He trod carefully around an open sewer grate, breathing through his mouth. Overhead, white sheets and shirts hung from a

THE PHAROS OBJECTIVE

stained clothesline, and dusty fans whirled in the open windows.

He turned one corner, paused and, glancing over his shoulder, he expected to see something out of place, someone following him. He scanned the crowds, the hundreds shuffling away from the markets like ants back to the colony after a fruitful campaign. He saw nothing out of the ordinary. Relaxing his shoulders, he summoned a weak smile and wondered whether he hadn't let the paranoia go to his head.

Then suddenly he felt it. He was certain of it, sure he was being tailed. And the tension crawled up the back of his neck. *Could be anyone,* he thought, imagining narrow faces pressed against car windows, eyes blinking at him from shadowed doorways. There was no reason to expect danger now, but he sensed it nonetheless. Perhaps because they were getting so close.

The Pharos protects itself.

But from us? He shook his head, turned and kept walking. No, the Keepers were the protectors. *We're only doing what's right, following the plan.*

Seeing no one in the next alley, a cramped space between the walls of two butcher shops, he opened the closest door and ducked inside. Within, the dark hallway was lit by a single naked bulb and littered with old newspapers and chicken bones. He walked to the only door on the left wall.

There was a keypad next to the handle. The door itself was made of heavy iron with large hinges set in a reinforced frame. The Keeper typed in a five-number sequence, whistling softly, and shot a quick look around at the shadows that seemed to gather at the other end of the hall.

Just as a hissing sound emanated from the door and the handle clicked, he had a surge of doubt, and the suspicion that he had just made a terrible lapse in judgment. He glanced down, and instead of opening the door he pressed the cancel button, then smeared his hands across the keypad, ensuring that no one could determine which keys had just been pressed. *Can't be too careful.*

The Keepers hadn't survived this long by being reckless. The greatest danger had always come from within, from the choices of the other Keepers; and there was only so much you could do to avoid such events. One had to choose carefully, that's all, as his father had done with him.

He lowered his hands and flicked his right wrist. Choices.

A slender blade that had been concealed up his jacket sleeve descended from a wrist strap. The smooth ivory handle settled comfortably in his grasp, and the feel of the cool grip calmed his pounding heart. He strode toward the shadows, wishing they had installed more lights overhead, despite the obvious protection such a dingy, dark location afforded to their secret entrance.

Something glinted in that darkness. An eye? A weapon? He strode faster, crouching, preparing to leap.

Then came a whisper. And another. Quick and powerful.

Deadly.

Two bullets punched through his chest and stopped him cold. The dagger clattered to the floor, a second before his knees. He looked in astonishment at the spreading stains from two meticulous holes in his left breast.

Footsteps.

A woman peeled herself away from the shadows, dark hair, a flash of bright green eyes, dressed all in black.

And smiling.

She placed the silenced Beretta into a pack over her shoulder and stood over the Keeper as he slumped to the floor, gasping, choking on his own blood.

"Too bad, Wilhelm," she said. "Now I'll have to do this the hard way."

Nina Osseni bent down and rummaged through Wilhelm Miles's suit coat, found his wallet, then searched his lapels for the microphone. She pulled the receiver from his right ear and placed it in hers, then secured the microphone on her turtleneck, stood up and opened the wallet.

She cleared her throat and tapped the dime-sized microphone.

"Hello?" She faced the metal door and took deep, quick breaths. "Hell-oo."

The earpiece crackled. "Who is this?" A man's voice, confused, but somehow still confident.

"I'm sorry," she said, "but I don't believe you're in a position to ask questions."

"I see. You'll indulge me, then, won't you?"

"Perhaps, but be quick."

"Am I to assume Mr. Miles is no longer with us?"

"Yes."

"Am I also to assume that you're standing outside our entrance, since you've obviously found and deactivated our hallway cameras?"

"Two for two. Now, my turn."

"Yes, of course."

"I have a message from my employer."

"We know all about your employer," said the voice in her ear. "And we know all about you, Nina Osseni."

Nina froze.

"We've tracked your employer's actions for some time. We know what he did to the Renegade, and we've been expecting you, actually, for quite some time. What took you?"

Nina sighed. "Well, well. My employer wants you to stay out of our way. You can do so voluntarily, or we can ensure it. We know your identities, every Keeper. We know—"

"And that's supposed to scare us?"

"Yes, Mr. Gregory, it should. As it should scare your son and daughter. And Jonathan Ackerman and Hideki Gutai and Annabelle Marsh and . . . Shall I continue?"

"No need," said Gregory. "You've made your point. But you must understand. If you know so much about us, you know our legacy. Our history. We are Keepers, and if we are struck down, others have been prepared to take our place. We have endured for two thousand years, protecting the secret, guarding the treasure."

Nina laughed. "Guarding? Is that what you call it? Is that why you're following the Morpheus Initiative? Or is it that you want the same thing we do?"

"What we want is only our right. We are the heirs to this legacy, not you."

"You've had two thousand years to claim that legacy and you've failed." Something shifted behind the door, stealthy footsteps.

Nina reached for her Beretta.

"No," the Keeper said, "we didn't fail. The Pharos won. There's a difference."

Nina cocked her head. Sure she heard movement beyond the door, perhaps guards readying themselves for an attack, she stepped back into the alley.

"Time for me to run," she whispered, hoping that Nolan Gregory hadn't alerted any other security who might cut off her escape out in the street.

"Nice of you to drop by," he said. "I hope we'll have the pleasure to meet in person soon."

"Count on it," she said, then tossed away the microphone and the earpiece, just as the door clicked and the hinges squealed.

Her would-be pursuers found the alley empty. Nina Osseni had vanished into the heat and the heart of the city.

When he next glanced at his watch, Caleb was pleasantly surprised. One hour to go. Then he looked down at the floor, at the seven scattered pages and the elaborate illustrations his subconscious had been drawing for the past sixty minutes.

Free-drawing, his mother called it. Kind of like the free-writing other psychics did while in a trance. With Caleb and others like him, especially those in the Morpheus Initiative, free-drawing was the key— the key to the past, the key to the present, the key to anything you set your mind to, giving it free rein like a dog off its leash in a great open park. Sometimes it returned empty-handed, other times it came back with something you really wanted, something valuable.

He stared at the drawings. Each one held a recognizable scene, something familiar. In some cases, he had drawn these very images before, years ago as a frightened kid hauled along with his baby sister on exotic romps around the world with his mom and a bunch of weirdoes claiming to see things.

Sheet one: a dizzying spire, so high it scraped the clouds, with a burning flame at its peak and a beam striking out below, seeking out the next target among the fleet of Roman galleys braving the greedy reefs. Two ships were ablaze, sinking as men leapt into the sea.

Sheet two: a smaller, much more modern light-house erected atop a hill beyond an apple orchard while below, a rusty iron ship with a lantern on its mast approached from the horizon.

Sheet three: a rugged mountain range and a series of caves, one with bars and withered arms reaching out from the darkness. In the sky hung a five-pointed star behind a crudely drawn fence. The entire picture was dark, drawn in deep lines and angry shading, as if he had wanted to be finished with it as soon as possible.

Sheet four: a girl in a wheelchair at work in a lab, peering into a microscope. Caleb frowned. What was that about? He had definitely drawn Phoebe, but as far as he knew she had never had an interest in biology or chemistry. What could it signify? He shook his head and considered the next one.

Sheet five: another ship, a naval clipper with striped sails—red and white, Caleb saw with sudden clarity—braving a dangerous sea while fleeing a small armada hot on its trail.

Sheet six: a finely detailed caduceus, a thick staff entwined with knotted snakes facing each other with huge glowing eyes.

And finally: a turbaned man standing atop a windswept dune, gazing at the ruins of a once-great tower, and a small flame burning at its peak while the stars blazed in the night sky. Caleb stared at this one, then back over the other six for a long time.

The minutes passed, his vision blurred, and it seemed another trance beckoned, just within a breath, a finger's reach, a blink. He caught the whiff of jasmine, the thick pungent aroma of hashish, and the musty signs of old, wind-eroded stones.

Then the door whirred, the speaker crackled, and everything in his mind dissolved into a pale sheen of white as Waxman, lowering his head, stepped inside the chamber.

"Time served, young man. Ready for parole?"

Caleb blinked. "No, but how about dinner?"

An hour after Caleb checked into his new hotel he was struck down with a violent strain of food poisoning. He and the other members of the Morpheus Initiative had eaten at the same café outside of the mosque of Abul Abbas al-Mursi, but it seemed Alexandria had only intended Caleb as its target. He had been sitting next to the only one who actually seemed interesting, a Mediterranean beauty named Nina-something. She had tried to get him out of his shell, even bought a round of Ouzo shots, but Caleb passed on the drinks, already feeling queasy.

He'd avoided his mother's gaze and tried to shut out Waxman's ceaseless lecturing, going on just to hear his own voice talk about the glory of past missions or the strengths of the visions the group had achieved.

Maybe it was the food, or maybe Caleb really just didn't want to put on a happy face for this gaggle of psychic misfits, so his body supplied the best possible excuse for his absence. Unfortunately, this bug left him unable to think, much less sit up to reach the cache of books he had brought along. The fever took hold quickly and didn't let up for two brutal days and nights. People swam in and out of his vision, in and out of his consciousness, darting around the hotel room. But other times he was left extremely lucid, if unable to speak or move. He remembered his mother appearing frightened at first, then increasingly haggard. A pale face wavering in the watery blur of his room, a blur in which he could see every detail: the petals in the flowery curtains, the watermarks on the stained wallpaper, the cracks in the ceiling that mirrored the spider web lines in his mother's skin, and the red jagged lines against the whites of her eyes.

Once, as Caleb tried taking a sip of water from the bedside cup in the middle of the night, he felt another presence. He saw a dark figure standing beside the rectangular outline of the door, head bowed, long arms at his side. Menacing, yet motionless. He was a blur, a melding of form and shadow, darkness and deep tones of gray and green. A low mumbling emanated from his throat, but in

Caleb's fevered state the words meshed into gibberish that echoed off the walls. Caleb trembled, and saliva dribbled down his chin as fresh chills ran over his body. Pajamas formerly stifling now felt like frost-covered rags. And the presence, whatever or whoever he was, appeared to be pointing at him and trying to speak. Then the door opened and blessed light stabbed inside, chasing away the image. Caleb was at the same time grateful and frustrated.

Helen entered and curiously paused on the threshold, as if she had caught the scent of something familiar, yet impossibly frightening.

Caleb fell back against the soaked pillow, the room spun, and he drowned in a frothing whirlpool of dreams . . .

. . . *as he grips a wooden rail on the prow of a ship heaving upon turbulent waves. The surf pounds against great rocks, and only by furious rowing do the men manage to pull up to the embankment. And with a shout of thanks to Triton, they scramble overboard.*

The rain spits upon them as they jump into the shallows and trudge to shore. His cloak is drenched, his armor unbearably heavy. Titus—his name is Titus—looks up as the others rush past, and there he sees it for the first time up close: a hulking shadow, black against the churning clouds, a brooding tower defying the angry storm.

Far, far above, the seething flame of its beacon burns against the swirling winds, and the great mirror sends a crimson beam through the pelting rain, stabbing over the sea through the infinite folds of night.

Titus hurries forward with the others, his legion part of a small team of reinforcements for Caesar and his personal troops. In the pounding surf, the howling wind and the driving rain, even the sound of his own boots upon the granite stairs are muffled. He runs between two immense statues, an old king and queen greeting arrivals, then into a dark courtyard. Once more he turns his face up to the merciless rain and has the impression that the glowing tip of the Pharos is tickling the thunder-clouds until they erupt in a laughing cacophony of light and sound.

Inside, the men shake off their cloaks, remove their helmets and dry their faces. Their leader, Marcus Entonius, orders Titus to follow him into a nearby doorway while the others set about their tasks. Hastening to obey, Titus has time only for a glance around the torch-lit interior to notice the winding ramp, the weathered statues clinging to the precipitous walls, the central shaft and the cauldron ready with oil.

He follows Marcus, trotting close to his torch as he is led through a winding labyrinth of passageways, one door leading to another exactly the same. It seems they double back, then forward again, before they finally descend a small ramp and turn into a tunnel-like chamber that drops sharply to a spiral staircase.

The stairs descend endlessly. The steps feel worn, as if water has coursed through this shaft for centuries. After circling for what seems like hours, breathing in the acrid smoke from Marcus's torch, Titus's legs nearly buckle beneath him.

The well opens into a massive, brightly lit chamber. They approach two guardians, enormous Egyptian statues carved out of black onyx— an Ibis-faced god with a long staff and a writing palette to one side flanked by a female statue wearing a peculiar half-moon headdress and holding a large book to her chest.

Titus respectfully bows his head to these native deities and steps between them. Ahead looms an imposing red granite wall covered with strange carvings and images. Centered and most prominent rises a large staff with twin snakes wrapped around it and facing each other at the top. Standing before this symbol is Gaius Julius Caesar.

Titus kneels as Marcus bows his head. "My Lord."

Caesar slowly raises his left hand. In his right he holds an unbound sheaf of papyrus. The flickering torchlight from two braziers mounted on opposite sides of the wall illuminate scrawled lines and symbols on the papyrus similar to the images on the walls.

Titus peers at the wall ahead, observing seven strange symbols enclosed in raised circles spaced around the great snake-entwined staff. He recognizes some of them as ancient Greek signs for the planets.

Caesar turns. His eyes are haunted, glazed and exhausted. Titus has heard whispers that since his taking of the Pharos, he has been rarely seen, spending all his time inside the lighthouse. Doing what, no one would say. Some of the men whisper that the ancient gods have trapped him inside their shrine and will not let him go until Rome has left their land. Others claim Caesar has found an ancient source of power and seeks to wrest it from the gods. Still others believe he has discovered Alexander's lost treasure.

"Titus Batus,"—Caesar clenches the papyrus tightly in his hand—"your skills are needed. These papers were in the possession of this tower's keeper, an old, pathetic man who, with his son, alone kept the fires burning and directed the great mirror above."

"What, only two—?"

"The boy is dead." Caesar says sharply. "He fled, and when we caught up with him, down here, he was trying to throw these"—he holds up the papers—"into the flames. We had to stop him."

"What are they, sir?"

Caesar shakes his head. "Whatever these scribblings represent, that boy died for them. We brought his father here, and the old man actually broke free, lunged for the papers and tried to tear them up."

Titus frowns, looking from those sheets to the wall again.

"Titus. Get the answers from the old man. He is secured in the living quarters upstairs. Use whatever means necessary." Caesar turns his back and regards the wall once more. His shadow leaps from his body and dances obscenely across the wall, mimicking his stance and mocking his ignorance. Behind him, Titus imagines the two Egyptian statues expelling low, indifferent sighs.

"Yes, sir." Titus stands and extends his arm in salute. "I—"

But then a trampling of feet pounds out from the stairwell and four men rush into the room. "My liege, Egyptian forces are approaching. Twenty ships."

Caesar lowers his head as if a great weight pulls on his neck. He looks at the papers trapped in his fist and then considers the wall once more.

Marcus glances from the messenger to his leader. "My Lord, we do not have the strength to withstand such an assault."

Caesar sighs. "Very well. We leave for the

safety of the palace and wait for Mithradates and reinforcements. I will return once we have the situation in hand. Bring the old man with us."

"Sir," says another soldier on the stairs, "it is too late. He has chewed off his tongue and drowned in his own blood."

Caesar swears. He pushes past Titus, muttering a curse on the local gods, and stomps up the stairs. Titus follows the others, the last to leave the silent chamber. Turning one last time, he meets the unnerving stares of those two snakes carved deeply into the granite wall. In the flickering light, they appear to slither around the staff, turn their heads and warn against his return. Then Titus risks a glance at the female statue, who seems to be smirking, confident in the secret clutched tightly to her heart.

Caesar's forces leave Pharos Island, fleeing from the lighthouse on the few ships remaining after the Egyptians caught them unprepared. Several Roman galleons are already floundering, however, as too many men cram onto their decks. The Emperor's vessel, too, sinks and men are crushed by planks and become entangled in arms and legs, ropes and moorings.

Titus swims feverishly, finds a floating piece of wood, and kicks his way toward a distant boat. Up ahead, in a flash of lightning, he sees the purple cloak of his leader. Caesar struggles, trying to swim using only one hand. In the other, he holds aloft the papyrus sheets.

A flash.

And then, leaving the brilliant afternoon sun, Titus enters the central palace. Caesar stands on the balcony above the great square as the Fourteenth Legion waits in the hot sun for him to pronounce the words they all expect—that they would be moving out.

Alexandria is in Caesar's hands again. Pothinus and Achillas, instigators of the rebellion, have been executed, and Ptolemy XIII died trying to escape. Lovely Cleopatra rests comfortably on the throne, her gambit of capturing Caesar's heart a success.

Caesar leans on the railing and stares across the harbor. He gazes over the waves to the lighthouse, with its mirror reflecting the sun's rays back at him. Titus has the sense that two great warriors are regarding each other in a contest of wills, deciding whether to continue the struggle or to bow out in mutual respect for the other's prowess.

Caesar looks away. He stiffens at a touch from the alluring Cleopatra, her olive skin shining in the sunlight. "You must go," Titus hears her say. "Your enemies stretch your forces thin. Seek them out, one by one, and consolidate your empire once more."

Caesar nods and gazes one last time at the

lighthouse, acknowledging it as an opponent he cannot overcome and determining to press ahead more vigorously in matters he can. "Here," he says to Marcus Entonius, standing at his side, "take these papers to my father-in-law. They shall be safe in his personal library until I can return my attention to their mysteries."

"My love," Cleopatra says, "why not leave them here at the museum? Our scholars can study the symbols and put their great minds to the task of unlocking their secrets."

"No. The harbor fire makes it clear that they are not safe here. These scrolls must be preserved."

"But all the original books are safe. Only the copies were lost."

"It is decided." He raises his arms to his men and they shout up at him, reaffirming their loyalty and their readiness to leave.

Cleopatra lowers her head, but when she steals a glance at the Pharos, Titus swears he sees her smile.

10

Caleb awoke from the dream at the same time the fever broke. It was mid-afternoon on a nameless day. He struggled out of bed, weak to exhaustion, and in the sunlight filtering through the curtains he found a bowl of raisins, nuts and bananas on the table.

Still in Alexandria. How long had he been out? What was happening back in New York? He needed to check back soon. He could only imagine if he were stuck here past the start of the semester. How would his students fare with Lombardo or—God help them—Henrik Jenson as his substitute? He had to get out of here as soon as he was cleared to fly, if not sooner. Pain he could handle. He wasn't quite sure about his tolerance for his mother or her crazy friends.

With a full stomach and confidence that the food would not be coming back up, he made it to the shower. After dressing in sweat pants, sandals and an old T-shirt, he left the room and took the stairs down to the lobby. His head still felt weak, lost in a fog, but he kept moving, taking a short break against a wall as he made his way to the conference room. He forced a smile to a rotund, dark-skinned maid who gave him a wide berth and then he opened the door.

Around a long table littered with papers, pencils, tape recorders and half-full ashtrays sat the ten members of the Morpheus Initiative. A video camera on a tripod was set up in the corner to record everything that transpired. Helen sat at the far end of the table, peering at four pages spread in front of her, and George Waxman stood behind her, busily taping sketches to the wall in groups that seemed to be related by their subject matter. He wore a white polo shirt with a turned-up collar and starched blue jeans and cowboy boots, like he had just stepped into a country bar, the kind with peanuts on the floor and a mechanical bull in the corner. He turned at the sound of the door.

"Caleb. Good of you to show up, finally." He pointed to an open chair. "Take a seat. I didn't realize you university types had such weak constitutions."

Caleb's mother offered a tired smile. "Feeling better, hon?" She wore a multicolored local shawl and big red plastic sunglasses pushed up on her head. She was radiant, her face tanned and her eyes shining. She had the poise and grace of a deity. In fact, in silhouette she looked like an Egyptian goddesses painted on the crumbling walls around this city, like Isis maybe, or Caleb's local favorite, Seshat, the wife of Thoth and the goddess of writing and libraries.

This blasphemous comparison made Caleb even angrier with her for intruding into his imagination, weaving herself into the tapestry of the ancient religion he had found so fascinating and liberating. Caleb opened his mouth to speak, but suddenly felt overwhelmed with nausea. Weak and his head spinning, he staggered toward the table. He smelled menthol. Smoke clogged his lungs and stung his eyes, a blinding light . . .

. . . *and he is descending the narrow spiral staircase again, rounding the final bend as the statues of the god and goddess come into view, leaning toward him with wide, staring eyes.*

Hands held him upright. Someone guided him to the chair and he slumped forward, turning his head and taking sharp breaths.

"Okay," said Waxman, oblivious to Caleb's condition, and stretched and walked back to the wall. "Let's see where we are. Caleb, you can just listen for now and play catch-up later. The rest of the team has just come back from the morning session with their impressions of the assignment, which we've now taped to the wall. They were each asked to concentrate on a single object and draw whatever came to them." He set his burning cigarette down in an ashtray as he adjusted his shirt and regarded the drawings again. Helen frowned and moved the ashtray away from Caleb.

Waxman continued. "You were all directed to focus on a symbol, one familiar to most of you. It is a staff with snakes wrapped around it—"

Caleb sat up straight.

"—the caduceus, symbol of medical practice everywhere." Waxman adjusted his collar. "I'm sure everyone had preconceived notions of its meaning, but that'll simply be another factor to account when we analyze your visions." He looked down his glasses at everyone before taking stock of the pictures on the wall.

"Okay, what do we have?" continued Waxman. "Xavier, you drew what look like spheres or balls circling around a snake. Consistent, but unusual. Not sure what that means, yet."

Caleb's breath came out in shallow, choking puffs. Flashes of his dream returned with pounding clarity . . .

. . . *showing him the subterranean chamber, Caesar's shadow thrust impotently upon the wall, the snake heads eyeing him with indifference.*

With the back of his ballpoint pen, Waxman tapped the next sheet. "Two of you, Tom and Nina, drew something like a door with bars across it, and above this Nina sketched a flame and wrote something . . . that I can't quite read."

At the other end of the table, with her lustrous hair tied back behind her head in a yellow scarf, Nina Osseni cleared her throat. Caleb took deep breaths, trying to ground himself in just one world. Sensing the pull again from the other side, he forced all his attention onto this woman. She seemed cat-like, calm and calculating. Her eyes scanned everyone sitting around the table, like she trusted no one and was ready for an attack to come from any angle. "I wrote 'Light,'" she said, "just because I had the impression that the flame was different somehow. Like it wasn't meant for warmth, but for illumination only?"

"I see, Nina. Thank you." Waxman chewed on his pen and took another step to the right. Caleb watched his mother, saw how her gaze followed Waxman, like he was some kind of god, or hero at least, in her eyes.

"Then," Waxman continued, "we have five mostly unrelated drawings: Mary drew waves with some kind of wreckage or bodies floating in the water; Elliot sketched a tower tipping over on its side; Amelia drew a temple-like building with lots of pillars and put a gate around it; Victor drew a pyramid in the desert, near an oasis; and Dennis . . . I don't know what this is."

"Sorry," said a heavyset bald man, sweating and smoking across from Caleb. "I didn't get a good impression of anything this time around. I had the sense of something choking or smothered under heavy layers of, I don't know, something black and hot." He rubbed his forehead and took a sip of Pepsi. "Sorry."

"Don't worry, Dennis." Waxman smiled. "It's not an exact science. Good days and bad."

Helen held up one last drawing. "Then there's mine," she said, "which, admittedly, is biased, since I know the ultimate target."

"True, so while we can't count yours as a valid blind experiment, it's telling nonetheless." Waxman gave her a light pat on the shoulder.

Caleb narrowed his eyes, then tried to focus on his mother's picture. She had drawn a series of doors, one after another. Seven in total, with some kind of dog or jackal standing guard before each one. But what pulled his eye was something she had drawn in the upper corner, away from the doors.

He stood, reached over Helen's shoulder and snatched the sheet from her. He held it up, staring at the smaller image of a crudely drawn mountain, its top blown off. Jagged lines rolled down its sides toward two separate sites that looked like domed houses, one on each side of the mountain.

Waxman was frowning. "What are you doing?"

Helen tried to grab it back from him. "Honey," she said, "just sit and listen for now."

"I know what this is," Caleb said, and the room quieted down. He stumbled forward, took a piece of tape and stuck her picture on the wall, overlapping Tom and Victor's drawings.

"Looks like a volcano erupting," said Dennis, chewing into a Mars Bar.

"It is." Caleb glanced back to the drawing and he pointed to the rightmost pillared structure threatened by the zigzagging lava flow. "Mom, what is this you've drawn over this house?"

Her face reddened as everyone looked at her. "A book," she said at last.

Caleb smiled, took a step back and sat down. "In my fever, I had a dream."

Waxman and Helen both sat quietly, inching forward. Caleb expected one or both to tell him to be quiet, to let them get on with their important analysis and the next phase of the experiment, but in their stunned silence, he continued. "I know what she's drawn. I know what the caduceus represents and how it relates to the treasure."

"Treasure?"

"In a minute, Dennis." Helen snapped her chewing gum. She leaned back in her chair, crossing her arms. "Okay, Caleb. Go ahead, enlighten us."

Caleb pointed to Helen's drawing. "Vesuvius. It erupted in seventy-nine AD, burying both Pompeii and Herculaneum." He indicated the two houses she had drawn, believing she had intended them to represent two distinct cities. "It happened so fast that people died in their sleep or even walking on the street. All the buildings were encased in seventy feet of volcanic ash and mud, and buried until excavators rediscovered the city by accident in the eighteenth century."

"Lava!" Dennis exclaimed. "I knew it. I—"

"We all know about Vesuvius." Waxman coughed and lit up another cigarette. "How does this information help us?"

"My mother drew a book over one of the cities."

"And . . . ?" Helen led, getting annoyed.

Caleb's voice faltered a little. *Am I on the right track?* Everyone was looking at him, and he was sure, with the exception of Waxman, that none of the others believed he had any real psychic abilities, let alone that he shared their vaunted remote-viewing powers. He gathered his confidence. "She drew a book. That's the key. The key to the doors, the gates, the caduceus—in short, everything the rest of you have drawn."

"What do you mean?" Waxman leaned forward. Caleb could see the bright blue of his eyes, and he imagined that something black slithered and crept behind them, patiently waiting for a moment to strike. He had the sudden impression that Waxman knew exactly what Caleb was talking about, and was simply hiding it from these people, waiting to see what they could find out on their own.

Caleb took a deep breath. "There was a large personal library in Herculaneum. With few exceptions, such as at Athens or here in Alexandria, most libraries in those days were the possessions of wealthy individuals with a passion for collecting books. The library at Herculaneum belonged to a man named Lucius Calpurnius Piso."

Someone coughed. Others looked around the table.

"Who was he?" Helen asked at last. She leaned forward in her chair, and her eager eyes met his.

Caleb let the question hang for a moment. When no one else answered, he said, "He was the father-in-law of Julius Caesar."

Around the room interest piqued, but still the blank stares remained. Nina seemed to be watching him more intently, hungrily even, and it took all of Caleb's willpower to pull his eyes away from hers.

He took another breath. "In my dream I saw Caesar flee the lighthouse, holding papers he had stolen from its keepers."

Helen stood up. "Did you see the caduceus? The snakes wrapped around a staff?"

"Carved on a door, about eight feet high. It's the symbol of Mercury, by the way, of Hermes, and before that the Egyptian equivalent, Thoth."

"God of Medicine," Waxman said, eyes beaming.

"And writing," Caleb added. "They believed he was the one who gave language to mankind and taught us everything from astronomy to medicine and farming. He also counseled the other gods and judged the dead. And it was rumored that he put all of this knowledge into a series of books, the greatest of which he called the Emerald Tablet."

The room was quiet, so quiet that Caleb could hear his heart thudding against his ribs. Everyone was looking at him through the haze of smoke.

Helen cleared her throat. "So Caesar may have taken some kind of important papers from the Pharos Lighthouse?"

"Yes," Caleb answered, his voice cracking. "And unable to decipher the cryptic words and symbols drawn by the lighthouse keepers, he ordered the scroll sent to the library at Herculaneum. His father-in-law's library. With all of his attention then focused on Rome and other various campaigns, he forgot all about it, and those papers were still there when Vesuvius erupted." He glanced around at his attentive audience. "Anyway, it could've happened that way."

Waxman was grinning like Caleb had never seen anyone grin. "*The Villa of the Papyri!* Found in the 1750s as workers tunneled under Herculaneum. A team of archaeologists have been trying to open and restore the scrolls recovered from the volcanic rock for years."

Caleb triumphantly sat down and returned his mother's glowing smile. A sinking feeling nagged at him, though, tugging at his victory. *How did Waxman know about Piso's library?* From what Caleb understood of his background, Waxman was a mathematics teacher from Cleveland who had begun a project to document paranormal abilities after receiving visions of his dead mother. His published articles had caught the eye of an archaeological team pursuing sunken ships in the Caribbean, and he had formed a group of like-minded psychics, people like Helen, who had scored well on such tests. Despite all his worldly exper-ience, book smarts never appeared to rank high on his resume, although somehow he had managed to come up with a fitting name for the team, as Morpheus was the lord of dreams, whose mother was the goddess of visions.

Now, at Waxman's direction, the room burst into a frenzy of activity, of discussions and rev-elations. Helen and Waxman set about explaining to the others the nature of the real subject, filling them in on the Pharos Lighthouse and the sup-posedly hidden chamber below.

"We know now what the visions are showing us: there's a sealed door with the sign of the caduceus on it, and there are seven symbols around the staff, which might represent seven keys or puzzles to solve before the door can be opened."

The next phase, Waxman said, would be to see if there was anything at Herculaneum that could help them. "We know that a series of earthquakes destroyed the bulk of the Pharos, with the last great quake in 1349 toppling what was left."

"And," Helen added, "we can assume that the shifting earth, the collapsed structure and tons and tons of limestone blocks have made it impossible to tunnel down to wherever the original entrance may have been."

"So isn't this all just a moot point?" asked Dennis. "What do Caesar's papers matter if we can't get into the Pharos chamber?"

"We've been scuba diving," Waxman said, nodding to Victor and Elliot, "but with limited success. We'll need to focus our energies on that front, see if any of you can find a way in from the sea."

"What about Qaitbey's fortress?" Xavier Montross asked. He was in his thirties, with a thick head of orange-red hair. He was shaped like a soccer player, muscular and lean. He never smoked, drank, or consumed junk food, and always sat as far as possible from anyone else, as if he feared contamination. "Anyone check inside there? Snoop around down in the basement?"

Something about his eyes made Caleb anxious,

as if of all the psychics assembled here Xavier had something, some speck of real power, the ability to shred Caleb's own meager gifts. He had always given Caleb the creeps. But fortunately, Xavier was the most reclusive Morpheus member, rarely speaking his mind or voicing his visions.

Helen shook her head. "We have detailed surveys of the structure from the Alexandrian government. Looks like there's nothing but bed-rock accessible from any location. Unless there's a hidden entrance or tunnel somewhere."

Caleb coughed, and his voice cracked again. "We could try sonar and see if we could locate hollow chambers?"

"It may come to that," Waxman said, "although getting permission to excavate the fortress or damage the foundation in any way would be extremely difficult, given the level of protection it enjoys as a Muslim historical site."

"So we're back to the sea route," Helen said. "We know from early writings that the designer of the lighthouse, a brilliant architect named Sostratus, used all sorts of advanced building techniques, including hydraulics, winches, gears and pulleys. We also believe there had to be vents in the harbor where the seawater could funnel in and out to power the internal mechanisms."

"Such as traps," Caleb couldn't help but say.

Waxman shot him a look of caution. "Yes, there

are those rumors. And maybe Caesar's papers reveal exactly how to bypass them. If you did have a true vision, maybe Caesar found the door to the lower chambers, but either couldn't open it . . . or feared springing such traps if he didn't open it in the right way."

Helen stood up. "If we can find and decipher that ancient document, which miraculously may have been preserved in Vesuvius's eruption, we might just have the key to the treasure."

Dennis scratched his head. "What's this treasure again? A ton of gold or something?"

"We don't know, exactly," Helen said. "It could be Alexander's spoils from his conquests across Asia and India. Legends are vague. All we know is that whatever it is, it's valuable enough that many have died trying to find it."

And, Caleb thought ruefully, recalling the father and son who had died before letting Caesar have the scroll, *to keep it hidden.*

He took a deep, cleansing breath and looked down at his shoes. As the others talked and made plans for a visit to Herculaneum, he noticed a leather case resting by his feet. *Waxman's bag.* It had several folding compartments, but one had been left open slightly, and inside was a folder of formal-looking typed pages. At the top right margin of one sheet was a stamped seal—*an eagle's head in profile atop a banner with a radiant sun in the middle.*

Caleb's blood went cold as ice water. The tiny hairs stood up on the back of his neck. He looked up at Waxman. Close to Helen, he was talking and waving his hands, flicking ash into the air as she returned his enthusiasm and pointed at various drawings, making connections.

The eagle . . . the sun and its rays . . . He had seen that image, again and again, leaving bloody trails in the nightmares of his father. Seeing it here tied his stomach into barbed-wire knots.

Helen's smile dropped when she saw Caleb's face. But he had slipped out of the chair and was backing away from the table, from Waxman. He turned and stumbled out of the room, muttering that he needed to find a bathroom. Around the corner, he staggered into the men's room, collapsed into the first stall that smelled as if it hadn't been cleaned since Vesuvius blew its top, and his stomach heaved.

Caleb struggled to the sink, washed his face, then looked into the mirror. Standing behind him, against the wall, was a man with long stringy hair over his face, his head down, arms at his side. He wore a faded-green khaki jacket, dirty pants and muddy boots.

His hands were trembling, his whole body shaking. A mumbling, throaty ramble came from his mouth. Caleb turned, a scream forming—

—and saw no one. Unable to look in the mirror again, to face either that haunting intruder or the prospect of his own insanity, Caleb crept out of the bathroom, staggered up to his room, collapsed on his bed and descended at once into a gratefully dreamless sleep.

11
NAPLES, ITALY

They arrived at the Bay of Naples on an afternoon favored by sun, warmth and the ever-present scent of olives wafting over the calm waters. The Royal Palace, its immense southern facade of red and gray, with hanging trellises and countless windows, could be seen a mile away as they stood on the front deck of the tourist-laden ferry.

After docking, they walked down the ramp and passed through a small plaza. Waxman efficiently handled the customs procedures, then strode ahead with Helen, who only glanced back once to make sure Caleb and Nina were following. Helen's urgency showed in the way her arms swung forward and back and the strides she took bounding up the plaza stairs.

Her enthusiasm was catching, Caleb thought.

Despite the nagging fear that Waxman had tricked him, that this was all part of a setup to get him back into the group, and despite the stationary in the briefcase—and the certainty that Waxman was more than he seemed—this *was* exciting. He couldn't help but feel that unavoidable thrill, that rush of adventure scholars only fantasize about while locked away in their libraries or rectangular classrooms in front of bleary-eyed students.

He and Nina tried to keep up, but soon decided on keeping their own pace. The other members of the team had stayed in Alexandria with instructions to continue remote viewing, focusing on the harbor and a way into the chambers under the lighthouse.

Caleb felt more than a little awkward being around Nina; he hadn't had a girlfriend in two years, nothing more recent than a few passing crushes from infatuated students. But compared to those innocent and naïve flirtations, Nina was a lioness, a tempting and refined young woman with skin like molasses and eyes so green they blinded him to the very fact he was staring. He had been caught snatching glimpses at her more than twice during the ferry ride. She had merely smiled, amused by his fawning interest.

"Let's keep up," she said in a low voice, nudging him with her elbow as she pulled ahead. She wore a summer blouse, red and white, colors that reminded him of the billowing sails of a visionary

DAVID SAKMYSTER   105

boat, and shorts that showed off her golden legs ending in high-heeled sandals. Mirrored sunglasses nestled on the soft-gelled curls of her thick black hair.

Caleb picked up the pace, his pulse rising in time as he caught up, painfully tearing his eyes away from her body as she climbed up a marble staircase toward the palace.

Up ahead, Helen and Waxman were talking about how to document this part of the project. "If we find what we're looking for, the discovery will be documentation enough of our success," Helen argued.

They crossed the square as pigeons flew away, parting biblically before them, then resuming their settled positions after they had passed. Caleb held the door open for Nina, whose bright lips peeled back into a playful smile before she slipped through, and gave a lingering glance to the palace grounds, to the lush lawns, manicured rose bushes and polished statues on the terrace overlooking the shimmering harbor.

Once inside the palace, Waxman directed them away from the crowd of tourists and went to a side door where a dour-faced man in a blue suit waited impatiently. When Waxman introduced himself, the man looked quite relieved.

"Giuseppe Marcos," he said. "Director for the Biblioteca Nazionale, the largest collection of books in Italy outside the Vatican archives, here in the Royal Palace." Caleb took a look around, marveling at the architecture and contents of this first hall alone. Apart from its great collection of Renaissance artwork and sculptures spanning several centuries, the palace also contained the Officina dei Papiri, which analyzed and preserved the ancient scrolls recovered from nearby Herculaneum.

Despite his lack of personal charisma and his occasional stumbling over English vocabulary, Marcos had a fluid, beautiful voice; in another life he could have been a tenor in the Royal Opera. Nina seemed to adore hearing him speak, sticking close, making the man uncomfortable. Giuseppe briefly covered the palace's construction in the early seventeenth century, begun as a suitable resort home for Spain's King Philip III who, ironically, had promised to visit Naples but never quite got there.

Waxman, in his usual tactless manner, cut off the history lesson and the tour. "Can we move on? We're short on time, and we came to see the laboratory."

Apologizing, the guide led the way, glancing over his shoulder frequently. "This is very irregular, no? We do not get many visitors to see the papyri, or the library. They think it is, how do you Americans say . . . *lame*."

"Others might," Caleb protested, "but I'd like to

see your library very much." He was salivating at the chance to actually touch the leatherbound spines of books hundreds of years old. He pictured lonely monks working away in dusty monasteries, copying down the Classics while the world toiled in ignorance through the Dark Ages.

Giuseppe smiled. "Well, you will get a look, sir. But I must say, Mr. Waxman and Ms. . . . ."

"Mrs.," Helen said. "Mrs. Crowe."

Caleb saw Waxman make a face Helen missed.

"Or just Helen," she added. "Please, Signore Marcos. I realize what we're asking is very unorthodox, but we have good reason to believe that a certain scroll in your Herculaneum collection is of great archaeological interest to Alexandria."

"I respect that, Miss—eh, Helen, but I fear you may have come all this way for nothing."

They passed from one marble-tiled corridor into the next, where large tapestries hung side by side, presenting dull-faced members of Bourbon royalty observing the humble approach of visitors through their ancestral home.

After stepping through a mahogany doorway, Caleb's heart skipped a beat when he saw a wall-spanning series of bookshelves. He tried to peer around Waxman's shoulder to see the rest of the library foyer.

Giuseppe said, "You must understand. Of the two thousand or so scrolls recovered from the excavation at the Villa dei Papiri, we have only succeeded in opening some fifteen hundred. And that has taken two hundred years."

They entered the library wing. Then quickly, before Caleb had a chance to peruse the titles or even to see how deep the shelves went, they hurried after Marcos down a central staircase. Caleb grinned and followed quickly. The smell of ages past, of old, musty paper, was exhilarating to him.

Giuseppe stopped at a brightly lit, bookshelf-lined room that reminded Caleb of his high school library. "The Officina dei Papiri," their guide said. "Here we work on the scrolls. It is a difficult process. First, we paint the burnt exterior of the rolls with *gelatina*. When it dries we separate and unroll them, sometimes only millimeters at a time. This is a new process, developed recently by Norwegian papyrologists. It is much better than the previous method—a machine designed by Antonio Piaggio in 1796."

He made a depressing face.

"But you must understand the situation: hundreds of scrolls were lost when the first excavators tossed them into the trash heaps. They believed the pieces *carbonizzati* to be lumps of coal. Also, early attempts to open the scrolls, they destroyed many. If the scroll you seek is not among those already opened, I fear your odds are not very good."

Caleb saw his mother's expression fall.

Nina sighed.

Giuseppe pointed to where seven men and three women, all in white coats, peered into microscopes at tiny fragments. Others worked at aligning blackened shreds on a steel table. Another woman held a magnifying glass and examined some fingernail-sized fragments.

Caleb cleared his throat. "What if we were to give you some help and tell you where this scroll had been located in Piso's library?"

Giuseppe made a perplexed face, as if he feared his knowledge of English had failed. "What do you mean?"

Helen offered a weak smile. "We may be able to tell you in what part of the library this particular item was stored at the time of the eruption."

"That," he said, looking at them sideways, "would be impressive indeed. I should like to know how you came by such knowledge. However, it would still do no good. All the recovered scrolls were found in great heaps, buried by five-hundred-degree mud, then compressed through time."

Waxman coughed. "So you're telling us you can be of no help?"

"I am sorry. As I said, you are welcome to look through the scrolls we have already managed to catalog. Mostly we have discovered the writings of Philodemus, a first-century philosopher. Apparently a friend of Piso—"

"So you've come across nothing unusual?" Helen asked. "Maybe something astrological?"

Giuseppe shook his head. "Regrettably, no. Such findings would be of great interest to me personally." He spoke under his breath so the others wouldn't hear. "To be honest, philosophy has always bored me. I spend many, many hours dreaming of finding some treasure map or magical incanta—"

"So," Waxman interrupted him again, pointing to a room in the back, where great shelves were stacked with the assorted chunks of what appeared to be black rock, "in there might be what we need, but your little team here won't get to it for, what . . . decades?"

Giuseppe nodded. "Manpower is short, and the process is—"

"Difficult," Helen said with a sigh. "So you said."

"*Mi dispiace.*" Giuseppe shrugged and sighed. "There is always hope that new techniques will aid our search. Some new application of MRI technology perhaps? But until then, this is the way we must work. We know there is also another section of the library still buried, and we are waiting for permission to excavate. Maybe we find thousands more scrolls."

Caleb hung his head so he didn't have to see the expression on his mother's face.

"But it is ironic, no?" Giuseppe smiled, and he

seemed surprised that his guests didn't join in the joke. "Don't you see? Vesuvius, the very event that caused such destruction, also preserved these scrolls. They exist far beyond the normal lifespan of papyrus and ink. Frozen in time, just waiting"—he motioned to the lab and the shelves and the people all diligently poking and teasing the material free with tweezers—"waiting here for future generations to give new life to history."

Caleb lifted his head, and gave him a smile. "Just like the Dead Sea Scrolls and the Nag Hammadi texts were preserved in caves or underground."

"Yes, yes. These scrolls are like . . . who is it, Rip Van Winkle? They go to sleep for a long time and wake up to a different world. And best of all, they escape the elements and the persecutions, the *fanatismo* of book burning and intolerance of the Dark Ages."

Caleb thought for a minute, and was about to give away their real purpose. He was about to say how the same thing applied to the lighthouse: if there really was some kind of treasure down there, the earthquakes had sealed it in and prevented intrusion by another ten centuries of curiosity-seekers and treasure hunters. *Sealed it in, possibly, until technology—or our developing psychic powers—could offer a way inside.* Maybe that time was now. As much as he hated to admit it, he was starting to feel the contagious sting of his mother's obsession.

Waxman pulled Helen out by the elbow. In the stairwell he said, loud enough for Caleb to hear, "A wasted trip, then, unless we can RV the exact scroll and then wait for these guys to unroll it and hope we can actually read something of what's left."

"I know. But there has to be another way." Helen looked away from him and met Caleb's eyes. "We'll review the scrolls they've already trans-lated—"

"But it doesn't sound like they've found it." Waxman shook his head at Caleb as he walked past. "Thanks for the wild goose chase."

After they all went back up the stairs, Caleb returned to the library. He thanked Giuseppe and shook his hand. Then he lingered for a moment, looking about the room with envy. Every one of those scholars in there, peering into the creases of time . . . he wanted to join them, wanted to pull up a microscope and hunker down for hours, days and weeks, sifting through the past. But that dream would have to wait.

He found Nina in a courtyard, standing between the paws of a massive marble lion. Sunlight danced among the ferns and tomato plants, and a large iron fountain bubbled nearby. The scent of espresso carried on the breeze from a street-side café. They were surrounded by three-story walls lined with gorgeous balconies and doorways beckoning into splendid rooms. Through two archways in the western wall Caleb could see the colorful sails of the pleasure boats basking in the glittering Bay of Naples.

Helen and Waxman were standing in the shadows under the east section, engaged in a heated discussion. Helen waved her hands, at times pointing in their direction, then to the ground. Her bright shawl made her stand out, even among the European tourists in their colorful outfits and wide-brimmed hats.

Nina playfully put her hand into the stone lion's mouth to feel its teeth. "So what do you think they're talking about?"

Caleb shrugged. "Probably blaming me for slowing down their project."

"Probably," she said, laughing and petting the lion's head. "Sorry Caleb. Just kidding. You know, your mother thinks you're the most powerful psychic she's ever seen."

"What?"

"It's true." Nina tilted her head, resting it against the lion's mane as she stared around the courtyard with a contented eye, as if she imagined herself a princess and this whole palace was hers. "It's true. I heard them talking earlier, on the boat. She told Waxman that you seem to pick up things without even trying, unlike the others. Visions just come to you."

"Only the ones I don't want," he muttered. "Visions of . . . my father, images everyone says can't be real. What about those?" He glared at his mother. "How could she think I'm so talented while she denies those visions?"

"I don't know." Nina closed her eyes. "Maybe . . . maybe she does believe you. Did you ever think of that?"

"What do you mean?"

She shrugged and peered into the lion's mouth this time. "Maybe she sees him too."

"What?"

"But she can't do anything about it, so she tries to shut them out."

"Of course she could do something!" Caleb's hands were fists at his side. "She could tell the State Department!"

"And they'd believe her?" Nina's fierce eyes, like jade buttons, held him in place. He had barely talked to this woman before, and now to speak so bluntly, like they were old friends . . . or as he imagined Phoebe would be speaking to him if she were here. Phoebe was always the logical one to poke holes in his fantasies—at least as far as Dad was concerned. "Why would they believe a woman who claims to be seeing her dead husband?"

"Because she—I could tell them where to look!

I've seen landmarks that they could search for. A river by a hill. The layout of buildings on the hillside. They could triangulate by the shadows or the direction of the sun, anything!"

Nina shrugged, stood up and stretched like a cat. A silver necklace sparkled and drew his attention to the curves around the V in her dress. The eye-tattoos on her bare shoulders seemed to stare at him. "Maybe you're right."

"I am." Caleb turned from her and plodded over to the fountain. The chaotic bubbling and splashing calmed his nerves. She had him thinking, questioning, second-guessing his anger. He glanced sideways and for a moment Helen looked over and met his eyes. Something passed between them, a mutual softening of emotions maybe.

Then Nina was at his side, digging into her purse for change. "One Euro," she said, looking at the shiny coin. "Whatever that's worth these days." She tossed it in, closed her eyes and whispered to herself.

"What did you wish for?" Caleb asked.

She gave him a wink. "Not supposed to tell, but I'll let you know. I wished that your mother gets *her* wish. That we find it."

They're all the same, Caleb thought. *Every one of them.*

"We need to find it," Nina whispered. "So we can go home."

"What?"

"I want to go home," she said. "I don't care about the treasure. I don't even want to know what it is anymore. I just want to go home. I miss my family. We have a cherry tree orchard in Virginia. This time of year the air is filled with the scent flowering blossoms, the buzzing of bees, and the sound the wind makes through them at night."

Caleb blinked, gaping at Nina in a new light, as if the sun striking her features now revealed an even deeper beauty emerging from the shade. "I had apple orchards," he said.

"Really?"

"Apple trees. Back home, in Upstate New York. Haven't you been there, with the group? Waxman said he's been using the house as a base."

Nina blinked at him, smiling. "Nope, haven't had the pleasure. I'm new, but it sounds divine. Bet you had some delicious apple pies every fall."

"Twice a day," Caleb said. "After lunch and for dessert. At least until Dad left and Mom, well . . . she got caught up in this crowd. No offense."

"None taken. I'm—well, this is all new to me."

"So you really can see things?"

Nina blushed. "Yeah, sometimes, but I don't think I'm all that good at it. Can't control it very well. Still, Waxman seems to think I can help."

"I'm sure you can," Caleb said. "But just be careful of him, Nina. He's . . . not what he seems."

"Really?" Her voice cracked. "How do you know? Did you see something?"

Caleb shook his head. "No. Don't worry about it. I'm probably just overreacting." He looked over Nina's shoulder to where Waxman was holding Helen's shoulders and talking in animated tones.

"Sorry about your father," Nina said. "I heard he was interested in the Pharos too. He would have loved to be here."

"He came to Alexandria a couple times right after I was born. Did a lot of research and even made a couple dives himself. At least he told me that much. Sometimes, while we were up in our little lighthouse—a museum now, really, since they put up a new one a mile away at the pier—he'd tell me all kinds of stories about the Pharos, about Alexandria at the time of its construction, about Sostratus and the Great Library and the temples and everything."

Nina folded her arms, chilled suddenly. "Maybe you'll see it soon. Like it was in your mind."

"Maybe," Caleb said, remembering the all-too brief glimpse he'd had while nearly drowning, and his gaze grew distant.

Nina absently scuffed the sole of her sandal over the thin layer of gravel on the flagstones. "What are you thinking about now?" she asked.

Caleb blinked, smiled. "Actually, thinking about Dad still. How he'd take us out to see the other landmark historic property on our land: 'Old Rusty.'"

"Old what?"

"Rusty, it was my sister's favorite thing. An ancient, rusted lightship. You know, the kind they used to send out in the foggiest of nights, with lanterns on its masts, to guide ships into the harbors. Phoebe loved the sound its hull made when we threw stones against it, and then we'd run before anyone could catch us. We used to sneak aboard, make up stories and pretend to be in great sea battles, captain and first mate, raiding the high seas."

Nina sighed. "Sounds like you had a one-of-a-kind childhood. But you're right, you should have been allowed to grow up there without racing all over the world with your mother."

Caleb smiled. "Well, too late now."

Nina closed her eyes and turned her face toward the sun and breathed in its warmth, then looked back to where Helen and Waxman were still arguing. "Do you think we'll find the way in to the lighthouse vault?"

"Nope. I think old Sostratus hid it too well."

Nina looked depressed. "Then they better accept defeat soon."

"They won't. My mother won't, either. She's obsessed."

"So was your father."

Caleb winced as if she had reached over and smacked him across the face. He thought for a moment, remembering his father's eyes, the tenderness in his voice, the way he would crack open a book, spread out its spine, and sometimes take a deep sniff of the pages, savoring the old smell of the paper. "Yes," Caleb said, "but for a different reason. He didn't want the treasure, didn't care about money." Caleb was getting excited, and felt a strange energy fueling his cells. "Dad just wanted knowledge. He loved everything about ancient Alexandria, and he wanted to understand the lighthouse completely. Just as he was intrigued with the library and . . ." A strange connection tugged at him—a spark of a great inferno waiting to be ignited. Suddenly he was certain that his father had known more than he'd let on.

The sun ducked behind a cloud and the courtyard flickered into shadow. In mid-thought, nearly at a revelation, he noticed someone watching them, standing in the opposite section from Helen and Waxman, beside a pillar in the deeper shadows.

Who is that? How long has he been there?

He waited, narrow and trembling, with long arms and ragged hair, so out of place amidst the tourists who just walked by, snapping their pictures, ignoring him.

Caleb's blood went cold and the hair on his arms stood on end. He shuddered.

"Caleb?"

"Do you see him?" he tried to raise his arm to point but couldn't.

"See who?" Nina asked, whipping her head around.

The sun reappeared, dazzling off the stone tiles and the limestone pillars. Caleb blinked and the figure was gone.

Someone's throat cleared. Caleb looked up and saw Waxman with Helen standing beside him. "Let's go," he said. "We'll see if the team has fared any better."

When he walked past, Caleb looked at his mother and saw that she had taken off her glasses and was staring across the courtyard, squinting.

"What?" he asked.

She shook her head, blinked and put her glasses back on. "Nothing, come on." She took one last look around. "I still think what you saw in your dream is the key, Caleb."

"You do?"

She nodded. "But it's just so frustrating. The Pharos is taunting us from the past, giving us scraps and keeping the larger secrets to itself."

Caleb looked warily at Nina. "Maybe," he urged, "we should let it keep them."

Helen chuckled and pushed a strand of hair from her eyes. "You've got a bad attitude, you know that? What would your father say?" She rubbed his head in a rare display of affection, and then followed after Waxman.

Caleb gave Nina an "are you coming or what?" look, to which she smiled and followed after Helen and Waxman. He couldn't help but take her in once more before he threw a tentative glance over his shoulder to where the figure had stood, watching.

Before they boarded the ferry, Waxman used the payphone to call the other Morpheus members who had remained at Alexandria. When he hung up, he was smiling.

"They've found the entrance!"

12

Nina asked Caleb to wait for her by the pier with Waxman and Helen, telling them that since they had another half hour before the boat left she wanted to get a few more pictures first.

Quickly returning to the palace, Nina entered the south stairwell and, pretending to admire tapestries and framed royal crests, she blended in with the tourists, murmuring to a group of Americans about her favorite exhibits and commenting on the grandeur of the palace and the grounds. Eventually she made her way back to the lower levels, where she waited for her target to emerge from the lab.

Only a few minutes had passed before he appeared. Gregor Ullman. She sized him up in an instant: bald, hawk-faced and slightly overweight, rolled-up white sleeves and a new pair of Levi's. He had a Bic pen behind his ear and a toothpick in his mouth. Nina smiled, but she was no one to judge. She only carried out the sentences.

"*Scusa, signore?*" She stepped into his path, interrupting what was either a trip to the restroom or his chance to call and update his colleagues.

"*Si?*" He stopped and smiled, admiring the frisky young woman moving in so close.

Nina licked her lips and set a hand on his chest, while her other hand swept up and around and plunged a hypodermic needle into his neck. Ullman staggered, gasped and shot her a look of dawning recognition. He tried to call out, but only whispered something indistinct, and collapsed at her feet. With a quick glance around to make sure no one was in sight, Nina took his legs and dragged him around the corner into a storage room.

Gregor Ullman awoke to find his wrists secured with duct tape, and the barrel of a Beretta pointed at his left eye. A dull pain registered in his legs, but in the drug's aftereffects, he couldn't quite place the source.

"Hello, Mr. Ullman." Nina sat on an upside-down plastic bucket, with her legs crossed, smoking a cigarette. "You know me, I'm told, so I'll skip the introductions and get down to it."

Ullman grunted and coughed as a cloud of smoke rolled into his face. *She didn't tie my legs*, he realized, and at once he sprang at the chance to escape. With a shout he tried to lunge forward, but only collapsed, howling in sudden, blinding pain. He rolled onto his back and looked down in horror to see the bright red slashes through the back of his pants.

She had severed his hamstrings.

Nina sighed. She hated this part of the job, and really didn't like the sight of blood. At times like this, she reminded herself of the importance of the mission, the nobility of the cause. What they were doing, what she was a part of, would help preserve everything she cared about, everything she loved. All her life she had sought a way to stem the advance of time, to hang onto beauty and the perfection of youth; and when she had been singled out for this opportunity she knew it was her chance: an opportunity for a different sort of immortality.

Of course she had lied to Caleb, tossing him a sympathetic tale about her childhood home and orchards, a story to snare him in her web. It was a secondary mission, but in all likelihood the most important. Caleb, after all, was the key, and she and Waxman had to get him to realize it. They had to prod him, guide him, get him to see, truly *see*. But it had to be soon. And it would be, if she played her part perfectly.

She bent down and looked into Ullman's straining eyes. "The morphine I mixed with your tranquilizer will help, but only for a few more minutes. I need you calm and able to answer questions." She stood up and stepped toward him. "Tell me what I need to know, Keeper, and I'll call for an ambulance on my way out."

Ullman groaned and turned his face toward the cold floor. "What do you want?"

"Tell me," she whispered, bending down and putting out her cigarette right in front of his face, "if Water is the first symbol."

"What?"

"You heard me, and you know what I'm asking. Water. Is it the first symbol?"

"I don't know what you're talking about. You're mad."

"And you're dead if you don't tell me the truth." She stood and placed her spiked heel against his neck. "Is it Water? Or Fire?" Nina held her breath. She needed him to confirm the first symbol to validate what their other informant had given up. Torture was never perfectly reliable, but in that case her boss had felt reasonably certain of the information they had elicited. *But not certain enough.* He wanted a second confirmation.

"The first code . . ." she repeated, pushing down on his neck, "is it Fire? Is it Air? Earth?"

Ullman coughed. His legs twitched, his arms

flayed about in his pooling blood. "I told you, I don't—"

She increased the weight on his neck.

"Aaaaaah—all right, all right!" he hissed, bringing his hand to his throat as Nina eased the stifling pressure. "It's Water . . . Water! But you won't get in. You don't know the rest of the sequence. No one does."

"Don't be coy," Nina said. "Of course you know the sequence. What you don't know is how to bypass the defenses."

"And you do?"

"We will, soon." *Very soon*, if Morpheus's remote viewers continued with their hits, or if Caleb found his sight. But she guessed that the Keepers were in the same boat as far as the scroll's recovery—hoping for a miracle. She tapped the barrel of her Beretta on the floor in front of his nose. "So you say it's Water. What if I said I don't believe you?"

"I would say I don't care. I already know my fate."

"Such pessimism." Nina sat down again. "How long have you been here in Naples, Mr. Ullman? Well, not you, but you know what I mean—the Keepers. How long have you known?"

"About the scroll?" Ullman gave a wheezing chuckle. "Be serious. As soon as the Villa was rediscovered, we put a man on the inside."

"All that time," she clucked, "and nothing to show for it." She sighed and shook her head in disappointment. Caleb probably had gotten closer to it in his one lifetime than six generations of Keepers. She checked her watch. "Well, Mr. Ullman, it's been a pleasure. Your leader claims each of you has a successor lined up. In your case, I hope you haven't delayed that obligation."

Ullman laughed again as he looked up at her with a bland grimace. "See you soon."

Nina frowned, tightened the silencer on her gun, aimed and fired, punching a hole through his forehead. She stood and contemplated the body, replaying the conversation, weighing his words, his gestures, debating whether his answer was reliable. In the end, she decided it didn't matter. She was thorough in these matters of life and death. If a second independent confirmation was insufficient, she would simply seek another.

They returned to Alexandria just before midnight. Exhausted, the others retired upstairs to their rooms. Caleb fully intended to do the same, but there was something he had to do first. Today, after all, was the anniversary.

Phoebe.

Eight years ago.

Looking ahead at the others, Caleb saw his mother who, if she had even thought of today's importance, had given no indication. She was in the thick of the group, Waxman at her side, still talking, going over plans and relating visions.

Caleb headed to the hotel's lounge, where subdued techno music droned in contrast to an elegant mahogany-walled interior lit with evenly spaced blue-flamed oil lamps. He wanted to call his sister, needed to hear her voice, wanted to apologize, again. He checked his cell phone; the battery was almost dead. There might be enough juice, but in his head whirled an uncompromising swarm of thoughts about Alexandria, the Pharos, Caesar and Herculaneum; the impossibility of their task of recovering a vulcanized scroll from the ashes of a two-thousand-year-old library; and discovering the entrance to something that may never have even existed, except in legend.

He reached the bar, a smooth black surface that reminded him of the tomb door back in Belize. He stood before it, staring at the surface as if paralyzed.

"Martini," said a voice behind him, "and whatever this guy's having." Caleb spun around as Nina slid into the seat beside him, crossed her legs and smiled. "Good idea, ditching that crowd." She looked fatigued yet infused with an indefinite sense of vigor, a nervous hyperactivity streaming through her every muscle, as if she had just been on a thrill ride and the high hadn't yet worn off.

Caleb shook off the chill and leaned against the bar. The large bald man making Nina's martini gave him a questioning glance. "The same, I guess," Caleb said, then turned to Nina, whose penetrating stare made him so weak he leaned back and slipped into the chair. Cool air from the overhead vents breathed fresh life into his lungs, and seemed to pull out the heat and humidity.

"Needed a little drink, I suppose. Been a long day."

"And it's not over yet." Nina held up her glass. The vodka glowed a cerulean blue with a lamp shining behind it. When Caleb received his drink, she said, "A toast?"

"I love toast," Caleb said, wearily. He felt stupid, but relieved when she smiled. "Raisin, Texas, wheat . . ."

She leaned forward until he could smell her perfume—a deep mix of carnal power and animalistic subtlety. She clinked her glass against his. "How about . . . to us?"

"Us?"

"To us," she whispered, "you and me. To us, finding the treasure first. Finding it and then getting the hell out of here."

Caleb lowered his glass. "How?"

"Upstairs." She drained her glass. "Come with me, I know a way."

"A way to what?" Caleb choked as he drank too much too fast, trying to keep up with Nina.

"A way to get the mind working." Her green eyes sparkled. "It's a tantric thing, a combination of meditation and physical exhaustion that's been known to—"

"Wait." Caleb put his hand on her wrist. "I don't want any more visions. Especially tonight, of all nights, I can't—"

Nina gripped his hand, and then settled her other hand on his thigh, squeezing slightly. She whispered, "I know, Caleb. I know."

"What do you—?"

"All about you . . . and Phoebe. I came down here because I know what day this is, and I know what it is that you're facing tonight . . ."

Caleb's heart was pounding, his flesh chilled in the cool air, his temples throbbing, as he stared dumbly into Nina's eyes.

". . . something you shouldn't have to face alone."

He couldn't pinpoint exactly when it had happened, at what point in the candle-lit darkness of Nina's suite the visions had actually exploded, blossoming like a pinwheel fireworks display, because he had long since lost track of time.

The memories blurred together: the door opening, Nina pulling him inside, both stumbling into the room, her fingers tearing at the buttons of his shirt, his already under her skirt, sliding under a silk barrier. Their lips mashed tight, tongues in a desperate duel. The bed had been nothing more than a prop to be used much later, after the walls, the couches, the tables and the floor had been put to punishing use. Nina had relentlessly and skill-fully pushed him to further and further acts of extreme physical exertion, exploits he had never even contemplated, positions so exotic his muscles screamed even as the pleasure intensified.

And when they couldn't move any more, she coaxed him gently into a mode of breathing and visualization. Her legs locked around his back, they sat up, face to face, breath to breath, eye to eye.

How long they had kept this position, with only barely perceptible synchronized movements, as if they thought with one mind and moved with one connected will, Caleb had no idea. But at some point, the green of her eyes had leaked out into the darkness and swirled into the shadows, twisting like serpents. And then the floor had given way and his spirit was tugged, gently at first, then ripped free and thrust into a kaleidoscopic world of sensation.

The images came fast, full of vivid clarity. Caleb never knew exactly how remote viewing worked. Specialists in the field of parapsychology theorized it was some variation on Jung's collective unconscious theory—that all the memories of everyone who had ever lived or ever would live out there, and anyone could dip into that collective pool and perceive anything in the mixture—people, places, events—anywhere in time and space. In such visions one used all their senses, fully experiencing their environment.

Caleb's own belief was that it had something to do with the fundamental nature of reality.

Intriguing experiments had revealed that quantum particles shared some sort of telepathic bond; one particle instantaneously changed its characteristics when another, no matter how distant, was altered. Another theory held that the observer's consciousness acted on these particles, implicitly changing them because, in a sense, the particles were not truly independent or distinct from the greater reality of Mind. What this and other properties of quantum behavior implied about the universe was astounding. The early alchemists—and further back, the disciples of the Egyptian Mystery Schools—adhered to the belief that everything from the smallest particle to the most massive planet was all related, one seamless tapestry. "As above, so below" was their sacred creed. They re-created the heavens structurally on the earth, and they read into the stars the nature of things terrestrial. The spiritual was a direct extension of the physical, and it could be accessed if one knew the proper codes and ways of belief.

Maybe it was true. On some level, everything *was* connected. And that's why, when Nina and Caleb entered the last trance before their descent, they shared the same visions. Unconsciously they tapped into something that revealed, in a succession of chronological scenes, what they needed to see. It started with a sense of impending disaster, and then the earth . . .

. . . begins to tremble. Three men sit atop the lighthouse. They are dressed in heavy cloaks and turbans, warming themselves by the great fire. It is Naseer's turn to make the descent and haul up more fuel, but he is too afraid to move. So he waits with the others for the quake to stop, praying.

Outside, beyond the four renovated pillars surrounding the roofless circular platform, the stars burn fiercely, trying to compete with the smoke churning from the pyre. The bitter winds rise, snatching at their clothes and scattering the smoke, but the sea lies peacefully slumbering under the blanket of a hundred ships, the entire Muslim fleet, preparing to launch at dawn.

Naseer and his two friends have been manning this lookout post and tending the fire for three years. They meet each other's bloodshot eyes, and whisper their personal prayers to Allah. "It is happening again."

"No, Farikh, it is too soon. The earth shook only twenty years ago. My father was at this post, and he said the quake only succeeded in knocking free part of the lower balcony and a few stones from the east side."

"That only means the lighthouse has been weakened. A hundred years ago the highest section fell off, and we have been building these fires on the ruined top of the second level ever since."

"God willing," Alim-Asr says, "it will hold again

this time."

"Perhaps we should make our way down," Naseer whispers.

But it's too late.

The tower rumbles and sways. One of the pillars cracks down the middle. Naseer springs to his feet and races to the west edge. Balancing on the shifting floor, he risks a look down. A dozen stones tumble free from the midsection, consumed by the darkness. He spins, fighting his vertigo, before his knees buckle with the floor beneath him. He reaches for his friends—

—but they are gone. Naseer is left alone, holding fast to the one remaining pillar on a jagged section of the floor while an open space yawns before him and a stairway ends in the night air.

The fire is gone. Only darkness and smoke have taken its place. He perceives movement, an immense shadow sliding down and away. Screams rise from the precipice, but are cut off by a rumbling of masonry and the baleful whimpering of an old giant casting off its dead skin.

He blinked, and . . .

. . . it is now daylight. He is somewhere else. Someone else. Dazzling sunshine spreads over the metallic azure sky. The ships are gone, the harbor quiet but for a lone sail. The city's beachfront looks different, with new domes and mosques, pillars

and minarets dotting hills as far as he can see.

He sits astride his horse, a beautiful Arabian with a bejeweled purple saddle and harness. It paws at the ground and shakes its mane in the shadows cast by giant slabs of stone. To the east, the cracked monoliths and the enormous piles of granite and limestone lead a twisting trail to the ruined heap of the once-proud tower.

It still ascends nearly one hundred feet, and its foundation seems strong and defensible, buttressed on all sides by a low barrier, broken in places but repairable. Its lower levels breathe with potential. Many rooms are still intact despite the crushing weight of the collapsed superstructure. He hangs his head and can only imagine the way it once was. Forty years have passed since the last great quake finally brought down its magnificence. Forty years since a flame has burned at its top and led mariners to safety.

He listens to the wind and the crashing of the sea over the ancient blocks, and he imagines the wondrous fragments lying just ahead in the pounding surf—the great stones, blocks and statues that had so long enjoyed the breezes and the awed stares of countless visitors. He turns as a man approaches.

"Lord Qaitbey." His lieutenant slows his horse and bows. "The men are ready. We have two hundred horses, enough rope and pulleys and

carts. And stone-cutting tools."

Qaitbey nods, satisfied as he looks over the ruined structure. He notes the placement of the fallen stones, the edges worn by rain and wind. "Do what you can to build it up," he orders. "We must defend Alexandria."

"As you wish."

Qaitbey turns again to the haunting, desolate ruins, and he gazes into the few remaining windows and a half-collapsed doorway. A chill runs down his spine as he prepares the next question. "What of the descending staircase and the chamber below?"

His man coughs. "We know no more, My Lord. It ends at that wall, the one with the devilish carvings. That snake and the staff . . . Your men, Lord, they . . ."

"They are afraid?"

"Yes. They know the legends. They fear what awaits below to defend the treasure. The hundred horsemen who were slaughtered."

Qaitbey nods, lost in thought. Legends are of no concern. His purpose is to protect this city from the Turks and to avenge past evils not to trespass into vaults locked away for good reason. Without turning, he instructs his lieutenant, "Cover the stairway entrance with a false wall, a slab of granite controlled by a secret lever on the eastern wall of the second floor."

"It shall be done."

"Then," Qaitbey adds, smoothing his horse's mane, *"kill the men who build it, and swear yourself to secrecy."*

After a moment of silence, he consents. "Understood, My Lord. I so swear."

"Thank you." Qaitbey makes his voice heard above the rising winds. *"What is down there must not be found, not by the likes of unworthy ones such as us."*

"My Lord," he bows.

"Others will find it, infidels to whom the symbols mean something. And may they be cursed by what lies within."

The wind dies and the crumbled remains of the Pharos quiver in silence, anticipating the hammers and chisels that will come and shape the blocks and pillars into a new form, a dwarfish, stunted relic of its former glory.

When Caleb opened his eyes Nina was breathing heavily, staring back at him. Her breasts still tight against his chest. She exhaled and lifted herself slowly off of him.

With a sigh he fell backward onto the rug, the muscles in his arms like wet rags. "What did you see?"

"A man in black," she whispered, hugging her knees to her chest, as if suddenly feeling exposed, "on a horse, watching while hundreds of men and animals worked at building that fort—that place we were at last week."

"Qaitbey," Caleb said. "What else? Did you see a door?"

She nodded, wide-eyed. "I saw the switch, I know where they put it."

"It's still there," they both whispered at the same time.

"Why didn't anyone else see it?" Nina wondered. "No one else on the team?"

"Not sure. I don't think Waxman asked the right questions. He had them probing the harbor, not the fort." Caleb looked up. "They've been looking in the wrong place."

14

One hundred feet below the streets of Alexandria, beneath a dilapidated warehouse in the eastern section of the city and down a long corridor littered with construction materials, tools and concrete girders, with hallways that led into unfinished storerooms and antechambers, a polished set of steel doors parted slowly—too slowly for Nolan Gregory. He was late. The others were here already, impatient and, most likely, scared.

He squeezed into the dusty chamber lit by a succession of floodlights connected by yellow extension cords to a generator below the floor. Forty feet overhead, the domed ceiling caught the shadows of the occupants at the central table. Nolan eyed them as he strode into the room, and he

imagined them taking on their celestial counterparts in the freshly painted cobalt blue dome, soon
to hold a host of stars and zodiac imagery. He
buttoned his gray sports coat and quickly took his
place at the head of the long mahogany table.
Fifteen others sat around it, drinking tea and
whispering among themselves.

"Keepers." Nolan's voice was soft and controlled, as if humbled from recent setbacks. "Thank
you all for coming."

"Is this wise?" asked a gray-haired woman at the
opposite end of the table. "All of us in one spot?"

"No," Nolan said, looking over his dull-eyed
counterparts, "it definitely is not. But we have no
choice."

"We heard," said a younger man on his right,
"about Ullman and Miles."

"Horrible," said the man to his left, who was
perspiring despite the cool air filtering through
ducts along the floor. His gray suit coat hung on the
chair at his back.

Nolan hung his head. "Yes, we'll mourn their
loss. But now we must consider succession."

"But their successors are not ready," said the
older woman, slapping her hand on the table. "It's
too soon, and they were too young, not prepared
properly."

A younger woman, with short hair and sad
brown eyes, stared up at the unfinished ceiling.

"Who else is ready?"

"Mine are," said Nolan. "And if there are no objections—"

"Why does he get two?" asked the young woman.

"Because," the older woman replied, making a face, "Nolan can't decide which child he loves more."

Nolan Gregory shrugged. "They each have valuable strengths. I'm only volunteering them because I see no alternatives. It was unfortunate that our fallen colleagues were not prepared, but I am."

The first man who spoke leaned across the table and pointed to Nolan. "Then that will leave us one short if you are next to die."

"I'm aware of the math," Nolan said with an exasperated sigh. His attention roamed about the room, noting the alcoves built into the rounded walls and the hundreds of empty shelves; and for just a moment he set his imagination free, allowing it to fill them. He completed the vault, applied the finishing touches and imagined it full. Whole.

Soon, he thought. *Soon*.

"This is our most desperate moment," he said. "This new enemy threatens everything. We can survive without our full number for a time, but I maintain that what we have before us at this moment is an opportunity. With my successors in place, we may have a chance to get to the Renegade, to find the key, and claim our legacy."

"Assuming," the old woman said, hunched over, "we aren't all killed first."

Nolan crossed his hands in front of his face, simultaneously rubbing both temples. "My other reason for calling this meeting was for our protection." He looked up. "We're safe here, and here we'll stay."

The older man straightened up. "For how long? I have commitments—"

"—which will have to wait," Nolan said. "We stay here until the threat has passed, which I promise you will be soon."

"How do you know?" asked the young woman, her face flushing.

Nolan stared at her. He knew she and Ullman had been more than just colleagues. "I know, because our enemies are on the wrong track."

"What do you mean?"

"They've been misled," replied Nolan. "Misled about the codes. Someone—I don't know who—first told them the wrong sequence, and based on the recovered recordings from Ullman's body, he was able to think fast, and managed to strengthen the initial lie."

The old woman frowned. "But then, who started it?"

Nolan shook his head. *That is the real question.*

"It doesn't matter," he said. "However our enemies know about the door and the sequence, they have it wrong; and in their blind impatience, they will surely try it."

Smiles broke out around the room as the Keepers glanced at one another.

Nolan Gregory nodded and sat down with a heavy sigh. "Now, we only need to sit tight, and wait. Wait," he repeated, "for the Pharos to protect itself." *And then we can get back on track.*

He again stared over the incomplete shelves and the empty walls, and he listened to the echo of his voice as it traveled outside the room, down the desolate corridors and chambers of this venerable vault. *Now I have ensured it: my successors will be the ones to find the key, and they will bring the treasure here, to its new home.*

15

She waited in the hotel lobby café behind a wilting palm tree and a mosaic-tiled fountain. The others were still upstairs, those that were going on the descent, preparing. But Nina was already packed and ready. Now she wanted a minute alone with Waxman, and after calling up to his room five minutes before, he was on his way.

Of course, the merry widow had been with him up there. *Always with him*, Nina thought, stewing that she had to wait for her assignments until he had a chance to sneak around and come to her room in the middle of the night. He always stayed longer than necessary, which was fine by her. Waxman was powerful, and a skilled lover. Two qualities she desired in a man. But this time she only needed a minute.

She opened her makeup case, turned away from the lobby and started to apply, watching. The stairwell door opened and George came out, looking flushed with excitement, a book bag slung over one shoulder and a diving bag over the other. He came right up to the pillar by the palm tree and, glancing around the lobby first to make sure no one else from the group was lingering about, whispered, "What is it?" He stood on the other side of the palm's trunk, pretending to check through his bag for a lost item.

Nina brushed her eyebrows. "I'm not convinced." She waited for his reaction, then continued when he made none. "I want to find another Keeper and be more deliberate this time. I think I might have led the last one in my questioning—"

"I thought you were a professional," he said. "Did you lead him or didn't you?"

In her mind, Nina replayed Ullman's last words again, trying to recall the nuances in his voice, listening for any signs that he had misled her. Then she cursed herself for killing that first Keeper so quickly, reacting out of fear. She snapped the case shut. "No," . . . *but I can't be sure.*

"Well, the rest of them won't be so easy to find. Now that you've put the fear of God into them, they're scurrying under the rocks, afraid of their own shadows."

Nina shifted uncomfortably. "I know, but I can still get to them. We have the location of their families, and it would be easy to grab key relatives and convince one of them to—"

"No," Waxman said. "You did your job. You got a confirmation. I say we go."

Finally she nodded.

"Good," Waxman said. "And remember, if we get inside the vault, the others don't make it out."

Nina grinned. "Believe me, I haven't forgotten. And I assume you mean everyone . . .?"

"Yes. Make it look like the traps took care of them and only we survived."

"So . . . Helen as well?"

"Yes," he said without pause, "especially her. It'll be easy. Caleb already believes we're all doomed."

Maybe he's right, Nina thought. But at least Waxman hadn't made this mission personal. If he had asked to spare Helen, Nina would have had to question his priorities. Despite last night, Nina's priorities were intact. At least she could say that much, even though she had to admit she was tempted. Caleb had a certain darkness about him that attracted her, and a streak of individuality she saw as a challenge, something to tame.

"Okay," she said, and steeled herself for the coming tasks, the culmination of their project, and hopefully the end to all this mess of novice psychics, codes, legacies and secrets. She glanced over her shoulder. But Waxman was gone, already heading to the front desk to call up to the rooms and bring everyone down to the waiting jeeps.

16

On the way to the elevators, his pack slung over his shoulder, Caleb stopped. Room 612. The door was open a crack, and someone was peering through the gap, watching. The door opened a little wider, and a patch of red hair emerged from the shadows, then bloodshot blue eyes darted up and down the hallway. *"Danger."*

Caleb took a step to the door. "Xavier?"

"Danger," he repeated. "I'm not going with them." Shirtless, still in his striped pajama bottoms, Xavier Montross looked like he had been through a four-night bender. His hair disheveled, eyes dark, bits of food stuck in his teeth.

"Did you see something?" Caleb asked. "Is that why you're not going?"

Xavier gave an almost imperceptible nod, retreating back into the shadows.

"Wait." Caleb reached out as the door closed. "What was it? What did you see?"

The latch clicked and a bolt slammed home. The eye view on the door flickered. Caleb imagined Xavier pressed close, breathing the sour breath of an anxious man. "Xavier!"

From under the door, his voice, like a desiccated whisper came, "Climb, Caleb."

"What?"

"I'll see you again . . . at the . . ."

"What?"

". . . mausoleum."

Caleb knocked on the door. "Xavier?"

Down the hall, the elevator doors opened and Helen stuck her head around the corner. "There you are!"

Caleb shuffled away from the door, shaking his head. *The mausoleum?*

"Come on, lazybones!" said his mother, holding open the doors. "This treasure isn't going to find itself!"

"How did George arrange this?" Caleb asked Nina as they stepped out of the jeep before the deserted lot around Qaitbey's fortress.

Normally, the promontory was crawling with tourists and peddlers, couples enjoying the view and sitting in a revitalized courtyard, sipping cool drinks by transplanted palm trees. Some waited for their chance to tour the empty fortress, now a museum, although there were no artifacts inside and nothing to look at but the empty hallways. Normally, they would have had to sneak in during the early hours after midnight or attempt a brazen break-in. Now, apparently, they had other means.

Nina smoothed back an unruly wave of hair, gave Caleb a knowing grin and said, "It pays to have connections."

"But this . . ." He looked around, amazed. Armed Egyptian soldiers stood guard outside, beyond the perimeter of the jeeps, keeping onlookers away.

Helen overheard them. She gave Nina a frowning look and said, "It's what I've been working on, Caleb, building relationships with the Council of Antiquities. And George's monetary influence helps."

"Of course."

"Let's move, people!" Waxman spread his arms and turned in a full circle in the breeze. Seagulls took off behind him, circled and alighted on the castle's ramparts. "Today is an historic day! For archaeology, for history, and for the new trail we're blazing in paranormal research. Follow me, if you please."

The members of the Morpheus Initiative

followed through the outer gate, one by one, Waxman and Helen in the lead. They crossed the deserted courtyard to the inner citadel and mosque. Once, from these windows, arrows had rained down upon Turkish ships.

Inside, the fort was cool and refreshing. Caleb let his fingertips dance along a granite wall and took a moment to consider that they were possibly touching a remnant of the great Pharos Lighthouse. "This archway looks older," he noted, catching his breath. "And those pillars—they have to be part of the Pharos."

"I think you're right," Helen said, up ahead, her voice breathless.

Out the open window, three seagulls had followed them and were circling, screeching. Caleb had the sudden fear they were sounding an alarm, protesting an unwarranted intrusion. He looked past them into the harbor where a fleet of boats, dinghies and random vessels of all colors and types were moored, pointing toward Alexandria, waiting for some great pronouncement from Cleopatra, perhaps, or Caesar himself.

"Ready, Caleb?" Nina pinched playfully at the back of his thigh, then took off down a plain corridor that narrowed like the inside of a tomb. Waxman, Helen, Victor, Elliot, Mary, Amelia, Tom and Dennis waited, expectantly. Helen nodded, smiling.

"Your show, kid," said Waxman. "You saved us from going in through the water vents and braving the currents, so this is your vision, go with her. Lead the way."

Helen paused, counting. "Aren't we missing one?"

"Xavier?" Waxman said, glancing around.

"Got the kid's stomach bug?" Elliot asked.

"Or he's hung over," said Victor.

Or, thought Caleb, *he's the only smart one in this bunch.*

"Well, we're not waiting for him," Waxman said, a little ruefully.

After adjusting his knapsack to the other shoulder, Caleb followed Nina, moving through the first hallway. "Wait up! Do you even know where you're going?"

"Sure, I've seen it, remember? The stairs should be just past the mosque." The hallway suddenly opened into a large chamber. They both peered at the beautiful dome three levels up. A single dove flew around the red brick ceiling, circling gracefully. "There it is," she said, pointing to a faint outline in the far wall. "That's where the door will open when you pull the lever."

"When *I* pull the lever?" Caleb put his hands on his hips.

"I'm not a glory hound, you get the honors," Nina said, sliding up to him, giving his leg a squeeze. "After all, you did all the hard work last night, you deserve it."

Blushing, Caleb looked up the stairs. "If it's even still there." They went up to the next level and walked side by side through the slanting shafts of sunlight down the narrow sandstone corridors. When Caleb realized their strides were matching, step for step, he almost burst out laughing. He felt like they were the fort's defenders, marching on patrol.

At a shadowy recessed area in the western corner beyond a chain with an "Off Limits" sign preventing public access, Caleb dug out his flashlight, switched it on and cut through the darkness. The beam continued inside an alcove about the size of a supply cabinet and illuminated three fist-sized rectangular slabs of rock, all about waist high, protruding from the wall. He had a moment's hesitation. He had not seen three. He had not even seen this arrangement.

"Come on, slowpoke. It's the middle one," Nina said, leaning forward. She gripped the lever with both hands, pulled it up, then to the left and down. A grating noise echoed below, and Nina smiled into the flashlight beam. "You didn't see them do that?"

Caleb slowly shook his head.

She patted his shoulder as she walked by and said, condescendingly, "Now, now, it's okay. Just keep practicing."

They squeezed into the narrow opening beyond the massive, three-foot-wide door. It had opened just far enough to let one person through, and they inched forward in the darkness, letting their eyes adjust. Caleb wondered how someone could bring any kind of significant treasure out this way.

The flashlight beam played off a narrow space and a wall just ahead of them. Caleb aimed it down. The shaft of light, alive with the thick dust stirred by opening the door, illuminated the steeply descending stairs.

"Ready?" Waxman's voice dwindled and was quickly swallowed up by the dust and gloom. "Go on, Caleb."

"How did I get into the lead role, here? I'm not even a member of this team."

"You've always been a member, Caleb." His mother's hand on his shoulder. "But if you don't want to go first—"

"Fine, I'll do it."

"I'll understand," Helen said. "Belize, and—"

Nina gripped his arm from the other side, digging her fingers into his flesh. "Don't listen to her," she whispered. "This is your time, make it up to Phoebe now."

He started down.

"Should have brought sweaters," Helen said, and Caleb cursed his stupidity. A cold, stale breath rose from the depths, chilling them to the bone.

"How deep do you think it goes?"

An image materialized in Caleb's mind. It was like an architect's diagram—the tower, hollow and inscribed with its ramps and statues and fuel transport hoists and the same thing projected beneath it, as if a mirror were held under the design.

"As above, so below."

Waxman looked up. "Huh?"

"Just a feeling." Caleb took the first tentative step. "Sostratus might have built this according to the Hermetic tradition, representing below what is above."

"So you're saying we might be going four hundred feet down?"

"Maybe." Or maybe the door he had seen was almost two hundred feet down, then there would be another stairwell or shaft to take the visitor to the "beacon," the light—the treasure at the bottom.

Or maybe he was way off.

They descended toward the mystery slowly, one long step after another. Nina walked behind Caleb, clutching his t-shirt with one hand and steadying herself against the cold wall with the other. The subterranean gloom did its best to resist the feeble light cast by the flashlight, but they could see well enough to continue.

Around and around. Caleb counted seventy-two steps before the wall disappeared and the last step ended. They stood before a great darkness and had the sense of an overwhelming space ahead. The flashlight pointed down at their feet, at the dust and pebbles. The beam trembled, and Caleb realized his arm was shaking.

He felt Nina's hand on his, and together they raised the light. It stretched across the floor, dipped into a rectangular pit, then came up the other side and struck the far wall. He moved the light higher, and his jaw dropped. There were the carvings—signs and stars, circles and moons. Shadows played among the shapes, danced around symbols, letters and images too far away to see clearly. Then he found the center and traced up the length of a painted vertical staff that had two brilliant, green-scaled snakes wound about it. He followed their coils around until they converged. Great fangs and eyes locked onto each other.

"Wow," Dennis whispered, and pushed through the group to the front.

"Wait," Caleb urged. He had a terrible premonition as a grating sound echoed in the chamber like something opening or sliding apart. He felt a shifting in the floor, and he quickly moved the light to his feet. One of the blocks had settled under their weight, but only a couple inches. A hissing and gurgling sound came from the pit ahead, and a *whoosh* like escaping steam whistled above. Dennis stumbled back as cries of fear and confusion rose.

Caleb whipped the light around in a frenzied sweep. He saw a crescent moon, then a bird-like face and a long sloping beak. Another pair of eyes peered at them knowingly, and huge arms clutched a giant book. Faces turned on great stone bodies that swiveled, expelling the dust of centuries.

"Statues!" Caleb shouted, taking another step back with Nina, overcoming his fright. "Only statues." He remembered his vision of Caesar and how the immense statues of Thoth and his consort Seshat had flanked the entrance to this vault. But he wasn't clear whether they posed any threat.

"How are they moving?" Waxman whispered, inching closer.

"Steam power?" Caleb replied, slowly panning the light from one to the other, willing his heart to settle down, his breathing to relax. "Just physics and hydraulics. Inventors back then were into making statues seem alive. It was a trick to thrill the worshippers—"

"Or scare the piss out of trespassers!" Victor offered.

"Did it work on anyone?" Elliot asked, stifling a chuckle.

Caleb tried to smile. "Okay guys, looks like the welcome is over. Let's go in." He played the light over the two statues one last time, then bowed his head as he passed between them. It might have been a trick of the light, but it almost seemed as if

Seshat moved again as he passed, as though she bent at the knees and lowered her head in honor of his arrival.

They approached the wall. Four more flashlight beams appeared, heavy with collected dust, and darted over the floor, the walls, the ceiling. The team members gave the rectangular pit in the center a wide berth. From its depths Caleb thought he could hear plunks of tiny stones hitting water. He looked closer and saw that the pit had a set of stairs coming up from the watery gloom.

There was a tug at his arm and he moved the beam back in front of them. Before he knew it they were right in front of the wall, staring up at the great caduceus, with those snakes now appearing to eye him with quiet indignation. Caleb took a deep breath, and when he exhaled, his breath sparkled in the dusty air. He counted seven symbols surrounding the staff, each carved deeply into the limestone and bounded by a raised circle.

He figured someone could grip the symbols by their outside edges and turn them one way or the other, like wheels. "Should have brought floodlights," he whispered, fumbling in his bag. "Hold the flashlights steady."

"Why?" Waxman asked.

Caleb took out his camera, aimed and pressed the button. The room lit up. His eyes dazzled, and he suddenly remembered a night years ago on the hill overlooking Sodus Bay as the first bright fireworks rocked the night. He snapped another picture, then a third. Each time moving the aim a little more to the right until he was sure he had captured the whole wall. Strange symbols and images filled his vision until he could barely see even with the pitiful flashlight beams.

Waxman looked over his shoulder, and with the light blinding off the limestone wall, his face was draped in shadow, but pinpoints glittered in his pupils. He looked like an Egyptian demon ready to plunder the ancient treasures of the gods. "Guess we should have consulted Caleb from the beginning. Apples don't fall far from the tree, do they, Helen?"

Caleb swallowed and glanced at the two of them as Waxman reached out and traced the path of the snakes on the wall. He had found a crack in the wall, a vertical split right down the center of the staff.

Nina moved closer to whisper something in Waxman's ear and pointed at one of the signs on the wall. More footsteps approached, and more beams of light roamed the wall. The others gathered in a semicircle behind Waxman. "Give me a minute," he said, after whispering something back to Nina. He traced some of the symbols.

Again Caleb was struck with the certainty that Sostratus had designed this tower and its antecedent, the "below" extension, according to the matching principle. If the visible and familiar were above, then this was the occult—the hidden and mysterious. Yet, according to the mystical tradition, it should still consist of the same basic elements. He would then expect this door to lead to the second level, the octagon-shaped section, and once inside, another stairwell would take the visitor down to the final level, ending in a small pillared chamber.

As Waxman viewed the symbols, Caleb had the notion that he was looking for one in particular; and once more, he sensed that George hadn't been completely honest with his mother, or with the rest of the group—with anyone except for Nina Osseni. Seeing them talk, whispering together, hit him with a feeling of something stronger than mere jealousy.

Waxman pointed to the inscription ten feet up, above the caduceus. "It says, in Ancient Greek, something like, 'Only the golden ones may pass through.'"

"'Golden ones'?" Helen stepped past Caleb and shone her light across the lettering. Caleb's beam joined hers, and he saw a peculiar symbol at the end of the Greek inscription.

I've seen that before, he thought, recalling treatises on alchemy, illustrations and symbols in his father's study. Reluctantly, as if its importance demanded he figure this out now, he lowered the flashlight beam from that character down to the caduceus and made a slow clockwise circle around it, highlighting one symbol after another. "Seven symbols," he said.

"So?" Victor asked.

Caleb shrugged. "Mystical number and all. But I think . . . looking at those signs, they're representations of the planets. Some double as symbols for elements. I see the sun and the moon, then . . . Venus, Mars, Jupiter, Saturn and Mercury."

Helen frowned, scrunching up her face as she tried to look closer. "How does that help us?"

"Alchemy," Caleb said, thinking back on bits and pieces of things he'd read, ideas tying back to Ancient Egyptian magic, methods of controlling the material world and preparing for the afterlife.

"Alchemy? Turning lead into gold?"

"Something like that."

"So what are the golden ones?" someone asked as Caleb tried to see into the gloom. It might have been the heavier one, Dennis.

Waxman tapped his flashlight against the wall and listened to the echoes.

Caleb cleared his throat. "It could just mean, 'those who are pure, those who are worthy.' In its earliest form, alchemy was the study of spiritual transition. Isaac Newton, Francis Bacon, and all their predecessors, when they discussed turning things into gold, they weren't necessarily talking about a physical, elemental transformation, but about obtaining spiritual perfection."

"Hokey, kid," said Waxman. "Even for you." He regarded the door again, and then Nina said something inaudible, to which Waxman nodded, and

then said, louder, "No, I'm thinking this is just
another typical Egyptian curse, the usual scare with
no teeth. They loved to put curses all over their
tombs, especially the valuable ones. Threaten
looters with a curse, and maybe you'll get to rest in
peace."

He aimed his light at one symbol, about knee-
high on his left, and Caleb had the sudden certainty
that this was the one he had been searching for, the
one Nina had pointed out. Jupiter. The planet
associated with Water.

Nina tentatively backed away, but Waxman
told her to keep the light still, to illuminate the
symbol while he tucked away his own flashlight.
He reached out, grasping the outer edges of the
sign.

"What are you doing?" Caleb asked. "Nina,
George, wait! You're not seriously going to try this."

When Waxman glared over his shoulder his face
was a mask of annoyance and anger—such anger
that Caleb took an involuntary step back.

Waxman grunted and started to turn the symbol
clockwise.

"I don't know about this," Helen said. "Maybe
we should wait."

Retreating another step and bumping into
Dennis, Caleb said, "Egyptians were known to back
up their curses with actual defenses."

Waxman laughed. "No one else saw any traps in

their visions."

"You didn't see the way in, either," Caleb countered. "Which only means you weren't asking the right questions—again." A blinding light stabbed into his eyes as Nina turned the beam on him.

Waxman hissed through his teeth. "Enough, Caleb. You can go back up."

The light pulled away, leaving painful flashes in Caleb's vision. He couldn't make anything out. He heard a scraping of the small wheel within its granite setting. Rubbing his eyes, he took another step back and completely lost his bearings. "Nina?" He started to call to her, but a heavy *clang* drowned out his voice. Fuzzy shapes appeared out of the glare. He looked up and saw two giants looming over him. One appeared com-passionate and sad; the other's bird-like expression had darkened into something like rage.

Caleb turned away from the stairs, back to the chamber, and there was his mother, to the right of Waxman, and Nina, standing directly in front of the caduceus.

Another *clang*, and Caleb blinked. Then, in an unfocused haze, he saw five figures gathering around the seal. The crack down the middle expanded into a dark, widening line the width of a pillar.

"We did it!" Waxman shouted.

Nina stopped and looked back, but her look of

triumph melted when she saw Caleb's face. He seemed to want to say something witty, something to make them all pause and regroup. But he couldn't find his voice. He squinted and tried to see beyond the parting doors, but so much shifting sand and dust were drizzling down on the intruders. Then a horrible grating reverberated off the walls of the chamber. The walls, the floor, the ceiling, groaned as though the harbor was pressing down upon them—millions of gallons of water compressing their little chamber all at once.

"Nina!"

She turned to him, reaching out—

—just as a torrential wave of blackness erupted from the gap in the door, exploding into the room.

Caleb had a glimpse of five figures consumed and swept backward like ants in a flood. Helen and Waxman, just off to the side, out of the rushing water's path, turned and ran toward the safety of the stairs.

The flood took Nina head-on, lifting her in the air in a watery death-grip, and then drove her into the granite floor. Another surging wave rushed in and flung her toward Caleb. He grunted as she slammed into him and they both hurtled back into the colossal leg of Thoth. Caleb struggled to hold her wrist as he gripped the statue's staff.

Nina coughed and tried to force out a watery

scream. She was nearly ripped free by the freezing water crashing over them again and again, swirling and pulling as it rose. Caleb choked on wretched-tasting seawater mixed with the dust of ages, but he could feel the statue's contours below his feet. He pushed off its midsection and hauled himself up, only to be hit by another angry wave. With a burst of strength, he pulled Nina higher as he fought to work his way up the statue to stay ahead of the rising flood.

Finally he locked his arm between the staff and the statue's upraised hand and could go no higher, his head hard against the cold ceiling, when the room plunged into darkness, the final flashlight beams swirling under the dark tide. He thought of his mother and the others and could only imagine the worst, their bodies tossed about, dashed against the stones, consigned to this, their final resting place hundreds of feet beneath the surface.

His lips were almost pressed against the ceiling—the last inch of air left. He took another gasp and then his head was completely below water. In seconds his lungs began to scream, his heart thundered and he almost gave in to panic.

Then suddenly, it was as if someone had pulled the stopper out of a giant bathtub. The water started receding with a huge sucking sound, a swirling in the darkness. Caleb could breathe again. The water descended quickly, very quickly, and soon he could make out the dimmed, submerged flashlights before they disappeared altogether, flowing out through the tunnel. Sucked out, Caleb thought, with sudden dread, along with his mother, Waxman and the others.

"Caleb!" Nina gurgled, coughing up pints of water. Her wrist started to slip through his weakening grasp, now high above the chamber floor and without the buoyancy of the water to support her weight. Her voice was weak when she said, "Don't—don't let me go!"

"Hang on!" The blackness around them seeped into his skull, blanketing his consciousness. He heard a buzzing, and he was back there—in the jungles of Belize, in that tomb, holding onto his sister.

His grip on Nina slipped another inch and she screamed. Her feet dangled in mid-air, kicking absently. She clutched wildly at his body, and in her frenzy grabbed his arm, tearing it from its grip on the statue. But in sheer reflex, he shook her off to free his hand and regain his broken hold. The following scream was an echo of Phoebe's familiar cry from years ago. Then there came a wet thud and a sickening snap that resounded over and over, drowning out the grating of the closing door.

"Nina!"

He fought the cold and fatigue and struggled to stay conscious. He made his way down the statue, sliding, scrambling, then dropping the final few feet. He landed knee-deep in the swirling water and reached down to feel around for anything but the stone floor. The currents pulled at his legs, and if it had been any higher, he might have been swept toward the pit. But he was able to stand firm.

"Nina!" His hands fumbled about. He dropped to his knees, splashing, reaching in the darkness. The water was down to only five or six inches, but rushing quickly and powerfully toward the drain. "Nina!" He crawled, rolled, swung his arms wide in a frenetic effort to find her.

Lights appeared—two of them—streaming down from high up the stairs, falling on Caleb, and then flicking around the room, scoping out every niche, every square foot of the water-cleansed chamber.

"Find Nina!" he screamed, as the streaming floods exiting through the gap in the floor and the great door sealed shut again, the caduceus once again whole. "Where is she?"

"Caleb." His mother's footsteps, splashing in the last few inches of draining water.

"Nina!"

"Caleb . . ." Helen knelt next to him, placed her hands gently on his shoulders. Her touch calmed him, even as he realized there was nothing left to do.

He whimpered, and rested his forehead against the cold, wet floor.

He never remembered much about the next few minutes. He didn't know if he had blacked out or just stumbled about in a daze. There were only vague recollections of a kind-eyed, bird-faced goddess blinking at him in the darkness and shifting ever so slightly, the noise of her motions keeping him conscious.

His mother helped him up while Waxman continued searching for Nina. Then someone was helping him, carrying him up the stairs, stumbling every few steps. Except in his delirium he wasn't under the sea in Alexandria, he was in Belize, climbing the broken stairs, carrying his sister's broken, unconscious body, and praying that Phoebe—if she was still alive—wouldn't wake up, wouldn't wake to the agony. Wouldn't come back to a world where she might never walk again.

They dragged Caleb out to freedom and, taking deep gulps of the cool Mediterranean air flowing through Qaitbey's vacant stone hallways, he slipped away from his mother's arms and rolled over to gaze at the dome high above, at that one lone dove, still circling, singing out its cry of loneliness.

17

The next few days were lost in alternating surges of pain and guilt, sleepless fits and frantic attempts to see his mother. Every time Caleb slipped back into consciousness, prodded by a succession of stern doctors and narrow-faced nurses, he saw Waxman speaking with Egyptian authorities, reporters, and other men in dark suits.

Finally, he had some time alone with his mother. Red-eyed and sullen, she spoke without making eye contact, and only once, briefly, she set her hand on Caleb's. Her other arm was in a cast and she had green and blue bruises all over her face. Caleb learned soon enough that his mother, Waxman and Victor were the only ones to make it out alive, the only ones luckily carried toward the stairs, where they managed to climb out ahead of the rising water. The others' bodies, mangled and deformed, with shattered skulls and broken bones, were found later that night after a six-hour rescue mission by the Egyptian Coast Guard.

But Nina . . . Nina's body hadn't been found yet. Caleb couldn't think about her, not now. All he could think about were the others, and he kept dreaming that it was up to him to tell their families how they had died, and for what.

He was alive. His mother was alive. On one level he was relieved that she had survived. On another, he couldn't get past his fury at another treasure hunt gone horribly wrong. Just like Belize, except this time it wasn't his fault. Or was it? His visions—and Nina's—had brought them to this fate. Never mind that it was Waxman's impatience and bludgeoning optimism that had gotten most of the Morpheus team killed.

"Well, that's one thing anyway," Waxman said, slipping into Caleb's room behind Helen. He was little worse for wear. A couple bandages on his forehead and his wrist in a cast. "The Egyptian government just thinks we all went for a dive after visiting the fort. And since the tide is so treacherous around that area, well, we were unlucky. They're convinced enough of the danger that they've decided to drop breakwater stones in that section."

Helen spun around. "What? They can't do that. What if—?"

"Easy," he said, hands out in a settling gesture. "This will just discourage other treasure seekers. We can still get to the tunnel. They didn't find that, fortunately. I didn't tell them about the entrance we'd found, and while the rescue operation was under way I went back and closed the door, resetting the lever. It's there for when we need it again."

Caleb blinked. "'For when we need it again'? Are you serious? After what happened?"

Waxman was about to say something when Helen pushed him out of the room. "Later," she said, shutting the door before turning to her son. "Caleb. This is a tragedy, the worst outcome possible, but we can't just run from it."

"Yes we can!" His lungs groaned with the effort.

"Then their deaths will have been for nothing." She bit her lip and looked down. She sat in the chair beside the bed and slumped forward. And then, finally, Caleb realized she was still dealing with the guilt too, still trying to succeed at something, to make it up to her husband, to prove his life hadn't been a waste.

"It won't be soon, Caleb. But someday, someday we'll try again. We'll work at it, work at deciphering those images on the wall. There have to be clues to the way in, and—"

"Take my camera," Caleb said with disgust. "For

all the good it will do you. It's supposedly water-proof, so maybe the film survived." He sighed. "Take it. Hopefully it'll prove that you can't get in. Face it, Sostratus was too good."

Helen was about to say something, but whatever it was, a nurse interrupted her as she came in to draw blood. When she pricked Caleb's arm he immediately felt woozy, and he fell into an ascending tide of death.

When Caleb awoke it was night, the curtains drawn. An IV was still stuck in his arm, the entry point throbbing in counterpoint to the pulse in his head. And a man was looking down on him.

He was dressed in a gray suit. He had soft eyes and a head of thick gray hair, like snow, with straggly caterpillar-like eyebrows. His lips were moving, but Caleb didn't hear any words—nothing but a sound like the rush of water.

The man raised a scolding finger, and for an instant the water gurgled away and the room quieted down. He leaned forward and whispered, "The Pharos protects itself." Then he stood and made a curious bow.

Caleb blinked, and it was daytime. His arm was free, the IV gone. He sat up in bed, blinking again. His mouth felt like it was full of sand. Turning sideways, he slid out of the bed until a wave of nausea forced him back, and then he tried again. He stood up this time, made it to the window and looked down. Two stories below there was a small field with a soot-stained marble statue of some Egyptian patriot pointing toward the sea. Overhead, a lone dove circled, then landed on the statue's head and stared up at Caleb's window. Then Caleb noticed the man.

He stood in the field, looking down at a flat stone set in the grass. He was familiar, but not the one who had visited the previous night. This man wore a dirty green jacket and had long hair, stringy and unwashed, down to his shoulders. He knelt and set a single white flower upon the stone at his feet.

Caleb's mouth opened. What had once been fear gave way to curiosity. But then the figure stood and turned around, looking up, right at Caleb. He raised a hand and pointed, first at Caleb, then down to the stone. Then he touched his chest.

Caleb rocked back, so startled that he didn't even get a good look at his face, but he bumped into the bed, turned and saw his mother silhouetted in the doorway.

"What are you doing out of bed?"

Caleb pointed to the window, eyes wide, and speechless.

Helen limped past and set her good arm on the windowpane. She looked down. Caleb hesitantly peered over her shoulder, already sure of what he'd see.

The field was empty.

She turned, shrugging. "Phoebe's on the phone, asking for you."

Caleb had to sit again. "I can't talk to her."

"You're her big brother. You saved her life back in Belize, no matter what else you think. Go, talk to her."

"I'll talk," Caleb relented. "But then that's it. This quest is over for me—once and for all. I'm done. Unless you enlist the help of a dozen military divisions and a thousand tons of TNT, I'm finished. I'm leaving."

"You can't—"

"I can. I have a job. Classes to teach. Books to publish." Caleb stood and walked to the door. "It's over, Mom. It's over."

"Dad wouldn't have given up," she whispered, and her words froze him to the spot.

Caleb hung his head. Out in the hall, the fresh air felt soothing on his skin. "Dad's dead. Or don't you remember?"

"Caleb—"

"He's dead," Caleb repeated. And now he finally believed it. He did, and he felt an utter vacancy in the place the hope of his father's return used to occupy. It was always like Dad had been there waiting in the corner of Caleb's mind. *Waiting for me to find and rescue him.*

But that chance had passed.

"Dead," Caleb said again. "Like your obsession. Like the myth of this treasure. Like everyone who goes after it."

He closed the door—on his mother, on the quest. On his lost youth. On hope. He put them all behind him and walked away, toward his future.

At dusk, as the other boats, schooners, trawlers and pleasure cruisers headed to the docks, and their passengers geared up for a night out at discos, bars and restaurants, George Waxman took the sleek four-seater speedboat in the opposite direction, to the center of the harbor and his waiting yacht.

Minutes later, he descended into the lower quarters, still fuming. "Get upstairs," he barked to Victor, who he found standing before the recompression chamber window, peering inside. "Go up top and keep watch."

Victor turned, a bruised cut on his forehead, still red and turning purplish around the stitches. "For who? Helen will be with her boy, right?"

"It's not her I'm concerned about. How's our patient?"

"Unresponsive. But alive."

"Good."

"She rose sixty feet in less than a minute, lungs half full of seawater, and . . . I don't know, boss, shouldn't we get her to a hospital?" Victor paused at the stairs, his voice cracking, betraying perhaps some newly kindled desire of his own.

"No," Waxman snapped. "We need to leave soon, and I need to have her close. In case . . . in case her injuries, the blow to the head, made her forget her priorities. Or otherwise experience a lapse in judgment."

"Understood."

When the footsteps had retreated, and Waxman was alone with the sound of hissing gas and the vibrating echoes of the generator, he cupped his hands to the portal window and peered into the chamber.

"Sleep tight, Nina."

BOOK TWO
—THE LIBRARY—

THEODOTUS.   *What is burning there is the memory of mankind.*
CAESAR.   *A shameful memory. Let it burn.*
                       — Shaw, *Caesar and Cleopatra*

Caleb Crowe hadn't seen his sister in more than five years. It was Christmas, and he had just finished grading midterms. Now he was off to the Museum of Natural History to wrap up his research into the vanished Alexandrian library; and then he was looking forward to finally sitting down to the book that had been impatiently waiting for him to write.

He had his coat on and he was reaching for the door when Phoebe called. She was at the entrance to his apartment. His heart pounding, a thousand questions in his mind, he rushed out of his room and ran down four flights of stairs, out of breath with excitement, recalling that awful day, that tragic descent around a much longer—and older—staircase three years ago.

He stepped out of the stairwell and there she

was in the lobby, two upperclassmen holding the
door for her before heading out to a football game
in the quad. Phoebe wheeled herself inside, gave
Caleb a smile, and then spun her wheelchair in a
full circle. "Like the new model?" She adjusted the
chair's controls and sped over to him. She wore a
heavy fleece turtleneck and faded khakis, with a
plaid blanket over her legs. Her dark hair had
grown longer and had been recently colored, with
streaks of auburn highlights offsetting her eyes, soft
and shining, without a hint of recrimination.

"It suits you." He looked her over, shaking his
head in dismay. She was radiant, excited, just like
he remembered her before the fall. "Where's
Mom?"

"Merry Christmas to you too," she said. "She's
out in the car."

Caleb glanced out the window to see the silver
Lexus at the end of the path. Two shapes inside, the
windows open a crack and cigarette smoke filtering
out into the air.

"We were in the city, so I made them bring me
to see you." She rolled closer and pulled out a red
gift-wrapped package from under her blanket. "I
didn't want another Christmas to pass without
seeing my big brother."

Caleb felt a pang of guilt and had to lower his
eyes as he took the gift. "I don't deserve this."

"You do."

"I didn't get you anything."

"Hey, I surprised you by showing up. What can I expect?"

She reached up and touched his hand. "I don't have long," she said. "We're on our way to Philadelphia. George—Mr. Waxman—has some contacts he wants Mom to meet. Some friends in occult studies who might shed light on the symbols you found on that door under Qaitbey's fortress."

Waxman.

Caleb's blood boiled. He thought about Nina and the others—those unfortunate pawns Waxman had brought down into that place to drown. "Still trying to figure out the Pharos code . . ." he said. "Have they made any progress?"

"Do you care?" Phoebe didn't wait for Caleb to answer. "Actually, we've interviewed two dozen different psychics. Still trying to repopulate the Morpheus Initiative. And George wasted a lot of time trying to locate that other guy who went missing in Alexandria. Xavier-something."

"Montross?" His skin broke out in a surprising chill. "With all of Waxman's influence, he can't find one guy?"

"Yeah, weird. It's like Xavier just vanished off the face of the planet."

Caleb thought for a moment, remembering the red hair and the haunted eyes peering at him through the crack in a hotel-room door. "Or, he really doesn't want to be found."

"Well, anyway, the search goes on. Some of the candidates are good, some not so much. We brought them in, set them to work, but they've found nothing, nothing but unrelated gibberish. Their drawings make no sense, they don't correlate with anything we know."

"Maybe you're not asking them the right questions."

"Or they're just bad psychics."

Caleb smiled. "What about you? What have you seen, assuming you're helping them?"

"I am. But mostly . . . I don't know, I guess I haven't known what to look for, or what questions to ask, either."

"How's college?" he asked, changing the subject.

Her face lit up. "Great. U of R has a nice handicapped-friendly facility. I stay on campus and all my classes are in one building connected to my dorm. I've got a head start on my thesis already, and I'm interning with Professor Gillis, helping him translate a collection of cuneiform tablets from Babylon."

"Sounds wonderful," Caleb said. He hadn't realized she had developed such similar interests. Suddenly he regretted the years they'd been apart.

"It's not bad," she said. "Except for when Mom basically kidnaps me and makes me help out with her research." A couple underclassmen walked by, hand in hand with their girlfriends, and Phoebe wistfully watched them go.

"I'd hoped she'd give you a break," Caleb said, looking out the window again at the figure in the passenger seat.

"She has, mostly, but I've asked to be kept in it."

Caleb opened his mouth to ask a question, but when he saw her eyes, the hard lines around the edges, the lost years in her smile, he knew why she couldn't let it rest. He urged her toward a seating area, where he pulled up a chair and leaned forward to be at her level. "I'm sorry, Phoebe. I really am. I think about you all the time."

"Even though you never call?"

"Or write."

"Or write," she said. "You've read my letters?"

"Of course." And it was true, he couldn't set them aside. Even though she was the link to his past, the sole connection to his mother and to a life he desperately wanted to forget, he just couldn't close himself off to her completely. And she wrote so well, so full of enthusiasm about everything, as if despite her disability she was thrilled to just be alive. She experienced life with the zeal of a heaven-bound spirit sent back to Earth for one last romp.

"So maybe you'll write back sometime?" she asked hopefully, looking over her shoulder as a horn sounded. "Or visit?"

"I will," Caleb promised.

She nodded and then backed up, first wrapping her scarf around her neck. Caleb followed her to the door. Outside in the cool wind Waxman stood, wearing a black trench coat. He opened the trunk for Phoebe's wheelchair.

"Has he moved in?" Caleb asked.

"More or less," Phoebe said. "I ask Mom about it every once in a while. She seems to really like him."

"Did you ever . . .?" Caleb paused, unsure how to phrase the question.

"Remote view him?" She gave a little laugh. "Nah, too creepy. You?"

"Haven't done it at all in a long time."

"Too bad. But it's not one of those 'use it or lose it' things. If you want to get back to it, I'm sure it's waiting for you."

"No thanks."

"You sure? I bet you and I could figure this thing out in no time."

Caleb opened the door for her and felt the suddenly bitter wind whip at his face. "Thanks for the present."

With a speed that surprised him, Phoebe reached up, took him by the wrists and pulled him down for a big hug. "Take care of yourself, big brother." She started to wheel away, then stopped. "One more thing, are you dating someone?"

Caleb blushed despite the cold. "Nope. No time. Studies and all."

"Geek."

"Why'd you ask?"

"Just curious. I thought of you once, and I went into a quick trance and saw you with a girl, someone with long blond hair and green eyes."

"Blond? No, no one I know," Caleb said, truthfully. He hadn't thought too much about girls since he'd been back to the States. And he only had a few other teachers he could even call friends. He steered clear of parties, and Columbia was such a big campus one could easily escape notice. And he preferred it that way. "But I'll keep an eye out for this mystery girl."

"Do that," Phoebe said. "Because I felt she was bad news. Some kind of threat to you. That's all." She rode down the walkway as frosted leaves blew across her path and great elm trees swayed toward her. The morning clouds hung pregnant and low, dark but complacent.

"Merry Christmas!" Caleb called out, and just then his mother's head appeared from the other side of the car. He saw her face, her lips moving, mouthing an apology or an accusation, Caleb wasn't sure. But suddenly he saw something he hadn't seen in three years—a huddled figure, a man trembling in a tattered green coat, long stringy hair over his face. He was standing across the street, by the corner of the brick building. The shadows seemed deeper around him, as if he had enlisted them to his side. He stared at Caleb. With the door open, shivering against a renewed blast of cold air, Caleb stood motionless. He smelled gunpowder, or fireworks, and imagined hearing a band playing a somber dirge on the field. The figure in the green coat raised its hand. At first Caleb thought it was pointing to him, but then he realized the finger was directed toward the car.

Toward Waxman.

Caleb heard mumbled words and realized it was Phoebe saying goodbye. He blinked, opened the door all the way and was about to come out when the light shifted, the shadows scattered, and the man was gone, as if he had been inhaled into the earth.

Caleb retreated into the lobby and stared at the gift in his hands. When he looked up, the car had driven off, and only the swaying trees and the courtyard lawn and the eight guys playing touch football remained.

Back in his room, he peeled open the wrapping paper. He stared inside the box for a long time. Then he cursed them—cursed his mother, cursed Waxman, and even Phoebe, although he didn't really mean it. She had framed the three photographs he had taken *down there*. The inside of the Pharos chamber—three panels of the great seal, cropped and edited so the entire wall appeared seamless, along with the symbols and the images that had stymied their advance and killed most of the team.

If Caleb had ever wanted to get back into the hunt, Phoebe had just given him the means to take the first step.

2
ALEXANDRIA—MARCH

Nolan Gregory sat in a wicker chair on his son's seventh-floor balcony. The apartment, while somewhat light on luxury, had a strategic view from its western side, at least for certain interested people. Nolan had observed this very scene every night for almost two decades, beginning with every move the bulldozers had made below, every truck carrying away the ruined pieces of old warehouses, apartments and abandoned shacks. Now, he gazed with pride at the glass domed rooftop of the massive library, marveling at the crowds, the tourists, the scholars.

"It's been five hours," his son said from inside the screen. "Can I at least get you another drink?"

Nolan shook his head as he continued to watch. "No, Robert. I'm fine. I should be going." In his mind he visualized the layout below the dome, remembering the excavation of the sub-levels, the laying of the foundations, the steel girders. He thought of the precision needed to connect to their sub-level, already in place one hundred feet below. So much to think about, so much to supervise. All from behind the scenes of course. A dozen firms had been brought in, capital from so many organizations, interested benefactors, governments and private donors. Consultants, architects, linguists, sociologists.

Such a project. It had easily consumed the last twenty years of his life. Two decades that had seen his children grow from precocious teenagers to successful adults, each with their own lives—his son here, his daughter overseas.

But each of them Keepers. Valued colleagues.

The screen opened and Robert came out, leaned on the ledge and looked down. His blond hair rippled in the soft breezes. His piercing blue eyes followed his father's gaze, looking down at the structure with something more like jealousy and impatience. "I'm uncomfortable with your plans for the Key's retrieval," he said.

"I know," Nolan replied, "I know. But it's the only way. We've been lucky so far. Lucky the son has turned his back on his talents, and lucky he's distanced himself from his family. He's given us time."

"Must we move now?" Robert asked. "Waxman is getting nowhere. He's given up."

"Wishful thinking. He's only biding his time, still hoping the other psychics can help him. Fortunately, Helen and Phoebe Crowe haven't succeeded, but it's only a matter of time at this point. One of them will find the Key if we don't get it first."

Robert lowered his head as the smell of curry and raisins filtered out from the kitchen, where his mother was busy making their evening meal. "So it has to be this way."

"Yes."

"And she has agreed?"

Nolan sighed, again gazing at the shimmering reflection of the sun's setting light off the glass dome, and he told himself that whatever the personal risks, it was worth it. "She's ready."

3

NEW YORK CITY—OCTOBER

The remainder of Caleb's research, six months before a fury of writing and revisions, passed in a blur of old books, dank library archives, endless hours in museums and the rare-book sections of various universities. He needed his own place, needed the isolation and quiet to see the project through. And so he holed up in a Manhattan 72nd Street studio apartment, one where he just barely met the rent payments by clerking in the Classics section at the New York Library during the summer. But that was all about to change.

Six months ago he had secured an agent, a publisher, and a $50,000 advance on a work entitled *The Life and Times of the Alexandrian Library*. It was the culmination of reams of notes, anecdotes, theories and research. Advance praise was extraordinary; it was being hailed as "a classic with epic non-fictional characters that seem so lifelike it's as if Caleb Crowe has actually stepped back in time and observed the places and events in person."

There was, of course, some truth to the statement. Although he had sworn off using any form of psychic abilities since Nina's death, sometimes his subconscious, overwhelmed with the intensity of the research and late-night writing, took over with its own agenda. It would yank him into a waking dream to stroll among philosophers in white robes, their voices echoing off the alcoves as they spoke to rapt pupils. He would wander the ten colossal chambers of learning, savoring the breath of ancient truth exuding from the scrolls held therein. He would peer out the windows, looking past the dark silhouette of the Pharos Lighthouse and up into the heavens where his fellow scholars had mapped out the trails of the gods.

He had rubbed shoulders with Euclid, drunk wine with Claudius Ptolemy, dissected corpses with Aristarchus, charted the cycles of Venus with Hipparchus, and tinkered alongside Heron. And all of those experiences—the sights and sounds, the flavor of those revered halls and the luxurious museum grounds—they all made their way into his book as revelations and wonders and theories that modern scholars and critics were fast to admonish;

yet something about his forceful style and the strength in his words proved irresistibly satisfying to readers.

Today was his first book signing, at a trendy café in Soho on a late October afternoon. A steady, drizzling rain tapped against the windows, and the cabs squealed out front while shoppers scurried by. The thick aroma of coffee permeated the air. Caleb's stomach was tangled up in binding knots, and his voice was on the verge of cracking. More than forty people had packed the small room, a host of multicolored umbrellas and rain slickers—and one bright orange shawl beneath a grinning face.

Phoebe was there, in the back of the room, hands folded, a copy of his book in her lap. The lustrous metal handles on the chair glistened with raindrops. Her surprising appearance—the first time Caleb had seen her since Christmas—was all he needed to gather his courage, to relax and let the words flow.

He spoke of the incalculably valuable storehouse of knowledge lost in the library's destruction. Briefly, he highlighted the acquisition of books from around the world and how the library and the museum served as the world's first university. He touched on the great names associated with the museum and the scrolls. He spoke of Kallimakhos and his innovative cataloging method that led to the current card catalog system; then he turned to speculation of what major works had been lost forever. According to surviving memoirs, biographies and other histories, among the lost works were plays of Homer, Plato and Virgil; mathematical treatises by Euclid; medical texts that described treatments for what remain today incurable diseases. Then there were metaphysical texts, spiritual guides to awaken the soul and expand one's consciousness.

Next, so as not to bore them completely, Caleb turned to the major theories about the catastrophic destruction of all this knowledge, delving into the bloodshed and intolerance that had brought all these works to flames. He spoke of Caesar and the later Roman emperors who, in their zeal to crush Alexandrian rebellions, had inadvertently or consciously torched sections of the library. He spoke of Emperor Theodosius's decrees that had incited the Christian mobs in 391 AD, and even touched on the questionable theory that Arab conquerors had depleted the library's scrolls as a means to heat the city's steam baths, citing the famous order of destruction from the caliph of Cairo: "The scrolls either contradict the Koran, in which case they are heresy, or they agree with it, so they are superfluous."

About halfway through his presentation, Caleb looked up and saw another bright face watching from the counter beside a gold-plated espresso machine. A blond-haired woman looked across the room through narrow-rimmed glasses. She wore a neat gray suit over a tight yellow blouse. For some reason, despite the enthralled stares of the others, young and old packing the tables and chairs, her attention made Caleb uncomfortable.

But he continued, drawing a welcome smile from Phoebe, who held up his book and made a signing motion. He hurried to wrap up his talk, reading from the last chapter, ". . . The mob burst into the Serapeum, shattered the meager defenses of the scholars and priestesses inside, then proceeded to tear down statue after statue, demolishing urns, altars and artwork. A trio of young men guarded an arched doorway on the east side." His voice cracked here as he pictured the scene in his mind. After all, he had witnessed it first-hand . . .

. . . *as one of the mob. He finds himself urged on with vitriolic hate and burning venom as the Patriarch Theophilus stands behind them, waving his blazing cross and shouting passages from Leviticus. He storms past marble columns, swinging a torch in one hand and a twisted tree branch in the other. He howls as he strikes down one youth, crushes his skull, and falls upon the defenders. The others surge at his back and push him through the door into a large chamber with a rounded ceiling. Across each wall are hollowed-out alcoves overflowing with neatly packed scrolls, trembling like bees in a hive.*

With a shout for God and for their Patriarch, twenty of the zealots race across the floor, brandishing torches and crying with delight. The room cowers before their shadows, moving in a twisted parody of an ancient orgiastic dance. Gleefully the men hurl their torches into every corner, igniting anything that will burn.

He barely makes it out, coughing and choking on smoke, trampling on the bodies of men and women, "protectors" of the temple of learning. He takes one last look at a statue of Seshat holding a book to her chest, toppling as four monks run, cheering. Then a burst of flame roars out of the archway, the roof collapses, and a dozen rioters are crushed.

He trips, catches himself, then stumbles over debris and falls at the feet of Theophilus, who holds up a blazing silver cross with both hands and shouts to the heavens, offering up to God their glorious victory.

With stinging eyes, he looks out over Alexandria and witnesses other pyres burning into the huddled night, smoke clouds rising, rising, occluding the stars and blurring the lights of heaven.

Across the harbor, beyond the pall of death and smoke, the lighthouse beacon flickers as if blinking away its tears.

Caleb closed with a brief but chilling postscript on how the early Christians had solidified their hold on the city, vanquishing first by edict and then by violence all record of the early learning. They had forbidden the study of the classics, burning remaining copies of scrolls and assaulting those who still practiced the old beliefs. In many ways, this body of classical work—the robust philosophical ruminations of the past—had shaped and molded and even nurtured Christianity; but now, in the ultimate betrayal, the fledgling religion was stabbing its mentor in the back.

He focused on Hypatia, the familiar classic tragedy of the last great symbol of enlightenment. How this respected scholar-author and teacher had been pulled from her chariot by the incited mob and torn limb from limb, her flesh carved from her bones with stones and shells, then burned and fed to dogs. Only, Caleb added a minor detail he alone knew, having seen it in one of his visions: ". . . At the end, through a haze of blood and flayed skin, she looked toward the Pharos, and as they beat and clawed and ripped at her body, she seemed to reach for it as a last refuge, or perhaps something more. A necklace was torn from her neck—a chain with a gold charm of the caduceus."

Maybe it meant nothing, Caleb told myself, or maybe . . . she had been down *there.*

He closed the book and took a deep breath. His mouth was dry. He eyed a full glass of water balanced on the edge of the podium. Phoebe stared at him, open-mouthed. Then, the woman at the counter began to clap, and the room erupted into applause.

Caleb spent the next forty minutes signing books and thanking people for braving the nasty weather. He listened to boring stories of the customers' favorite authors and travels and anything else they wanted to talk about. Finally, the crowd thinned and people made room for Phoebe, who rolled up to his table. She held his book to her chest, hugging it fiercely.

"Oh, Mr. Famous Author,"—her pony tail wagged back and forth as she shook her head— "won't you sign something clever in my book? Something sweet, and maybe give me your phone number?"

Caleb walked around the table and gave her a crushing hug. In the corner of his eye, the strange but beautiful woman at the counter sipped an espresso and watched him carefully. "I didn't know you were coming," Caleb said. "How—?"

"It's in all the papers back home, big brother. You know how dull the *Sodus Gazette* can be. They ran out of shore-erosion stories and interviews with the apple farmers, so they had to look elsewhere for news."

"Great. So Mom knows."

"Of course. She's been following your career, while respecting your need for privacy. She and Dad—"

"'Dad'?"

"Sorry, Mr. Waxman—"

"They got married?"

"Yeah." She lowered her eyes. "In March."

Caleb groaned.

Phoebe looked down at her hands. "I know you hate him, but really, he has been good to Mom. He's supported her, and kept the house going. They've published articles together, worked on some other special projects. It was like they were living together anyway, so—"

"So she just gave up on Dad. Went with this loser."

"Caleb." Phoebe sighed. "Don't bring up Dad again. You know he's gone. You said so yourself."

He turned his back, walked around the four remaining copies of his book and slumped in the chair. The smell of espresso, jasmine and cinnamon hung in the air, blown about by the door opening briefly.

"Caleb,"—she leaned forward on her elbows—"listen to me. They bought advance copies and found in your book some stuff they think might help with the Pharos."

"I don't care," he whispered.

"You do care," Phoebe insisted, holding up his book. "You still see it. It's stuck in your mind, if only in your subconscious. And you've seen things the rest of us haven't. Gone places we never thought to go."

Caleb shrugged. "It was for a different purpose. The library is what matters to me."

"Just like the lighthouse mattered for Dad."

He shook his head. "What could be more important than the search for lost knowledge?" Caleb placed his hand on the cover of his book, feeling the smooth, velvety texture around a picture of a magnificently arched building atop a hill. "The entirety of human knowledge was contained at one point in Alexandria, and . . . and I've seen glimpses of it. That should be—should've been our focus. That's all I care about."

Phoebe straightened and pulled her shawl tighter around her shoulders. She spoke through pursed lips. "Earth, fire, air, water. The four elements, each represented by a planet—Venus, Saturn, Mars, Jupiter." She spoke slowly, carefully, watching Caleb's reaction. "Then, Mercury, the Moon, the Sun. Those are the seven symbols around the caduceus. They're set in grooves that allow you to turn each symbol."

"Phoebe—"

"Mom thinks maybe if you spin them in the correct order, the seal will open."

Caleb laughed out loud. "Really? She thinks it's that easy? That the grand tower designed to last forever and guarded by ingeniously deadly traps would have only a simple combination lock on the door?" Caleb started to laugh again, but then noticed that woman at the counter looking down her glasses at him. Patiently waiting, it seemed, for him to finish.

Phoebe sighed. "Anyway, we don't know what the symbols really represent. So there's no way we'll get in."

"And that's why Mom and 'Dad' want my help."

Phoebe nodded.

"I suppose you've tried more trances, remote viewing?" He took a sip of water.

"No luck," she said. "Couldn't see anything else about that door, besides another glimpse of Caesar, as you had seen him. We're stumped. We tried focusing on that scroll again, over and over. And, once we got a hit on something strange; I saw a castle atop a sheer cliff, and a man in a red cloak being led up to it in shackles. But we couldn't make sense of that."

Caleb frowned. "You never saw Naples or the Herculaneum library again?"

Phoebe shook her head. "I told you, we're stuck. But you know Mom, she'll never let this rest. And now, with Waxman around full time, it's like there are two of her."

"Sorry to hear that. Hopefully they aren't always asking you for help. Do they still have the Morpheus Initiative?"

"No. Disbanded earlier in the year. Although, that Victor guy still hangs around." Phoebe tried to smile. "It's hard to attract new volunteers once they've learned what happened in Alexandria. The prospect of violent death kind of dampens the volunteer spirit."

"Yeah. So, what about you?"

Phoebe nodded. "Keeping busy. Still translating a steady supply of museum pieces—tablets and medieval parchments, that sort of thing." She gave Caleb a weary look. "Most of the time I go to bed with a raging headache."

"And how's the . . ."

"Disability? I get by. I'm used to it." She raised her arms and pretended to flex. "Getting huge biceps. Handicapped bathrooms have always been a real treat, and it's just a blast taking an hour to get my pants on in the morning." She shrugged. "Same ol' same ol'."

"I'm sorry."

"Stop it," she scolded. "Listen, if you're not going to come back with me and help us out, can you at least sign my book?"

Caleb reached for it, opened the inside cover, thought for a second, then wrote something he imagined he might regret. In the end, he felt he had to reward her effort, at least in some little way. He wrote: *To my little sister. To my Sun and my Moon. The other elements—the other planets—are mere shadows, diminishing before your light.*" It was just a guess on his part, but if the seal *was* a combination lock, the order should have some relationship to the orientation of the planets, maybe their distance from the Sun.

After a kiss on the cheek, Caleb walked Phoebe to the door, opened her umbrella, and hailed a cab. He helped get her inside and then packed her chair into the trunk. He leaned in before he closed the door. "My email address is on the back cover," he said. "Write me more often, and we'll talk. I promise. And I do miss you."

She blinked and chewed her lower lip. "Miss you too, big brother."

Caleb walked back into the café, smiled at a few lingering patrons, and made a beeline to the counter where the woman was still sitting, smiling. As he came closer she set down her cup and extended her hand.

"Great job," she said. Her eyes glittered like jade stones. Sharp bangs fell over her face and tickled her lips, which were a shade of crimson that seemed too striking for her smooth face.

"Thanks." Caleb took her hand, and she gently moved her fingers against his, surprising—and intriguing—him by this sudden seductiveness. She wouldn't let go.

"Sorry I was late," she said. "Doubleday has a habit of telling its publicists last minute where they're supposed to be. But now that we've met, you and I can work out the schedule, and I won't leave you hanging again."

"Excuse me. You're . . ."

"Oh, I thought you knew. I'm Lydia Jones." She squeezed his hand a little tighter. Caleb felt his eyes drawn to the flash of skin just above the open buttons on her blouse. Instead of looking lower into the tempting shadows, he focused on the glittering charm—an Egyptian ankh, a cross with a loop over its arms.

"Again," she said, pulling her hand away at last, "sorry I was late, but I'm glad to see you handled yourself brilliantly. Great reading style, although we may want to shorten your intro in the future. Some people walked out early."

"Understood," he said, still staring at her charm.

"Ahem." She touched his chin and lifted his eyes to hers. "See something you like?"

"Sorry," Caleb stammered, blushing fiercely. "Your charm, the ankh. It's just, you know, Egyptian mythology . . ."

"Oh." She touched it. "Yeah, I'm kind of the specialist on ancient history authors. I get stuck with all of you dusty guys. This thing was a present from an old client, a one-book-wonder on Egyptian culture and symbolism. Anyway, let's grab something to eat and map out your next readings. Hope you're hungry."

"Famished," he said, following her to a table.

From somewhere in the cramped storerooms of his memory, Phoebe's warning came whispering back. A blond with green eyes. But Caleb felt drawn into destiny, and as he sat beside Lydia and breathed in her jasmine essence, exotic like a drifting evening breeze over the Nile, he couldn't explain his reaction, feelings of desire, unlike anything he'd experienced since Nina.

They ate and talked, and Caleb stole glances at her whenever he could, thrilled at this new partnership.

4

Across the street from the Soho bookstore, the rain slammed against a three-story brownstone and fell in torrents around a green awning that covered the man in the long raincoat from all but the wind-driven sleet.

George Waxman tried again to light his cigarette and finally succeeded. He took a deep breath of the menthol-flavored smoke and waited for his associate to cross the street. Yellow cabs raced by, pounding into rainwater-filled potholes, and Waxman winced with each splash, imagining an old woman hurling insults at him and screaming: *Your fault! Yours ...*

Waxman clenched his teeth, nearly biting

through the cigarette, and his tongue. "Go away, Mother."

Listen to me, boy!

Across the street, the man with a folded newspaper over his head waited for another series of cars and buses to drive past.

"Shut up."

Sorry, boy. I'm waiting for you.

"Leave me alone."

Like you left me? In pieces? After you caused the accident? You, crying, always wailing in the back seat. Your no-good father took one look at you and ran off with some whore, left me with your shrieking and whining, every waking moment.

"Mother, not now—"

Yes, now. The intersection, the bus . . . I know you remember it, I know you do.

"Please. I have work to do."

Oh yes, your precious work. You think it will ease your conscience?

"No, mother. It's too late for that. I was only four years old the day you died—

The day you murdered me.

"But I can still save others."

The rain hissed off the sidewalk and guzzled into the drains.

He put his hands to his temples, then covered

his ears and pressed as hard as he could. The image burned into the back of his eyelids: his mother's head, severed as a jagged piece of that bus tore through the driver's-side window, her eyes locked on his, lips still moving,

Victor Kowalski ran across the street, dodging a silver Honda. His pants were soaked and his shirt sleeves drenched. He had a leather case strapped over his shoulder.

The rain continued to pound out words on the canvass awning: *You won't be rid of me, Georgie. Even if you get past your precious lighthouse door. Even if you get the treasure.*

Waxman froze. His mother had never talked about that before. For years her voice had haunted him, but she had never taken her comments beyond direct, guilt-provoking insults.

"What did you say?" He held out a hand to stop Victor from speaking.

A sound like laughter dripped from the brownstone walls and fell from the overflowing gutters. *I see your future Georgie. Oh yes. Soon, we'll have something in common. What comes around goes around, boy. Oh yes.*

Again, the laughter.

"Mother!" Waxman hissed, then all at once the rain stopped, and the whispered voice with it.

"Sir?"

Waxman cursed, fuming at the dripping rainwater, the puddles, the filling drains. Then he glared at Victor. "What?"

"It's her. Lydia."

Waxman looked over his associate's shoulder, back to the bookstore, where Caleb Crowe sat with his publicist at the coffee counter. "You're sure?"

"Yes. Using a different last name, but still her." Victor's eyes held that cold metallic glint common to people like him. Killers. Loyalists. As long as Nina was still out of commission, Victor was the best Waxman had to work with.

"Get me a report by eight p.m., and a transcript of what she said to him before you left."

"Sure," Victor said, wiping his dripping forehead. "Sorry I couldn't stay longer. It looked like she was getting suspicious, and I didn't want to risk Caleb recognizing me."

Idiot. Who couldn't blend in at a bookstore? "Fine," Waxman said. "But begin surveillance; I want to know everything they say. Everywhere they go. Her, especially."

As Victor walked away, Waxman lingered a moment, wishing he could trust him more, wishing he had confidence in the man's abilities the way he had trusted Nina. She was sorely missed, in many ways.

He lingered on, until the rain came again and the whispers returned. They grew louder, more malicious, and Waxman felt a renewed chill down his spine that spread through his legs, numbing his feet and tingling his toes. He moved forward, stamping his feet. The whispers followed, and in every puddle he walked past he thought he saw his mother's scowling face.

"Wait," Waxman called, jogging after Victor. "We'll share a cab."

5

SA EL-HAGAR, EGYPT—MARCH

Six months later, with Lydia now his research assistant as well as publicity agent, they began work on a sequel, a comparative study of libraries in the ancient world. The plan was to chronicle such storehouses of knowledge as King Ashurbanipal's library at Nineveh and the Greek Pergamum, which Marc Antony had diminished to replenish Alexandria's library for his queen. It was at the Temple of Isis in the ancient city of Sais that Herodotus and Plato had claimed the god Thoth had relocated the entirety of the world's wisdom, all the ancient tablets and scrolls from before the flood. Some psychics, including Edgar Cayce and Madame Blavatsky, had even claimed that the refugees from sunken Atlantis had brought their advanced knowledge with them to civilize Egypt, and that

Thoth had been one of their representatives, later revered as a god.

This new book touched on the legends that the Great Pyramid also had been built as an impregnable storehouse, a library to withstand time, natural disasters and the elements. Of course, Lydia would have liked first-hand evidence, and after learning of Caleb's talents, she had pressured him into trying to gain psychic validation of these claims. He had given half-hearted efforts to please her, but nothing substantial had come of it, and they went on in their normal course of research.

On the back cover of the new book they were going to put Lydia's favorite quote from Plato's *Timaeus*—a quote that signified their book's theme on the true essence and function of libraries: *Whereas just when you and other nations are beginning to be provided with letters and the other requisites of civilized life, after the usual interval, the stream from heaven, like a pestilence, comes pouring down, and leaves only those of you who are destitute of letters and education; and so you have to begin all over again like children, and know nothing of what happened in ancient times.*

It was their central thesis that these ancient libraries, filled with scrolls, clay tablets and other writings, had arisen out of the urgent necessity of preservation. With advanced knowledge of the heavens and the earth, knowledge even of man's gross depravity, there must have been great trepidation—a sort of cosmic paranoia—about the loss of all that accumulated wisdom of humanity. Libraries, Caleb and Lydia postulated, had been originally built as magnificently constructed, earthquake- and flood-resistant structures, so that after any such upheavals, through cosmic or man-made actions, the history of human advances could be regained, and civilization could progress, rather than devolve.

To research this encyclopedic work, Lydia and Caleb set out together across Europe and the Middle East, ending up in Egypt, doing book signings for his previous book along the way. It was fairly typical for a publicist to accompany an author for part of such tours, but with Lydia it was different. Everyone knew it was different. For the past few months, they had been living together, writing and researching all day, making love at night. They enjoyed elegant dinners on the publisher's tab and took in the occasional show or concert. But mostly, they stayed in and worked.

And fell in love.

For Caleb, the past year had been a whirlwind of twin passions: Lydia and history. Both had become entwined about him like hungry snakes, alternately pulling and squeezing back in an exotic tug of war. Neither side lost, but neither won. He shared them and matured with them both.

The book was a huge hit, translated into ten languages, and the rush of travel felt so invigorating, unlike those frustrating trips with his mother, during which he had sat brooding on the sidelines, angry at the disturbance in his life, as if he had known that other factions were waiting for his attention.

Time hurtled by, and somehow, from the depths of his dislocation and melancholy, he now found himself fulfilled. He was standing upon the ruins of an ancient Egyptian temple, hand in hand with the woman he loved. They had just wrapped up the research tour, appropriately closing with the most ancient site referenced in their new book: the crumbling town of Sa el-Hagar, the dynastic city of Sais.

Located on a branch of the Nile that flowed through the Delta, like at Alexandria, Sais was once a proud, bustling city that boasted its own share of philosophers, historians and priests, and a connection to an ancient source of secret wisdom handed down by the priests of Thoth and stored here in the temple.

The winds blew reverently through the half-collapsed columns, and sand skittered about Caleb's feet with the scarabs and lizards. The buzzing of gnats had grown past annoying. He and Lydia both wore white scarves and khaki pants, heavy boots and wide-brimmed hats. Lydia's face was tanned evenly, and she seemed tirelessly radiant, even with those thick oval sunglasses that reminded Caleb a bit too much of his mother when he was young.

"So what about now?" she urged, poking him in the ribs as the sun ducked behind the hills. A lonely motorboat made its way up the murky Nile, and a white-robed passenger waved to them.

"Are you serious?" He looked around. "Can't you wait? Our hotel is—"

"No, silly." Lydia took off her glasses and her deep green eyes sent a chill down his spine despite the heat. "I meant, what about trying your remote viewing here? Now that there's no pressure. The book is written, our research done. You can relax and just, I don't know, see what there is to see."

He tried to smile. "Doesn't work that way. It's something that just happens, whether I want it to or not. And actually, in my family's experience, psychic abilities seem to manifest more intensely after traumatic experiences. Stress encourages the power. My mother only started seeing visions after her father died. And Phoebe's powers seem to have gotten stronger after her injury."

Lydia pouted and kicked at the sand. She leaned against a pillar decorated with faded hieroglyphs.

"Besides," Caleb added, "I gave up actively pursuing those visions. That was a part of my childhood, a piece of my former life that only brought misery."

"Just try," Lydia pleaded, tugging at his sleeve. "For me? We're at the site of Isis's temple. You may never get this opportunity again!"

He looked into her eyes for a long time, then finally nodded. "Nothing's going to happen, though."

"Not with that attitude."

He shrugged, stepped around Lydia and leaned on a pillar, touching its rounded limestone surface and tracing the glyphs. Focusing on the chiseled grooves, he started to translate, picking up a portion of a hymn to Isis, praising her for begetting the sun, and suddenly he smelled smoke . . .

. . . *and burning oil. Thick, oppressive. In the light of the braziers and torches, men with shaved heads and long blue robes are kneeling on a marble floor and inscribing letters onto long strips of papyri. A great arched roof spans overhead, brilliantly painted with a scene from the* Book of the Dead *in which Thoth judges the souls of the departed and greets a royal couple.*

"Manetho," someone calls. And he finds himself looking up, shocked to hear the Egyptian language spoken as it was over two thousand years ago. "We are almost finished," says Vutan, one of the Hermopolis priests coordinating the translations.

"Good. Ptolemy Philadelphus will be pleased. These must go to Alexandria in all haste."

He takes a moment to look around. They are deep under the earth, several levels below the main temple. Thick pillars support the roof, and strong walls, ancient walls built thousands of years ago, seal in this chamber. Two narrow air shafts lead up to the surface and serve to recycle the air. The materials here below are safe from the erosion of time that affects papyrus scrolls. And there are other earlier texts stored here, some inscribed on clay, others hammered into copper sheets and rolled.

And there ahead—two enormous, squat pillars. One of them plated with gold, the other with emerald. Deep, perfectly chiseled symbols carved over every inch.

Manetho has spent two decades studying these, the most ancient histories. He has used them to chronicle the kings of Egypt from the dawn of time until now. He has written treatises on magic, on philosophy and science; he has learned the ways of the heavenly bodies and the motion of the earth. But still, there are passages on these two pillars, lines of inscrutable text he cannot translate. And the priests will not reveal those secrets. Not yet, they say. Even though his name, Manetho, means 'beloved of Thoth,' they feel he is unworthy to know this most sacred wisdom.

There are dozens of translators at work, each copying partial sections only, undertaking the difficult tasks of translating the symbols into Greek, striving to keep even the phonetic elements the same. Later, these fragments will be integrated by a master craftsman and magician on ten tablets to be named The Books of Thoth. *The wisdom from these pillars, Manetho knows, was translated from the one great artifact he has never been allowed to see—a tablet of pure emerald, what the priests claim is a miraculous, multi-layered book containing the most sacred wisdom.*

Manetho has promised to collect both this tablet and the translation, and transport them to the Ptolemy's new library. Even then, he will be accompanied by priests to prevent even a glimpse of the ancient words on the Emerald Tablet.

"Thank you," he says again and clasps his hands together. "I will be outside, taking my supper. Call for me when you are finished." He makes his way up the winding stairs, thinking upon all he has learned, questioning this legacy of learning.

For some time, he has sensed that plans were underway to move this knowledge, for the library's safety has become compromised. The common people know of its existence, and while protected from the elements, the library can not be safeguarded from ignorant and malicious men who seek power.

Once outside, standing under the host of

heaven with the great temple at his back, he looks up at the stunning constellations, at Osiris standing proud above the mighty Milky Way, at Sirius blazing at his feet. Manetho turns, and in the starlight he reads the inscription on the temple entrance: Isis am I, I am all that was, that is, and that shall be and no one of mortals has ever lifted my veil. *And below this:* Only the Golden Ones may enter and see the truth of the world. *And then, a familiar but powerful symbol:*

He thinks about the priests below, furiously translating and preparing the most ancient of books for the new library, hammering all that has

been recorded into tablets. And Manetho sup-
presses a chill, knowing that despite all his
learning, all his understanding, he is still con-
sidered impure, unworthy to pass beyond the veil
and see the truth—

Caleb snapped back into the present, trembling
in Lydia's arms. After he had related his vision, she
exclaimed, "But that would have been amazing to
include, assuming you accurately saw through
Manetho's eyes."

"Right, but that's just it. I can never be sure of
the accuracy of what I see." He was still shell-
shocked, slow in getting to his feet. "And even if it is
true, how could we have footnoted it, *Psychic
vision, Caleb Crowe?*"

"You're right." Her smile broadened, then she
frowned. "So, the 'Golden Ones . . .'" She eyed the
columns, picturing how the roof and the inscription
would have appeared. "What do you think that
means?"

Caleb sat and leaned against a pillar. He
pictured the symbol again, remembered seeing it
with a similar warning under the Pharos. He
recalled what he had told Waxman four years
earlier: "In the alchemist tradition, handed down
from the surviving Hermetic writings, gold is the
purest form of matter. So if you were to pass
beyond the veil of Isis here, or beyond the doorway
with a similar warning under the Pharos, I assume

that you would have to first be somehow tested—purified and deemed worthy."

Lydia laughed. "Oh, then we're definitely not getting in, not after what we did last night."

"Seriously, there are many early religions that expressed the world around us as a veil, a thin covering over the real world, which only initiates of the hidden mysteries could part."

"What initiates?"

Caleb shrugged. "Egyptian mystery schools trained students in certain ways that elevated their spiritual essences, made them question the nature of the world and learn truths about reality."

"Didn't I read somewhere that Jesus might have spent time in Egypt?"

"That's a theory," Caleb said. "The Gospels are silent about the period of his life after the 'kid in the temple' incident and until he returns to Jerusalem and starts his ministry. Some occult sources claim he learned the backdrop of his teachings in the temples of Isis and Osiris, from the high priests of Delphi, that he had access to occult wisdom, and that he—"

"—passed beyond the veil," Lydia finished.

Caleb slowly got to his feet. "Many of the Gospel verses are word-for-word translations of much earlier Egyptian sources. The first line of John is nearly verbatim from one of the Pyramid Texts, a hymn to Amun-Ra found in a two-thousand BC tomb. The Sermon on the Mount reads almost like a carbon copy of a speech Horus gave to his followers. And images inscribed on a temple wall in Luxor show Horus's birth, surrounded by three solar deities who followed the star Sirius, with a previous panel depicting Thoth announcing the news to the virgin Isis."

Lydia held up her hands and he stopped, unsure whether he should continue. She said, "Hey, don't worry. I won't hit you with charges of heresy. I haven't been to Church in ten years."

Caleb had never known that about her. In fact, he didn't know much about her life before they'd met. They had been so caught up in researching ancient history that they'd had no time for investigating the more recent past. Every so often she would question his relationships with his mother or with Phoebe, and she would ask about the Morpheus Initiative. Every once in a while Caleb would get a letter from Phoebe inquiring about the book or just updating him on their fruitless attempts to break the Pharos Code, and Lydia would ask how their search was progressing. Thankfully, she had never asked about his father. And sadly, Caleb rarely thought about him.

At least that part of my past is over.

Caleb took a deep breath as a trio of buzzing gnats flew about his face. Lydia helped him up, and they walked out of the ruins toward the distant tourist area and the two cabs waiting patiently for fares.

"So, if your vision is true," Lydia began, "then we have an even more tragic picture of what was lost at Alexandria."

Caleb stopped. For a moment, the sunlight skipped like a dozen flat stones across the Nile and he had a flash of clarity, a moment of understanding, as if he had somehow restored a waking connection to the historical vision. A rush of faces passed before his mind's eye, a tumultuous crowd of men and women. He had the certainty that they were all involved in a grand legacy, a noble plan, a cosmic secret. Plato's words echoed in his mind: "*. . . you have to begin all over again like children, and know nothing of what happened in ancient times.*" Then it vanished as Caleb saw something out of the corner of his eye—a blurry figure in the distance. He squinted. There on the opposite bank stood a man. Out of place, looking like the stump of a diseased palm tree. He was so narrow, so motionless—until he lifted his arm, and pointed at Caleb.

The air shook, an invisible ripple extending out from that finger to Caleb's heart. He jolted back, spun and Lydia just barely steadied him.

"Do you see him?" Caleb shouted, frantic, pushing away and running toward the river. "There!" But the far bank was empty. Only desolate shrubs and a jumble of rocks. Caleb turned to see Lydia giving him a frightened look.

She came to him, held his hands, kissed his sweaty forehead. "Let's get you back to the hotel."

VENICE

Whatever had let loose his visions at Sais, whatever jolt had restored the sight, it was responsible for releasing a chain of successive dreams of such realism over the next week that Caleb and Lydia decided against returning to the States until they had sorted them out.

Caleb filled one sketchbook, then another. He tried to force daytime trances to get more clarity, and he again slept with a coffee cup full of sharpened pencils and a pad of paper next to the bed. Lydia would sit quietly by his side, run book errands, and bring him water and food. Watching and biting her nails from the shadows.

Finally, he gave up; the visions were not progressing past the point he had already reached. Lydia coaxed him into talking, and he described what he'd seen, the same rush of images he had been privy to back in the harbor in Alexandria. In an excited, breathless voice, as the song of cicadas drifted on Mediterranean breezes through their window, he said, "It starts on Pharos Island. Alexandria. I believe it's two hundred and seventy-nine BC. Just before Dedication Day."

"Dedication of what?" Lydia asked.

Caleb smiled and told her the story of what had come in pieces and jumbled images, like video clips in his mind. The story of Sostratus and Demetrius, the tour of the lighthouse, the cryptic words of its builder . . . all the way to the point where Sostratus had led his visitor down those stairs. But then it ended. And despite his attempts to go farther, to venture below through the vault door with Demetrius, the visions wouldn't oblige.

"Maybe you need to give your mind a rest," Lydia proposed. "A vacation."

Before returning to Alexandria, where they'd hoped Caleb's visions would continue and lead them to further answers, they took a month's vacation on a cruise up the Nile, visiting the Valley of the Kings, Luxor, Karnak, Abydos and other amazing sites he had only read about. Caleb's dreams were filled with enormous pyramids, sprawling pillars, cyclopean roofs, rows of hieroglyphs and painted wall reliefs. Then they spent a week in Cairo, at the museum and in the markets and among the Pyramids. But before embarking on the last leg of the cruise and making their way to Alexandria, they went to Venice.

To get married.

They crossed the Mediterranean, passed within ten miles of Rhodes and then Malta, and continued past the tip of Sicily and up the coast of Italy. Caleb pointed out the Bay of Naples and the Royal Palace, where he could almost see the scholars in white coats still teasing millimeters of carbonized papyrus from the Herculaneum scrolls. They went around the boot of Italy, circled back and continued north past Tuscany until they entered the canals of Venice. While Caleb ordered dinner, Lydia secured a room on the eastern side of the city, overlooking St. Mark's piazza. And that night, under velvety purple skies, they were married.

Facing each other in a gondola, as the full moon painted them in ghostly auras, they said their vows before a priest, in Latin. They held hands and kissed, and people cheered—people on the bridges, people in their homes looking down, people at the edge of St. Mark's.

They celebrated with a wonderful seafood dinner unlike anything Caleb could remember. And then there were three bottles of wine, some Chianti to wrap up the night before they stumbled back to their room. Dizzy, Caleb promised Lydia they'd consummate the marriage in the morning, and she giggled and agreed as she pulled up the sheets.

Under the covers, away from the lights from the cathedral, she whispered in his ear, "I have to tell you something."

Caleb laughed and kissed her fiercely. He felt her nakedness entwining around him completely. He could not have been happier. His only regret was not the suddenness of their decision to marry, but the fact that he hadn't told Phoebe.

"What is it?" Caleb whispered back, nibbling at his wife's lips.

"Something about me," she said. "I need to tell you—"

"Can it wait?" he asked, trying to stop the room from spinning. He wished he had taken some aspirin. Mildly curious about what she had to say, he suddenly imagined that the alcohol had freed some inherent block, and a small window had opened, which he could peer into and learn whatever dark secrets his new bride harbored.

"No," she said. "It can't wait. But . . . I don't know if I can say."

"Tell me," Caleb insisted, barely able to keep his eyes open. But at that moment, his stomach lurched, the room spun even harder, and he ran to the bathroom, which happened to be down the hall, shared by six other guestrooms. Fortunately it was empty, and when he returned to the room, Lydia was snoring. He slid under the covers and fell fast asleep beside her.

In the morning, the phone woke them up.

Lydia got to it first. "Wrong room," she said, slamming the receiver down. Her hair was a mess, and sheet lines were written over her face. She turned to Caleb. "Ugh. Sorry, I don't think that was the most romantic of wedding nights."

"No." He groaned. "But the ceremony was nice."

"Sure was." She sighed and looked out the window, closing her eyes and feeling the cool Venetian winds. "Let's get something to eat and go see the cathedral."

Caleb got up, then sat back down, the room still pitching. He put his head between his hands and groaned. "Was there something you were going to tell me last night?"

She shot him a glance of surprise. "I don't . . . I don't think so."

"You're not already married, are you?"

She walked over, bent down and gave him a long, lingering kiss. "Yes, that's it. I'm actually married to the prince of Monaco, and when his royal soldiers find out what you've done, your death will be unspeakably cruel." She smiled and tousled his hair. "Of course I'm not married. You know I've been waiting for you." Her eyes, like emerald pebbles, searched his face, his eyes, his tangled hair. "I don't remember what I said last night, honey. But I do remember you saying something about consummating our marriage?"

He grinned and pulled her back onto the bed.

Inside St. Mark's Cathedral they jostled in and out of crowds, shuffling from the gorgeous statues of one saint to another, from one sprawling mosaic to the next, only to find themselves standing before a wall-length image depicting, of all things, a lighthouse.

"Didn't you know about this?" Lydia asked, and for a moment Caleb had the suspicion that she had directed him to this spot on purpose, maybe to get him thinking about the past again.

"I did, but I forgot. I remember something in my father's research about one of the earliest surviving depictions of the Pharos being found here." Caleb traced the tiny facets making up the image. "Not quite to scale, and smaller than I've seen, but that's it."

"Why is it here?" she asked.

"St. Mark was thought to be martyred in Alexandria. And later, in 829 AD, Christians made a daring raid into Alexandria, stole his body out from under the Arabs and buried him here, under the main altar. Along with his body may have come the legacy of the Pharos, and one of few surviving pictures of what it really looked like."

Lydia raised her eyebrows. She poked Caleb in the side and hugged his arm. "Sorry for bringing it up, but I just thought . . . well, I had an idea about our next book."

"No." He looked her in the eyes, and his smile faded. "I'm not digging up those memories. I'm not going to—"

"—continue your father's work?"

That was it. She had a knack for knowing how to hit him where it counted. He pulled her aside and they made their way through a tour group snapping pictures. They walked past somber statues of the saints and elaborate woodcarvings, up a flight of stairs and finally exited back at the piazza. The pigeons whirled and flitted around the crowds, the picture-takers, the musicians, the souvenir peddlers. The flapping of their wings seemed to create a breeze that stung at Caleb's eyes.

"Sorry," he said. "But, even despite my recent visions of Sostratus and the lighthouse . . . I'm just not ready for this discussion."

"But we're married," Lydia said, smiling devilishly. "Good times and bad and all that. Don't you want to keep your wife happy? I need a new project. And in case you didn't read your contract, Doubleday needs another book out of you within two years."

"Doubleday can wait," he said, putting on a

cheap pair of black sunglasses he had bought in Cairo. "They can wait forever if it means going back to my mother's obsession."

"It doesn't have to involve her," she said. "You have your own notes, we have all the research we need. We can go to Alexandria next week and start."

Caleb kicked at a pigeon that came too close, missing by several feet. "Why the lighthouse, Lydia?"

"Because," she said, barely above a whisper, "you're dreaming about it. And not just that, I think it fits with our research. And I think you know this."

"What do you mean?" His throat tightened up. His heart started pounding.

"You know . . ." she whispered. "You haven't admitted it, but it's the only thing that makes sense."

His vision was getting blurry. Across the plaza, something tugged at his vision, the only clear image in the tide of activity. Beneath the Campanile clock tower, standing just at its base, was *that man*, the figure in green khakis with long hair over his face.

"Caleb?" A blurry Lydia tugged at his sleeve. She was still talking, trying to convince him of something. He heard her speaking about impregnable strongholds, great seals, and something else.

He blinked and wrenched his attention away from the figure, the first time he was ever able to do so, and stared at Lydia. "What did you say?"

"Aren't you listening? I was talking about what you saw through Manetho's eyes. The legendary writings of Thoth, said to contain the mysteries of creation, power over life and death, and knowledge of heaven and earth. Fragments of its message may have found their way into alchemy and the Arcanum, and formed the backbone of the Rosicrucian and Freemason movements."

Caleb licked his lips, glanced back to the clock tower, but couldn't find that enigmatic figure anymore.

"Caleb, honey . . ."

Blinking Lydia back into focus, he sighed and said, "The Emerald Tablet."

"Along with the collection from Sais. Transported and hidden away—"

"—in the Alexandrian library. I already—"

"Didn't you hear me before?" Lydia moved her face to within inches from his, her full lips lustrous in the sunlight, tempting. "I don't think the tablet was brought to the library. I'm betting that to find it you have to look to the other architectural wonder of Alexandria."

Caleb's mouth opened, and suddenly, everything shifted. The world sparkled and everyone was surrounded by a floating nimbus, but only for a moment, then it was gone, like a flash of insight.

The seal, the great door, the traps. Could it be—?

"What do you think?" Lydia asked. "Worth writing about, at least? It's a novel theory: the Pharos not only served as a beacon and an architectural wonder, *it was a vault*."

Caleb looked at her as if she had just stepped out of a lamp and had offered him three wishes. *How could I have not seen it before?* The implications were staggering. Everything they had witnessed and perceived had to be viewed again under this chrysalis. "The treasure—"

"—isn't what you thought."

"It's something even more valuable," Caleb said, and in that instant, a flash from beyond ripped through his core, revealing . . .

. . . *a dark convoy of camels, covered wagons, dozens of slaves lifting great bronze chests. The three dark pyramids dwindle at the horizon, black against the tapestry of night,* . . .

"A caravan," he told her, slipping back to the present, "heading away from Giza." The bright sunlight streamed onto his face as Lydia touched it and brushed back his sweaty hair. He sat on the rim of a fountain, a bubbling, dribbling marble façade. The choking smell of fish and dirty water entered his nostrils. He blinked and saw them . . .

. . . *carrying a secret cargo under cover of night, tracking the Nile, a man in black robes supervising the operation.*

"Do you know what year it was?" asked Lydia.

The flow of the Nile, the passing of hills, trees and great stretches of desert. Then, through a marvelous gate into a sprawling city full of wondrous temples and obelisks, a stadium and so many people, the caravan takes back routes through the darkened alleys and emerges onto a stretch of streets and warehouses in a harbor. And there, across the water, a dark shape rises from an island. Half-assembled, it stands and waits for morning, for the hundreds to resume work on its construction.

"Had to be around 300 BC," he said, still watching the images flashing through his mind. "The Pharos isn't completed yet."

"What else?" Lydia prodded. Her grip on his thigh was fierce.

Caleb shook his head, resisting the onslaught of the present, the pigeons, the tourists, the accordion and singers in the distance, the tolling of the great clock tower all pulling at his consciousness. "They led the caravan past the Palace District, past the Temple of the Muses. Across the Heptastadion, to the Pharos." He held his head in his hands and took great gulps of air. Another flash and he saw that figure again, the leader of the caravan, dressed in black robes and a deep hooded cloak . . .

. . . *stop at the first step leading up to the Pharos. All around him are great blocks, ropes, pulleys and workbenches. Discarded tools of the craftsmen. He pauses on the next step while at his back the convoy comes to a halt, and all the slaves look down at their feet.*

A man appears above. In flowing white robes he glides to the top of the stairs. "Welcome. You have what was promised?"

The man in black nods. "I do. It is now in your safekeeping, Sostratus."

"This collection will be but the first of many."

"It is the oldest, the most important."

"Then it shall be the safest."

The man in black surveys the massive, half-finished structure masterfully etched upon the canvass of the heavens. A light mist drifts over the rocks from the sea and cools his face.

"The ancient resting place of Thoth has been emptied. Guard his treasures well."

Another gulp of air and Caleb was back.

"Wow," Lydia said with a look of dismay. "No matter how many times I witness that, I still can't get used to it."

"Me neither," he said, wheezing.

"I believe you." She lifted her head, distracted by something across the plaza. "Listen, I'll go grab you an Orangina and ice. You need some fluids."

"Okay." He watched her go, then reached into the fountain, cupped some water and splashed it on his cheeks and forehead, feeling momentarily blasphemous for disturbing the sacred waters, before slipping on his sunglasses again

A minute passed, then another. Finally, he looked up toward the drink stand. A trio of pigeons swirled over its roof and flew up and away. The stand was empty. Caleb stood and glanced around, feeling a sudden bout of anxiety. But there she was, a short distance away, talking to a man in a gray suit with a beret tilted on his head, over bushy gray eyebrows. Then the recollection struck like a hammer blow and Caleb remembered him.

The hospital! Standing over my bed.

"The Pharos protects itself . . ."

Before he thought twice about it, Caleb was sprinting. The pigeons scattered at his approach. He bumped into a pair of Asian tourists, and kept running. Lydia turned as he closed in. The man lowered his head and swiftly walked away.

"Honey?" she called as she stepped toward him in a way which seemed to cut him off from following or even getting a better look at the stranger. She caught him around the chest. "Are you okay?"

"That man! Who is he?"

Lydia looked around. "What, that old guy I was just talking to? Don't know. He asked me how much a gondola to the museum costs, and—"

"No!" Caleb shook his head, pointing after the departing figure, now stepping into a boat. "You knew him. You were talking. What did he want?"

"I told you." She gripped Caleb's shoulders, that same fierce grip as before. "Caleb, you're acting weird. Let's get back to the hotel."

"No!"

Lydia took a step back. "Hey, I'm sorry I brought up the lighthouse. I didn't realize it would make you this crazy."

He glared at her. "I'm not crazy. I know that man. I've seen him before."

"And that's not crazy?"

"No! In Alexandria. He . . . he visited me in the hospital. Gloating that we had failed."

Lydia looked over her shoulder at the gondola oaring away, joining three others cutting into the canals. "You can't be serious. You think someone's following you after all these years?"

He glared at her over the ridge of his sunglasses. "Lydia. Tell me now. Tell me if there's something else going on here. Believe me, I'll find out."

She laughed and gave him a pinch. "Threatening me with your powers? Are you saying I'll never be able to have an affair, because you'll be remote viewing my every move?" She pushed back her hair, still grinning. "Guess I should have covered that in our wedding vows. Come on, my love. There's nothing to hide."

She offered the bottle of Orangina and led him out of the plaza. Her fingers caressed his, but he did not return the gesture. He was thinking of Phoebe's warning, years ago.

A girl with green eyes . . .

But by the time they arrived back at the hotel, he had cast the incident in a different light. He'd been hallucinating, imagining the worst. He'd been miserable all his life, and now that he had found a shred of happiness, his subconscious had to dredge up reasons for the dream to fail, to engineer his fall. He wouldn't let it succeed.

He had a renewed purpose. As it happened, that purpose now brought him back on the same path as his mother's. But he planned not to tell her. Not yet.

This time, the quest is mine, and I have a new partner.

Victor Kowalski sat on a bench beside the fountain and pressed SEND on his cell phone. Careful not to look back at the departing new-lyweds, he held the phone to his ear, fixed his sunglasses and pretended to stare up at the church's extravagant architecture. He was dressed in a light blue blazer and gray sweatpants, and wore a Yankees cap. Two cameras hung around his neck, and he was chewing three sticks of strawberry gum. Typical tourist.

The ringing stopped and he heard Waxman's voice. "Yes?"

"She's made contact."

"In person?"

"Yes."

"Then things are getting serious. They must be close."

"I was positioned near enough to overhear." Kowalski snapped his gum. "She told our old friend it wouldn't be long."

"So they're headed there next?"

"Yes, although the kid doesn't know it yet. They'll be in Alexandria by next week."

"Good work. Tail Mr. Gregory, but don't get spotted. I prefer to have them think we've given up."

"So, no action against him until . . .?"

"Until Caleb gets us in."

Victor flipped the phone closed. He stood and made his way to the pier, where he hailed a gondola.

He might as well follow in style.

7
ALEXANDRIA—JUNE

"Our meeting in Venice was stupid. Too dangerous," Lydia said when the man emerged from the shadows in the nightclub alley. Caleb was back at the hotel, a block away, finally resting after nearly two sleepless days of research and work on the codes. They had settled in at Alexandria a month ago, and had started to work immediately.

"I hadn't expected him to be so paranoid," Nolan Gregory said.

"He has a right to be," said Lydia, "after your dramatic appearance in the hospital. Was that necessary?"

"We will see, in time, what was necessary."

"That's not something he'll ever forget."

"All I know is that we need to keep Caleb on the

path. Continue to steer his thoughts and dreams back to the Pharos. Otherwise—"

"Yes, yes I know. Otherwise, we'll never succeed," Lydia said impatiently. Then, quietly, with urgency, she added, "But he's making progress. He's seen them—the founders! Sostratus and Demetrius. And much more."

"Good, good. You must now make him see the rest."

"Why not tell him to the truth about who he is?"

"No. When he finds that out for himself, he'll understand, and then he'll lead us to the Key. Any other way could invite a disaster." Gregory pulled his face back into the shadows. "And another millennium of darkness."

A cab's horn blared into the street, and a trio of laughing young women went running out of the club to their ride.

She sighed. "I fear I may have to do something drastic."

"You have my confidence. I trust you will know the time."

Turning, Lydia walked slowly east toward the hotel. Cars rumbled past, and the warm air played with her blouse and tickled her neck. Out in the harbor a few lights twinkled. Dim flickering beams cut through the night over Qaitbey's fortress.

Lydia took her time, walking and thinking. And

fighting back her emotions.

She put a hand to her stomach, and began to cry.

The advance from Doubleday paid for Caleb and Lydia's hotel suite for the next month. The first book was still selling well across Europe, but only to limited success in the States, probably because they hadn't had a chance to do any further promotions there.

Their room overlooked the harbor. And outside, across the Boulevard de la Rosette, they could reach the causeway and walk to Qaitbey's fortress within an hour. The museum was a short distance away, as were the Municipal Palace and the Zinzania Theater. Near the harbor, where most archae-ologists believed the old library once stood, now proudly stood the Bibliotheca Alexandrina—the modern version of the historic library. With construction finishing in 2006, it comprised ten levels, four of which were built underground to further protect the contents from environmental forces. Adjacent to the library was a science museum and planetarium.

But as exciting as all these attractions were, Caleb and Lydia had little time for sightseeing. Caleb had enlarged the photos of the great seal Phoebe had given him for Christmas years ago. He posted them on a wall and tacked up a bed sheet to cover them when he and Lydia went out. They spent hours each day analyzing every inch of the image, studying every carving, every symbol.

He sent Lydia out repeatedly, sometimes several times a day, for journal articles or books they couldn't access online. Most of these she had to order from contacts at the UK Doubleday offices. They acquired some rare seventeenth-century texts on alchemy—Paracelsus, Geber, Hollandus and Kircher. They consulted works by Francis Bacon and Isaac Newton, Madame Blavatsky's three-volume compendium, and so many other books of arcane knowledge. The trick, as always, was to focus on the truly inspired, those derived from the most ancient writings.

Their hotel suite quickly began to look like Caleb's boyhood room back in Sodus. Dog-eared copies of books were scattered about, and stacks upon stacks of heavy tomes covered the floor.

One day late in September, while Lydia was taking a nap, face-down on the couch as several fruit flies buzzed around a plate of dates and prunes on the coffee table, Caleb sat cross-legged before the wall, considering the enlarged photographs. He imagined he was there again, before the grand staff and the entwined serpents surrounded by seven symbols.

Those symbols were all familiar now, old friends, after fine-tuning his knowledge of alchemy, immersing himself in the subject for the better part of a year. The first four were Water, Fire, Air and Earth and their corresponding planets, Jupiter, Saturn, Mars and Venus. These were the principles of the denser matter, what the alchemists called the elements of the Below; while the realm of the Above hosted the intangible essences of soul and spirit. The remaining three symbols were the Moon, Mercury and, finally, the Sun, often represented as salt, quicksilver and sulfur, signifying the coming together of Above and Below into a new, immortal form of pure essence. The Gold of the soul, the Philosopher's Stone. Quintessence.

It took Caleb a long time to finally accept the obvious: that the sequence might be the key. But no matter which way around the staff he read the symbols, they were not in the right order.

When Lydia awoke she found him staring at the sign in the lower left corner.

"It's a combination lock after all," he said.

"Great." She yawned, then perked up. "So what's the combination?"

Caleb's eyes were out of focus, and in his mind he pictured a cosmic scene of . . .

. . . *the planets of our solar system whirling about the sun in their elliptical orbits*. He spoke slowly, dreamily. "Working backward from the most distant planet they could see with the naked eye, Saturn came first."

"Why backward?" Lydia interrupted.

"The sun was the center of everything. The light they all aspired to."

She nodded, as if the truth had been obvious all along. "So then, Jupiter's next?"

"Yes. Then Mars. Then Venus, which is also the symbol for the material of Earth. Then Mercury, the Moon and finally the Sun."

"Wait, why not the Moon before Venus? It's between Mars and Venus, right?"

Caleb shook his head. "I'm guessing that would stump, or kill, most people who thought they'd figured it out and dared to try. No, in the tradition of alchemy, the Moon occupies an elevated station. It's the second largest object in the sky, dwarfed only by the Sun. Its influence, while subtle, is just as indispensible to life on our planet. And, as if we needed more confirmation, in the alchemical process of turning something into gold, the Moon represents Silver, the stage just before achieving perfection."

Lydia smiled thoughtfully. "Okay, so if we spin the seven symbols in the proper order, we can open the door without releasing the water?"

Caleb considered that for a while, but it still didn't make sense. He thought about the alchemist's instructions, the order for transmuting imperfect material into perfection. And finally something clicked into place.

"That's the wrong question."

"What?"

"Trying to avoid the water trap—avoiding any of the traps—seems like the wrong way to look at this."

"How do you mean?"

"Bear with me a moment. First, let's consider how the water trap was sprung. Waxman set it off when he turned the Water symbol." Caleb focused on the symbol for.

"He started with Water," Lydia whispered, "but that's wrong."

Caleb nodded. "Saturn is farther away from the Sun than Jupiter."

"So it needs to be Saturn first, or Fire, then Water."

"Calcination, then dissolution." His scalp broke out in a sweat. *Could it be that simple? As long as you know the right sequence of the visible planets?* "The problem," he said, "is that we know that when the door opens, a devastating flood is released. For that much water to emerge so quickly, the opposite chamber has to be already filled up, waiting for the doors to open."

"What chance does that give us, then?"

"Maybe we've overlooked something." Caleb scanned the photos again and came back to something he had puzzled over earlier. "There," he said, pointing, "all by itself above the left edge of the seal. It looks like a ring set in the limestone about eight feet above the ground, with a crescent moon symbol above it."

"So?" Lydia reached for the bowl of fruit on the table and popped a fig into her mouth.

Caleb stroked the ragged stubble on his chin. "So why is it there? And is there another one somewhere? I can't see the other side of the door, but maybe I didn't photograph far enough. The crescent moon, it's a symbol for Seshat, Thoth's wife."

Lydia nodded. "She's the goddess of libraries and writing, I know that. But—"

"She was also the mapmaker and the designer of the king's cities, his temples, and so on. One of her symbols is the rope, and in certain Egyptian hymns she was praised for 'stretching the cord,' or measuring out distances in the king's temples and palaces."

Lydia looked from Caleb to the photo. "So we get

a rope?"

He nodded.

"But why? What do we do with it?"

"The first task of the true alchemist is to purify himself, to burn away and dissolve his ego. To blast away the imperfections."

"You mean . . ." Lydia drew in a sharp breath and beamed. "We're not supposed to avoid the traps."

"Like I said."

Caleb stood and started pacing. "Think about it . . . the water trap is an effective defense because of its sheer violence. A million gallons of water rush through the door at once and batter around everything that's not weighted down. The room fills with water, but drains quickly. My guess is, if you're secured well enough you can withstand it—hold your breath until it drains, and then you're fine."

"But why?" Lydia asked. "Why build the trap that way? Surely there has to be an easier way past the seal?"

"Yes, but you have to think like they did. Egyptian mystery schools had a different way of teaching—through intuition and experience, symbolism and reason. Imagine an initiate going through this ordeal. Surviving such a watery onslaught would be a transformative, cleansing experience. It would prepare him for the next stage in the process of enlightenment. Think of people who survive a tsunami, clinging to trees, watching their lives, their whole history, wash away. They can't help but to be transformed by it."

Lydia licked her lips. "Only the worthy," she murmured. "So what comes first?"

"I hate to say this, but I bet there's a fire-oriented trap we need to prepare for. Remember the legend about the Muslims who were tricked into almost destroying the lighthouse? The Arab treasure hunters released the tide of seawater and were swept into the harbor, but the few survivors described other horrors: fire, the floor falling away . . ." He thought about it. "I'm sure they didn't even try the symbols; they just attempted to break down the door."

"And maybe that sets off *all* the traps in sequence?" She walked up behind Caleb and slid her hands around his waist. She pressed her lips to his neck and he smelled figs, along with a hint of her ever-present jasmine perfume. His skin danced with excitement, both from this new revelation and from Lydia's touch. "Can't you try to RV the chamber? See the fire defense?"

Caleb's throat tightened as if choking on a thick crust of bread. "No, I don't think so." It was one thing for visions to visit directly, but quite another to actually invite them in. It wasn't a step he wanted to take just yet.

"So we'll just chance it?" Lydia asked. "Get a

rope, or a bungee or something, a harness. And then just pray we're worthy enough?"

"I'd rather do this by myself," Caleb said. "I don't know if two of us can make it through, and . . ."

"And," Lydia gave him a gentle squeeze, "you haven't forgiven yourself yet for Phoebe."

Or Nina.

Or any of the others.

Caleb tried to pull away but she held him close. "It wasn't your fault," she whispered. "And now's your chance to make it up to her. We'll get through that door, you and I. But you'll need my help. I'll bring cameras and flashlights, and you'll have another set of eyes to catch anything you might miss, and—"

"And it will be twice the danger," Caleb said, relenting. "But I know you won't give up. Besides, I don't really want to go alone."

She smiled with him. "So what are we waiting for?"

"Nightfall." From his occasional visits after a walk about the city, he knew Qaitbey had become a major tourist site of late, and guards patrolled regularly during the day. At night it was lit up from all angles to provide a visible backdrop of its imposing strength, but Caleb figured they could still slip into the courtyard, hug the shadows and get in to the mosque if they were careful. But they had no special connections this time, so they would have to use bolt cutters on the padlock.

"Good," Lydia said. "Then we have time." She pulled him away from the wall, toward the bed.

It was a moonless night, the air still thick with humidity, resisting the Mediterranean breezes. The stars shone fiercely above the waves, and as Caleb and Lydia crept through the arch in the sandstone wall, Caleb glanced up at the constellations, imagining for a moment he was a Roman soldier storming the great lighthouse, marveling at its flaming beacon thirty stories overhead. He could picture dozens of statues and winged creatures perched on ledges and atop windows punctured into the face of the great tower. And the simple, cunning dedication greeting visitors: *Sostratus of Cnidos dedicates this lighthouse to the Savior Gods.*

As silently as possible, he and Lydia stayed in the shadows and ran along the wall to the inner citadel. Four silent cannons observed their approach, and Caleb could almost hear their muffled explosions, subdued echoes from the conflicts of a bygone age. At the back gate, he rummaged through his bag for the bolt cutters, but paused as Lydia knelt by the padlock and told him to give her some light. "We don't want them posting a guard in case we need to get back down there in the future." A few twists and gentle stabs with two pins held in her nimble fingers, and the lock clicked open.

"Where did you learn that?" Caleb asked.

She merely smiled and winked.

He heard a noise—a soft, padded footfall—and his heart lurched. Pausing at the threshold, he looked back but saw nothing moving in the starlight-speckled courtyard.

"Come on," Lydia said, and glided through the sandstone halls with a purpose, like this was all second nature. Caleb's sense of unease returned. First, the incident in St. Mark's Square, then the lock-picking, and now this feeling that somehow she'd been here before.

"Are you seeing someone? A girl with green eyes . . . ?"

He put his imagination behind him and followed Lydia's flashlight beam, which steadily led the way. She climbed to the second floor, and when he joined her he peered out the arched, barred window to see the sparkling lights of the city and the brilliant floodlights around the new library. After a moment's reflection, they made their way to the great mosque. The heavy water-proof backpack, stocked with all their supplies weighed him down, and when he switched shoulders, he saw something white fluttering above, against the red brick dome.

Ahead, in the darkness before a bend in the corridor, he heard his name. It sounded so much like Nina's voice. Suddenly Caleb was overwhelmed with the sense of foreboding he'd felt before, the same dread that far below his feet the secrets of the Pharos slumbered without a care, secure behind its defenses.

Again, that lone dove flew around and around the dome overhead, flirting with the trembling beam of light. Caleb's mouth hung open and it happened again. A shift in perspective, a jaunt into a different medium where everything was a little more real, a touch colder, his senses sharper. He saw a man . . .

. . . *in flowing white robes. "Come, Demetrius. It is time for you to see." Two great Egyptian statues flank the entrance to a grand chamber lit by a half-dozen torches inside glass lamps set high on the walls. A pair of long chains rest on the floor, one hooked to the wall above the inscribed door, the other clamped to the feminine statue's moon-shaped headdress. Four slaves are securing the chains and preparing a large, circular harness that could hold several men. "This is why you have come."*

Demetrius, out of breath, holding his side, moves past the enormous onyx statues. "What is that?" he asks Sostratus, pointing to a pit in the floor.

"Drainage vent."

"And that?" He faces the great wall ahead, observing the pair of winged snakes coiled three times around the staff with an inscribed sun symbol above their heads. Six other arcane symbols surround the staff.

"The great seal." Sostratus turns and points to a spot on the ground. "Stand there."

In the flickering torchlight, Demetrius only now notices the symbols on the floor. One following the other, seven symbols painted and carved on seven large granite blocks leading to the sealed door. He steps onto the first block and reads the sign. "Lead?"

"We both will stand here," Sostratus says as he joins him. "Then we shall move forward, block by block. At the next stone we will be secured by these chains."

Demetrius looks to the next sign, two feet closer to the seal. "Tin?"

Sostratus lowers his head. "You will understand."

"Hey!" Lydia shook him. Her face loomed over his, her soft hair tickling his skin. "Tell me you just saw something."

Caleb leaned on her shoulder. The room was stuffy, oppressive. The dove had stopped its flying and perched somewhere overhead. "I think I've just been shown the way. Or at least, past the first two stages."

Caleb's legs were weak from descending the
cascade of stairs, and as he stepped on each one he
imagined they sighed with audible reminders of his
guilt, mocking echoes of Phoebe's pain, and their
separation. Then he thought of Nina, and here he
was, attempting the same feat that had killed her,
with another woman he loved.

I hope I'm better prepared this time.

For someone experiencing firsthand what she
had only previously imagined, Lydia remained quite
calm. As they stood before the great seal, she
shrugged when Caleb asked how she felt. "Just like
the pictures in our room," she said, shining the
flashlight back and forth, then up the vertical crack
in the door, aligned with the caduceus. "So this is
it."

She walked up to the wall and then shined the
light back across her tracks, and Caleb saw for the
first time the alchemical symbols for the metals,
each about two yards square, taking up seven
mammoth limestone blocks. Starting at the door,
Caleb recognized them: Sulfur, Silver, Mercury,
Copper, Iron, Tin and Lead.

"There they are," Lydia said, shaking her head in
wonder. "Guess none of you thought to look down."

SULFER

SILVER

MERCURY

COPPER

IRON

TIN

LEAD

"No, we'd have seen them. The flood must've washed away the dust covering them." Caleb aimed the light now at the wall, at the symbols around the staff. "Anyway, I think I understand. Each element corresponds to a planet and a stage in the seven steps of transformation. But this adds a new wrinkle. I believe we'll need to turn the symbols on the door in the right order to get this started; then we'll need to come back and stand on the first block, wait for whatever happens, and then move forward accordingly."

Lydia stood before the seal, careful not to touch anything. "The symbols . . . protruding from . . . Wait, I see where you can grasp them by their edges and turn each one."

"Not yet," Caleb said, digging into his knapsack for the ropes, harness and carabiners. "Let's get set for the water trap."

When they had secured the first clip to the ring on the wall and the second to Seshat's statue, they clipped the other ends to their harnesses, so all they had to do after passing the first test was to step forward, slip on the harness, tighten it and wait for the water to come.

They stood together at the door, shining both lights on the caduceus. Caleb saw that one symbol at the end of the upper inscription, the symbol assigned to the Golden Ones. It seemed to pull at his consciousness, to hang there as a marker of denial, a guardian that expressly denied him passage. And now, more fully versed in alchemy and familiar with the symbols, he was even more certain that this was a mistake.

"That sign," he said, pointing, "I know it now."

"What is it?"

"Exalted Mercury." He stared at it and his breath quickened. "An upward-pointing triangle symbolizing Fire—in this case, the sublimated state of distilled consciousness rooted in the Above. And within that triangle, the symbol for what they call Exalted Mercury, which is essentially the Mercury symbol with a dot in the center, signifies that it has become the One Thing perfected."

"The One Thing?"

"The Philosopher's Stone. The center of every-thing. Our minds and personalities come together as one unifying, powerful thought."

"And the triangles on either side? And the star below?"

"Water on the left, Fire on the right. With the star below, signifying the union of Fire and Water, the permanent coming together of the Above and Below."

Lydia nodded. Caleb couldn't tell for sure, but in the shadows he imagined her giving an oddly satisfied smile.

"Sure you want to do this?" he asked. "I don't know about you, but I don't feel like we've passed the test, like we're in any way ready. We don't know what else to expect. If the water trap requires us to be prepared in some way, maybe all the others do too. I didn't see far enough in my vision."

Lydia stared at her shoes.

Caleb fidgeted. "I'm sorry, but I don't know what Sostratus did next."

"Hopefully, your inspiration will come again and help us when we need it."

"I don't think so." Caleb was again overcome with a terrible apprehension. And then, just as suddenly, he had the feeling someone was watch-ing them. Someone not in this room, not even in sight. Someone . . . "Phoebe," he whispered, and a deep chill seemed to rush in from unseen vents.

Is this what she saw—the time it would all turn for me?

A grinding sound echoed off the four walls. It seemed he had lost a minute of time, a minute in which the world had moved on without him. Lydia was kneeling at the base of the door, sniffling. She grunted with effort as she turned one of the signs— Saturn, the symbol for Fire.

"Wait!"

But she had stood up and reached for another symbol, the one Nina had turned first. Jupiter/ Water. Again the grating, scraping sound.

"It's too late," she said in a choked cry as she twisted the next sign: Mars/Air. "We're about to see if you're worthy." She shot Caleb a look, and in the trembling flashlight beam he saw tears streaming from her eyes. "I'm sorry, Caleb."

He reached for her and tried to yank her arm away. "Come on. We can still—"

"I didn't finish the sequence!" she shouted as she pushed him off, thrusting him away with surprising strength.

Off balance, Caleb tripped and fell back. Dropped the light. And in the spinning beam he imagined the walls shifting, closing in. Thoth and Seshat moved, turning as before and contemplating the two intruders. And there was Lydia, reaching for another symbol. She finished with the Venus/Earth sign, and then reached for Mercury.

Caleb scrambled forward and dove for her. "Stop! We'll come back when we know more!"

She twisted out of his way and kept him at bay with her kicking legs. "It's too late!"

"What are you talking about?"

She grasped the Moon and, when her eyes settled on his, they looked cold and hard. "We've been waiting for you Caleb, but you let us down."

He took a step back. He couldn't breathe.

She spun the Moon, then reached for the crown above the snakes—the Sun. "We can't wait for you to snap out of your psychic exile. I'd hoped to free you, but I've failed."

"Who are you talking about?"

She gave Caleb a look of pity. Turning her back on him, she rotated the Sun. "As always Caleb, you haven't asked the right questions."

She lowered her head. "Remember me. Remember that I loved you."

"Lydia . . .?" He took a step toward her.

"Back up, and get ready." Her head inclined sideways. "You told me once how your mother's powers were triggered. Your sister's too."

"Lydia!"

"Welcome, Caleb, to your personal trauma."

"What are you—?"

A rumbling passed through the blocks and sand

fell in thin veils. The wall rattled. Three fist-sized holes opened on each side of the door, and six plumes of gas hissed out. Pungent methane, strong and powerful, streamed from the openings. Caleb reached for Lydia, but she ripped her arm free, switched off her light, and darted to the side.

"Lydia!" In the sudden gloom, Caleb reached for his flashlight and speared the beam madly back and forth, catching a glimpse of her legs, rolling into the shadows, but then he heard a tortured cry of sharp rocks scraping together.

A spark in the darkness.

He cursed and leapt back two steps and curled into a ball, hugging his knees on top of the symbol for Lead.

Calcination.

A rush of heat, a burst of searing hot light. "Lydia!"

And the room became an inferno.

It was as if he knelt in a protective container. The entire chamber swirled in a fuming cyclone of volcanic fire, gases igniting and flames roaring all around. But Caleb was safe, barely uncomfortable from the heat. And then he felt it: all around the block he was crouched on, a rush of fresh air propelled upward, a maelstrom of wind creating a barrier. The stone block had lowered and compressed, and the gaps surrounding it expelled a rush of fierce, steam-laden air.

And as quickly as it had begun, it was over. The whoosh of flames subsided and Caleb stood, unscathed. He had only a moment to take stock of the smoking room and realize that even if Lydia had somehow survived the blast, neither of them would make it past the next trap.

The cords were gone, incinerated.

Coughing from the noxious fumes and the choking heat, he spun the light around, desperately looking for some sign that Lydia might have survived, terrified he'd see a smoking corpse.

Then he heard the door grating again, and now it started to open as if pushed from the other side by a pair of monstrous Titans. He took one last look around the room, saw the melted flashlight against the edge of the pit, smoke and embers rising from its depths.

Then he turned and fled, racing to the ascending stairs and bounding between Thoth and his mistress, just as the great door burst open and the ravenous flood roared in.

Three steps at a time he climbed, never looking back. The water chased after him like a rabid jackal, snapping at his legs. He splashed up the next flight of stairs, dragging his feet through the rising water, and then lunged and collapsed on the cool, dry steps above.

He screamed and slammed his fists against the

unyielding granite.

He aimed the flashlight back down. The waters were receding. He followed them back down, step by step. He walked between Thoth and Seshat, trading a wounded glare for their scolding expressions. His feet splashed on the limestone blocks as he played the light around the room.

He waited, poised to flee back up the stairs at the slightest hint of a new trap. He watched and counted the seconds, counted the beats of his devastated heart, urging it to calm.

Nothing else happened. The door remained open, a yawning cavern of blackness, defying even his powerful flashlight beam. All his other supplies had either been reduced to ashes or swept away in the flood. He was left alone with nothing but his mind, as clear as it had become.

He waited. And then he thought, *I'm not on the next block, not putting weight on the Iron stone.*

Suddenly, the door closed with a quick, efficient snapping back into place. On the seal, the wheels all spun back to their original positions as if nothing had happened.

Caleb switched off his light. Alone, he hung his head and embraced the silent darkness.

Acceptance did not set in for another week.

A week in which Caleb had divided his time above and below the harbor. He'd read the papers every day, fearing the worst. After the first day he had rented a boat and cruised around the peninsula, looking for anything that had washed up. As always, Fort Qaitbey had brooded staunchly, baking in the sun as a few tourists lingered about beyond the outer walls. He'd resisted venturing again below, but the chamber beckoned, whispering for him to come back, to dwell there forever. To ease the loneliness of those ancient halls.

The guards had replaced the padlock, and without Lydia's lock-picking skills, he'd had to break it to get back in. Knowing he was embarking on a hopeless effort, he couldn't help but feel like Sisyphus rolling his boulder to the top of a great hill only to have the gods kick it back down. Even so, he'd smuggled in a small generator and a half-dozen hurricane lamps and combed every inch of the chamber, in vain.

Under another moonless night's sky, with Jupiter, Saturn and Mars aligned fittingly in a row along the horizon, Caleb crept back inside. Since he had found a mechanism for opening the fortress's secret door from the inside, he closed it behind him, so he knew he wouldn't be disturbed. Carrying enough food and water for a week, he descended into the vault. He slept in a roll with a jacket as his pillow. He brought a handful of texts on alchemy rich with imagery and illustrations to aid his interpretation of the next stage. He worked and slept and ate by candlelight. He existed for one purpose only: to study the wall.

To become worthy.

To become Golden.

Again and again he thought about Lydia's last words. He wondered how she could have deceived him, and he contemplated the breadth and depth of her conspiracy. Who was that man she had been talking to, the one who had chastised him after Nina's accident? Had Lydia manipulated him into marrying her from the start? Had she worked to become his publicist, then prod him towards the research, pushing him further and further? Had she hoped to spark his psychic talents in order to get the treasure herself?

"You're asking the wrong questions," she'd said. And he knew it, but he couldn't get his mind around the right way of thinking.

All day long, as tourists ambled overhead, he stared and stared, pondering every sign, every etching on the floor and wall. And time after time he endured the flames and the flood, securing himself with steel chains, enduring the heat and standing against the onslaught of frigid water. He reeled as it ripped passed him, tore his clothes and scraped his flesh. He staggered, but held fast, digging his feet in, lowering his head and yielding to the torrent. He held his breath as the waters devoured him, and just when it seemed his lungs would burst the water level dropped in a rush. In the darkness he felt as if he'd ascended and emerged into the clear night air, reborn.

Calcination and Dissolution. Caleb endured them both, and survived.

And then he stepped forward while the water finished draining. His boots splashed to the next stone, and he stood over the symbol for Iron. He breathed deeply, clearing his head and accepting whatever destiny the Fates had woven for him—

—until the ground shifted. The gaping doorway ahead hissed and a wind blew forth, sending shivers across his raw flesh.

Fire. Water. Now wind. Air. He stood, poised, expecting some great gust to hurl him into a wall of rusted spikes. He was prepared for the brutal piercing, an ignoble death, an end to his hopeless existence, but he merely teetered and stood his ground. He dried, and the shivering subsided.

As the water evaporated, Caleb felt a residue deposited from the water and the fire caked on his skin, on his hair, eyelids and cheeks, covering the tatters of his shirt and ripped jeans. It had the consistency of baking soda. *Something to do with the Separation Phase,* Caleb thought. In alchemy, it signified that his old life had been burned away by the masculine energy of fire, then washed clean by the feminine strength of water, leaving him with the combination of the two.

Renewed, but somehow certain that he had not yet passed the full test, he considered taking a step forward onto Copper. The next stage was Coagulation, in which the alchemist was supposed to earn the Lesser Philosophers' Stone, to be imbued with a greater sense of purpose and clarity, to see the way through to the realms of the Above. To set foot on the path to immortality. To Gold.

Instead, Caleb stepped back onto the glyph for Tin. For an instant, he was certain such a backward motion would trigger another deadly trap.

Nothing happened.

He was impatient, and growing angrier with the mocking sense of nothingness that pervaded the room. The parted doors teased him with a false sense of progress that made him furious. But he knew for sure he wasn't ready. Yet, finally, in desperation, he bolted and ran, determined to make it through regardless of what was expected of him.

It started closing as soon as his weight lifted off the block. Caleb leapt for the narrowing aperture—

—and collided with the wall as it sealed. The seven signs wheeled back to their preset positions, and something beyond the great door made a low, wheezing sound like a heavy sigh.

Over the next few days Caleb attempted it eight more times.

Every time the same. The fire, the water, the air . . . and then nothing. He read and reread everything he had on alchemy. He studied the teaching of Balinas of Tyna, who had claimed to have mastered the Emerald Tablet, and who had performed miracles, healed the sick. He studied all the theories about what the tablet was supposed to contain. All of these interpretations had become infused in his mind, into his very breath. And yet he came no closer to wisdom.

And despite Lydia's belief in his eventual transition, nothing happened. He may have passed the first two tests, but he still felt trapped in the flames of Calcination. He couldn't let go. Not of her, not of his past, not of his fears.

And I can't draw down a power I never really had. His visions had always been passive, reactionary. And try as he might, immersing himself in the depths of the lighthouse sub-chamber, opening his spirit to its mysteries, he was denied and could go no further.

She was right, he had failed.

10

On a crisp, surprisingly cool morning, Caleb checked out of his hotel and made his way to the airport.

The authorities stopped him at customs, and he spent eight hours with the local police. He detailed how he and Lydia had gone on a cruise, and he insisted that she had been swept away during a dive. They asked why he had never reported her missing. Caleb couldn't come up with a good excuse. They called the hotel, where the manager only fueled their suspicions by relating the odd nature of Caleb's nocturnal comings and goings, his reclusiveness since the sudden absence of his lovely bride.

Caleb didn't blame them. Because of his vague

and rattled responses, they seemed sure he had killed Lydia, and he was prepared to spend the rest of his life wasting away in an Egyptian jail.

As it turned out, it wasn't that bad, but it was bad enough.

Egyptian laws were incredibly complex and quite often subjective. He asked for a trial, begged to be shown the evidence against him. Where's the body? he demanded. Witnesses? A motive? Caleb told them to look for a man in a gray suit, with matching hair. He knew her. They had planned her disappearance together. Set him up.

The police didn't budge, and they told Caleb they could hold him indefinitely if they felt like it.

Doubleday sent a lawyer on Caleb's behalf, but his efforts proved ineffective. Caleb began to believe even the lawyer thought he was guilty. Their star publicist, and his co-author, was missing, and Caleb was the sole suspect. It didn't make good press. His book sales plummeted. They took the stock off the shelves. Cancelled further printings.

And left him to rot. Day after day, month after month in a dank cell.

He asked for his research materials and they refused.

He begged to be allowed a few encyclopedias. A book. Anything.

Again they refused.

It was killing him, this separation from books. More than anything else, even more than his own imminent mortality, he longed for a book, a newspaper, a magazine. He had never been apart from his life's blood for so long. He missed the feel of pages, the touch of a leather spine; missed the smell of the binding, the sound an old book would make as it opened.

Finally, he pled for pen and paper, and they grudgingly obliged. And on a cool day when the wind blew gently through the barred window of his cell, he began to draw. Just random images at first. Then the visions came.

He asked for more paper. They gave him scraps at first, but then a guard with a shred of compassion smuggled in a thick sketch pad. And Caleb drew.

For hours on end, skipping meals, neglecting his body, avoiding sleep, he drew. Pain and hunger were mere inconveniences compared to his insights, compared to his growing sense of purpose. The days and weeks flew by and his portfolio grew as he allowed his practice to become an obsession. Every night he looked over the day's output, and then never looked at the pages again. He awoke every morning and meditated—just sat and listened to his breathing and his heartbeat, learning to tune out the cries of the other inmates, the banging on the walls, the shrieking, the pleading and find a measure of peace residing deep within. He was lucky to have his own cell, but it would not have mattered. He was passing onto a new level of being.

And he continued to draw.

Eagles and suns, gates and stars. A river flowing beside a large complex of stone buildings. He sketched his father, or at least his recollection of him. He no longer suffered pain, but his essence remained for Caleb to capture and put to paper. The signs were the same. Caleb didn't understand them, but this time he didn't try.

And he drew.

Once, he awoke to see that dreadful man in the green khakis sitting cross-legged in the shadows of the cell, just beside the door. He breathed heavily, as if he were sleeping. He stared, propped up on his scrawny arms. Caleb told himself it was only a dream, but he knew better. He finally called out.

The man breathed in. Wheezing. The darkness at his head shifted and Caleb froze. He knew the man was looking right at him. A mumbling sound reached him from the darkness, and Caleb smelled something—iodine and alcohol.

"Caleb," came the word, grating, guttural. "Go . . . home."

Caleb sat up and looked closer. The darkness wasn't quite as dark as he had first thought. He could see the grimy wall, the blood and vomit stains beside the urinal.

The room was empty.

Caleb slid back onto the cot and reached for his pad of paper.

He had more images to draw.

A government lawyer stopped in one day. He was polite and smart-looking in a tailored white suit, but he acted disinterested. Looking around Caleb's cell at the piles of discarded sheets of paper, he asked what he liked to draw. Caleb only smiled and replied, "Whatever comes to me."

The lawyer left, and Caleb took up the nub of his pencil and went back to work.

Another month passed. At least, he thought it was a month, having given up keeping track of time long ago in this Alexandrian jail while the world outside went on. He had thought about Phoebe a lot. But he knew, somehow, that she was okay. His mother too. They were both fine, though unfulfilled and desperate. Still driven for answers beyond their grasp.

He knew it. He saw it all, and more.

Knowing that it might prove fatal to look upon the dead, he attempted to remote view Lydia anyway. He fasted for almost a week, and even the normally callous guards were getting uneasy about his health. They didn't want someone dying of their own volition.

In Caleb's haze of detachment, his body yielded

to his soul, merging, coagulating; and deeper visions came. It was as if he had immersed himself in something of the transcendent, like he had gone skinny-dipping in the cosmic pool of consciousness.

He thought of the mystic Balinas and he laughed. A long beard hung down Caleb's chest. His hair was matted and in stringy clumps. His skin was full of sores, lice and ticks. *If I only had a mirror . . . maybe we'd look like twins.*

But he didn't care.

His consciousness existed elsewhere. Caleb Crowe was gone. In his place emerged someone new. Someone focused, dedicated. And he saw things—some he wanted to see, and others he never asked for.

When he thought of Lydia, when he really thought of her—the scent of jasmine, the touch of her silken skin, the way the ankh had dangled on her chest—he saw a rush of images: the Great Pyramids lit up at night; a congregation of people in gray cloaks, mumbling to themselves about keys and doorways, about lost secrets and betrayal; a massive, fanciful construction project along a familiar shoreline—an upward-sloping structure that looked like a sheared-off dome with thousands of windows and dedications from every modern language on its walls, with hundreds of workmen, cranes and hoists assailing it from all angles. In the distance, a dozen men and women in dark gray suits stood atop a ridge, watching in silent appreciation.

One of those figures, a blond-haired woman, turned away from the others. Her face was hidden in shadow, the sun burning at her back. But it seemed she looked in Caleb's direction, and she gave a secret, almost unnoticed nod of her head.

He saw Phoebe next, seated alone in a specially designed chair, peering into a microscope in a dimly lit lab. She wrote with her left hand and moved an ancient fragment delicately with her right.

Then he saw his mother standing outside the family's lighthouse, looking out over Sodus Bay. She held an apple in both hands and rolled it gently back and forth as if willing from its skin memories that were long lost, but definitely not forgotten. Down the hill, the rusted lightship had received a facelift. People were walking across a remodeled pier, snapping pictures of the old boat, but Helen paid them no heed. She glanced up once at the lighthouse beacon, and in her eyes flashed a distant recollection, as though she expected to see Caleb's father waving back at her.

Then Caleb saw Waxman. Saw him again and again, like a recording slowed down on a VCR. Unbidden visions swirled around in a choppy soup, pictures of Waxman's childhood, tormented dreams of his mother. She had inflicted her wrath on everything he did. Interfering in all aspects of his life, turning him into a loner. Waxman had studied all the time. He'd trained by himself, pulled away from friends, from strangers, from life.

Then Caleb saw him enter a familiar white building beside a winding river.

Overhead, an eagle soared, circling, then rising above the sparkling sun.

At the doorway, Waxman turned as if aware of someone's snooping gaze. *"You're asking the wrong questions,"* he whispered, and Caleb snapped out of his vision, jerked awake, gasping for air. His mouth was a desiccated old prune, his limbs too weary to lift.

Two armed guards stood in the doorway. "You're free to go," one of them said, and handed Caleb his knapsack.

"Get a shower," said the other, "and something to eat on your way out."

Caleb didn't know it at the time, but he should have figured it out. It was too easy. He'd had help. Probably a simple phone call had sprung his release.

He didn't ask any questions. He just went with the flow and tide of Fate, accepting this sudden transition in his life and hoping that the long months of confinement had somehow prepared him for something meaningful.

So, after several weeks of recuperation, after

cleaning up, after eating and nursing himself back to health, he prepared to leave Alexandria.

"Caleb, go home."

While he waited for the porter to get his single bag, he looked out the hotel window at the Bibliotheca Alexandrina, nestled impressively between the beachfront and the mass of white hotels and offices. He held out his palm to block the glare from the sun glinting off the windows of the dome, and in the spots dancing his vision, he imagined the ancient structure after which it was patterned. And it filled him with hope.

A knock came at the door. Somehow, when Caleb opened it, he wasn't surprised by who had come to find him.

11

A year ago, Caleb's first inclination would have been to run. But now he stood firm, calm and settled. He focused on what was important. He saw Phoebe's face light up, that big grin and her teeth biting her bottom lip. A touch of her handrest controls and her wheelchair shot forward, zipping around Helen and rolling right up to Caleb. She threw her arms around his waist.

"Missed you, big brother."

Caleb held her, squeezed her with an emotional intensity that surprised him. "Do I have you guys to thank for my release?"

"George," Phoebe said, nodding back to the threshold of the door. "He worked for months with the authorities, finally pulling enough strings."

Waxman offered a weak smile. "You can thank me later."

Phoebe squeezed Caleb's arm. "By the way, where was my invite to my own brother's wedding?"

"Sorry," Caleb gulped. "It all happened so fast."

"Even after my warning," Phoebe said, shaking her head. "Was it her, the girl with the green eyes?"

Caleb nodded.

"I tried to tell you—"

"Shhh. Later, okay? Now's not the time."

She took his hand and looked at her brother with new eyes. "Come on, we have a lot to tell you. You're going to be amazed."

Caleb held his ground, and the wheels on her chair spun. "No, I don't want to go with them."

"Caleb," Helen walked into the room. She was thin and pale, her hair cut short and dyed a California blond to cover her gray. Her eyes were lined with crow's-feet, hooded but no less crystalline. The blue shook Caleb, and he felt an electric current spark when she touched his arm. "Jail! My poor boy. We were so worried. And they wouldn't let me see you."

"Hello, Mother." He gave her a peck on the cheek. "Why are you here?"

"You shouldn't have gone down there without us," she scolded. Waxman sauntered over, his hands in the front pockets of his suit pants. He wore a black turtleneck under his navy blue jacket, and his hair seemed just as wild as Caleb remembered, only now flecked with gray. A lit cigarette was trapped like a worm dangling from his lips.

"Listen, I just want to go back to New York and sleep for a month."

"You'll want to hear this," Waxman said.

Caleb stared at the gold band around his ring finger as he lifted his cigarette, then he looked blankly at Helen. "Speaking of not being invited to weddings . . ."

"Caleb," Phoebe pinched his arm.

Waxman turned his head to watch a pair of hotel maids walk past in the hall. He put his arm around Helen's shoulders. "I told you he hasn't changed."

Caleb slung his bag over his shoulder. "I'm going. Thanks for the jailbreak."

"Caleb,"—Phoebe wheeled into his path—"we know where it is."

"Where what is?"

Helen smiled. "Don't be modest, Phoebe. Tell him how you found it."

"Okay," Phoebe said, beaming. "You were right, Caleb. We weren't asking the right questions."

"About what?"

"The scroll. Caesar's scroll."

"I saw it," Phoebe said, "by refining the question. Remember when I said I kept having visions of a castle on a steep hill, and a prisoner in red robes being led up to it? Well, I decided to follow that lead. I remembered that those ancient scrolls were coveted by aristocrats in the nineteenth century, and it was considered fashionable to have one among your personal treasures, even if you could never read it."

Caleb's heart started to race. "Of course. But still, the possibility that just that one scroll, of all the thousands . . ."

Phoebe continued. "I decided to work from the assumption that it had been removed from the collection. I asked to be shown how Caesar's scroll was taken from Herculaneum, *and then I saw it.*"

"Saw what?" Caleb asked. He started to feel faint.

"That man again, in long red robes and fur-lined lapels. But this time, he was standing before a series of machines. Several blackened scrolls, coated with a silvery substance, were stretched out, hanging partially unrolled and glued together where they had started to rip."

"The Piaggio machines," Caleb said, recognizing the description. Vatican scholar Antonio Piaggio had invented the device in an effort to stop the wanton destruction of the scrolls by other investigators. It was the only thing that worked until the 1970s, when the Norwegians came along with their gelatin solutions.

Phoebe nodded, and her eyes glazed over, as if

seeing the vision all over again. "Someone came up to this red-robed man and said, 'Welcome, Count Cagliostro, what brings such an esteemed visitor to inspect our work?'"

"Cagliostro," Caleb whispered. "He was an alchemist, a magician of the old Egyptian mysteries. It fits. He would have been drawn to this scroll, but how did he—"

"'A dream,' the Count said, walking from machine to machine, ten of them with scrolls in various stages of unrolling. 'A dream told me there was something I needed to see here.'"

Phoebe blinked, and quickly focused on Caleb. "Cagliostro stopped in front of one scroll that had only been opened about an inch. He bent over, gasping as he peered at a faint symbol and a few visible letters."

"What symbol?" Caleb asked, although he could guess. *Exalted Mercury* . . .

Phoebe shrugged. "I didn't get a clear enough glimpse of it. But anyway, he sent everyone from the room, then carefully removed the scroll from the machine, boxed it up and hid it under his robes. He took a random scroll from the hundreds on a nearby table and set it up on the machine. He began to clumsily unroll the first inch when a group of priests walked in, ushered by one of the papyri officials. Discovered in the act, he ran. Fled the library and disappeared into the shadows of the palace corridors.

"My next vision was of Cagliostro in shackles being led up an uneven rock path beside a sheer cliff to a fortress overlooking a valley. The castle, with its turrets and walls, stood against the rough winds and made me think of Qaitbey."

She let out a deep breath and rubbed her palms together. "And that was it. I did some research and found that Cagliostro had been imprisoned at a castle, the same one I'd seen, jailed on charges of heresy."

"He was tricked," Caleb said, "into performing an ancient Egyptian rite of initiation on two Vatican Inquisition spies, who then arrested him. Classic entrapment."

"So you know."

Caleb nodded. "He was first imprisoned in Castel Sant'Angelo in Rome, but after trying to escape, he was moved to the fortress you saw."

"San Leo," she said, pouting. "I spent days looking through Italian guidebooks trying to find a picture that matched, and you knew it all along!"

"Sorry, but at least you found it. The question is, what does that vision tell us about the scroll?"

"That's what we're going to find out," Helen said. "If you'll join us, we've got a flight already booked. It leaves in the morning for Venice."

"But—"

"I saw one more thing after that vision." Phoebe

wheeled closer, almost running over Caleb's foot. "A church with Roman-style arches and a bell tower. I found it quickly, in the same guidebook, fifteen miles from San Leo Fortress, in the town of Rimini."

"The Tempio Malatestiano," Waxman said, pronouncing the Italian very slowly.

"What does that have to do with it?" Caleb asked.

Waxman sighed. "We think Cagliostro may have had a connection to that church. And since he knew the authorities were after him, he might have stashed the scroll somewhere inside."

Caleb suddenly felt exhausted from it all, and actually missed the solitude of his prison cell. "What do you want from me?"

"Caleb, you have to take my place," Phoebe pleaded, thumping her chair's wheels. She leaned forward. "They need a good psychic to go along, one that's more mobile than I am."

A refusal formed, but then Caleb let out his breath. He imagined her down in that tomb, her hand reaching up, begging him not to let go. He remembered the feel of her fingers slipping away, and the dwindling of her scream before she hit the bottom.

He could not deny her this. He took a breath and glanced from her to his mother. In his mind flashed a vision of excavators in Herculaneum, chipping away at the volcanic rock and sediment, retrieving scroll after scroll. The possibility that they'd found just the one they were looking for and that it might hold the secrets of the Pharos—and the answer to Lydia's death—proved an irresistible temptation. He saw Julius Caesar again, bathed in torchlight, standing before the defiant caduceus, the scroll in his hand.

This was a chance to discover what Caesar could not, to pass beyond, into the one place he had failed to conquer. To reveal the secrets of Alexander the Great. *And perhaps to reveal the truth about ourselves. Why my family has these powers, these visions.*

Despite his transition, or perhaps because of it, his path was clear. He wanted the same things: to see whether the Pharos hid merely a treasure of gold and silver, or whether, beyond the door, lay all the secrets of the human race. The mysteries of the spirit and the soul, secrets that had survived a brutal two-thousand-year war waged upon them by the twin armies of ignorance and evil.

His mind calmed and his pulse settled. "And you've already booked our flight?"

Waxman smiled. "I may not be as good a psychic as any of the Crowes, but I did foresee you'd be coming with us. We leave in the morning."

So they had one night to rest, but unfortunately

there was little time for it. A deep breath of stale hotel air filled his lungs as Caleb rejoined the others in the main suite. They were discussing the scroll.

"If we can get our hands on it," Helen said, "and unroll the remainder . . . there's a new technique out of BYU that has been successful in restoring damaged ancient scrolls. And our University of Rochester is getting in on the act, with Xerox and Kodak contributing equipment and funds for analysis of the Dead Sea Scrolls."

"The cameras are there if we need them," Phoebe said. "We can photograph the scrolls at various wavelengths—say, ultraviolet at 200 nanometers or infrared at 1100—to see which will best differentiate the ink from the background."

"That's all assuming you can still manage to open the scroll."

"True."

"After we return from Italy, why not come back with us?" Helen asked. "Everything's ready back home. We've got the house set up for research, a quiet room for introspection and drawing. The Morpheus team comes over twice a week, so we can use their skills as well."

Caleb groaned. "I thought the Initiative was disbanded."

"New members," Waxman said, puffing on his cigarette.

"Come on," Phoebe urged. "You can get the

pleasure of joining me aboard Old Rusty. The museum is closed again, but you can still see the exhibit."

He blinked at her. "It was turned into a museum?"

"Didn't you read my letters?"

"I was a little busy. Anyway, no, I'm not going back there with you."

Still that voice from his dreams . . . *Go home* . . .

"I told you," Waxman said under his breath. "Useless as ever."

"No," both his mother and sister said at once. Helen moved over and looked into Caleb's eyes. She scrutinized his face, every line and crevice, and he started to turn away when he noticed her eyes were filling with tears.

"You look like him," she said, and brought her hand to Caleb's chin. Her eyes held his, and her lips moved, just barely. "I miss your father," she whispered so only Caleb could hear. "And I'm sorry."

"What do you mean?" The room dimmed slightly, as if the lights flickered, and the air shimmered and everything seemed less tangible, less real.

"You know. I—" Suddenly she stopped and frowned, and her face took on the look of a hunted animal. Her eyes darted around and finally settled on a corner, near the television.

Caleb followed her gaze, and for just an instant Caleb saw him, the tall man in the green jacket, matted hair over his face. Just standing there, trembling in the shadows. And then, he was gone.

"Did you—?"

Helen snapped her head back and stared wide-eyed at Caleb.

Waxman moved in between them, pulling her aside. "Listen, kid. We need to show you something, something about your late wife. After that, if you still want to bail on us, that's your call. Just see what we've discovered."

Phoebe wheeled herself to one side of a rectangular oak table where Waxman sat in front of a black laptop. Helen leaned in over his shoulder and turned the screen in Caleb's direction. On the monitor was a blurry black and white image, a photograph taken of a group of people standing between the forepaws of the Great Sphinx.

"This picture," Waxman said, "came from an unpublished book called *Keepers of Nothing*. It was written by a man named Alex Prout, an author known for his paranoid, disjointed and unconvincing beliefs in all manner of nutty ideas."

Phoebe cleared her throat. "His first book was titled *George Bush and How America Collaborated in the Upcoming Alien Conquest*."

Helen smiled at Caleb. "Anyway, you get the drift. In this latest book, however, Prout seems to have hit on some actual facts."

Waxman tapped the monitor. "After we learned of your incarceration and the charges against you, we started looking into the background of Lydia Jones."

"How much did you know about her past," Phoebe asked, "before you up and married her?"

"Not much," Caleb admitted. "I didn't want to share my history with her, so it somehow felt wrong probing into hers."

Looking away, Helen said, "We found her credits as a publicist, and that got us started. One of the books she had marketed was written by a respected Egyptology professor from the American University at Cairo. When we took a chance and dug into his history, we came across some serious criticisms of his work, all coming from the website of Alex Prout." She raised her eyebrows. "Seems this professor was a regular target of his."

Waxman lit up a cigarette. "We got a copy of this photo from Prout's website. The manuscript for his new book was in his possession when he was mugged in Central Park late last year."

"He was strangled to death," Phoebe said. "His papers torn to shreds and scattered into the East River."

"Fortunately," Waxman added, "he was so paranoid that he backed up the whole thing to a secure website every time he worked on it."

Caleb frowned. "Then how did you get them?" He leaned closer and stared at the picture. There was Lydia, dressed in a gray suit, head bowed reverently, leaning against the Sphinx's left paw. Surrounding her were three other women and thirteen men. But Caleb zeroed in on one man. It was the same face. The same hair. She had been talking to him in St. Mark's Square. He was the one from the hospital.

He pointed, and before Waxman could answer the earlier question, Caleb said, "I've seen that man!"

Waxman nodded. "Lydia's father."

"What?"

"Nolan Gregory. The Egyptology professor, the author. Sixty-two years old. Jones is an alias. Your wife's name was Lydia Angeline Gregory, born in Alexandria."

Caleb pulled out a chair and slumped into it. His head hurt. The two cups of coffee had only added to the throbbing. All his muscles were cramping, not yet having recovered fully from his confinement.

Waxman continued. "Prout investigated this man, Nolan Gregory, and bribed a few of his acquaintances into giving up this picture. He believed it was the only photograph of the current members of an ancient society known simply as The Keepers."

"Guess what it is they're keeping," Phoebe

challenged, before tossing a handful of airplane peanuts into her mouth.

Caleb stared at the photograph again, and Lydia's eyes dreamily stared back at him. "The Pharos Treasure?"

Silence answered. Caleb could hear the ticking of the clock in the next room.

Helen stood up. "The rest of Prout's book goes on to describe his discoveries about this group. He claims these Keepers are all descendents of high priests and scribes from the Ptolemaic Dynasty."

Caleb looked up. "The legends of Thoth. The Books of Manetho and the Emerald Tablet . . ."

"Lost when your library burned," Helen said. "We read your book too."

"Nicely written, big brother," Phoebe said, raising a can of Sprite. "Although I notice you didn't give any credit to your sister in your dedication."

"Sorry." He stared at the screen again. "So . . ."

"So," Helen continued, "Prout believed that the members of this group pass down their secret legacy to one family member each generation."

"And this legacy?" Caleb asked. "What is it?"

Phoebe fidgeted in her chair. "The truth about a storehouse of wisdom that could change the world."

"Crazy nonsense," Waxman said. "Usual stuff about Atlantis and ancient technology. Radical power sources and miraculous medical techniques. That sort of crap."

"It's the truth," Caleb said, "if you believe Plato. Or Herodotus. Both claimed that old priests in Egypt recounted the demise of a prior civilization, and that Thoth had brought the whole of their knowledge to Egypt and started again." He took a breath. "Which is why you see such a high degree of civilization in Egypt right from the start, with their hieroglyphics, farming, astronomical lore, culture—"

"Whatever," Waxman muttered. "The point is these guys know something. But Prout's book never actually mentioned the lighthouse. He believed the Keepers moved this stuff to Giza and buried it long ago under the pyramids or the Sphinx."

"He quoted the psychic Edgar Cayce," Phoebe said, crunching on peanuts. "And his visions."

Caleb held his head in his hands. Closed his eyes and felt it—felt what had been building behind a wall of denial every bit as secure as the one below the Pharos. A wall that now cracked, splintered and erupted into a flood of anguish. "Lydia . . ." he choked, "she was a Keeper. Using me all this time . . ."

". . . to get inside the Pharos vault," Helen finished. "Whatever they know, they don't have the way in. Not anymore."

"Although" Waxman added, "they've been trying to find it for years. Centuries, maybe."

Caleb shook his head and bit his knuckles,

thinking. "No, something's not right. These people are supposed to *keep* the secrets, keep them safe. That's their mission. My vision of Caesar in the lighthouse confirms it."

Helen nodded. "That's what I said. I remembered your dream of the father and son. They had the scroll and died to save it, to protect the secret."

Caleb scratched his head. "But since then, that scroll was lost." He stood up and started pacing. "Which means the other Keepers have lost the way in. They may not even know what it is they are guarding anymore."

"There could be other copies of the scroll," Waxman suggested.

"Doubtful," Caleb countered. "The way those two were defending it, I'd bet that was the only one."

"Caleb," Phoebe said, "we haven't heard what you did under Qaitbey. How far did you get?"

"Not far enough." He told them about the symbols on the floor, their meanings and how he had made it past the first two.

"Yeah," Waxman said, "we found those symbols too. Three years ago, we went back and mapped out the whole chamber, took photos from every angle. But those symbols . . . never could figure out their importance."

"Did you see the rings?"

"Yep," said Phoebe. "But didn't imagine what they were for. Not like you. Maybe you've turned out to be the better psychic?"

"Not really," he said. "It's still nothing I have control over." He took a deep breath. Thoughts were flying about in his mind. He remembered Lydia's last words, spoke them under his breath, *"We can't wait for you."*

"What?" Helen asked.

"It's what Lydia told me before she died."

Waxman closed the computer. "Well, it sounds like the current generation of Keepers feels it's kept the secret long enough; they want the treasure for themselves. They've tried with Caleb, and failed. We need to be on our guard. They may try again to break through."

"Let them," Caleb said, and those words came back to him, words Nolan Gregory himself said: *"The Pharos protects itself."*

Waxman shook his head. "These clowns might screw it up and make it so no one else can get to it."

"Do they know you might have found the scroll?" Caleb asked.

"Not unless they have us bugged."

"Isn't that possible? Not to sound like Prout with his paranoia, but—"

"No," Waxman said. "I checked."

"How?"

He shrugged. "There are ways. Trust me, they don't know what we know. That's what frustrates them."

"And it might be why they're stepping up their activities," Caleb said. "They can't very well protect anything if there's a bunch of psychics running around, seeing their way past the defenses."

"We're cheating," Phoebe said, grinning.

"Or maybe," Caleb said, again thinking of Lydia's words, "maybe we're only fulfilling the prophecy, achieving what the original designer had anticipated."

"What do you mean?" Helen asked.

He shrugged. "Just a thought, but in alchemy the goal is to achieve your own personal contact with the One, the infinite."

"God."

"Yes, but not necessarily the Judaeo-Christian version of a meddling, demanding, all-powerful figure. The early Hermetic beliefs conceived of an omnipresent energy which infused everything, quickened every atom, every star and scrap of matter as well as thought. As Above, so Below. Everything's connected. It's all spiritual and divine. Unfortunately, our material bodies and the temporality of this world somehow interfere with that connection, distracting us. Alchemy, including the Emerald Tablet and the sacred texts, is a way to restore the lost connection. And if you succeed and regain that contact with the divine, if you're freed of the impurities of this false world, you perceive all truth and can do and experience things that seem miraculous or supernatural."

Phoebe thought for a minute. "Like what we can do?"

Caleb nodded. "Think about it. This is the only thing that explains the existence of our abilities. How can we see things in distant lands or times, just with our minds?"

"Because reality isn't what it seems," Helen said, nodding. "It's all connected."

"Exactly." He looked out the window again. "Many religions carried on the Hermetic message, transforming it slightly here and there and incorporating its beliefs into their own. Buddha maintained the world was an illusion, a veil pulled over our eyes to blind us to our inward spirituality. Early Gnostics and Copts taught that we lived in a material prison created by an evil god, and only through meditation and purification could we pull our spirits free."

"Excuse me, but how did we get off track?" Waxman threw his hands up. "Why are we in the Twilight Zone? This is about treasure, not religion."

"It *is* about a treasure," Caleb said. "But not what you and Mom have been thinking you would find. It is knowledge of man's inner divinity. The power of life over death, of spiritual freedom.

"Alexander the Great went into the Egyptian desert and found the tomb of Hermes, of Thoth, and took the ancient tablets he found there. When he emerged, the oracle proclaimed him king of all the world. Alexander studied these tablets, and the teachings clearly went to his head; eventually some of his own generals began to fear him and moved against him. But he and his followers had hidden the treasure, maybe under the Great Pyramid at first, as Cayce claims, then according to Herodotus and Plato, in the temple of Isis at Sais, and then ultimately moved to Alexandria.

"And," he continued, "at a pivotal moment in man's history, when we had a choice between two paths, we chose darkness and subjugation over light and freedom. Copies of these books were rounded up and destroyed. The practitioners were demonized, tortured and killed by the thousands. Yet all through history these secrets have been preserved, hidden away, surfacing only in veiled disguises—in Renaissance art, in symbolic literature like the Grail legends and chivalric poetry. In short, they were hidden in plain view."

"What?" Helen asked.

"In plain view," Caleb repeated. "It's one of the other tenets of Alchemy. '*Conceal in plain view what is secret.*'" He closed his eyes and thought again about the sealed doorway, and for a moment he thought he had it. The answers were right there.

Or very close. Then the opening revelation faded.

"Throughout history," he continued, "the lessons of the Emerald Tablet and the philosophical practices continued, working their way into art, into culture."

"The Tarot," Phoebe said, smiling. "See, I did read your book."

"Thanks, at least someone did. But you're right, the Tarot represented in image form all the elements of Hermetic ascension, depicting the path to divinity veiled as a game. It's why the Church banned it in 1403, seeing it as a threat to their spiritual dominion. But like many pagan belief systems, it was found to be easier to co-opt and assimilate such an attractive ritual. The Church reintroduced the deck, but excluded the Major Arcana, the representations of the steps in the realm of the Above. Those were the cards which represented spirituality and communion with the divine. And they also removed the Knights, in opposition to the Knights Templar, most likely, and left us with a deck of just fifty-two cards. Four suits signifying the four elements in the Below stages of transformation, with the Joker, or the Fool, who represented the initiate before beginning on the path to enlightenment."

Phoebe nodded. "Loved that connection you made. Spades are swords, symbolizing separation and representing Air; Diamonds are the coins of the

Tarot, reflecting Earthly desires; Clubs came from the Greek symbol for Fire; and Hearts were the Water of emotion."

"Now we're talking about cards?" Waxman was becoming exasperated. "Caleb, I swear I liked you better when you were in prison."

"George . . ." Helen scowled at him, then turned back to Caleb. "How does this help us?"

"I don't know if it does," Caleb said. "I learned everything I could about the Tarot, about alchemy and the study of the tablet, but I still couldn't get past the third step before the door. I don't know what it wants. Unless . . . maybe the vault was designed in such a way that only those who sought enlightenment, only the purest, could enter."

"You, pure?" Helen said. "You're a good boy, Caleb, but—"

"They had pinned their hopes on me," he said. "Lydia sacrificed herself for their cause—or at least her version of it. She thought only such a trauma would accelerate my spiritual advance toward enlightenment, or purity, in a sense, expecting that I could then fine-tune my talents and open the vault."

"Why couldn't they figure it out for themselves?" Waxman asked. "If this tablet thing was translated into Arabic, transmitted around the world after they saved some early books from the Christian fanatics, surely others have had access to the spells or whatever?"

"Apparently something's missing," Caleb said. "The Philosopher's Stone. The Holy Grail. They can't find it, although they've come close. No alchemist has ever been able to truly perfect the process and obtain it. Maybe that's because the actual physical copies of the books are not available. The early legends maintain that the material the Emerald Tablet was written on had something to do with the powers it could grant. Or else, maybe there were translation errors."

Waxman shrugged. "Whatever. In any case, Gregory and his gang want what we have, or what they think we might have. We have to figure this out first."

"Why do you care so much?" Caleb asked, turning to Waxman. "I mean, if the vault doesn't hold riches and gold and everything; if this turns out to be nothing but a collection of old books, won't you be pissed? You'll have wasted your entire life."

Helen leaned over the table. "Caleb, if it's what you think it is, we'll transform the planet. We'll be heroes."

"Rich heroes," Phoebe added, smirking.

"Good enough for me," Waxman said, crossing his arms over his chest.

"All right," Helen said. "Caleb, will you help us again? It'll be like old times."

He tried to smile. "I don't know. I guess, as long

as it's not like it was when we were kids, with Phoebe and me staying in our rooms while you adults have all the fun."

"Not this time," his mother said.

Caleb lowered his head and sighed. "I'm in."

12
RIMINI, ITALY

The valley hugged the base of a precipitous mountain range, its tips shrouded in dark clouds. From the chiseled landscape and the jutting hills, Caleb could see where Dante had received the inspiration for his description of Purgatory in *The Divine Comedy*. A short ride past Rimini led to Fortress San Leo. They could have driven up and toured the museum and the old prison and military barracks, but from the details of Phoebe's vision, there would be nothing there of any help. By the time Cagliostro had been imprisoned inside San Leo, he had already disposed of the scroll. Maybe he had been tortured in the castle, and Caleb could possibly attempt to view his confession, but that seemed like a long shot.

Instead, with their driver taking the turns at

breakneck speeds, they made their way into town, to the church Phoebe had seen. Finally, they rode through a grand Roman arch crowned with medieval battlements. It was the first of its kind built north of Rome, their guide explained, and initially dedicated to Augustus in 27 BC. They passed a white marble bridge, built by Tiberius, then drove into the bustling resort town, just as the sun sank below the red rooftops and the vineyard-studded hills.

Cafés, hotels and nightclubs flew by as their driver took the narrow roads at even higher speeds while looking over his shoulder and telling his passengers where to eat, how to find quiet areas on the beach, where to get the best wine. He told them, "Most vacationers gone now for the season. The town very quiet tonight. No more celebrations."

"Too bad," Caleb said.

Then, though they didn't ask for it, the driver offered a quick history lesson, relating how Rimini had emerged from Byzantine rule in 1320 as an independent city, and was lorded over by the Malatesta family for over 200 years. The last ruler, Sigismondo Malatesta, had taken upon himself the great work of expanding the Franciscan chapel at the center of town in 1447, in which he decided to house the crypts of his ancestors. The great Florentine architect and precursor of da Vinci, Leon Battista Alberti, had designed the exterior, incorporating Roman arches and grand pilasters. The interior, however, was what had caused such consternation and debate for centuries to come. Within the sacristies and chapels, pagan sculptures, zodiac emblems and mystical designs merged with Christian décor, crucifixes and Madonnas.

Malatesta never quite finished the reconstruction, as his political fortunes had turned and the papacy closed in, confiscating his lands and power. "Some say his true purpose in re-designing the church was for the love of his life, Signora Isotta, his third wife." The driver turned and grinned at them, his oily mustache fanned across his face. "You will see everywhere sculptures of the 'I' and 'S' twisted together, for 'Isotta' and 'Sigismondo.' Much like the young people write on trees, no?"

Caleb nodded, smiling, but the imagery had him considering alternatives. *An entwined S . . . like a snake . . . around an I, or central staff . . .* Scholars had theorized about this church and that symbol for two hundred years, wondering what cipher Malatesta might have intended. The prevailing notion of a tribute to his wife was certainly romantic, but Caleb had the feeling there had been other forces at work, forces that had perhaps influenced Cagliostro and led him to trust that his secret would be safe here.

Finally, they passed through the Piazza Tre

Martiri and pulled up onto via Garibaldi. "There it is," said the driver. "Tempio Malatestiano. The old Chapel San Francesco."

Helen thanked the driver and offered a large tip, then told him not to wait. They stood before the arched doorway and admired the great façade with the bell tower in the background.

"Now what?" Caleb asked, looking at his watch. It was six o'clock.

"We go in," said Waxman, eyeing the doorway, and then looking around at the landmarks as a general would scout a battlefield before an attack. "They close at seven, so we only have an hour to see if it's here."

"And if it is?"

Waxman gave Caleb a sideways glance. "I'll figure something out."

Caleb lingered outside for several minutes, observing the intricate architecture, the host of varying symbols. Wreaths, vines and flowers, an elephant—apparently the symbol of the Malatesta family—and then, of course, the S-and-I image repeated several times.

Again he thought of the caduceus.

"What is it?" Helen asked over his shoulder. She had moved in close, and he could smell her perfume, like a floral overabundance attempting to hide something musty and old.

"I was just thinking. About how it looks like a

snake coiled around a staff. Or, remember the
Garden of Eden? The serpent was demonized
because he offered Eve the gift of knowledge."

"Good and evil," she whispered. "Knowledge of
everything. All from the fruit of the Tree."

"Exactly." Caleb pointed to the symbol. "It all
stems from fear—fear that we might learn too much
about this world, about ourselves. Look at the tower
of Babel story; God punished us when we all got
together and spoke the same language and—"

"—built a tower challenging the heavens." Helen
ruffled his hair as if he were still a little boy. "You
and your theories. So much like your father. You
read too many books, you know, both of you."

"Did you really expect me to be that different
from him?"

"Never," she said with a softening smile, "and I
wouldn't want you to change. Come on, let's go
inside."

He followed her in, craning his neck at the
massive arch as he walked into a stuffy chapel, a
hint of incense on the air, with sacristy areas on the
left and right, and rows of candles down the middle,
flickering before several Rosary-carrying locals and
a few tourists snapping pictures. The crucifix above
the main altar was the most solemn image in the
church. The rest of the artwork—lace, sculptures
and paintings of Roman cherubs and young children frolicking, scenes of angels dancing on the

columns and the figures of the zodiac around the planets—all seemed more playful.

They walked slowly, Waxman leading the way, toward the altar. Caleb could tell by the heaviness in his steps he was expecting to stop any second, hoping either mother or son would drop to their knees in the throes of some great vision. But nothing happened as they stood before each alcove, each chapel, and admired the intricate ornamentation, marveled at the consistency of the classical themes, and were humbled by the grace of the Roman architecture.

After a half hour they had circled the interior twice. Caleb left Helen and Waxman to whisper among themselves when an usher came by and told him that the church would be closing in fifteen minutes.

Caleb continued circling until he stood at a chapel dedicated to the Archangel Michael, which depicted the evil serpent's death at his hands. Below a host of other angels, Isotta's tomb, beautifully sculpted, was set back against the wall.

Lingering, Caleb stared at the marble coffin for a long, long time. It seemed the candlelight flickered steadily brighter and brighter, flashing against the walls. He was aware of a representation of Diana riding a chariot, holding a crescent moon above two horses on the wall to his left. She seemed to be driving him onward, urging haste.

When Caleb focused again on the tomb, he saw something that wasn't there before . . . *the shadow of a robed man kneeling and sliding the lid back upon Isotta's resting place.* A flash of red on his cloak was all Caleb caught before he blinked and the vision faded.

But it was enough.

"Come on, we have to leave," Helen said, suddenly at his side. "I guess we'll have to try again tomorrow."

"No need," Caleb whispered. "It's here, in Isotta's tomb."

Waxman gasped. "You did it, kid? You saw it?"

Ignoring the desire to tell him he wasn't a kid any longer, Caleb nodded and walked away under the watchful gaze of the dying serpent and the triumphant expression of the Archangel.

Caleb and Helen ate under hooded lanterns at an outdoor restaurant at the Piazza Cavour across from the gothic-styled and newly renovated town hall. A circular fountain built by Pope Pius III stood in the center of the Piazza before a beautiful neo-classical theater.

"Where's your husband?" Caleb asked when she came down from the hotel to meet him. She wore a blue sundress with a black shawl thrown over her shoulders and secured it with a golden butterfly broach.

"He's resting. He said to start dinner without him."

Caleb took her hands. At first she resisted, with the shock of his abruptness. "I need to apologize—"

"Caleb—"

"—for the way I was. For the way I walked out on you and left you with Phoebe."

"You didn't walk out on us."

"Yes, I did," he whispered. "It was my fault. I was angry, confused and lost."

"You were just coming to terms with losing your father."

"I did lose my father. But I still had my mother, and my sister." He pulled her close and hugged her, squeezed until she sobbed. "Dad never would have wanted me to desert you. I—I guess I understand that now."

"But your visions . . ."

He shook his head. "I think Dad knew it was too late for him. He was sending a warning, that's all. Not a cry for help."

"A warning?"

Caleb nodded and sat back, looking into her eyes. "I don't understand it all yet. I was close, in that prison. My consciousness opened, my spirit traveled to places I couldn't imagine. I don't really remember it all, but I saw my whole life differently."

She gave Caleb a sideways look as she wiped her eyes. "Were you brainwashed by the Krishnas over there?"

"No." He laughed. "But I feel like I underwent some kind of spiritual jump-start. And I saw the fool I'd been when we first set out on this quest." He lowered his head, and the image of a Tarot card fluttered in his mind's eye—a vagabond character, full of unwarranted confidence and illusionary dreams, cocky and selfish. "I've been many things since, only now I hope you'll forgive me."

Helen reached for him. "Thank you."

It was a comfortable embrace, but all the same, Caleb had the unnerving certainty that it would be the last time he would hold her before another tragedy befell them. Before the Pharos would claim another victim from among the loves in his life.

"So what's keeping George, anyway? Is he that tired?"

Helen looked down at the crumbs on her plate. "Caleb . . ."

Just then a cab wheeled around the piazza and came to a squealing stop. The front passenger door flew open. Waxman reached around and opened the back door. "Get in!"

Helen stood and dropped a handful of bills on the table. "Don't say anything," she warned when she saw Caleb's eyes widen.

"He didn't—"

"Don't," she repeated.

Waxman patted the breast pocket of his jacket,

squeezing a lumpy-shaped item, and all Caleb could think of was a shattered work of art back in the church, a desecrated tomb.

"They won't miss it," he said after Caleb shut the door and slid in beside his mother.

"How did you get in?"

"Bribed the guard to take the night off," he whispered so the driver wouldn't hear. "I won't tell you any more until we're back in the States."

"Assuming we get through Customs."

"We'll make it," he said giddily, smiling as he fixed his hair in the mirror and then reached for a cigarette.

Caleb hung his head and slumped away from his mother as she tried to move closer. Closing his eyes, Caleb searched his feelings about his role in this theft and discovered that, surprisingly, his excitement for the discovery outweighed his sense of guilt.

They were closing in on the truth.

13

ALEXANDRIA

Nolan Gregory stood in the darkened vault, with just the running floor lights to see by. He preferred it this way. The stars were just visible, backlit in the deep blue of the dome, and he could almost believe he was outside, standing on a desolate beach without the dust and haze and noise of Alexandria.

Seven flights above the dome, the library was closing. They were turning off the lights on the inside while lighting up the exterior glass panes. He sighed and sat quietly, listening to the hum of the generators and the battery of IBM servers running below the floor.

I'm getting old. Too old for this international cloak and dagger shit.

Soon he would have to go to New York. His informant in Italy had indicated that the San

Francesco church had been vandalized, and Nolan could only take that to mean that they had been successful.

They had found the scroll.

Caleb's focus was returning. Lydia's death and his incarceration must have triggered his abilities, just as she had believed it would. Gregory shook his head ruefully. For so long, the Keepers had thought the scroll was still in the collection at Naples, and needed to keep a man inside looking for it, when all that time, Cagliostro . . .

Interesting, but it didn't change things. He bit his lip and turned away from the scornful sight of the constellations.

It won't be long now.

He wondered which would come first—the scroll's translation or Caleb's revelation? Nolan wasn't sure exactly what was on the scroll, other than that it at least explained the seven codes and how to pass them. But that much they already knew. Was there more? What did it say of the Key? The two-thousand-year-old question.

Right now, he had no choice. No other Keeper could be spared. He was the oldest, the most expendable. *And God knows it's going to be dangerous.*

He would have to stay close, to be there the instant they had a translation or any other breakthrough. And then it would be a race against

Waxman and his considerable resources. He had debated for months whether to reveal himself to Caleb, but in the end he had come back to the original premise that like an initiate of the Egyptian mystery school, Caleb would only achieve enlightenment through self-discovery and direct experience. Without that progression, the Key might be forever lost.

It was time.

Nolan buttoned his jacket and straightened his sleeves. When he next returned, if he came back at all, this chamber would all be different. Full, thriving, alive with wonders. An accomplishment to honor, if not rival, the genius of Sostratus.

14

After waking from a fitful nap, Waxman unbuckled his seat belt, stepped into the aisle and made his way toward the back of the plane. Caleb was sitting in the row behind him with Phoebe, whose wheel-chair was stored up front. He had his eyes closed and headphones on, listening to one of the in-flight music stations.

Cocky kid, Waxman thought. *It's about time he contributed. And now it's Phoebe's turn. Time for the cripple to pull her weight.* Their last hope was that this damned scroll could be opened, and that it had something useful on it. But he had to be careful; lately it felt like he was on shaky ground with Helen. Every day, everywhere he went, it seemed he trod in Philip's shadow. Several times he had caught Helen staring at the photographs in her room, the ones she would never remove, the ones he would never again make the mistake of asking her to take down.

All in all, it could be worse. She was still a beautiful woman, and she let him have his hobbies, tolerated his absences and asked no questions. In many ways, she was the perfect wife. And what better way to keep an eye on the project? To fan the flames of Helen's obsession with the Pharos Code, and to be ready to pounce at the moment of revelation. In one fell swoop, by marrying Helen, he had ensured himself access to vital information before the Keepers could ever learn of it.

And that was all that mattered—that, and finding the treasure. *Soon.* Whenever he felt like they were losing ground and would never succeed, he closed his eyes, imagined the vault opening for him.

In the lavatory, after squeezing through the narrow door and sliding the occupied slot over, he took a deep breath and stared in the mirror, right next to the No Smoking sign and its vapid threat of fines and jail time.

He reached into his shirt pocket for his pack of menthols, turned on the water, took out his lighter and pulled one cigarette from the pack with his teeth. When he looked up, the mirror had fogged over, thick puffs of steam exhaling out of the sink. Odd that the water could be so hot . . .

Waxman was about to wipe the mirror clean when lines started appearing on the glass. Smears and curves formed as if a finger slid along the surface.

MAMA

Cursing, Waxman put out his cigarette, then smeared the fog clear off the mirror with his jacket sleeve. "Leave me alone!"

Something in the drain gurgled and bubbled up with the steam that promptly fogged up the mirror again.

I WILL DO NO SUCH THI—

Waxman wiped the mirror clean again and turned off the water. "I'm done talking to you. We've found what we needed, and soon I'll do what I was born to do."

SODUS BAY, NEW YORK—NOVEMBER

It took the better part of three weeks to unroll enough of the scroll to obtain some fragments to analyze. Phoebe was able to secure a lab and a couple interns at the University of Rochester to assist; and together and in shifts, they worked around the clock, applying thin coats of gelatin, separating the layers and prying them apart piece by piece. Phoebe slept there five nights a week, supervising, and Caleb visited every day.

While this was going on, Helen and Waxman continued their remote-viewing trials at home. They brought in new psychic candidates, and worked at applying their abilities to the remaining five signs. The new recruits were showed the great seal, the alchemy symbols and the symbols for the planets. As always, the context was difficult to capture without leading their imaginations.

Mostly they failed, and the potential hits were far from revealing. Waxman grew frustrated and impatient, and he took to leaving for days at a time. "Doing research," Helen insisted. Caleb bit his tongue and kept quiet. He never broached the subject with her. Things were going well between them, the best they'd ever been, and he didn't want to rattle that cage by questioning her husband.

So the days passed. Caleb spent hours walking the leaf-strewn hills below the timid lighthouse, fighting the chill from winds blown over the bay. This particular November morning, he reminisced on the years he'd been away, and he determined to make up for them, to infuse his spirit with the breath of these massive willows, with the feel of the frosted ground beneath his feet, with the sound of the wind and the birds.

He visited the docks and strode along the pier toward Old Rusty. Every morning after his cup of coffee, he came out to toss a rock at its steel hull, just to hear the dull, echoing thud. He thought of Dad. He imagined his father at his side, like it used to be for such a short time. He remembered being taught how to throw a curveball. "Go on," his father would urge. "Sure it's a historical treasure, this old lightship, but it's ours to watch over. And if I want my boy to use it for target practice, damn it he will."

Even now that memory made Caleb grin. He

looked at the dents in Old Rusty's lower hull, the red paint chipped away and nearly invisible above the barnacle-crusted waterline. The whole ship was eighty-four feet in length, with two steel masts twenty feet high, painted red, with a glass-enclosed oil lantern at each masthead. He thought back on the history of lightships, from the early Roman galleys with baskets of oil and wicks, to the last two centuries of naval use. From 1820 until 1983, more than a hundred lightships were in use along the United States coastlines. Eventually these old relics were phased out and replaced by permanent lighthouses or electric buoys.

This one, Old Rusty, had been here for more than thirty years, decommissioned after serving faithfully at various posts off the Northeast coast. It was listed on the National Registrar of Historic Places, and fell under the watch of the family of lighthouse keepers here, to Caleb's father, and to his father before him.

Caleb crossed the ramp, stood on its cast steel deck, and peered into the large wooden deckhouse. Inside were controls for a steam chime whistle and a hand-operated 1,000-pound bell, along with framed sea charts, wheels, tables and cupboards. A few years ago it had been opened to the public as a museum, and Phoebe had worked inside part time, collecting donations and dishing out various historical anecdotes. Caleb wondered if they couldn't apply for a grant to improve its condition a little. Slap on some paint, restore the deckhouse, smooth out those dents in the hull . . .

For some reason, that simple notion, so distinct from code-breaking and world-spanning quests, seemed idyllic. But he smiled and let that dream rest for now. He said goodbye to Old Rusty, and when he stepped off the pier he saw Helen up at the house, waving her arms. She seemed agitated.

Out of breath from the climb and sweating despite the temperature dropping and the wind picking up, he finally made it back up the hill. Before he could ask what the matter was, his mother's words reached him on the breeze.

"Caleb! We found something."

"Another ring," she said, "this one on the ceiling. Something we never noticed before." She led Caleb into the family room, where dozens of pictures were hanging on each wall. In the kitchen he heard the psychics taking a break, talking and laughing.

Helen pointed to two pictures. "We asked them to draw images concerning the Pharos chamber and the sign for Iron. Both Roger and Nancy have drawn what looks like a man suspended upside down. It seems to match the image and orientation of the Hanged Man on the Tarot."

"This is above the third block," Caleb said excitedly. He pictured the chamber again and tried to imagine being there. Having just endured the torrential flood of the second trap . . . *he unhooks the harness and steps onto the next stone, feels the white powdery residue coating his skin and clothes. The air blowing around him, legs balancing, holding fast against the wind . . .*

"Suspended . . ." He thought about it, imagined twisting back and forth. To what purpose? He thought of the Tarot again, and from what he remembered of this card's symbolism, it had to do with letting go, giving in to God's will. Continuing the themes of Calcination and Dissolution, this was a logical step in releasing the initiate's preconceptions, his ego. But it also had to do with self-sacrifice. Martyrdom. He thought of Lydia, whose death had come about because Caleb couldn't see the way past this step.

He slid into a kitchen chair and lowered his head. "I don't get it. The symbolism of that Tarot card is 'to win by surrendering.' But how does that help us?"

Helen took down one sheet of paper and held it in front of Caleb. "This might be a clue." She pointed to something the second person had drawn: a series of blocks crumbling around the hanging person. "What if the next trap has something to do with the floor falling away? And to survive it—"

"—you have to be suspended in the air." Caleb rubbed his eyes and squeezed them tight, trying to see inward. "But what sets it off? I stood there for almost an hour one time, and nothing happened."

"Did you step forward, toward the door?"

"No. Away." He could see his foot lifting, starting to move forward. But it was as if he had a notion of self-preservation, and pulled it back and turned the other direction. "I guess I just felt there was no point going forward if I hadn't experienced anything at this stage."

"That may have saved your life."

Before he could respond, a flash of white light and a burst of heat exploded inside his head with the image of . . .

. . . *Sostratus leading his guest out, returning through the great seal and into the main chamber. The door closes slowly, the snakes again facing each other across the staff.*

"The traps will be in place as I have described," Sostratus declares, and directs Demetrius's gaze down at the inscribed stones underfoot. "You have seen my vault below. You have seen its defenses."

"I have seen." Demetrius is pale, and shaking. "But I fear that with such defenses, what we place inside may never be found."

Sostratus smiles. "No, my friend. Human nature, such as it is, will always lead men to yearn for the truth. And the legends we create will live on. The grandeur of this lighthouse will endure, serving as a beacon for generations long after its light no longer burns."

"And how will you ensure that what it guards will be sought after? If no one knows . . ."

"Ah," Sostratus says, stroking his white hair, "they will know, because you will tell them."

"I?"

"Yes, you and those whom you select to keep this knowledge."

Demetrius shakes his head. "No, Sostratus. That will not work. How can I find enough trust-worthy individuals? And, how do I get them to pass along the information?"

"They will pass it on to a son or daughter, one per generation." Sostratus places a heavy hand on his friend's shoulder. "Choose your Keepers, Deme-trius, then spread them over the world. Those selected will keep the secret. They will know what the lighthouse's true purpose is, and what it protects."

"These Keepers . . ." Demetrius takes a breath. "What makes you think they will not try to steal the contents for themselves?"

Sostratus shifts his arm around Demetrius's shoulder. "My friend. That is precisely what I am counting on."

As suddenly as it had begun, Caleb was torn from the waking dream. He clung to it and focused and tried to keep his mind wrapped about it, but the visions scattered through his grasp like fireflies on a warm summer night.

"No," he stammered, trying to stay in the dream. "I saw them."

"Saw who?" Helen was leaning close, pressing her cool hands to his burning forehead. "Caleb, you terrified me. I've never seen someone fall into a trance so suddenly. You were shaking, so pale. And your eyes—"

"I saw them," he repeated. "Sostratus . . . and Demetrius."

"The architect and the librarian?"

Caleb blinked away the remaining imprints of the two men and the great seal. "I've had several visions now of the two of them together as the Pharos was being built."

Helen stood up and took a step back. In the kitchen the others were washing dishes and talking over the noise. "Maybe you should go back into the trance, if you can. Find out more."

He took a deep breath. "You know I'm no good at forcing visions."

"But this sounds like the connection we've been seeking!" She glanced at the kitchen and motioned for someone to stay away for a moment longer. "Caleb, if you can learn more, it might confirm the presence of the books you think are hidden there."

"The books I *know* are there," he corrected. "We don't need confirmation of that. What we need now is to understand the puzzles, find a way past the traps. From what I saw, Sostratus constructed the vault and the door, then he built the traps around them and set everything into place. I don't think I'll get a view of anyone getting past them. I don't think anyone ever has."

"Someone must have. There's the scroll."

"Which might only be one Keeper's attempt to pass the door. Maybe he failed, or maybe only some of the answers are in it."

"Did you see any of these Keepers?"

"I think I saw Sostratus create them." Caleb frowned. "And I heard something about his plan for the treasure's release. He was relying on man's inner nature—the Keepers' greed, their curiosity—to one day seek out the treasure and find the way in."

"Sounds like a lot of presupposition on his part."

"But it was something Sostratus would do. He was tricky like that."

Helen urged the others inside and had them take their places again around the table. "Okay, that was symbol number three, and we think we might have the answer we're looking for."

"We hope," Caleb added.

"We hope," she agreed, giving him a wary smile. "Let's continue, people. Four more to go."

Caleb took a breath and settled back in his chair, for the first time in his life eager to join one of these sessions. As the others took their seats, he thought again about what his mother had just said.

"Four more to go . . ."

All of a sudden, Caleb was struck with the certainty that she was wrong. *We're missing something.* And then he realized what was bothering him. The sealed door with the caduceus was only at the halfway point, maybe a little more. If the adage *As Above, So Below* held, then there was still a long way to go before they reached the beacon—the fire, the light of truth—where Sostratus surely hid his vault.

And if seven clues were needed to open this door, what would be next? Caleb tried to picture it, but saw only darkness. There would be the octagonal section, ending in the cupola and the pillared room with the mirror.

"Octagon," he whispered, shivering in a sudden chill.

Helen looked up, first at Caleb, then to the kitchen, where a brisk wind blew through the open door.

Waxman was standing there. His face was rosy. He stank of menthol. "Caleb," he said. "I've just come from the University. Phoebe's asking for you. She's finished unrolling the scroll. "

16

Caleb bounded up the steps just as the first snow-flakes began to fall. At his back, across Elmwood Avenue, Mount Hope Cemetery sprawled over two hundred acres, its monuments and time-worn markers standing as mute soldiers among the rolling hills and saluting into the twilight. He took one last look, waved to the cab driver who had just dropped him off, then flung open the door and ran into the university's archive center.

He had left Waxman and Helen at home to continue working with the psychics. He'd told them that realistically, poring over the fragments, taking the pictures, scanning them into the computer and playing with the resolution could take days before a translation was possible. But the real reason he had come by himself was that he didn't care to share space with Waxman. The man still got under his skin, and of course he had never quite accepted Waxman's role in his mother's life. Caleb liked to think he had become more tolerant, but this was one instance where he had reverted to the petty emotions of a child. He just didn't like the man. He respected that his mother saw something in him, although what that was Caleb couldn't tell. There never seemed to be any real affection between them. They acted like business partners, and maybe that was part of the problem; Caleb didn't make an effort because Helen never acted like he was her husband.

So Caleb convinced Waxman to stay in Sodus while he made the trip, promising to call as soon as they discovered anything significant.

He rushed down empty halls, pounding each step as hard as he could, relishing the sound of his echoing shoes, as if he were trying to banish any malevolent spirits lingering about. At the end of a long corridor, he took the stairs down three flights, past eerily blinking hallway lamps, then through the fourth door on the left.

Inside, Phoebe sat in her work chair in front of a laptop on a long table. The other interns were gone, sent home hours ago. Four binocular microscopes were set up along the table, and a large glass strip covered the unrolled fragments of the blackened scroll. Observing the shreds and scattered pieces, Caleb marveled that anything could be salvaged from of it.

"About time, big brother." She had her hair in two pig tails, and she wore a red turtleneck with little reindeer embroidered on the collar. "Come on, see the fruits of modern technology."

"Tell me you have a translation." He walked around the table and pulled up a chair.

"Not yet, but I've scanned all the photographs taken at different wavelengths and uploaded them onto my laptop. I think I'm close, but need your help in interpretation." She pointed to her screen and clicked with the mouse to shrink the image. "There are fifteen of these fragments. Here's the first one." She called up a tattered-looking strip. The lettering appeared blue, with the background now in white.

Caleb grinned. "Perfect! Thank Mother Nature for preserving this for us in volcanic ash."

"Yeah, never mind all her children that she killed in the process."

"Cycle of Life, sis." He jabbed her with an elbow, hoping she knew he was kidding.

"Anyway. Here's the symbol for Lead, and there's the one for Tin."

"And there," Caleb pointed, "near the one for lead . . . a cone drawn around a figure of a man who looks like he's praying."

"Right, the next section is badly torn, and not much could be recovered, but next to the sign for Water we see the figure again, bound with two chains."

Caleb's excitement mounted. "So far, this scroll is two for two. Whoever drew this at least got that far. Wait, was this how the scroll began? Wasn't there any introduction, any words to the reader?"

"Nothing," Phoebe said. "Nothing but the word 'Pharos' and then that symbol . . ."

"The one for Exalted Mercury."

"Yeah, that. Well, it seems more like a cheat sheet to be used by someone who already knew how to get into the chamber and what they were supposed to do once they got there."

He tapped his fingers on the table impatiently. "Then Cagliostro, having seen only the first inch, knew this for what it was."

The lights flickered for an instant, and Caleb's eyes darted to the door, a window set in the middle. *Did someone just walk by?*

"So the third symbol," Phoebe continued, "Iron . . ."

"It shows a man suspended above the floor." Caleb quickly filled Phoebe in on what the psychics had just discovered.

"Three for three. So far so good." Phoebe clicked again, and enlarged a section. "Fourth. Copper. Here, it's like the writer couldn't draw what's going to happen, so he wrote, 'Go below.'"

Caleb leaned back and rubbed his temples. He had a fleeting thought that maybe it meant the seeker was supposed to go down the stairs to the external vents and wait, but that didn't make sense. There wouldn't be enough time to then get to the next stone.

"What if—?" He began, but saw movement to his left. A face at the window, looking in, then it was gone just as quick. Caleb leapt to his feet.

"What is it?"

"Somebody's outside." He started toward the door.

Phoebe grabbed his hand. "Don't worry about it. Evening classes are letting out." She tossed her hair and batted her eyes. "I'm sure it's just one of my many admirers."

Caleb took a breath and sat down again. Something about that face . . . *the white hair, narrow, hawkish eyes* . . . He had seen it only for a second, but he knew who it was.

Nolan Gregory.

"Keep working on it," he told Phoebe as he stood up again. "I need to check something."

"You're going to leave me in here all alone?"

"I'm sure you can handle yourself, along with any 'admirers' who might come looking for you."

"Fine, I'll solve all the puzzles myself. You just go. Have fun chasing shadows."

Caleb tore open the door and stepped into the empty hallway. He stopped and listened. To his right, up the stairs, a door closed. He took off in that direction, bolted up the stairs and out into the lobby, where he saw someone dressed in gray rushing out the front door.

The walls seemed to close in, narrowing as he ran. Caleb slammed into the door and burst outside. Four steps at a time, then onto the street. He chased the fleeing man across Elmwood Avenue. A black Lexus screeched to a halt just as he hurdled the front fender, before being blocked by a passing transit bus. "Come on, come on, come on!"

Seconds later he was across the street and racing up the hill. Caleb bounded the waist-high stone fence the other man had just climbed, and tore through the cemetery in pursuit. Snow had begun to fall in earnest, a driving sleet from the wintry evening sky. The shadows had grown long and jagged, and the tired elms sloped longingly towards their departed leaves. He chased Gregory through the older section of the cemetery, weaving around worn monuments and moss-covered stones, side-stepping miniature obelisks and urns, crosses and pillars. For an older man, he was in great shape. Caleb, on the other hand, was wheezing and cramping up his left side within minutes. But adrenaline kept him going.

Gregory looked back once, then sprinted toward

the eastern boundary.

"Mr. Gregory!"

He connected with the path and lost his footing on the icy pavement, slick with scattered leaves. Caleb was almost upon him, but he dodged him and ran out through the gates.

He raced into the street, onto Mount Hope Avenue.

"Mr. Gregory, please!" The old man turned, and in an instant Caleb saw his eyes shining their defiance—

—and then he disappeared in a flash of white batted against the grillwork of a Ryder truck. The air split with the sickening sound of crunching bones, followed by a squealing of tires. Caleb's heart lurched but he kept running, now chasing the flopping, rolling body twenty feet away. Nolan Gregory lay twitching in the gathering snow.

Caleb held up a hand and shouted, "Call 911!" and then knelt beside Nolan. His face was clean on one side, a bloody, shredded mess on the other. One eye was missing and his nose had been crushed. His mouth opened and a dripping cavity full of shattered teeth tried to speak.

Caleb touched his shoulder, but then took his hand away, afraid to cause the man any more pain. "You didn't have to run," he said, making fists out of his hands. "I just wanted to know . . . wanted to ask you why." He leaned forward as the snow turned to freezing rain, mixing with his sweat and running into his eyes.

"Why Lydia? Why sacrifice your daughter? Why me, damn it? Why!"

Sirens wailed in the distant, sleet-soaked dusk.

Nolan Gregory made a sound like laughter. "The Split," he said in a choking voice.

"What?"

"The Great Split . . . the Keepers. The Renegade, Metreisse. Fifteen eighty-seven." He let out a chuckle that gave way to an unearthly rattle, and his eye rolled back in his head.

"Gregory. Mr. Gregory!" Caleb grabbed his hand, squeezed it and leaned closer. He thought of urging him to stay conscious, convincing him that help was coming, but he knew it was too late for that. Instead, Caleb sat with him. It seemed the thing to do at this momentous transition from one world to the next. And he spoke, not knowing exactly where the words came from. He just started talking, telling his father-in-law about the Light, about the truth. About going home.

Caleb held his hand and rocked in the freezing rain. Closing his eyes, he felt the driving, frosted sleet. Soaking wet, he still felt warm, like a rush of heat radiated out from Nolan Gregory's hand up Caleb's arm and down his spine.

Red and white lights beat against his eyes, and when at last he opened them, police and firemen were running toward him. He stood and let go of Gregory's hand, then stared out across the battalions of tombstones, the dark sentinels observing without judgment. As he waited, Caleb repeated only one thing, whispering it over and over like a mantra.

1587. Metreisse.

17

Back inside, Phoebe was waiting at the door to the lab. When she saw Caleb she turned pale. "Are you—?"

"Fine."

"You were gone so long."

"Had to stay and fill out a report."

She searched his face, and then pointed to a nearby shelf. "Paper towels in there. And I have a spare sweatshirt around here somewhere."

"Thanks." Caleb slumped into a chair after grabbing the roll of paper towels. "What did you find?"

Phoebe offered a weak smile. She rolled back to the laptop, punched a few keys and turned the screen so he could see. "For the fourth seal, you're on your own. That fragment is too damaged. We'll have to hope for more visions. But the fifth is clear: Mercury. You need to bring something along with you. Stand on that block, place sulfur in the crevasses of the symbol, and light it."

Caleb gave her a curious expression.

She shrugged. "That's what it says; I don't know what it's supposed to *mean*."

After a moment's consideration Caleb spoke. "It means," he said, wiping his wet hair with his damp sleeve, "you've begun the process of destruction, and you're starting on the path to purification of your soul."

"If you say so." She tapped a few more keys and moved the mouse. "And then we come to number six: Silver, which corresponds to the Moon."

"Distillation," he said. "Dissolving the ego and increasing purity. Releasing the lunar energies, and . . . okay, your eyes are glazing over. What does it say to do there?"

"This is where the scroll starts to really break down. There's a big section damaged here, but it looks like it says to reflect a light onto the serpent's head."

"Reflect? Like, with a mirror?"

"Probably, although I wonder if a flashlight would do." She scratched her chin. "I guess the point is to illuminate the serpent with a connection, linking it to yourself."

"See? You are getting this stuff."

Phoebe grinned. "I try. Okay, now here's where you're going to kill me. The description of the seventh, the Sulfur or Gold puzzle . . ."

"Yes?" Caleb visualized the steps in sequence, putting together the path to completing the cycle.

"It's gone." She sighed. "I mean, there's nothing legible, other than the word for gold." She bit on one edge of her pigtail. "I'm sorry. I can work at resolving the image some more, but . . ."

Caleb slumped forward. "Despite that, Phoebe, great job. Amazing. We're almost there. But as much as I want to continue this, please look something up for me—if you're connected to the Web."

"Of course I am." She gave him a dirty look. "I'm a cripple, remember? I don't get to go out much. I belong to some chat rooms where everyone thinks I'm this professional tennis player. It's great."

"I'm sure it is." Caleb leaned forward. "Look up the name 'Metreisse,' and put in the date 1587."

"Okay. Spell it."

"I don't know. Yahoo it."

She tapped some keys. "Alright . . . there it is, first try." She looked a little closer. "The first hit is from a book by an English historian. Let's see . . . 'Henri Metreisse was an alchemist in the court of Queen Elizabeth the First.' . . . Never successful, of course, in turning anything to gold, . . . but it says here he counseled the queen to victory over the

Scots in several great battles. Oh, get this. He claimed to have clairvoyance, and could . . . He could see into the enemy's palaces, even overhear their battle plans!" She stared at Caleb. "A remote viewer!"

Caleb scratched his chin and fought the onset of chills. He'd have to find that sweatshirt. "What else? What about 1587?"

She scrolled down and then followed a link. "It says he was known to have convened with fellow alchemists. They met at Stonehenge during every Spring Equinox, but after the meeting in 1587, he never returned."

She reached into her bag for a can of Coke. "Want one?"

"Nope."

"Are you going to tell me what this is about?" Phoebe took a sip. "What happened out there?"

Sighing, Caleb looked up. "Nolan Gregory was spying on us. Spying on me . . . again."

"But, I thought Waxman checked us out for listening devices."

"Wouldn't matter," Caleb said. "Gregory was following me. He knew everything I was doing, especially anything connected to the Pharos."

Phoebe sat quietly, pensive. "Did you kill him?"

"What? No. He ran into traffic . . ."

Phoebe nodded. "So what's this about 1587?"

"As Gregory died he told me I was important

to them because of something called the 'Split.' Something that happened to the Keepers in 1587."

Phoebe tapped her fingers. "Dissension in the ranks? Keepers against Keepers? Maybe that's why he and Lydia wanted the treasure so badly. They have competition."

"Maybe," Caleb said, his eyes swimming out of focus, as if his vision were being pulled in another direction. "But there's only one way to be sure."

"You mean . . . ?"

"I mean, get out your pencils and paper."

Phoebe clapped her hands. "It'll be like old times!" She grinned. "Except now you're not such a dork."

They dimmed the lights. Caleb changed into the dry sweatshirt and pulled up a chair beside hers. They decided against a formal trance. This one would just be free-form. Experience the visions and share with each other what they'd seen.

"Ready, big brother?"

"Yeah." He took her hands. "Actually, no. Not yet. First tell me something. What did you see that time when I was in college? You told me about the girl with the green eyes."

She pulled her hand away. "Oh that. I was hoping you'd forgotten. Well, I liked to try to look in on you now and then. Not that I was snooping, I just missed you. But for a stretch of a couple weeks, every time I tried it was always the same: I saw you being pushed underwater and held there by this girl with green eyes. The weird thing was, though, she was weeping while she did it."

"Anything else?"

"Yes. I don't know what it means, but I kept hearing a baby crying. Wailing actually. The whole time while she was drowning you."

"A baby?"

"Yeah. Like I said, weird." She gave a wistful smile. "Probably I was getting your visions mixed up with my dreams."

He reached for her. "Oh, sis, I'm so—"

"I know." She sniffed, then pushed Caleb away. "So anyway, are we going to do this? Because if we are, you should prepare to get outmatched by your baby sister again."

Later, Phoebe would say she hadn't seen anything. Only a confused jumble of scenery, with no people. A land of hills, forests and rivers. And rain, lots of rain. She lingered too long in the setting, and when Caleb shook her, after what had seemed like hours, it was over.

Caleb's vision began at once, as if it had been waiting there, expecting him to join . . .

. . . *eighteen men and two women standing under the stars in a clearing, surrounded by a stone circle made of immense blocks. They are all wearing gray robes with planets and stars stitched onto the black fabric. Seven torches burn in a straight line toward a smaller stone to the north-east, upon which a large burning brazier sends its smoke into the air. Overhead, the moonless night is clear, the stars bold and close, peering down through the terrestrial curtain to watch the spec-tacle.*

One of the elders steps forward. He is a white-bearded, hunched-over man, but with a surprising vigor about him. "We are here to discuss how to handle Metreisse. I had hoped he would honor tradition and come to our gathering, but it seems he has fled."

"Kill him," says one in the back of the crowd.

"Find him first," says a woman leaning on a twisted staff entwined with ivy. "Find him and see if he's the one."

"We know he's the one," says the first speaker. "Who else could have learned the way past the traps?"

"Are we sure someone did?"

"Yes. Our watchmen reported seeing a cloaked figure enter the ruins of the Pharos last month during the lunar eclipse. This intruder was under-neath the structure for many hours. When he emerged, my spies say he sought them out, called them from their hiding places, then gave them something to tell us. 'Tell your masters that I have

found the final Key,' he said. 'And I will hide it for all time, as long as your interests diverge from our original purpose. I have not entered the vault, and no one else shall until it is time.'"

"How dare he?" someone in the front mutters.

"He dares," says the other female, "because he believes he follows the will of Sostratus."

"Sostratus lied," a new voice speaks up. "We all know this. Once, Sostratus did the world a favor and protected the great works from the centuries of coming darkness. But he did not intend us to wait this long!"

"And wait for what?" asks the first female.

"It is decided, then." The elder steps into the center of the circle and raises his arms. "We are to seek him out. As long as it takes. Seek, and retrieve this key, whatever it is. Determine how to use it."

"Do we have any idea where he went?"

"Only that he sailed east into the Mediterranean aboard a galley."

"Then that is where we shall start."

One man who has been silent up until now steps forward. "And if we fail to find him in our lifetime?"

The elder sighs and looks wearily at his feet. "Then the search will continue in the next."

When Caleb came back into the present, it was with calm, relaxed breaths. His eyes fluttered, and he blinked in the somber light. Phoebe sat in front of him, chewing on a Snickers bar.

"How is it that you're not fat?" he asked.

She grinned and made a muscle in her right arm. "Tennis, remember? What did you see?"

He told her.

"So, someone *had* figured out the puzzles, found a way past the traps."

"Someone with the gift," Caleb said. "We know Metreisse could remote view, or at least he claimed to have that power."

"And yet, if he found the treasure, did he really leave it there?"

"Seems like it. Or maybe, having viewed the way past the traps, he never actually opened the door. It sounds like he considered himself bound by his ancestors' pledge to keep the treasure safe."

"So how do we use this information? And what did Gregory mean by it?"

"I don't know," Caleb said. "It has something to do with me, though. And . . . what?"

Phoebe was gaping at her laptop screen. "Something just happened. My screen flickered like it does whenever a new program starts up. Weird."

She bent over the keyboard and moved to a new program. "Just checking something . . . Oh no!"

"What?" he stood behind her and looked down.

She pointed to the first item on the list. "The file. I had saved all the scanned photos in one big file, and someone just accessed it and deleted it.

It's gone."

"Where?"

"Checking . . ." Phoebe pulled up a couple files, checked her emails, then threw up her hands. "I don't know. It's not even in the temp folder any more. I could scan everything back in, but—"

"But someone else has it." Caleb leaned in. "Did they get it all?"

"Yep."

He cursed. "Who has access to your computer?"

"I don't know. I was online, so either someone came snooping and grabbed this file, or I had a virus put on my laptop at some point, a virus that let someone else spy in on me and steal what they wanted."

"That's just freakin' great!" he said, throwing his pencil. "The Keepers have it."

"Maybe," Phoebe said, frowning.

"What do you mean, 'maybe'? Who else could it be?"

"I don't know. But I'm worried that it could be someone in the Morpheus Initiative."

"Come on, those guys? They . . ." Caleb stopped and looked at her closely. "But you're not suspecting *them*."

"No," she said, shaking her head. "You know who I'm thinking about."

He stood up and grabbed his things.

"Waxman."

18

After several attempts to reach them and getting only voicemail, Caleb wheeled Phoebe out to the street and a waiting cab. The sixty-mile drive back to Sodus took two and a half hours. The roads were slick. The rain had turned back to snow, and there were cars in the ditches every few miles. Fortunately the cab driver had a four-wheel drive and a strong sense of self-preservation. Even so, they skidded several times and fishtailed twice into traffic, barely missing oncoming cars.

When the cab pulled up to the house, Caleb got Phoebe out of the cab and into her chair, then helped push her through the snow up the driveway.

"No cars," Caleb observed. "And no lights on inside."

"Shit," Phoebe said.

The house was empty.

"I don't believe this," Phoebe said once they were inside. "Not Mom too! She wouldn't just leave us."

"Unless she believed it was in our best interest not to come along." He continued looking around the kitchen and the living room, where new drawings hung on the walls and lay scattered about the tables. "I don't need to RV the scene. I can imagine Waxman telling her that it's best they go on their own and get a head start without us. I bet he reminded her about what happened in Belize."

"That's ridiculous," Phoebe said. "We're different now, and besides, look at my condition! For all of Sostratus's genius, I doubt he was progressive enough to include a handicapped access ramp for me."

Caleb continued digging through papers, scrutinizing the drawings. Everything lined up for the first six puzzles. "I don't see anything about the Sun, about that final block. You didn't—"

"No. The scan was incomplete. Scroll was damaged."

Caleb turned to Phoebe, and saw her sitting hunched in her chair in the dark kitchen. "Could they have gotten *anything* from that scan?"

"I don't think so," she said. "Unless Waxman

has some proprietary software or something that enhances resolution. There were fragments of the scroll missing, but some of what was there could be legible enough, and maybe a computer program could extrapolate missing letters from the position of the visible ones, and—"

"So you're saying they could have the answer?"

"Or worse. They might think they have it, and be wrong."

Caleb pushed his hair off his forehead and cast a reflexive glance around the room, not looking for anything in particular, but hoping—hoping they were overlooking something simple. "Mom wouldn't have—"

"Caleb," Phoebe cut him off, "look. A camera." One of three Helen usually had rolling to document every step of the process.

"What about it? They must have forgotten it in their hurry to get out of here before we got back."

"I don't think so. Hook it up to the TV." Caleb gave her a doubtful look. "Humor me, okay?"

Caleb hooked the camera up to the TV's input jack and turned it on. He rewound the tape until the time stamp displayed seven thirty, three hours ago, then pressed PLAY and sat on the couch beside Phoebe.

"Maybe we should make some popcorn," she suggested, without a touch of emotion.

"Shh. No talking during the movie."

On the screen, the living room sprang to life. Twelve people sat around the table, and at the left side, Helen stood, bending forward and holding up a sheet of paper. It was an enhanced photograph of the seventh stone before the door. The symbol for Sulfur. "Here is your target," she instructed. "Imagine standing on this sign and then experiencing the door opening. How does it happen? What do you see? Draw what you feel."

"Alternately," she said, "think about the hidden vault under the Pharos. Imagine the last puzzle, the final key. See it, and draw what you see."

Caleb scratched the back of his neck. "Mom seems a little rushed."

"Desperate," Phoebe agreed. "Better to let them just focus on the symbol and see where the unconscious leads them."

"Right, I think she either just confused them or sent them thinking about something else."

"We'll see."

Nothing happened for the next few minutes, as the psychics all sat in various poses, eyes closed or opened. The room was quiet. A few candles flickered in the background.

Caleb fast-forwarded until he saw some movement. Nearly a half-hour had passed. Some people were drawing, but others were talking.

"I saw my fingers covered in gold," one middle-aged woman with dark bangs said. "And then I reached out and touched the staff. The door opened—"

"I was also covered in gold," a bald man in his seventies spoke up. "And I shuffled to the door, leaving trails of gold dust sparkling in my path."

"I didn't see any of that," said another woman. "I just saw a ship. Actually it might have been several ships. They were all a little different in shape, but they all had red and white sails."

A man in the back, wearing a turtleneck, cleared his throat. "I saw a ship, too, and I drew it." He held up a sheet of paper. The ship had two masts, and roamed a sea beside a coastal town, where a tower guarded a harbor.

Another man walked into the camera's view. He bent over and whispered into Mom's ear.

"Waxman," Phoebe whispered. "Mom's shocked. Look at her eyes."

"People," Helen said. "I think we might be done here. It's clear the seventh puzzle is opened by one who's covered in gold, or at least it's on one's fingertips. Information from George here supports it. We have verification from an ancient scroll that says 'to pass the seventh, touch the staff with fingers of gold.'"

"What about the ships?" the man in the turtleneck asked.

"False reading," Waxman suggested. "Who knows?" He stretched like a cat, reaching for the ceiling. "I think we're finished. You people have done a tremendous job. You're excused until further notice. Expect a hefty bonus check in the mail in about two weeks, and if you wish your names included in the study, please let Helen know."

People started shaking each other's hands and saying goodbye. Helen walked to the camera and reached for the OFF switch. For a second nothing happened. Then her face appeared, full in the lens. Her eyes darted to the kitchen, then back to the camera.

"Caleb, Phoebe . . . we're going to Alexandria. George . . . George is . . . I'm sorry. This is something we both want, it's what we need to do. If we succeed, everything will change. I promise. I'll be there for you, and this will all be over. Love you both—"

Caleb stopped the tape and when he turned around, Phoebe was at the phone. She hung it up. "Nothing. Mom's turned off her cell phone."

"Or they're in the air." He looked around helplessly.

"Caleb?"

"Yeah?"

"I think Mom's in trouble. And I think she knew it."

"I know. My fear is that the next call we get will be from the authorities, telling us they're dead."

Phoebe sighed. "Mine too."

Snow knocked against the windows, and the storm rattled the lighthouse frame.

Caleb tapped his foot, staring into the distance.

"What are you thinking? Do we go after them, or just wait for them to call?"

He shook his head. "I don't think they have the right answers."

"To the seventh puzzle?" Phoebe asked. "It sounded right—"

"Not the seventh," he said. "I think that one's right. But remember Mom's instructions to the team? They came back with two distinct visions."

"One dealing with the gold, the other with ships."

"Right." He took a deep breath and pictured the lighthouse again, magnificently rising in its three tiers, and then he saw its mirror image below. "How did she phrase the second set of instructions? She said to visualize the last key . . . whatever that is."

"Right, so that's what they did. They saw the seventh sign, and—"

"What if the seventh isn't the last?"

Phoebe opened her mouth. "Oh."

Caleb started to pace, something that always helped when he was researching a book. "We know the treasure has to do with the writings of Thoth. And we also know the seven steps of alchemy lead to spiritual rebirth, the seventh being to make permanent that state of consciousness imbued with the eternal."

"The Philosopher's Stone."

"Right. But some sources also maintain there is an eighth stage. Beyond the seventh there is rebirth, complete transcendence. Setting everything in motion. God created the world in six days, rested on the seventh, then on the eighth, it all clicked into place. Same with Thoth. Eight is also the number of the octave, and Thoth was said to create the world through his voice, through music."

"Okay, I get it. Eight's a powerful number." Phoebe wheeled into the room. "But are we sure there's another door?"

"Think about it. The Keepers were furious with the Renegade, Metreisse. If there were only these seven puzzles, they should have been able to figure them out, being the studied alchemists they were. Instead, Metreisse, using psychic abilities, was the one to find the way into the vault. That makes it sound like the last door maybe isn't something that you can use your intellect to pass. It might be more conventional, requiring the right *physical* key."

Phoebe nodded. "And Metreisse fled on a boat, exactly what Mom's psychics had seen. But what does it mean? That the boat sank, and with it the key?"

"Maybe," he said, fearing the prospect of having to don scuba gear again at some point. Still, it didn't quite sound right. "Then why would the Keepers of today still be convinced that we have it?"

"I don't know."

But I should. I should know. Caleb rubbed his temples. *The answer is close, hidden in plain view.*

It wasn't the first time he had had that feeling, but again he couldn't make out what he was meant to know, and he cursed his lack of intuition. As far as he had progressed, he still hadn't transcended far enough.

Phoebe whispered. "Mom's in trouble, big brother."

"I know. We have to go. Maybe there's a chance we can get there ahead of them."

"Doubt it," she said. "Unless the storm delayed their flight."

"Let's hope for nasty weather," Caleb said, and went for the car keys.

19
ALEXANDRIA

The Pharos protects itself.

Somewhere over the Atlantic, while Phoebe was fast asleep beside him, Caleb had the sudden certainty that they would be too late. They'd had no luck at the Rochester airport. And not only did all the previous flights leave on time, but theirs was the first to be sidelined.

Two hours they'd waited for de-icing and final runway clearance, then they were off to JFK, where they had another hour's delay before boarding their flight to Alexandria, after a stopover in Paris. They had no way of knowing how much earlier Helen and Waxman had left. All they could be sure of now was that they would be too late.

He buzzed the flight attendant and requested a pillow and tried to sleep, knowing that he would need his strength.

It was ten thirty in the morning by the time they hailed a cab at the Alexandria airport. At eleven, they were stuck in horrendous traffic, behind slow-moving produce trucks, and held up by a gala event at the Bibliotheca Alexandrina, where huge crowds surged around a festival-like atmosphere on the grounds in front of the enormous glass-roofed construction. Caleb marveled at the blue dome of the planetarium off to the side, and he noted the sturdy construction, the reinforced concrete girders and the enormous walls of the main library. As they slowly drove past, he recalled reading that four levels were dug under sea level, protected from the sinking of the land on a raft of concrete.

Finally they made it to the causeway. Halfway across, Phoebe grabbed Caleb's arm. They were both sitting in the back seat, neither talking. Barely breathing. It seemed like they were in a funeral procession.

"Sirens." Phoebe pointed, and Caleb saw the flickering lights up ahead. He rolled down his window and looked out. In the sky, a lone helicopter sped away, rising up from the Pharos promontory.

"Bad accident," the cab driver said, his English surprisingly good. "I hear it on my CB radio. Scuba divers have . . . how you say . . . accident?"

"What happened?" Phoebe asked as they neared

the parking area for Qaitbey. Her face had gone pale, her shoulders trembled.

The cabbie spoke some words into his CB, and the answer came back, a garbled series of guttural consonants. "I am told an older woman was just lifted out in a helicopter, taken to hospital."

Phoebe's nails dug into Caleb's flesh. "Stop! Turn the cab around and take us there."

"Pardon?"

"Do it!" Caleb said, his mouth dry. "Did they say what happened to her?"

"Do not know. They find her on the rocks. No swimsuit, no air tank. They say she will probably die, I am sorry to say. Underwater very long."

"Was there a man with her?"

"Yes, yes. Man with her. He is OK. He must be very powerful man. He survives accident and calls police."

Caleb shot Phoebe a look.

She leaned forward. "Just drive to the hospital, please. Fast."

As they turned around, Caleb stared at the old sandstone turrets of Fortress Qaitbey, and he saw the red and blue lights flickering off its massive walls. For an instant, he could see a marble stairway ascending between two immense royal statues looking solemn and compassionate.

Helen was on the second floor. And as Phoebe

wheeled into the room and rolled beside her bed, Caleb glanced around for Waxman. His hands were tight fists, and he found himself grinding his teeth, fuming.

"Where is he?" he asked the first doctor entering his mother's room. "The man who brought my mother here, where did he go?"

The doctor, a dark-skinned bald man, shrugged. "Your father checked her in—"

"He's not my father."

"—and . . . eh . . . he left immediately. Said you would be along to care for her."

Son of a bitch.

Caleb went to his mother's side. His arm around Phoebe, he sat in a chair and they both held her hands. She was so cold. Her head was wrapped in bandages, and a tube had been inserted into her nose. An IV fed fluids through her right arm.

"What about a decompression chamber?" he asked. "Shouldn't she be in one?"

Phoebe shook her head. "The nurse told me she's too bad off. She needs the IV, morphine and rest. They chose to save her life." Her voice cracked and she could barely finish the sentences. "They say she won't wake up again, and if she does, she'll be a vegetable. The damage to her brain, a severe stroke from the pressure . . ." Phoebe blew her nose and rubbed away her tears. "She won't—"

"It's okay," Caleb whispered, even though he

knew it wasn't. "Mom's alive," he said. "And as long as she is, there's hope."

"What did he do to her?"

"We're going to find out."

Phoebe lifted her head. Her eyes were like steel ball bearings, cold and fierce. "Let's do it now. Let's *view* the bastard."

He took his hand away from his mother's and held Phoebe's. They had seen similar visions before, but never this direct, never such a match, detail for detail.

It started with the caduceus. The door parting, the seventh symbol unlocked. This vision tunneled through Caleb's consciousness like a sonic drill. He saw the great door ease open, and Helen and Waxman gave a shout of joy. Their skin glittered with a golden dust. They picked up their lanterns and a flashlight, and bounded forward. Caleb's mind's eye followed . . .

. . . *Waxman down another staircase. He shines the lantern's brilliant light around. "Eight sides to this room." They stand together in an immense, cavern-like chamber with high vaulted ceilings and what looks like two circular portals above, vents for bringing in the water used for the second trap.*

"We're in the octagon section." Helen pans the walls with her flashlight. "Caleb was right. 'As Above, so Below.'"

"Yeah, all credit and glory to your son, Amen!"

"Stop being so cynical. He's the reason we're here."

"No, you are. It was your dedication, your focus, your drive that kept this dream alive long after he deserted you."

"You're wrong."

"Whatever. We're almost there. The treasure awaits."

They circle around and around on smooth stairs, through thin layers of dust shaken free in the quakes. Here and there a crumbled stone lies on the stairs, and pieces of the wall have fallen in places; but soon the steps end and they walk onto a flat floor that leads to another door, this one with a single image drawn on its surface.

"That again! What is this?" Waxman shines his light up and down. *It's a modest door, about half as large as the previous one, and otherwise nondescript. The room itself is bare, with no artwork on the walls. Nothing inscribed on the floor. No rings, no pits. Nothing but red granite blocks.*

Helen shifts her weight, looking over her shoulder. "I don't know, but I think we may have it all wrong."

"Nonsense. Here's a handle on the door. Probably just pull on it and—"

"Don't touch anything!" She shouts and grabs his hand.

"Are you serious?"

"Do you even have to ask?" She takes a step back, almost to the stairs. "Did you forget what we just went through up there? Any one of those traps could have killed us, and when we find another door you think it's going to be as simple as pulling it open?"

Waxman exhales roughly, exasperated. "Fine, then RV this one. Let's do it now!"

"No. Let's leave, and think about this. Come back later, once we have all the information. We can analyze the scroll some more. We can probe our psychics, we—"

"—can't wait any longer! It has to be now."

"Why?"

Standing at the door, he wraps his fingers

around the handle. "Because."

"Why? Nothing's as important as our lives. We can wait!"

"No, we can't."

"What are you talking about? What about the thrill of the hunt, the research, the quest into psychic talents? I thought that was what made this all worth it, whether or not we succeed in getting beyond that door."

"No." Waxman glowers at her, then turns to the door, his hands in tight fists. "There's more, much more. I have to make it stop!"

"What are you talking about?" Helen takes one step up the stair, back the way they have come.

"She never stops," he whispers, brushing the handle free of dust. "Every minute, every day."

"Who are you talking about, George? Have you lost your mind?"

"Yes, a long time ago." He looks back, and his eyes are glowing fiercely in the lantern's brilliance. "But it ends now."

He grunts and pulls back on the handle.

"Wait!" Helen yells. "I think I see something—a hole above your hand. Maybe there's a key."

But it is too late. The room shakes.

Helen screams and turns. Waxman slips and falls. As he topples, a foot-wide block rips free from the side of the door right where his head was. It shoots out across the room and glances off Helen's skull, spinning her around, and she crumples onto the stairs without a sound. Just as quickly, the deadly trap withdraws and returns to its sealed position.

Waxman lunges for Helen. He lifts her and races up the stairs, gasping for air. This time, as he makes it back up through the octagon section, the great door slams shut in front of him. A grinding sound arises from the left, up high in the chamber. Then another echoes the first, from the other side.

The walls rattle.

Waxman shines his light up and directs it toward one, then the other portal. The great circular doors have been opened, moved by some major contraption of gears and levers.

"Oh no." For a moment he feels blood soaking his arms and his chest, flowing from Helen's head. She shakes and mutters something. A name. "Philip . . ."

The water bursts through the twin vents above, monstrous jets flooding the chamber. Waxman drops Helen and starts to run back toward the stairs when his feet are swept from the floor. He flies back into the wall, spins around before being yanked to one side, where another door rolls open at the floor level. In a rush of bubbles and churning water he blasts out the door into a circular, tube-like hallway. Rolling, spinning, gagging and choking. Another body bangs against him and gets *tangled in his legs, then a powerful slam and they are punched through into a wall of water. He grabs hold of Helen out of reflex, holds his breath, and they rise together, propelled by the exiting currents.*

He opens his eyes and his mouth to utter a bubbly, agonized scream as the sudden pressure overwhelms his head. But he remembers his training and exhales slowly, kicking furiously all the time.

Somehow, he surfaces alive, just as his lungs are about to burst. He emerges into the bright sun, surrounded by a sea of multicolored boats. Men and women scream and point and dive in to help.

Caleb fought to free himself from the vision, but he failed . . .

. . . and finds himself in a helicopter. This time, leaving the hospital landing pad.

"Your jet is waiting at the airport, sir," says a man in uniform. He has a crew cut, and is wearing a starched blue suit.

Then Caleb flashed to different place, much later, and saw . . .

. . . Waxman exiting a small black jet. He turns up the collar on his long coat and jogs across a runway toward a waiting black limousine. The night is cold, brisk. To the east, a faint glow announces the rising sun. Inside the limo, the driver rolls down the back window.

"Good to have you back, sir."

Another flash.

Waxman steps out of the limo and strides across the long walkway toward one of many white-walled concrete buildings in a vast complex. Over a low hill and beyond a line of trees, he can hear the rushing of icy water in a river. He passes through two glass doors and a metal detector, where an armed guard welcomes him by name.

He walks across a gray-and-black marble floor, past an early morning janitor using a waxer to polish the smooth surface of a huge seal, and for an instant the vision pans out, allowing a whole view of the entire emblem—

—the profile of an eagle's head, perched atop a sun with multiple rays bearing out in all directions, with familiar words written around its circumference. Then the vision zooms back in on Waxman as he uses a thumbprint scanner to gain access to a long, white hallway. Inside, he pauses and looks over his shoulder, as if convinced he has just heard someone following. Shaking his head, he continues walking, and stops at an unmarked door halfway down. Again he uses the thumbprint, then swipes a card to gain access.

Lights spring on, and a great war room is illuminated. Dozens of screens and monitors line three walls. The fourth wall is occupied by file cabinets. There is a map in the center of the long table, with a red dot over northern Egypt.

Waxman slumps into a chair and lowers his head. "Shut up, mother," he hisses. "I'll still win. I'll find it."

Then he begins to sob, of all things. He pounds the table. Again and again. And with each slam of his hand, Caleb's vision crumbles, tiny pieces falling away like leaves from a great branch, swirling around before his eyes, until . . .

It was gone. Caleb was sitting in front of Phoebe.

They opened their eyes at the same time. "Caleb . . ." she whispered.

How could he have not realized it before now? That letterhead in Waxman's case, the images in those dreams of his father. Remote viewing. Together they had received the sights they'd needed, and found the answers they'd sought. Caleb had drawn so many pictures of this same emblem, never putting it all together.

But it added up now. Waxman's ability to hack Phoebe's computer. His connections with local governments. The money to bribe officials. But what did it mean? *Why has he been using us? Why?*

They continued to stare at each other until Phoebe said what they were both thinking. "We never asked the right questions."

Then they both whispered it at once, as if fearing that to voice it any louder would give it power.

"CIA."

BOOK THREE
—THE KEEPERS—

For the malice of Ignorance surroundeth all the Earth, and corrupteth the Soul, shut up in the Body, not suffering it to arrive at the Havens of Salvation.

—Book of Pymander

1

In the four weeks following the revelation about Waxman, Caleb and Phoebe had very little time to think about what it all meant. Every minute was spent caring for their mother and arranging plans to get her safely back home. Working out the finances, transferring money, setting up home care.

While still in Alexandria, they slept in shifts in Helen's room at first, until Caleb finally convinced Phoebe to get a room at a nearby hotel. She was exhausted, weaker than he'd ever seen her. Every day she seemed on the verge of a total collapse.

"I know what you're feeling," Caleb told her at last, after he recognized the look in her eyes. "It wasn't your fault."

"What do you mean?" They were at their usual

table in the hospital café, subsisting on a diet of lamb gyros and falafel. Relatives of patients came in and out, some glassy-eyed after being up all night crying.

"Believe me," Caleb said. "I felt the same after . . . after that tomb took your legs."

"Let's be clear about something," Phoebe whispered through her teeth. "That tomb didn't do anything but serve its function. Waxman was the one who did this to me. And he's done it again, this time to Mom."

She was right. It was Waxman.

"I want him to suffer," she said, and stared down at her plate, her food untouched.

"I think he does suffer," Caleb said. "But I know what you mean. The question is, what do we do about him?"

"CIA," Phoebe said, her eyes darting around suspiciously, as if she were suddenly convinced they were being surveilled. For all they knew, they probably were. It was something Waxman would have done. She picked at her cucumber salad. "What did Dad have to do with them?"

"I don't know that he had anything to do with them."

"But the symbol—the eagle and the sun—you saw it all the time when you viewed Dad at that Iraqi prison." She took a breath and continued. "And I saw the same thing, plus that other sign, the star surrounded by a fence."

Caleb had been thinking the same thoughts, but for days now. "I saw something in that room Waxman went into at CIA headquarters."

Phoebe stared at him. "What?"

"A name," he said. "Stargate."

"Like the movie?"

"No, like the project." He leaned in close. "After the Freedom of Information Act opened up a lot of government files, some early CIA projects were declassified."

"And one of them was called Stargate?"

Caleb nodded. "In the early seventies the CIA began experimenting with parapsychology, after the Russians tried something similar. You know the military; they can't let the other guy get the leg up, especially in the Cold War." He took a sip of Coke. "I only know about it because of Lydia. She mentioned it once." Caleb paused. "As if she knew . . ."

"What?"

He almost choked on the fizzing liquid. "I wonder if she did know."

"About Waxman?"

"Think about it. Why does he want the treasure so much? Could he be a Keeper? A descendent of the one that split from the others? And was Lydia trying to warn me?"

"Or were they both using you?" Phoebe sighed,

and they sat in silence.

"So what about this Stargate thing?" she took up again. "And why was I seeing visions of it? Crude visions, but then again, I was just a kid. Maybe that was all I could understand."

"Or maybe you were meant to understand it later, when you were older." And for an instant he had it: someone wanted them both to know. Wanted them to know what the truth was, even though they would be suffering in confusion for years. Caleb was close to figuring it out, but still there were too many jumbled pieces of the puzzle rattling around in his mind.

He thought aloud: "Stargate attempted to use psychics the same way we use satellite imagery now. Remote viewing. The CIA gave the subjects certain targets—a Russian nuclear plant, Castro's palace, a downed US airplane—and then the psychics drew what they could see. They worked with maps and landmarks, and in some cases, the results seemed accurate."

"So what happened?"

"Apparently, the hits were not specific or conclusive enough. Or the government just didn't want to be seen as kooky. In any case, the funding was cut after the Cold War ended, and the program disbanded."

"Or it was just buried?" Phoebe asked.

"Waxman had something to do with it, and he

still does. He took the program offline, continued it secretly."

"He seems to still have the financial backing and the political connections."

"But why the Pharos?"

Phoebe shook her head. "Again, it comes back to the Keepers. Could he be the Renegade?"

"I don't know," Caleb said. "I can't believe he's one of them. It doesn't feel right. It seems more personal with him."

Phoebe adjusted the handles of her chair and polished a spot so her reflection squinted back at her. "Let's be careful. We know what the Pharos does to obsessions, and we know Waxman. He'll try again."

Caleb met his sister's eyes.

"He'll be back for us."

That night they moved her. In a special care unit, Helen flew back to New York City, then to Rochester. An ambulance was waiting to take her to Sodus, where a hospital-appointed nurse named Elsa met them at the door. They got Helen situated in her bed, hooked up the fluids and monitoring equipment and set up a refrigerator to stock her IVs. They filled a drawer with sheets, washcloths and linen. Finally, Caleb took Phoebe to her room, where he helped her out of her chair and onto the bed. She collapsed, letting out a huge sigh.

"At least Mom's home."

Caleb didn't want to complete the thought . . . *so she could now die with dignity, surrounded by the familiar elements of her life.*

"I don't want to give up," Phoebe said, as if reading Caleb's mind.

"I know."

"There's a chance, you know."

"Of course," he said. "The doctors even said it happens. These kinds of comas are not the most severe. She can still move, and might talk, even though what she says might not make sense."

"No, I mean there's a chance we can cure her."

Caleb stared at her. He knew what she meant. "The books. The treasure."

"Didn't you write about all the medical marvels that were catalogued in those days? The scientific advances that we're only beginning to rediscover?"

He nodded. "There were rumors of alternative medical practices and healing techniques that united body and mind to facilitate recovery."

Phoebe rolled to her side, closing her eyes. "Like I said, there's a chance." She sighed. "Sorry, big brother. I need to sleep. It's been a long day."

"A long month," he replied, taking a blanket and smoothing it over her body. "Sweet dreams."

"Be careful," she whispered.

"What?" Caleb asked, but she was asleep. He backed out of the room, turned off the light, and tiptoed past Helen's room, where he peeked in on her. Elsa sat in a chair beside the bed, nodding off while holding a copy of *Time Magazine*.

Back in the kitchen, Caleb sat alone at the empty table. His vision started to blur, and he felt a tingle of energy move up his spine, circling around and around like a snake, rising to the base of his skull.

He gasped and let the feeling run its course, knowing what was coming. The kitchen lost focus. Water took the place of the floor . . .

. . . *and great heaving waves undulate where the cabinets used to be. The table has changed to a wooden railing. He hears the call of gulls following overhead, and when he looks, a great white sail bisected with a crimson stripe blocks out the churning clouds and darkening skies.*

"Father," comes a voice at his side, and he glances down to see a boy, no more than ten, huddled in a blanket as if he just woke up and stumbled out from the quarters below. "When will we land again?"

"Not soon. It is not yet safe."

"Will it ever be safe?" The boy's face falls, but his eyes shimmer. A lone gull screeches overhead, and a raindrop falls on his cheek as the boat rolls from side to side.

"We will take on supplies in a month. But then it is back to sea."

The child frowns. "We must keep moving?"

"We must."

"Why?"

"You will know. In time."

"Will it be soon?"

"Perhaps." He feels such pain in his heart when he looks at his son, and he's only too aware of the wheezing in his lungs. He does not have much time. He curses the intervening years since he left Alexandria. He curses time and fate. But still, he accepts that this is the will of the One. It is true he waited too long to father an heir. But now it is done, and the boy is almost ready.

His son looks out to sea again. He stares at the formless gray horizon where a distant rainstorm connects the sea to the sky, the above to the below. It draws on his imagination.

It is a good sign.

He is almost ready.

Something jarred Caleb into the present, and the railing was replaced by the wooden edge of the kitchen table. The cold room took focus again. A hundred small, bright objects were swirling about the kitchen, dancing and fluttering, and at first Caleb thought someone had let in a horde of moths that were swarming about, searching for heat and light.

Then he saw that they were snowflakes. And he saw the open door. Two men in black coats were standing on either side of the table. Through the open door Caleb saw a black limousine waiting in the driveway.

"Mr. Crowe," said one of the men, "Mr. Waxman is waiting for you to join him."

Caleb stood up, as if rising from a dream and stepping toward the next chapter in a book he'd written long ago. He knew all the characters, understood the plot and accepted his role.

Caleb smiled. "Let's not keep him waiting."

The half-hour drive to the small airstrip outside of Oswego proceeded in silence. Seeing that Waxman, who sat across from him in the dark, was fit only to stare and to wait, Caleb closed his eyes and pretended to sleep. At the airport, they boarded a black helicopter, and mercifully the background noise was too great to allow for conversation. Caleb avoided eye contact with Waxman and used the time to meditate, to think on the past, to think about his father and what he might have been trying to tell him in all those childhood visions.

And he thought about the eighth sign. The final key.

He thought of Sostratus and Demetrius, of Alexander, Caesar and Marc Antony. Theodosius and Ptolemy, Hypatia, King Michael and Qaitbey. A hundred names and images drifted in and out of his mind's eye and brought a smile to his face, as if familiar friends were dropping by. He felt the tug of the other world several times, felt the ripple in the veil, but left it alone. Now was not the time. He breathed deeply and calmly, preserving his focus, waiting and saving his strength.

They landed at Rochester International Airport, and then boarded a private jet to Langley. Again, at first they didn't speak a single word to each other, sitting in chairs facing one another. Caleb merely smiled at him and stared at a point over his shoulder. Finally, Waxman broke. "How's my wife?"

"My mother is resting comfortably."

"That's good."

Caleb nodded.

Waxman tapped his fingers together. "Do you know where we're going?"

Caleb nodded again.

"How long have you known?"

Caleb shrugged. "Not long enough. I never trusted you, but I never asked—"

"—the right questions. I know." Waxman chuckled to himself smugly. "Don't worry, for what it's worth, you're still the best psychic I've ever come across. And I've seen a lot of them."

The plane tilted slightly and Caleb's stomach compensated. The plane had just cleared a mass of churning clouds and emerged into the stark, cool blue of the heavens, with slanting rays of sunlight dazzling off the wing.

Caleb smiled. "Was Stargate yours?"

Waxman reached for a glass of scotch and ice, looked down, then back up and composed himself again. "It was. It is."

"I see." Caleb folded his arms. "Then rumors of its demise were exaggerated?"

"Stargate was far too important to close. And the fools in the Senate didn't know what they had. They only wanted to cover their re-election chances. They couldn't fund this kind of research openly, so we had to go underground. You understand."

"Of course." Caleb watched him carefully. He saw the way he stole furtive glances, trying to size Caleb up.

I've surprised him twice today.

Waxman was probably hoping Caleb didn't know anything else, but he wasn't sure. Maybe Caleb had probed deeper into his past. What else had he intruded upon?

"Stargate continues," Waxman said, "with a smaller scope, a limited budget, and much less interference. They only ask for one summary report a year on my progress, which I purposely keep vague and conflicting so as not to attract any undue attention." He drained his glass. "You and I both know the phenomenon is real, and we know what it's capable of. I have bigger concerns than proving its validity to anyone."

"Bigger even than national security?" Caleb gave a little chuckle. "You could have been using us to see into North Korea or Iran, to find bin Laden or predict the next terrorist bombings."

"True, but I actually find such distractions useful. Again, political attention is directed elsewhere while I address the true security issues of our world. There is so much more at stake, and I am the one who will preserve us."

"Really? You're to be our savior?"

He glared at Caleb. "Imagine if the contents of that vault fell into the wrong hands. Men are basically evil, Caleb. You know this. Your precious alchemy books say as much. Why do you think the old high priests kept the sacred texts away from the masses? Why did they write in hieroglyphics that could only be read by the most educated and privileged? Knowledge must be guarded. Why, later on, was it punishable by death to even own a copy of the Bible?"

"Priests wanted to consolidate their power. Knowledge is power."

"Yes, but knowledge is also dangerous. Didn't Pope Gregory the Great say 'ignorance is the mother of devotion'?" Waxman shook his glass around and the ice chinked as it melted. He had returned the favor and was now surprising Caleb. "Tell me something. If you found your way into that vault, and the treasure was everything you believe it to be—the power of life and death, the power of creation, the power for men to become gods—what would you do with it?"

His eyes locked on Caleb's, and for the first time in his presence, Caleb felt like a little boy again, afraid to speak. The truth was, he didn't know what he would do.

Waxman grinned. "I'll tell you what the Keepers would do. What your lovely Lydia and her father would have done. They were going to keep the books for themselves. Create a new order of the elite. They were going to rule. Talk about the corruption of absolute power . . ."

So Waxman wasn't one of them.

"And you?" Caleb asked. "What will you do with it?"

Waxman smiled and sat back, stretching out his feet. "The only thing that's appropriate. The only way to protect the balance of life on this planet. The only way to ensure peace and security." His eyes blazed. "The only way to protect the billions of souls from undergoing the hell you and I experience every day."

And then Caleb understood.

Waxman made two fists, and his glass shattered. "Those books open the gates of hell, Caleb. Just a glimpse, thousands of years ago, partially restored the connection between spirit and material, between life and death—"

"—above and below."

"Exactly." He calmed down and gently picked a

glass shard out of his left palm. "The door only opened a fraction, and for two millennia afterwards, the Church and the armies of man have valiantly done their best to slam that door shut again. But once opened, the stubborn influences are hard to put back."

He kept talking, eyes glazing over and seeing beyond Caleb and the plane itself. "I believe a few intelligent men, kings and priests, understood the threat and tried their best to destroy these elements, or at least alter them so the rest of us wouldn't be tempted. Witchcraft, demonism, occultism—these were the names given to any study of the esoteric, any attempt to link the two realms and travel from ours to theirs or vice versa. We punished these crimes by torture, death and enslavement, but still the sickness remained, refusing to be eradicated. Secret societies continued the forbidden practices, and kept the fragile link operating, only barely." He gave a look of disgust. "In time the defenses were weakened, and now we have Ouija boards, séances, crystals, psychic hotlines and palm readings, New Age movements. And people are moving back towards such beliefs."

Caleb shook his head. "And the sacred texts under the Pharos . . ."

"If released, they will only lead people to eternal misery and damnation."

"So what will you do?" Caleb asked, already

fearing he knew the answer.

Waxman leaned forward, with unblinking eyes boring right into Caleb's soul. "Destroy them all. Every tablet, every scroll. Every single letter of every word."

Caleb couldn't breathe.

"Do you see? Do you, Caleb? What's a single terrorist hiding out in the hills? What's another bombing compared to the widespread, wholesale change in consciousness that will come if these books are released? Our entire way of life will be torn apart. There will be no privacy, no place to hide. And good, honest people will be eternally plagued by the shades of the other world, every day, every hour . . . every minute. Their pasts will be their present, and their sins can never be left behind."

Caleb found his voice, and decided now was the time to play his trump card. A glimpse he had seen, a flash of something, more like a peek behind a stage curtain just before the change of a set. "What is it *you* see, George?" He forced himself to smile. "Weren't you a good child? Mama's little boy?"

What happened next happened too fast. There was a primal scream, a flash of white hot light as Waxman rocked out of the chair, and suddenly Caleb tasted blood and felt a rush of flaring pain up the side of his face.

Then his world went dark.

2

CIA HEADQUARTERS, LANGLEY, VIRGINIA

When Caleb awoke, he was lying in something that looked like a dentist's chair, all stainless steel, with leather straps cinched around his arms and legs and neck. Four silver lamps on coiled stands surrounded the chair. They looked like the mechanical eyes from *The War of the Worlds*, and just as menacing. He struggled briefly and then relaxed.

"Welcome back," said a voice from the glare. Caleb squinted, but could only see a pair of black shoes pacing on a white floor. He smelled cigarettes. Menthols.

"Thanks," he muttered. "Did I miss the in-flight movie?"

"Cute. Listen, Caleb. You know where you are?"

"Not really. It's a little too bright to see."

"Don't give me that. You have other eyes."

"Yes, but they don't always work."

"Lucky for you." He paced some more. "You're in my lab at Langley. The only remaining office of the Stargate program. You and I are going to get to work very shortly. I don't expect this will take long."

"It's good to have realistic goals," Caleb whispered, straining his neck muscles. His head throbbed and he felt sick to his stomach.

"It's a simple goal," Waxman said. "An easy target."

"The last door," he said.

"It had that crazy symbol on it, and what looked like a keyhole. Nothing else in the room. Nothing on the walls, ceiling or floor." Waxman paused. "But then again, I'm guessing you already saw it. Am I right?"

"Yes." He thought now wasn't the time to be difficult. Not yet. He had to think, to see a way out of this. Unfortunately every scenario he imagined came up with him dead and Waxman entering that vault as a bringer of destruction. Caleb imagined the firemen of Bradbury's *Fahrenheit 451* coming with flamethrowers to incinerate all the forbidden knowledge of the ages.

His success, my failure, will be the final triumph of darkness over light, of ignorance squashing truth, he thought. It would be the last surrender of a noble plan designed to protect the one great secret, the answer to every aspect of our suffering and all our earthly yearning.

"So what's it going to be?" Waxman asked. "Help me willingly, or do I do what I'm best at?"

Caleb swallowed, and for an instant, a drawing popped into his thoughts: one of his earlier ones, of his dad in a cage, poked at with blood-red spears, while that symbol hung overhead.

And then he got it.

Finally. Completely. He understood.

With an agonized cry, twenty years of emotion erupted at once. His chest heaved, his muscles strained. He kicked and struggled and screamed and howled into the void.

"What the hell is wrong with you?" Waxman shouted. "I haven't even touched you yet."

"Dad," Caleb whispered, choking on the sobs. "Dad. You were here."

And the room fell silent. The pacing stopped. Even the humming of the electric lights seemed to fade into a soundless abyss.

Finally, Waxman spoke. "I thought I had that covered. He had no idea."

Caleb forced himself to breathe, to calm down, to concentrate, to go with the clue Waxman had just left him. "Dad never went to Iraq!" Caleb knew he was right. "You brought him here, but tried to convince him—what, that he had been shot down?"

After a full minute of silence, Waxman let out a deep sigh, like it contained a painful secret he had been dying to tell for years. "One of my many subjects in the early years was a man named Howard Platt. Worthless as a seer, he never followed directions and never located a single target. But one time, when I asked him about the greatest threat to our security, he spoke of the Pharos Lighthouse, something I hadn't even known about at the time. His ramblings were strange, but just a little too detailed to pass over. I had to follow up on it."

Waxman lit up another smoke and puffed out a thick cloud that filtered into the bright light. "My team of analysts rounded up all the information on the subject, and what came back as a possible hit was a certain thesis written by one Philip Crowe."

Caleb could only watch and listen.

"And that is how I came into your life, Caleb. At first, I had no idea of your father's psychic talents. I only wanted his knowledge of the lighthouse. Then I learned what he could do, and how he could be used. But first, he spilled his guts. He told me of Sostratus, of the library. Of the Keepers, and most importantly, the existence of the traps."

"But not how to bypass them." Caleb said, already admiring his father and thinking of ways he might be able to follow his lead, ways to give Waxman only enough rope to hang himself. Certainly Dad hadn't revealed the right order of the first seven traps. Or maybe he had deliberately misled him and said Water was first, hoping Waxman would try it and be killed in the process. If Dad had managed to keep that secret, then surely he hadn't mentioned the eighth puzzle, the final key.

Waxman grunted. "Philip was tough, I give him that. But he broke when I needed him to. He gave me the purpose I had been looking for, the way out of my personal hell. And he showed me the way to redemption—the redemption of the whole human race. Platt's ramblings led me to your father, and your father led me to the Pharos. And by God, I will destroy those books and save us all."

Caleb had to laugh. "I pity you."

"Pity, hatred, fear—whatever you feel about me—I don't care, so long as you give me what I need."

Caleb struggled again, then gave up and looked around. "So he was here for how long?"

Waxman made a dismissive motion with his hand. "Seven, eight years? And he *was* convinced he was in Iraq. We had film on the walls, sand everywhere, we pumped in the sounds of the desert, battle. Brought in Middle Eastern men to perform the beatings and torture, it was all perfect."

"But he was my dad," Caleb whispered, and a smile formed out of his rage. "He knew, and he tried to tell me, but I was too young to understand." *I wasn't ready.* Caleb thought again of his last vision of the sea and the waves, and a boat forever on the move. And suddenly, with a chill, he understood. "So, you knew all along. Knew it wasn't Alexander's gold."

"Of course."

"Then, my father knew . . ." Again Caleb saw that boat from his most recent vision and the father talking to his son. In a flash, he saw another boat, then a ship, then a galley, then a swift clipper—a succession of maritime vessels down through the centuries, all with some form of white and red coloring, at different ports, on different seas. Sometimes at night, with burning lanterns on their masts, lighting the way, always moving, always afloat.

"You're sure slow, kid."

Caleb's heart was thundering, his flesh crawling. He *was* slow. How had he missed it? With all the focus on his mother, and caring for Phoebe, he didn't realize what the visions were showing him.

"It's me," Caleb said at last. "You wanted me, after Dad died."

Waxman's voice shifted lower. "Unfortunate that he couldn't survive . . . the stresses."

"Or did he make you mad?" Caleb asked. "Maybe give you the wrong sequence for the codes?"

Waxman ignored him, and by his refusal to respond, Caleb knew he was right.

Good for you, Dad!

Finally, Waxman spoke. "For a time I'd hoped your father had chosen Phoebe. She would have been much easier to deal with, and just as capable—"

"—of keeping the secret," Caleb finished. *I can't believe it. Dad left me all his work, all those documents, maps and drawings. And the stories, all those stories.* "It's us," he said at last. "We're the Keepers. The true Keepers. The descendents of Metreisse."

"Your grandfather was one," Waxman said. "Then he passed the secret on to your Dad, and he should have given it to you."

"But he didn't." Caleb tried to glare through the light. "You took him too soon, and he didn't have time."

"Sorry about that, but I wasn't getting any younger, and your Dad resisted too much. Something I hope you won't do, for your sake, and for your sister's."

There it was. The threat he had been anticipating, but dreading. His time in the Alexandrian prison had been sufficient preparation for anything, he thought, and he was confident he could coax his consciousness from his body to escape whatever physical agony Waxman could inflict for as long as necessary. But he couldn't protect Phoebe. And he had to. He couldn't let her be hurt again.

"So, kid. What's it going to be?"

Caleb made up his mind. *Dad's shown me the way.* He would trust in fate. He would trust in the lighthouse. Smiling, he told Waxman he knew where the eighth key was, and he would take him to it. All the while, he kept repeating to himself the one mantra he could now call his own.

The Pharos protects itself.

Hide the secret in plain sight.

Caleb stood on the hill overlooking the bay at dawn. The small farmhouse lay covered in a thin layer of snow, and icicles hung from the lighthouse railing, forty feet up. Phoebe sat in her chair in the kitchen, and Caleb could see her through the open door, watching carefully. Two men stood at her sides, wearing dark glasses. Caleb got the message, loud and clear.

"Your dad never spoke of a ship," Waxman said, squinting through his own dark glasses down the hill to the ice-covered bay glinting with sunlight, sparkling in the frosty air.

"Maybe," Caleb said, his lips curling up, "you never asked him the right questions."

Waxman turned his head and glowered. "Well? Are we going?"

Old Rusty creaked and groaned as Caleb set foot upon her deck, treading carefully on the icy surface, with Waxman following. His breath cascaded around his face, and his hands shivered in his coat pockets. But his soul was soaring despite the threat to Phoebe. And he smiled.

At last Caleb arrived, standing on his legacy. He couldn't help laughing, and wanted to spin and leap about like a young boy. He longed for those days chasing Phoebe around the deck, hiding behind the red-and-white-striped masts, ducking into the wooden deckhouse. So many memories. *And then Dad, urging us to play here. He knew it would stick in our minds.* He had talked this ship up as their property, a member of the family, even though it had been de-commissioned and docked for good. Its red hull was streaked with barnacles and muck, the paint chipped, the steel rusted. The masts were bent and covered with seagull excrement. Old Rusty had sat here all this time, waiting patiently.

"What's its name?" Waxman asked, and for a moment Caleb shuddered.

"Don't know," he said truthfully. "Old Rusty is all we ever called her. And boats are feminine, George. She's not an 'it.'"

"Shut up and take me to the key."

Caleb bowed and swept his arms toward the door to the deckhouse. "After you."

Following Waxman, Caleb glanced up the hill, and could see the tiny figures in the kitchen. Phoebe watched nervously. He waved to her.

She'll understand, he hoped.

"There it is," Caleb said, pointing to the large gold-plated key, about six inches long, hanging over the cast-iron stove. The deckhouse interior was a mess. After they had closed down the museum, the items in here just collected dust. The windows were grimy, caked with dirt and sand, and now ice. The compass over the steering wheel was shattered, the tiny bunk bed cots brown and molded.

I used to nap there, he thought with disgust. *Phoebe on the top.* After playing all morning, they would make hot chocolate and sip their drinks and tell each other grand stories about their naval conquests in the East Indies or some exotic port, and then they would snooze for an hour before running back up the hill for dinner.

Waxman warily pulled the key from the wall, as if expecting a booby trap, some vicious metal contraption to slice off his hands. Caleb was surprised he didn't make him take it down.

Waxman slipped the key into his pocket, after first looking it over. "Doesn't look that old," he said.

"Probably re-cast several times," Caleb said.

"Although I wouldn't know. I only just figured this out. Thanks to you."

Waxman frowned, unsure if Caleb was complimenting him or still hiding something.

Go on, Caleb thought. *Take your prize and go.*

"Phoebe dies if you're lying to me," he promised.

"I know."

Waxman eyed Caleb carefully. "I still don't trust you."

"Sorry. What more can I do? This ship is the legacy Dad left me. There's the key."

"We'll see."

"What do you mean?"

"I mean," he said, tapping the gun in his other pocket, "you and your sister are coming with me."

Before they left, Caleb said goodbye to his mother. Elsa sat cowering in the corner, but he convinced her everything would be fine. They would be back soon, and if she could just continue to care for Mom, he would be grateful.

So he knelt by his mother's bed and he kissed her forehead, ignoring Waxman clearing his throat in the doorway. "We'll be home soon," Caleb whispered. "I love you."

When he stood, he thought he saw a flicker of awareness. But her hands didn't move, and her chest barely rose.

Caleb turned and walked out, but stopped and looked first at a picture of his grandfather and his Dad, shaking hands while Old Rusty lay in pristine condition, sparkling in the background.

4

ALEXANDRIA

Phoebe and Caleb stood on the pier outside the entrance to Qaitbey and watched the frenzy of activity in the water and all around the causeway. Helicopters circled overhead, news trucks stood idling with camera crews filming scenes of the fort and the shoreline, running their pre-segments. They pointed out the new Alexandrian library, its brilliant steel-reinforced glass rooftop blazing in the sun. They spoke of its predecessor and lamented the loss of knowledge, but hoped this new building could regain some of that former glory. Emergency vehicles stood off to the side, ready if necessary. Four police cars and two ambulances were in position.

"It's all a sham," Phoebe said, wrapped in a black shawl and trembling in the morning winds.

"Waxman has it all planned out."

Caleb nodded and recalled Waxman's words from an hour earlier, just before he'd gone into the sea with his team of six divers. They had chosen the underwater route, going in through the ascending passage so as not to give away the Qaitbey entrance and encourage future investigations. Waxman had announced to the public that his team of archaeologists had reached a breakthrough and discovered an entrance point that seemed to fit with the legends.

"This is going to end the controversy before it even begins," Waxman had told Caleb, with his mask hanging around his neck. "There won't be any more Alex Prouts running around claiming conspiracies." And there it was, confirmation of Caleb's suspicion that it hadn't been the Keepers who had killed Prout.

"We'll film our dive, and then we'll document the dramatic descent to the final door, and inside . . ." Waxman made a grinning, devilish face. "Just like Capone's vault, that televised fiasco back in the eighties? I'm going to take the fall on this one. I'll be the laughing stock," he said, thumping his chest like a primitive. "There will, of course, be nothing inside."

"Because you will have already removed and destroyed everything."

"Precisely. And that will effectively put an end to

all future searches. Nothing spurs on the spirit like a little mystery. Take that mystery away, and people are left with only what they can see and hear and touch. And life will go on as it always has, as it should."

"If you say so."

He scanned Caleb's face. "Just so you know, you and your sister are going to be watched by my best men. A lot of them. They will be in the crowd, disguised as spectators. I would suggest keeping quiet and staying put. I don't trust you anywhere else."

"And after?"

Waxman spit into his diving mask and rubbed it around to coat the plastic. "After? I haven't decided. You're free to go, of course. But I would strongly suggest you get out of the publishing business for good. Or maybe turn to children's books. A word of this in any public forum, even a Web blog, and all bets are off. I'll start with your sister."

Caleb nodded. "Just so we understand each other."

"I think we do."

"Oh, and George?" Caleb called after him as he was getting into the motorboat with his diving team, their cameras and equipment.

"What is it now?"

"Good luck!"

Waxman patted the gold key secured with a chain around his waist. "Got it right here."

"I think I can feel her here with us," Phoebe said.

"Me too." Caleb held a hand to his eyes and looked up, imagining the great Pharos Lighthouse taking shape, a shimmering mirage, glowing and superimposed over the existing fort, rising in all its initial splendor. And he imagined his mother at the observation balcony, with her big red sunglasses and her hair tied in a kerchief, waving down at him.

"Don't worry," he said to Phoebe, and to his mother, if she could hear. "The Pharos protects itself."

5

"Caleb Crowe,"—Phoebe turned her chair sideways and looked up at her brother—"that key was made in 1954 to fit the lock on the steering column."

"And it was just what I needed."

"So where does that leave us?"

Caleb crossed his arms over his chest and stared over the choppy waves. The divers had been under for close to an hour. His guess was that they were in the main chamber by now, at least exiting the water tunnel and approaching the first sign.

"We wait," Caleb said.

"What are they going to find?" Phoebe asked.

"You know what they'll find. Do you want to watch?"

She looked down at her hands. "In a minute. First, tell me what you know. If they don't have the right key, then where is it? Or did Dad move it?"

"He didn't move it," Caleb said calmly, and he breathed in the crisp air and watched the gulls circling over the spot where the divers had entered the harbor. Overhead, cirrus clouds streaked across the sky. "It's still there."

"It is? Then, we'll have to go back and get it!"

"No, we won't. We have what we need."

Phoebe looked around. She looked at Caleb, at her chair, her feet.

"Actually, Phoebe, *you* have it."

"Me?"

"Yes, you. You were its part-time curator. You know Old Rusty's history."

"Of course, but what does that have to do with anything? Is the key on the boat or not? If it is, what could it be? There's nothing that old. Whatever that Keeper Metreisse stole and passed down in his family from generation to generation, from boat to boat, all those lightships can't be anything I'm familiar with. Maybe there's something in the hull, or stored in a hollow mast?"

"Nope."

"Big brother, you're really pissing me off. Okay, I give up. Tell me."

"You'll kick yourself."

"If my legs worked, I'd kick *you*. Tell me!"

"Thoth was intimately associated with the number eight, as we know. But also with music, with the octave. It is said he set creation going by the sound of his voice, by a single uttered word."

"Yeah, yeah. Get on with it. What about the key?"

"The key, Phoebe. The key isn't *on* the boat."

"But you just said—"

"It *is* the boat." Caleb took a deep breath and scanned the crowd, making sure no one had gotten too close, that no one could overhear. "It's all the boats we've seen in our dreams, all those red and white sails, all those dinghies, lightships, galleys and frigates. Metreisse figured it out. We know he had the talent as well. He experienced a psychic trance and went back, visited that last chamber, and he heard them speak the word. A single word. Then he planned, so his descendents would pass it on, ship to ship, as each one wore out. Generation to generation, every vessel—"

"—With the same name!" Phoebe shouted. "Oh, I do want to kick myself! Rusty's real name—"

"Let me guess," Caleb said. "Something Greek, or Egyptian?"

She smiled and folded her hands together. "Only the symbol for the rebirth of the land, the flooding of the Nile. The rising of the star, Sirius, also called—"

"Isis."

Phoebe nodded. "Wife of Osiris, mother of Horus."

"Thoth helped her reunite with her murdered husband, and brought magic to her kingdom. *Isis*. Just one word, spoken properly, and I believe the door will open."

"But can you say it properly?" she asked. "Egyptian phonetics were tricky, right? And that language hasn't been spoken in thousands of years."

"I'll find out," Caleb said. "I'll peer back to when Sostratus last entered the vault. I'll listen for myself."

"You can do that?"

"It'll be easy, now that I know to ask the right question." *Isis*, he thought, and had to smile, thinking back on the marble head he had first plucked out of the harbor's muck, the artifact that had started it all.

Together, he and Phoebe gazed out over the waves and listened to the roving helicopters. Cameras were flashing at their backs, video feeds running. The whole world, it seemed, held its breath. Caleb glanced back and thought he saw a face in the crowd he recognized. A man in a dark green coat, scruffy pants and black boots. Hair falling in unkempt strings over his eyes. But he looked . . . happy.

The crowd moved, surged, and the man was gone. And for a second Caleb caught a glimpse of another face he knew, a man with a bald head and dark glasses. Watching from a short distance away.

Victor Kowalski.

"Well, big brother?" Phoebe tugged at his hand. "I bet they're almost to the door. Want to take a peek?"

Caleb looked away from the crowd. "Should we?"

She squeezed Caleb's hand. "Oh, yes."

They strip off their tanks, fins and masks and bring their gear up the stairs, past the great statues of Thoth and Seshat, and place it out of harm's way. "Wait on the stairs," Waxman orders as he tests the chain and harness attached to the ceiling above the third trap. The seven men climb two flights and remain there, watching impassively.

Waxman strides to the great seal, steps over the chains that he and Helen had left for the second trap. He proceeds to turn the seven symbols in the proper order, and then calmly walks back to the first block, and waits. He passes through the realms of the Below: Calcination, Dissolution, Separation, Conjunction. He is relaxed, as if he has practiced this a hundred times. He ascends through the Above: Fermentation, Distillation, and finally Coagulation.

After the seventh test, he is covered with a fine gold dust that has drifted down from a sifting stone overhead. The scent of sulfur still hangs in *the smoky air, and water is heard trickling below, down the stairs and out the vent.*

And the great seal opens majestically at his touch, withdrawing and allowing him inside.

"Come!" he shouts, and his men follow, igniting their lamps and flashlights, bringing their torches and gas tanks. They leave the cameras behind. There will be time enough to film another arranged descent, once the room below has been emptied of everything but ashes.

Down the stairs, twisting through the octagon section. The tramping of their feet issue pounding echoes against walls unused to anything but the silence of the centuries. Dust follows at their heels, sparring with the brilliant shafts of light.

Then, the final room. The low-hanging ceiling. The non-descript door with the symbol for Exalted Mercury.

Waxman removes the key from his belt. "Here we go, men. What we do today we do for humanity's future. We close Pandora's Box for good."

He extends the key toward the hole as someone shines a light for him. "Goodbye mother," he whispers. He inserts the key partially, and it jams. "What . . .?" is all he can say. He frowns and withdraws it with a jerk, scraping the key against the inside of the hole. A tiny spark appears, nearly lost in the flashlight's brilliance.

Waxman lets go as the key falls, and he steps

back. A multitude of sounds arise at once: something hisses, like a flame has just ignited and is heating a small tank of water; sliding noises like thin metal flaps opening along the walls and on the ceiling.

Flashlight beams whirl around, stabbing at shadows, blinding his eyes. Waxman covers his face and tries to peek through his fingers when suddenly he is struck with something hot and wet, steaming. His fingers close around it, and over the hysterical screaming of the men around him, he realizes he holds someone's guts.

Something whistles through the air. He ducks, and a great scythe rips through the man standing behind him, cutting his head lengthwise and spilling out his brains. Another scythe, rusted and serrated, gleaming in the spastic lights, whispers across the room sideways, and two more of his men fall to the floor, in pieces, twitching, their mouths open in silent screams.

Waxman runs toward the exit. Somehow the blades have missed him. He still has a chance. This tower hasn't killed him the last two times. Surely, he has been saved for a reason. He thought he'd learned it, had understood that patience was needed. Patience and humility. He had proven both, and had come back this time prepared.

But it still wasn't enough.

He sees the stairs and he runs, but slips in a

rising pool of blood. His other hand catches at a protruding rib cage. He looks back and, there on the floor, his mother's head is lying along with the other grisly remains. And she's laughing, cackling and spewing out continuous insults.

He falls to his knees and faces the door, where that symbol stares at him, scolding, reinforcing his unworthiness.

Both blades emerge again, one after the other, and retreat into their resting places with barely a sound, their purpose served once more.

Quartered, Waxman makes a sound like a wet sigh, then slides apart.

A rumble vibrates from the walls, the stairs tremble, and a rush of sea water floods into the room from above, swirling, sifting, lifting, cleansing.

The Pharos protects itself.

"They're coming up!" someone shouted, and the crowd surged.

Shapes appeared in the water. Small, irregular forms that never really surfaced. Divers without their diving gear. The water stained red, a spreading, inky pallor, and the men kept floating up. Five, six, seven, eight . . . nine . . .

Then more.

A woman with binoculars screamed. The floating bodies were in pieces: a head here, a torso there, legs and arms jumbled together with severed chunks of flesh. The helicopters dipped, rolled and scattered. The ambulances' engines sparked to life, followed by their sirens.

And more screams shattered the morning air.

Eighteen Keepers, each wearing black Ray-Bans, moved through the crowd of spectators like a tide of gray death, each member keyed in on a target that, as soon as they had come into Alexandria, arriving ahead of George Waxman as his personal con-tingent, had been identified and secretly tagged with a chalk mark on the upper shoulder, visible only to those wearing the specially tinted sun-glasses.

The Keepers moved quickly, efficiently, and with a determination borne out of not just duty, but revenge. Each of them had a metal cap on their index finger with a tiny needle that had been dipped in concentrated tarantula venom. One jab would paralyze and induce convulsions, and sometimes—if it happened, it happened—death.

Simple pinpricks. Eighteen Keepers struck with subtlety and swiftness, poisoning and then moving on, disappearing into the crowd. Only one Keeper stayed a bit longer over her victim.

The bald man dropped to his knees, his hand at his neck where something had just "bitten" him. Victor Kowalski felt strange; a numb sensation, bitterly cold, almost ecstatic, cascaded through his veins. Suddenly, he couldn't move, and felt inertia pulling him sideways. People were screaming, rushing past him, pushing, trampling. He fell. Rapped his head on the flagstones, but felt no pain, just cold. So cold. Someone stomped on his arm, and still he felt nothing but a frigid arctic gale sweeping through his body, chilling his very core. His vision was stuck, looking straight up at a familiar face, someone wearing a baseball cap and gray sweatsuit, someone lording over him with a smile of retribution.

The exquisite rush sped to his heart, encasing it in ice, and the world drowned in bitter darkness.

"What do we do now?" Phoebe asked. Emergency units roared to the water's edge as the police herded the spectators away.

"We wait," Caleb said, backing away. "I think a few days, maybe more. The Egyptian authorities and the Council of Antiquities will place another ban on investigating the harbor. They'll declare that there's nothing down there but dangerous old tunnels. And the story will rest."

He exhaled slowly. "You can go back to Mom, if you like."

"No," Phoebe said. "I want to see this through. I can't help her there, anyway."

"Okay, then we'll wait for this circus to die down. We'll wait for Qaitbey to be alone again, sneak inside, and do this our way."

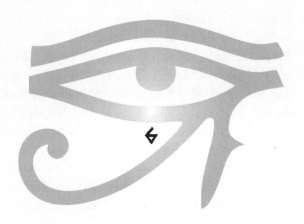

In the end, they couldn't wait for the causeway to empty, and the area around Qaitbey's fort was always either too crowded or guarded late at night. So they did the next best thing, taking a lesson from Waxman, and bribed the guard to allow them inside. Caleb made up a story about this site's importance to them. He said that he and Phoebe had been married here years ago, and they wished to recapture that feeling by spending a night inside. Maybe the guard took pity on them because of Phoebe's condition, but for two hundred dollars he agreed that it was quite romantic. He left them alone, locked up inside, and promised to let them out in the morning. Of course, Caleb knew they wouldn't be coming out the same way.

Beside a glowing battery-powered lantern,

Phoebe waited on the stairs and looked wistfully after her brother.

"Wish you were here?" Caleb asked after the water subsided and he coughed up mouthfuls of brine.

"No thanks!" she yelled back. "Comfy right here. You go on and get all dirty."

"It's going to be gold, not dirt!"

"Whatever, just hurry up. These statues are creeping me out." She stared at the spot under Thoth, where Nina had fallen years ago.

"Trying," Caleb said, removing the chains. He quickly splashed to the next symbol, then hooked himself to the ceiling, climbed and hung suspended, waiting for the ground to fall away. After it reset he took off the harness, dropped and stepped onto the next block. Immediately it sank, leaving him in a tunnel where the earth closed in and sticky mud clung to his skin. When the block rose again, the earth had hardened and he felt as if he wore a powerful suit of armor, a joining of all the elements into one, able to ward off any physical assault.

He stepped forward onto Mercury. He opened a zip-lock bag from his pocket, sprinkled the powdered sulfur onto the lines, lit it, and waited. A noxious gas rose from cracks in the boulder, mixed with the smoke from the sulfur, and swirled around his body. The earthly coating he had taken on began to bubble and crack. Tiny sprouts of green emerged from his arms, his chest, his face. Then these fell off, dropping with huge chunks of mud.

Fermentation over, he took the next step to Distillation, to Silver and the Moon. He withdrew the 200-watt water-resistant flashlight and switched it on. After a deep breath, he shone the light forward onto the heads of the snakes on the great door. Apparently made of quartz, their eyes glowed with an eerie orange hue. They sparkled and glittered. Caleb felt lightheaded, disconnected. It must have been the gas from the previous stone; maybe it contained some kind of hallucinogenic powder. Whatever it was, Caleb saw the snakes uncoil and lift off the wall, hover in the air, rear back and open their great jaws before slithering forward and wrapping around his legs, circling up his body.

He stayed perfectly still, recognizing that this was a test. It was an illusion, of that he was *almost* completely sure. An unbelievably realistic illusion. He felt their scales, heard their hissing. His breath shortened as they coiled around his ribcage, then continued winding around his neck, encircling his head, where they met at his crown. And still, he remained motionless, breathless, waiting.

Ten heartbeats passed. His head swam, the room spun and a strange, numinous aura ignited around his vision and bathed his mind in under-standing. *Here I am, the living caduceus, the embodiment of opposing energies: male and female, above and below, heaven and hell, black and white, good and evil . . . all of it. From these conflicting elements come oneness. Ultimate knowledge of everything from all perspectives.*

The only thing left was to make this state of awareness permanent, to become like a stone, the Philosopher's Stone.

Caleb stepped forward, the snakes greedily hanging on, but losing materiality as he accepted their presence no longer as a hindrance, but a strength. At the final block he dropped to both knees and spread out his arms. It had never occurred to Caleb that he needed to be in that position, and he surely hadn't gotten any hint from the scroll or any vision. It was just something that seemed right.

He knelt and waited. The snakes hissed gently in his ears, and he imagined words in their breath, whispered greetings, welcoming praises to one who had made a long journey and had arrived home.

Gold dust began to fall from the ceiling, a light coat clinging to his glistening skin, sticking to the residue of fermentation and distillation. It coated his head, his upturned face, neck, shoulders, arms and hands. It fell like a blissful spring rain. He even smelled flowers and fresh mountain air. The scent of jasmine floated by, and he thought of Lydia, then he smelled the bay back home in Sodus, and the

424   THE PHAROS OBJECTIVE

trace of old books permeating his little bedroom.

When it stopped, all too soon, Caleb opened his eyes. Standing, afraid to move too quickly and shake free any dust, he took the one remaining step to the door. The snakes had returned to their rightful posts, looking on with passive interest.

Caleb reached out with fingers of glittering gold and touched the staff, then flattened his palm. In the haze of the shadow-play it seemed he had reached into the limestone and actually grasped a three-dimensional staff.

He tightened his grip. And pushed. The door opened, grinding, both halves separating, welcoming him inside. "Your turn, sis," he called to Phoebe as he turned and jogged back for her.

"Not on your life!"

Over her protests, he lifted her up and carried her.

"You're filthy," she said, putting her arms around his neck. "And now it's all over me."

"Deal with it," he said with a laugh. "I'm not letting you miss out on this."

He took her over the inscribed blocks, through the open doors into the next high-walled chamber, and made for the flight of stairs leading down. Phoebe took one hand away from his neck and used it to wield the flashlight.

They descended slowly, carefully. He stopped once to set her down and catch his breath.

"Wimp," she giggled, then screeched as he swept her up and threw her over his shoulder. He trotted the rest of the way down and placed her gently on the floor, where she propped herself up on her side. She scooted away from a groove on the red-stained floor.

Caleb held up a finger to his lips and she nodded, trying to stifle her giggles and calm her breathing. Lowering his head, Caleb closed his eyes and directed his thoughts to this room, to its shape, its smell, its feel. And he asked to be shown a date long ago. To be shown Sostratus opening the door.

After two minutes passed, he started to worry.

Nothing happened. No images, no flashes of light, no trembling of the veil.

Another minute and he seriously thought of just trying it, saying "Isis" and seeing what happened. But then Phoebe gasped.

Caleb jumped and spun the flashlight to her. Then aimed it away. Her eyes had rolled back, and she was trembling, lying on her side. He had seen her do this only a few times before, in the grip of powerful visions. She had accessed the talent now, not Caleb.

"I see them," she whispered. "Don't speak. Don't say the name."

"Why?" he asked, dry-mouthed and chilled.

"Sostratus . . . he's brought someone else."

"Who? Demetrius?"

She shook her head, eyes still closed. "No. A woman."

"What?"

"A woman in a blue robe. Head covered with a hood. Hands at her side. She's facing the door, and Sostratus is waiting, head bowed."

Could it be, Caleb wondered, that the inflection had to be the right tone, had to be in the feminine voice? Yin and Yang. Male and female. Was this one last test? A final nod to the powers of the feminine, of intellect, feeling, compassion? The ultimate lesson? That true wisdom and power only comes from balance? Man and woman together before the great vault. Was this why Metreisse didn't open the door that first time?

Phoebe blinked and sat up. She smiled. "Did you bring me here for this purpose?" Caleb shook his head. "Then it's fate." She motioned him aside and crawled closer to the door. Closing her eyes, she took a breath and spoke the name, just as she had heard it. And the door opened, not with a grinding, grating sound, or any kind of fanfare. It merely whisked open as if someone had been waiting patiently, ages, for them to come.

Inside, they saw only darkness at first. Caleb started to aim his flashlight beam, but then a flickering light caught his eye.

"Put it out," Phoebe said, and he wondered if she still saw the past.

He switched off the beam, and watched as the room beyond started to glow. Four tiny lights about ten feet off the ground sprang to life. Small flames set in multi-prismed glass bulbs hung on the walls. He peered closer and could see narrow tubes attached to each, filling with oil from unseen reservoirs. They must have been triggered by the opening of the door, he thought. He started forward, then stopped and turned to retrieve his sister.

"Go on," she said, tears in her eyes, her lips quivering. "I can see from here . . . so beautiful."

And it was. A rounded ceiling, painted with vibrant colors, a mural of the heavens, the zodiac, the planets, lines of orbit crisscrossing with comets and nebulae and the overarching Milky Way. A golden border separated the heavenly loft from the four levels of alcoves, each stocked with scrolls and edged with gold and silver trim. A single desk, made of smooth black obsidian, occupied the center of a scarlet marble floor, and a lone chair, simple and plain, rested beside it.

Without any awareness of motion, Caleb walked forward and down the three steps into the chamber. The scent of jasmine and oil mixed with the ancient aroma of papyrus, preserved in this perfectly dry, moisture-free vault, evoked sweet memories of

Lydia. Everything was in the same condition as when it had been brought here, over two thousand years ago.

He turned, making a complete visual sweep of the chamber and thousands of scrolls blurred in his sight, each of them nestled carefully, sleeping safely in their alcoves.

Sometime during the next minute or so, he remembered to breathe. He heard Phoebe laughing and sniffling. "We did it."

Caleb couldn't stop smiling. He went to alcove after alcove and peered into the deep recesses to see even more scrolls packed away beyond those in front. He gently touched one, then pulled his hand away, afraid to damage it.

It's all here. All . . .

And then he saw it. On the desk. Sparkling. Emerald on black. The Tablet of Thoth, right there on the smooth surface, beckoning. It was thin, but proportional; flat yet somehow multidimensional. The writing went deep, and when he looked at the tablet from different angles, other layers became visible, with more writing, and even more beyond that. His mind swam, as if just seeing the cascading emerald layers was already affecting his consciousness.

There was something beside the tablet, something that shouldn't be there.

A tape recorder. And a piece of white paper torn

from a notebook with Hilton Hotel letterhead.

How can this be?

As he approached and saw the familiar handwriting, he knew. Caleb pulled up the chair, sat heavily, and took the paper in his trembling hands. He glanced at the clunky old tape recorder. He knew the batteries would be dead, but it didn't matter. He had already guessed what was on the tape: just one word, a woman speaking the name of Isis.

Choking back a sob, Caleb held the paper up to the light, saw the date, and realized it had been during the last trip his father had taken alone to work on his research just a year before his enlistment in the Gulf War.

Barely able to control the trembling in his fingers, Caleb read the words in his father's handwriting:

This is yours now, son. All I ask is for your pledge to guard this secret with your life.

7

The other divers' gear was still on the stairs, providing a convenient means of escape from the subterranean chambers. Caleb told Phoebe to practice breathing slowly through one of the mouthpieces while he fitted her with a suit, mask and vest.

They exited through the vent and ascended through the water gracefully, sharing one tank between them. Phoebe clung to Caleb's neck and he held her with one arm while passing the regulator back and forth. He let more air into the vest at a grudgingly slow pace, careful to ascend very slowly.

They stared at each other through their masks. They looked down now and then at the distant entrance port, at the breakwater stones and the hundreds of limestone blocks, the fallen reminders of the once-great Pharos. Here and there they saw a marble statue, limbs broken off, eyes dreaming as colorful fish darted about.

They rose together through the water into the rays of sunlight. The light seemed to gather and then scatter the bubbles before their ascent. Two feet from the surface, Caleb slowed and waited, not wanting this glorious feeling to end. But then a wave came along and nudged them upward and they were through, their vests fully inflated, and bobbed at the surface. He had purposely swum around to the other side of the fort to the beach for an easier exit. He kicked and swam and let the tide pull them in. About fifty feet from the shore, he became concerned.

"Who are they?" Phoebe asked in his ear.

Six white jeeps had pulled up onto the beach. They were arranged in a semicircle. The rest of the beach was nearly empty, and those few people that remained were being told to move away by men in gray suits.

"CIA?" Phoebe whispered. "How—?"

"Not CIA," Caleb answered, seeing more men and women emerge from the jeeps, a few of them with binoculars to their eyes.

"Then who?"

Caleb spit out a mouthful of water. He found his footing. A few more steps in the rocky sand and he could stand, wobbling, holding Phoebe in his tired arms.

Seventeen men and women stood patiently. Some with dark glasses, others shielding their eyes.

"I think," Caleb said, "this is going to be a reunion."

"After nearly five hundred years, we are joined again." The man who spoke was in his late thirties, strong and imposing, with broad shoulders, blond hair, blue eyes and thick, tanned skin.

Caleb held Phoebe in two feet of water, feeling the surf caress his calves. He scanned the crowd of faces. "Keepers," Caleb said, and bowed his head in greeting.

Someone made a motion and another man stepped through, wheeling an empty wheelchair. "We thought you might need this," he said, "after we realized you weren't coming out the way you went in."

Caleb put Phoebe down and got her positioned in the chair. "Thanks, I was getting a little tired there."

"Congratulations," said the first man as the others crowded around. "Are we to assume, due to your apparent health, that you have succeeded?"

Caleb stared at him. "Maybe we gave up."

The man shook his head. "After the first door is

bypassed, I don't believe giving up is an option. The trap would have sprung, as it did with your mother."

"Then there's no point denying it."

"Good. Again, congratulations. You have succeeded where we have failed for more than fifteen centuries. But now we are together again. The Keepers are reunited."

"What are you planning to do?" Phoebe asked, looking at all the excited faces. She eyed Caleb carefully, to see if he showed any sign of flight.

The Keeper smiled. "We would like to show you something. Assuming of course, that you wish to join us."

"We'll see," Phoebe said, crossing her arms.

"The seal is still open?" the man asked. "From the instructions we were given, if you succeeded, there is no reset program. You have to manually close the doors to reset the traps."

"We didn't close the doors," Caleb said. "Wouldn't want to go through all those trials again when we go back for the books."

"So you didn't take any?"

Caleb shook his head, feeling the dryness in his throat and trying to calm his pounding heart, hoping they would believe him. "Didn't think to bring any waterproof containers on this trip, plus there are so many scrolls down there."

"Good. We will bring them up." He nodded to a

woman next to him, who turned and left, taking a dozen of the group. They stepped into four jeeps and drove off toward the causeway, where a large black truck was waiting.

Two jeeps remained, and Caleb only now noticed someone sitting in the passenger seat of the closest one. A shadowy figure, watching them.

The Keeper who had first spoken noticed Caleb's attention. He stepped forward, into his line of sight. "I understand you were with my father when he died."

Caleb lowered his eyes. "Your . . . father? Nolan Gregory? Yes I was with him. I'm sorry."

"Don't be," the Keeper said. "It was his time." He reached out his hand. "You are my brother-in-law. My name is Robert Gregory."

Caleb numbly shook his hand, still eyeing the figure in the car.

"In my family's case," Robert continued, "my father couldn't decide between his two children, so he shared the secret with both of us."

Caleb continued staring at the silhouette.

"She wants to see you," Robert said. "But we needed to talk first, before your reaction might have spoiled things."

"She?" A lump formed in Caleb's throat. He couldn't breathe.

The jeep's door opened.

Phoebe gasped.

And Caleb's breath fled in a rush as Lydia strode toward him.

She stopped and took her brother's place as he stepped away. Her hands were folded before her waist. Her green eyes were radiant, her golden hair whipping about in the winds. Caleb smelled jasmine, strong, intoxicating.

"Caleb. I knew you would do it." He reached out his hand and she took it, squeezing it tight. "I'm sorry," she whispered.

"I know," Caleb said. "I think I've always known, somehow. As much as I admired your sacrifice, I secretly hoped you had tricked me. In the darkness you dove into the pit, then scrambled out the vent shaft."

"Where I had stashed an air tank and regulator the night before. You were stubborn, Caleb. You were trapped in a place that held you back."

"But we could have worked at it. Why the rush, why not give me more time?"

She glanced back at Phoebe, then her eyes met Caleb's again. "There was another reason. Someone else was going to come into your life, someone who would have sidetracked your true mission."

"Who?"

Phoebe gasped, fingers to her lips. "My dream . . . where Lydia was suffocating you. I heard—"

"A baby?" he asked.

And Lydia, with her eyes welling with tears,

nodded. "You have a son."

Phoebe and Caleb sat in the back seat with Lydia as they drove to the new library. They had brought a change of clothes, thinking of everything. Phoebe wore a yellow and black sundress, and Caleb had put on khaki shorts, sandals and a white button-down polo.

As they navigated the crowded market streets, Phoebe and Caleb looked through the photo album Lydia had brought of the first years of young Alexander's life. Caleb saw his son grow from a puny little cub to a brown-haired hellion covered with grape jelly and Saltine crackers. He seemed to love the beach and water and listening to Lydia read to him in his crib.

"He loves books," Lydia said. "Like his father."

"Then he'll love where we're going," Phoebe said. "How long has the library been open?"

"Officially, for ten years," Robert said. "Unofficially, in the subterranean levels, much longer. But it is still being stocked. All the works are backed up, digitized and stored in fireproof servers."

"What about earthquakes?" Caleb asked.

"Reinforced concrete girders across the structure. And deep in the earth we built the lower levels inside an immense vault on a series of rafters and posts to resist quakes and shore erosion. The angle of the windows overlooking the top six floors limit the amount of sunlight entering the library, further aiding in the preservation of the books. And, as I said, everything's duplicated and stored on servers at several locations across Egypt."

"And what about—?"

"We have it covered," Lydia said. "Armed guards, heavy security. Many benefactors, funding . . ."

"I'm sure they were equally confident about the previous library."

"So pessimistic," Lydia said, then glanced at Phoebe. "Was he like this as a child?"

"Worse."

Caleb groaned. "I'm just trying to gauge how sturdy this place will be, if, as I assume, you're going to use it to store what they're bringing up from the Pharos."

"We are," she said. "That has been our purpose all along. Keepers have been on the board here at the new library, securing funding through UNESCO and ensuring that the construction exceeds specifications. We knew, very soon, someone would find the way in. We had stepped up our efforts to find the Renegade. And your father, with his thesis, made it easy for us."

"Unfortunately," said Robert, "the CIA got to him first. A bad streak of luck, that. A little unfair, with Waxman's psychic help. They took your father away, and we were forced to wait. We had hoped, years ago, that maybe your mother had been given the Key, but instead we had to be patient."

"And prod you along," Lydia said.

"So it was all just for this?" Caleb asked her ruefully. He looked at his lap, reflecting, before he spoke again. "Any love in there?"

She stared back with a wounded look. "I hope you know better."

"I don't," he said, but then he looked at the album again, at his little son nestled in her arms. "But maybe I'll come to learn that, in time. If you're willing."

She reached back her left hand, where he saw her wedding ring, still glittering. "I am."

In the library, they walked down a massive ramp as Caleb wheeled Phoebe along. He marveled at the architecture, the perfect columns, the lustrous balconies on each of the six floors; the great windowed dome, the tracks of lights crisscrossing overhead; the rich mahogany shelves, tables and chairs.

He felt a burning need to linger here for days, weeks, months. As he turned around in a great circle, his heart thundered and he couldn't help but feel like Demetrius Phalereus stepping into his library for the first time, looking over the thousands of works from every subject on the planet.

Lydia gently took his arm and pulled him along,

toward a waiting elevator. She used a special key to gain access to a floor below the other four sub-sea levels. After nearly a minute of silent descent, they stepped into a long tunnel made of all white marble. Caleb felt like they were deep in a secret military installation. At the end of the corridor, a set of gold-plated double doors opened at their approach. Inside, the room was set up much as the chamber under the Pharos, except larger, and with twenty desks and polished wood chairs. Empty alcoves everywhere, flat screen monitors, computers, scanners, and a bank of servers. A similar vaulted ceiling arched overhead with beautiful cosmic murals.

"Here it is," Lydia announced. "We will keep the recovered texts here and invite certain scholars to have access to a portion at a time. A scroll here and there. And carefully, and only after great analysis, we will dole out the information as appropriate."

"Dole it out to whom?" Phoebe asked, leaning forward in her chair and looking around the room.

Lydia sighed. "To those who seek it. I expect we'll differ on this, but you must realize that such knowledge, with the power it brings, cannot just be made available to everyone, at once."

"Why not?" Phoebe asked, cutting Caleb off. She pointed to the servers. "You have everything you need. Scan all the texts, post them on the Internet, and let the world have at them!"

Lydia laughed, and Robert, who had gone down the stairs to sit at a table beside an empty alcove, snickered. "You can't be serious. No, we will decide when to release certain information. We'll catalog the sources based on their inflammatory potential, and release the knowledge in small doses gradually, but surely releasing it all."

"Over how long?" Caleb wondered.

Lydia shrugged. "We'll see how the early releases are received. Decades certainly, maybe centuries."

Caleb shook his head. "So we'll just have to trust your judgment?"

"*Our* judgment. Caleb, you're one of us now. Again."

He nodded, looking around. It was so tempting to have access to this, to everything coming along. The ancient treasure reunited with its library.

A cell phone rang, and everyone looked at Robert. "Hold on," he said, digging out his phone. Caleb was amazed it worked down here, but apparently they had set up additional receivers and transmitters for wireless connectivity to the outside.

"Yes?" he said, "we are. What do you mean? Look again." He frowned, gave Caleb a curious stare, and then glanced at Lydia. He hung up, stood and moved in close to her. "It's not there," he whispered.

Lydia's shoulders sagged. She turned to Caleb.

"The tablet isn't there."

He stared back at her impassively. "I didn't think it would be."

"What?"

"Didn't the legends claim it was moved before Alexandria fell to the Muslims? Moved back to Giza? I'm thinking it's under the Sphinx now."

"But your vision of Manetho . . ."

"Maybe I wasn't asking the right questions," he said. "I wanted to be shown how the wisdom left the Temple of Isis, not where it ultimately wound up."

Lydia continued staring at him, then looked to Phoebe, considering whether they were lying. Finally, she said, "We'll keep looking. It has to be there."

Caleb shrugged. "There were a lot of alcoves, it could have been hidden. Or maybe there's a secret wall or something."

She nodded. "We'll find it, wherever it is. But for now, we have enough to work with." She came over to Caleb, hesitated, then put her arms around his neck.

"Can I see my son?" he asked.

"My nephew!" Phoebe chimed in.

"Of course," Lydia said. "He's waiting upstairs."

8

SODUS BAY—CHRISTMAS DAY

With a deep sigh, Caleb leaned all the way back in the chair, put his feet up on the edge of his mother's bed, and turned to his side. He had been speaking to her for close to five hours, telling her everything, completing the story of their quest. Filling her in on the triumphant discovery.

Completely exhausted, he closed his eyes, just for a minute. Helen let out a sigh, and a soft murmur filled the darkened room. The lone candle had burned almost completely, the wick floating in a puddle of wax, and Caleb drifted toward sleep.

Then, he heard something. A rustling of the sheets, a creak in the floor. Wearily, with great effort, he opened his eyes. Someone stood over her bed.

The gaunt figure with the long, greasy hair and hunched shoulders. Green khakis. He bent over her. Words poured out from the darkness, whispers at once gentle and strange.

Caleb tried to rise, to lunge for him and drag him away. He'd plagued Caleb all his life, appearing, then disappearing. For so many years Caleb thought he was a manifestation of his own fears, or some subconscious guilt.

But to see him here, now . . . and to be unable to move!

Then the man did something that melted away Caleb's fears. He took Helen's dangling hand in his, and he gently caressed her skin. More whispers. His face right next to hers, he looked into her eyes. And then Caleb understood. Most times he'd seen this man, his mother had been around. And more than once, he knew she had sensed him too. But what visage, what presence would—?

"Dad . . .?"

The figure froze, as if he had been assuming Caleb was asleep. His head turned, ever so slightly—

—and the candle went out.

Another sigh, and the room suddenly chilled as the darkness dissipated. Finally finding his strength, Caleb fell out of the chair, turned and reached for the wall switch. The room sprang into light, and Caleb spun around, hoping to confront his father's apparition at last, to touch him, to apologize for giving up on him, for everything. But there was no one there.

The pictures on the walls watched soberly, and all those faces seemed to turn away, to provide him with solitude, to allow this moment to be alone with his mother. Caleb stumbled toward the bed and took the outstretched hand and the fingers that were already uncoiling from their last grip. Her eyes were closed, her lips moist as if just kissed. Caleb knelt beside her and put his head on her chest, and listened a long, long time, while tears started to slide unimpeded down his face.

SODUS BAY—JUNE
TWO YEARS LATER

"Hello, Mom." Caleb sat beside her stone and arranged the gardenias in a pattern matching those by his father's. He had petitioned the right people at the State Department, and with an agreement to forgive and forget, and a tidy sum for his loss, they released Philip's body from its unmarked grave behind Fort Meade. George Waxman's name had been stricken from all records related to Stargate and the CIA, and they disavowed all knowledge of his service.

"Just stopping by," Caleb told his parents as he squinted up through the eaves of a great willow in Forest Hills Cemetery. Here in the shade, and so close to the bay, it was a good ten degrees cooler than near the entrance road. He looked back and saw Phoebe chasing Alexander around.

"I hope you can see this," he said. "I still can't believe it, but the new treatments worked. They repaired Phoebe's neural connections and reconstructed the lower vertebrate, all according to the instructions from the Hippocrates Manuscript. We introduced that one quickly to the medical association, claiming that a boy playing in the caves outside of Cairo had discovered it sealed away in a jar."

Using the small shovel, Caleb piled more dirt around the flowers and sprinkled water from his bottle over the earth. Then he cleared the emotional block from his voice. "So much more will be coming out in the next year, you'd be amazed. I'm moving the others along as fast as I can, and it's working. The potential for hydrogen energy and innovations in robotics will astound the world. Amazing that the early thinkers considered these things only for sport. Imagine if necessity had weighed on their imaginations."

He touched Helen's stone, laying his palm flat against it. "Rest well, Mom. Phoebe's doing great, and your grandson . . . well, I have him for the next four months, and that will have to be enough time for him to experience some down-to-earth cooking and good old American culture. He's got a lot of games to play, TV to watch and books to read until I have to send him back to Lydia in Alexandria."

Caleb smiled. "Yes, I'll keep an eye on him there,

too. And, you'll be happy to know, we might be heading that way again very soon. Me, Phoebe . . ." then, in a whisper, ". . . the Morpheus Initiative."

He stood, stretched and watched the scene behind him, where Alexander chased after a Frisbee. "I'm reforming the group. Recruiting psychics, screening them myself this time. Waxman had the right idea, just the wrong motives. It'll be a good team, dedicated, professional. Going after the biggest stakes. Important relics, things that will benefit mankind."

Hands on her hips, gasping for breath, Phoebe laughed, saw Caleb and waved. Alexander shouted and Caleb thought he heard the words "Old Rusty."

"Dad," Caleb scolded, "he got that from you. Loves that damn rust bucket. Every chance he gets he's chucking stones at it, climbing through it, pretending to be Captain Nemo."

Dropping his voice a notch, Caleb leaned in toward his parents' stones. Carefully, keeping the words from the jealous wind, he whispered, "Alexander will be ready sooner than I thought." Caleb looked through the trees, across the narrowest part of the bay, to their little white lighthouse glittering in the sun. "It's waiting for him, down in our basement, beyond the root cellar door. Locked away behind what, I must say, are some ingenious puzzles of my own. Alexander will figure them out in time. But before that, I'll teach him what he needs to know."

Bowing his head, Caleb walked back to his sister and his son, back to the sunlight and the warmth. He paused at the rise and glanced back to the monuments.

"I promise, Alexander will make an excellent Keeper."

EPILOGUE

The patient's door opens with a sound like the hiss of an uncoiling python. The man outside wears a long overcoat, and a matching black hat all but covers the tangles of crimson hair matted in sweat beneath the fabric.

He takes off his gloves, slips them into a pocket. Before his next step, he glances over his shoulder at a heavyset man on the hallway floor, his neck broken. Outside, the Virginia sun has gone down for the day, and the quiet winds sweep across the sycamores, rolling over the Potomac—

—and three more bodies face-down in the water. Mercenaries, all of them, members of Waxman's old crew, still guarding the last vestige of a program long-since officially cancelled, following orders from distant bureaucrats interested only in keeping certain secrets in the dark. It wasn't a fair fight, but he has no interest in fairness.

Still hearing the echoes of the guard's snapping vertebrae, he enters the room. Despite what he's just done, he doesn't like death, not the look of it, not the smell, not the way it sounds. Just being in its vicinity brings too many unwanted memories.

Too many visions that just won't go away.

He turns his attention to the interior of the darkened chamber. The light from outside spills around him, seeking out the patient lying on the cot. IVs feed nutrients into her blood stream to keep her alive. How much longer could they keep her here? he wonders. Drugged up so she can't remember, so her powers can't surface? Forever? The men safeguarding this site on a skeleton crew, half-heartedly, had little idea of what or who she was.

A breath escapes her parched lips. Her head turns toward the light. Eyes flicker open.

Does she recognize me?

He thought she was an amnesiac, that her injuries beneath the Pharos stole her memories. But his visions—those he had started having back in Alexandria, before he deserted the Morpheus Initiative on the night of their ill-fated descent— showed him something else. Visions of the two of them together, glimpses even of this very moment, in this very room, doing what he is about to do.

He kneels beside her, takes her hand in his.

She blinks as her eyes focus. "You?"

Xavier Montross smiles, a twisted smile born of fiery visions and epic, exalted dreams. Relentless dreams, all his life showing him his purpose, what he was meant to find, what he was meant to be. So close now, almost within his grasp.

"Hello, Nina. Come, we have work to do."

END OF BOOK ONE

*For a preview of Book Two of the
Morpheus Initiative, read on . . .*

And so begins the

The Mongol Objective

PROLOGUE

NEW ORLEANS—25 YEARS AGO

The pencil, wielded like a wooden stake gripped in his little fist, speeds over the page, creating details here, shading in areas there, stabbing at the heart of his horrific vision. And as the drawing takes form, emerging from the chrysalis of his young mind, sweat beads on the boy's brow. He shakes his head to clear a thick lock of matted red hair from his eyes, awash in blue innocence the color of a robin's egg, as they lose focus, crack, then tremble with inescapable dread.

The pencil point breaks, and he absently reaches into a box of sharpened pencils on the rug beside him. He ignores the sounds from the babysitter, the fifty-year-old neighbor with her fingers to her lips, watching over him in astonishment that slowly turns to horror as the lines on his page darken and the images assume clarity.

Finally, the boy sets down the pencil, blinks and looks up at the sitter with tears spilling from his eyes, cascading down his puffy red cheeks. He lifts the page, tears it from the pad and holds it up for her to see.

As she takes it, he whispers, "Help them?" but the sitter only bites the knuckles on the back of her hand. She crosses herself and steps away, dropping the page. The sheet of paper descends, pitching side to side like a leaf, before gently landing in front of the child.

He tries to look away, but can't. He looks at it again, at the profile sketch of two people in an overturned car, a man clutching his chest, the woman next to him with her mouth open in a desperate scream as flames explode through the shattered windows, melt their flesh and char their bones.

Seconds drag into minutes. The sitter and the boy stare at each other, without a word.

The phone rings.

The boy slowly turns his head, and as the sitter goes to answer the call, he gets up, shuffles to the stairs and climbs. He struggles to ascend, every step a challenge. At the top, he enters his bedroom and closes the door before he can hear the cries from downstairs.

He sits on a small wooden chair in the middle of his room, and he desperately looks at the walls, trying to find just one bare inch, any small space that could serve as a refuge for his tortured soul, but the walls are completely covered. A haphazard assortment of pages, all rendered with his mad sketches, more than a hundred sheets of paper taped over the superhero wallpaper, attached crookedly, without a trace of aesthetic intent. Scribbled drawings from a dozen sketchpads, some pages clearly torn out in haste, overlap each other to form larger collages.

Each sheet reveals images no six-year-old should ever see, much less contemplate putting on paper. Drawings of men drowning, men burning, falling into deep pits crammed with long spikes, crushed under huge stones. Fires incinerating entire rooms. Acid chewing away at flesh. Severed limbs floating under water, heads bobbing along the surface. Amidst all this grotesque butchery, almost as background stage art, he's drawn enormous structures: colossal pyramids, crumbling ancient temples, a huge statue, an underground city. And in several frames, an enormous tower with a blazing light at its peak lords over a turbulent harbor. On each of these pages, it's as if the wondrous architectural structures are merely a backdrop for death and dismemberment, scenes of extreme, punishing violence.

The boy blinks and his eyes lose focus again. He reaches down and picks up a sketchpad and a pencil lying on the floor and starts drawing, even as slow, heavy footsteps approach up the stairs. He keeps drawing, sketching, shading, using light and shadow, creating a crude rendition of what looks like the top half of an enormous head, crowned with spikes, peeking out from a landscape of either sand or possibly ice. Tiny human forms are gathered around it, using shovels and pulleys.

And then the door creaks open.

"Honey . . . I have to tell you something. There's been an accident. Your father and mother were on their way home, and—"

The boy lowers his head, and his eyes focus momentarily, filling with uncontrolled emotion. Then he blinks the swelling tears away. He looks up to the window, the pale light suffusing around his pupils, and again the room loses focus as if he's staring at something a long, long way off.

"Xavier? Did you hear me?"

He directs his attention again at his latest drawing, then glances at the wall in front of him, concentrating on one sheet in particular, puzzled as to why this one should pull at his attention. Next to the muted image of a huge seal there's another drawing finished in colored crayons. It depicts a woman strapped to a bed, with two men crumpled on the ground around her, crimson splatters on their chests. A third man—a man with red hair—approaches.

"Xavier?"

The boy blinks again.

"Xavier honey, did you hear what I said?"

He turns his head and manages a smile. "Yes, but I'm sorry, I still have work to do."

Turning away from her, Xavier Montross picks up his pencil and flips to a blank page.

Author's Notes on the factual basis for
The Pharos Objective.

1) The central element of this novel is based on fact. Legend holds that King Michael III spread a rumor that Alexander the Great's treasure was hidden inside the Pharos Lighthouse, hoping the Muslims would destroy the lighthouse in their greed. Another Arab legend recounts that a hundred horsemen then stormed into the lighthouse to plunder its secrets, only to spring some sort of trap that swept them all out to sea.

2) The description of the Pharos Lighthouse, its size and the many marvelous elements inside, such as the automaton statues and the great mirror, come mainly from Hermann Thierschs' 1909 work, *The Pharos Lighthouse*, which he researched from a host of early Roman and Arab sources. The architect, Sostratus, cleverly signed his name upon this monument as described here.

3) There is an historic landmark lighthouse at Sodus Bay in Upstate New York. It was completed in 1871 and served as the residence for its keepers for the next eighty years. It's now run as a maritime museum, chock full of history. I, of course, took certain liberties with the layout and its current fictional use.

4)   A project incorporating parapsychology and archaeology took place in Alexandria in 1979. It was led by the *Mobius Group*, which utilized remote viewing to locate Cleopatra's palace and Alexander's tomb, among other lost sites. The fascinating story can be read in Stephen A. Schwartz's *The Alexandria Project*.

5)   The eruption of Vesuvius in 79 AD that buried Pompeii and Herculaneum ironically kept intact one of the largest collection of ancient scrolls—those owned by the father-in-law of Julius Caesar. Brigham Young University has been working with the Biblioteca Nazionale in Naples since 1999, applying NASA-developed imaging techniques to read the scrolls. The involvement of Count Cagliostro and his connection to the real 14th-century Rimini Church of San Francesco are my own creation.

6)   The three theories on the destruction of the Great Library at Alexandria are the prevailing, most logical conclusions, although there have been ardent proponents of one over the other. Modern consensus is as I have presented here.

7)   The CIA led many investigations into parapsychology, hoping to gain an edge in national defense during the Cold War, and these programs

have now been declassified. The Stargate Program was the best known, operating for twenty-four years, using the skills of early RV founders like Ingo Swann. Its proponents claim many successes, including viewing the location of downed pilots, predicting the rings of Jupiter before Voyager confirmed them, and scrying Russian nuclear facilities. Other information on remote viewing, including classes and lectures, can be obtained from the PsiTech organization at: www.remoteview ing.com and from Ingo Swann's website: www. biomindsuperpowers.com/Pages/1.html.

8)   The Emerald Tablet is part of a collection attributed to the Egyptian god Thoth (Greek Hermes, Roman Mercury). A selection of these writings that survived were assembled in the Middle Ages and compiled into *The Hermetic Arcanum*. These and other books were largely deemed heretical and banned, but formed the basis for the elements of alchemy and the foundation of many secret societies such as the Freemasons and the Rosicrucians. There are many great resources concerning the study of alchemy, including *The Emerald Tablet* by Dennis William Hauck (Penguin, 1999).

9)   The Tempio Malatestiano in Rimini, Italy, does indeed have mystery to go along with its storied past. The I-and-S combination on many

sculptures have puzzled scholars and philosophers alike throughout the years.

10) The new library at Alexandria (The Bibliotheca Alexandrina) was completed in 2002, and its precautions and construction are much as I've described here, designed to protect the world's wisdom against all catastrophes (at least natural ones . . .).

11) French and Egyptian officials are planning a new monument to take the place of the Pharos Lighthouse. Located about 150 meters from the coast of Alexandria, this new lighthouse will be designed by The National Center of Art and Technology in Reims, France. Designed in the form of an obelisk, this new lighthouse will measure 145 meters in height, 9 meters square at the base, and 6 meters at the top. The entire structure will be covered with glass and will reflect sunlight over the coast of this ancient city.

ALSO FROM
VARIANCE PUBLISHING

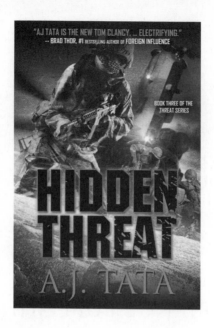

"Brilliantly crafted book and destined to be a top seller! Buy it and read it—it's that good."
-- W.H. Mcdonald Jr., author and founder of 'The Military Writer's Society of America'

"Every military thriller writer wants to be compared to Tom Clancy, but to be called better? That's what A.J. Tata is hearing . . . his books, filled with terrorist tales, are very realistic."
-- Paul Bedard, U.S. News & World Report

COMING 09-2010

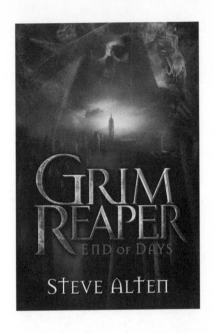

"...An instant classic!"
-- Washington Daily News

"This is Alten at his delicious best."
-- Andrew Tallackson, Entertainment Editor,
The News-Dispatch, Michigan City, IN"

"...An exciting read."
-- Booklist

COMING 10-10-10!

David Sakmyster is the award-winning author of over two dozen short stories and two novels, including THE PHAROS OBJECTIVE. In 2009 Dragon Moon Press published his epic historical fantasy tale, SILVER AND GOLD.